Other books in the Cat Star Chronicles:

THE CAT STAR CHRONICLES

REBEL

CHERYL BROOKS

sourcebooks
casablanca

Published by Sourcebooks Casablanca, an imprint of Sourcebooks, Inc.
P.O. Box 4410, Naperville, Illinois 60567-4410
(630) 961-3900
Fax: (630) 961-2168
www.sourcebooks.com

Printed and bound in Canada.
WC 10 9 8 7 6 5 4 3 2 1

For Kira
As one dream ends, another begins

Chapter 1

Other women paid for him,
only she gets to keep him.

————

THE CITY OF DAMENK NEVER SLEPT, BUT PARTS OF IT
did get a little drowsy now and then. Onca strolled down
a dimly lit street in just such a neighborhood, enjoying
the peaceful stillness. Talwat was a residential district.
No pheromones or subliminal advertising fogged the
atmosphere here, and it was quiet after dark, especially
in the hours just before dawn.

Although he'd taken this same route hundreds of
times, this day was unique. His most recent client had
seemed honored that she was his last before taking a
much-needed rest. She had smiled, tucked a lock of her
hair behind her ear, and told him to call on her if he ever
needed help. Allowing her to feel special had cost him
nothing, but really, it didn't mean a damn thing—even
her name escaped him now. That session simply marked
the end of a long stretch before the time when there were
no appointments, no ladies waiting for the use of his
body, and certainly no need to sleep at the Palace. He
was going *home*.

There were plenty of men who would have loved his
job and would never have considered taking a vacation.
Onca didn't see it that way. No matter how pleasurable

or lucrative it might be, it was still a job. He recalled hearing someone say that any occupation, no matter how much fun it was as a hobby, took on all the trappings and burdens of a job the moment money became involved.

That someone was right. Since his partners Jerden and Tarq had left the business, Onca had been trying to keep up with the demand, but he was finally forced to admit that even he couldn't maintain the pace forever. He had fucked six—no, *eight*—women that day. Although none had complained that he'd rushed them, he knew he had. Still, he doubted they would have blamed him for hurrying had they understood the circumstances. Onca's days began at ten and went until four the following morning, and he'd gone from doing one client every three hours to one every two—an hour with the lady followed by an hour to relax, plus an hour each for lunch and dinner.

It's a wonder my dick still works.

He didn't even have that excuse. One whiff of an aroused woman's scent, and he was ready to go again—all set to dive cock-first into a hot, wet pussy. He could think about it now, but without the scent, his cock remained flaccid. He'd even gotten to where he could stifle an erection if he smelled feminine desire in public, which was a useful skill for a Zetithian man to possess. Particularly one who worked in an area where the street pheromones had every passing woman panting with need.

He planned to put that skill to good use over the next few weeks. From now on, he was simply another inhabitant of a large city—anonymous and invisible. He had even donned clothing prior to leaving the Palace, something he'd rarely bothered to do before. For that matter, he didn't always go home. Roncas had long since given up trying to wake him after the last appointment, merely allowing him to sleep right where his client had left him. She would wake him in plenty of time to have breakfast and a shower before his first session of the day.

Poor Roncas. The tiny Zuteran woman would be left to deal with the calls from new customers, even though Onca had told her to stop making appointments two years ago, following his return from Jerden's wedding on Terra Minor. Instead of posting an announcement, she had opted to stay on for a week or two before taking her own sabbatical—no doubt deriving some sort of fiendish delight in telling desperate women that the resident Zetithian stud had taken an indefinite leave of absence.

She certainly didn't need the extra pay. Onca knew precisely how many credits she had stashed away, and her hefty parting bonus would allow her to live in style for the rest of her days. He could have lived like a prince himself, had he chosen to do so. However, he preferred a simpler lifestyle. Granted, he owned a house on Rhylos, which was pricey enough, but it was a modest dwelling in a neighborhood noted more for its peace and quiet than its ostentatious display of wealth.

Until the next moment, when the blessed silence was broken by running footsteps. The smack of two bodies colliding followed, accompanied by a masculine grunt and a decidedly feminine gasp.

"Let go of me, you creep!"

The man's chuckle raised the hair at Onca's nape. "Not likely, girly. You're mine now."

Onca sighed. A knight errant, he was not, although he *was* carrying a pulse pistol—something Jack had insisted upon if he persisted in pursuing what she considered to be a dangerous occupation for one of the galaxy's few remaining Zetithians.

"You'll end up dead," Jack had warned. "Rutger Grekkor isn't the only jealous man in the universe. You just watch yourself, bucko—especially when you're out on the street. And in restaurants, make damned sure you're sitting in the gunfighter's seat."

She'd had to explain what she meant by that, of course. Jack had made a study of old Earth's culture, with the result that her conversation was peppered with figures of speech that no one else understood, and she took smug satisfaction in insulting miscreants with thousand-year-old expletives.

Unlike the words now issuing from the captive lady's mouth. They were all explicit, succinct, contemporary terms—some of them having their origins on worlds far removed from Rhylos.

A highly diverse vocabulary for a lady.

Rounding the corner, he spotted the couple. A hulking Herpatronian with enough leather strapped to his simian body to satisfy the most perverse fetish held a struggling woman against the wall of a nearby dwelling.

At least, Onca assumed she was a woman. At the moment, all he could see of her was a mass of dark brown curls peeking out from beneath her captor's arm. Then it struck him that if her size was any indication, this was a young girl rather than an adult. Suddenly, the fact that he was armed was immaterial. A child must be defended, if only with bare hands and fangs.

However, since he *was* armed, he drew his pistol, set it for a light stun, and fired a shot, pinging the man in the ass. With a howl, the beast abandoned his victim and took off running.

If Onca had expected the girl to fall at his feet in gratitude, he would have been sorely disappointed by her reaction, which was more akin to the ire of a hissing, spitting cat.

"You idiot!" she screeched. "What the hell did you do that for?"

Onca stared at her, not quite believing his pointed ears. "Let me get this straight. You *wanted* that big ape to rape you?"

Her scowl was enough to scare off more than a Herpatronian; therefore, he concluded that she must *not* have been trying to escape. A quick once-over revealed a small, thin girl clad in skimpy strips of ragged green satin—attire that might have been alluring on a more voluptuous form, yet only made her look like an underage streetwalker fallen on desperate times.

"No, I did *not* want that big ape to rape me," she mocked. "I'm *trying* to find my friends."

"Peculiar method," he commented. "Unless, of course, he knows something you don't."

Her face seemed to crumble slightly. "I don't know whether he does or not. I'm trying to find out what happened to them. Three of them just…disappeared."

"Why didn't you go to the police? I'm sure their methods would be more effective—and less dangerous."

Bowing her head, she muttered something he couldn't catch.

"What was that?"

Her head snapped up, and she glared at him. "I said they'd probably lock me up if I said anything."

"You mean the police are in on this?"

"No, I mean…" With a wince, she sniffed in a breath, crossing her arms over her nonexistent bosom. "I'm the sort of person they don't like running around loose."

"Ah, I see." A homeless waif—and probably an orphan—which was one of the few things Rhylos prided itself on *not* having in abundance. "I agree. You *shouldn't* be running around loose. It's much too dangerous, as you can see. There are schools and orphanages for kids like you."

"I'm not a kid." She practically spat the words at him. "I'm twenty-two years old and I've been on my own since I was ten. I can take care of myself, thank you very much."

At least she had said *thank you*. Sort of. "Did you ever consider that the authorities might have picked up your friends? If they were living on the street and someone reported them…"

She shook her head. "I don't think so. I've seen *that* happen before. It's very official and well publicized. The cops like to advertise when they do something good—at least, something *they* think is good. This was different." Her arms were still crossed over her chest, and she hugged herself, shuddering. "All three of them disappeared during the night without a trace." She nodded in the direction her assailant had taken. "He was the first lead I had."

Onca refused to apologize. "Don't worry. I can report this little skirmish to the police myself. After all, I *was* a witness."

Squaring her shoulders, she glared up at him, sweeping her curls behind her ears in an angry, infuriated gesture as she stomped her foot. "You will *not*."

Onca's jaw dropped. "Mother of the gods," he whispered. "You're Zetithian."

He had originally taken her to be at least part human. Her eyes should have given her away—and they would have if he'd gotten a good look at them. The way she was glaring at him now, he could easily see the glow emanating from pupils that were vertical slits rather than round. Searching her face, he found other clues—her upswept eyebrows being one. "Smile, sweetheart."

"What?"

"I said, smile."

Although her grin was more an angry baring of her teeth than anything, it proved his point.

"Fangs too. Jack will have a shit fit."

"I beg your pardon? Who?"

"Jack—as in Captain Jack Tshevnoe."

"Should I know this guy?"

"Actually, Jack is a woman—a Terran woman married to a Zetithian man. She's, well…to be quite honest, she defies description. She'll be tickled to death to hear I've found another Zetithian."

"And why would she care?"

"Don't you kids hear *anything* on the street?"

"Some things." She sounded somewhat defensive. "The more important stuff anyway."

Onca couldn't imagine anything being more important to a Zetithian than the death of Rutger Grekkor. Onca had been one of a hundred refugees flying around in a starship for twenty-five years waiting for it to happen. This girl had obviously never heard any of the story.

"Zetithians used to have a bounty on them. Not sure how much was paid, but it was enough to have Nedwuts hunting us down all over the galaxy." He peered at her closely, noting the seedy, hunted look of a street urchin. "I'm guessing that's what happened to your family."

"Maybe," she conceded. "What's it to you?"

"Nothing, but it could mean a lot for *you*. There's a Zetithian trust fund paid out of the estate of the man responsible for destroying our planet."

"The whole *planet* was destroyed?" she echoed. "Really?"

"Really. If you want your share of the money, you'll have to come forward and claim it."

Eyes that had been wide open with curiosity a moment before were now shuttered and wary. "I don't believe it."

He shrugged. "It's easy enough to prove." If he lost sight of her now, he would probably never find her again, and Jack would never forgive him. The best way to lure her to safety was obvious. With the most disarming smile he could muster, he asked, "Are you hungry?"

Kim had never seen a man like this one. At least not since the day her family was wiped out by Nedwuts. He was like her father—tall and well-muscled, with hair that hung to his waist in spiral curls. In the growing light, she could see that his hair wasn't the same color as her father's. His had been dark brown, almost black, whereas this man's hair had a reddish tint to it. He also had green eyes rather than brown, but with the same glowing pupils. His ears were like hers too, curving upward to a point.

Those characteristics alone should have made her

trust him, and Kim certainly needed someone to trust. She and her gang had managed to elude capture for years, although lately their numbers had dwindled until only she and Jatki remained. The Kitnock girl had been Kim's insurance, shadowing her while she roamed the streets hoping to discover what had become of the others. No telling where she had run off to now, although if what Kim suspected was true, it was a safe bet Jatki hadn't been taken. When it came to sex slaves, there wasn't much of a demand for Kitnocks.

Kim eyed the man warily. Whether he was Zetithian or not didn't matter. In her experience, nothing was ever truly free. "What makes you think that?"

He was right, of course. She and Jatki weren't nearly as effective when it came to creating diversions as the entire gang had been, which made stealing food from street vendors difficult, sometimes impossible. She had been grateful in more ways than one when the Herpatronian had followed her as she skirted the brothel district.

It was hard to admit, but even knowing that was probably the best place to discover what had become of her friends, she had been afraid to go there, preferring to stick to the commerce and restaurant districts. Earning her keep with sex was possibly the worst fate Kim could imagine, and she had decided long ago that men were all pretty much alike. Except her father, which might be why she leaned toward trusting the man standing before her.

"Just a guess," he said. "I'm hungry as a bear myself, and I've got a nice batch of stew waiting for me at home."

"Your wife made it for you?" If there was a woman involved, she might actually get fed rather than fucked.

He shook his head. "Nope. Made it myself a while back. It's been sitting in my stasis unit, calling to me for several days now."

"Why haven't you eaten it yet?"

"Been too busy to go home," he replied. "I'm on my way there now, though." He smiled again. "Sure you wouldn't like to come with me?"

She rolled her eyes. "Get many girls with that line? It's pretty damned obvious what you want from me."

His eyes narrowed and his lips formed a grim line. "Yeah, well, you don't know everything, sweetheart. But if you're looking for a safe place to sleep and some hot food in your belly, you know where to find it."

With that parting shot, he turned and walked away. Although his motives were unclear, in her gut, she knew it was a ploy. Kim had never known a man to toss out a lure like that and then leave her to make her own decision. But then, she had never met a Zetithian man before. And he had just offered her the two things she wanted more than anything.

He might have been intuitive enough to know that, although she didn't get the greedy, self-serving vibe from him. Was it possible he actually wanted to help her? Even after mentioning police, schools, and orphanages? If he intended to nab her and turn her over to them, she could always escape—she knew others who had done it.

He hadn't gone far when her stomach betrayed her with a loud, persistent growl. She heaved a sigh. "What kind of stew is it?"

"Does it matter?" He didn't even bother to glance over his shoulder.

"Guess not." She considered yelling for Jatki, but immediately thought better of it. Her friend might still be out there, watching, and if this guy tried anything funny, it might be best to keep her options open.

Chapter 2

ALTHOUGH SHE WAS OBVIOUSLY TRYING NOT TO STUFF herself like a pig, she wasn't wasting any time making that bowl of *chupka* disappear, either.

"This is delicious," she said. "What did you say it was called?"

"*Chupka*," Onca replied. "It's an old Zetithian recipe—or so I'm told. It's not like my mother ever made it for me."

She stopped chewing for a second or two. "Funny thing, I remember some of the stuff my mom made. Didn't taste anything like this, though." Dipping her spoon into the stew, she had it in her mouth, chewed, and swallowed before Onca could comment.

"Different spices, perhaps."

This time, she only nodded her agreement. Onca wanted to know more about her and what she remembered of those days, but he was loath to interrupt her. He had never seen anyone so thin before—on this world or any other—and she was much smaller than she should have been. On average, Zetithian females were nearly as tall as the men, most of which topped out at about two meters. This girl was tiny. Unless she was lying about her age.

Twenty-two, she'd said. He would have guessed her at half that, although her mop of brown curls might have been responsible for that impression. Her elfin face reminded him of Bonnie and Lynx's daughter, Karsyn. *She* was smaller than average too, but then, Bonnie was rather petite herself—and she was human.

"You're a purebred?"

"I think so," she said between swallows. "Both my parents had ears like mine, and so did my sisters."

She was one up on him. Onca couldn't remember his family at all. Still, having been rescued from Zetith just before it collided with the asteroid that blew it to bits, he could safely assume that his pedigree was pure.

He had about a thousand other questions he wanted to ask her, which wasn't surprising considering he had never come across a Zetithian female in the wild.

In the wild… He had to laugh at his choice of terms. It made her sound like a rare species of fauna, which was essentially what she was. A *very* rare species. If she'd had her origins on any other planet, he wouldn't have been quite so intrigued. Yet he couldn't stop the questions buzzing around in his head. How had she survived—orphaned and on the street—from the age of ten? He couldn't begin to imagine the dangers she must have faced, not the least of which was keeping herself fed.

The climate was temperate, so shelter hadn't been a problem, but why had no one ever found her and taken her in? Then again, perhaps someone had tried. He'd been afraid for her—enough to intervene—and she had turned on him like a wildcat. She was certainly tough. He shuddered to think what kind of men she'd had to fight off before.

Closing his eyes, he turned away. The beast he'd rescued her from had easily been three times her size.

The mere thought of what he would have done to her made Onca sick. He wished he'd done more than ping the bastard—which she had chastised him for doing. He still didn't understand what she hoped to achieve. Yet another thing he would have to ask her.

Her spoon scraped the bottom of the bowl. She looked up at him with eyes so brown they seemed to absorb the glow emanating from her pupils. "Is there any more of this?" She drew in a breath, holding it for a second before she spoke again. "I'll fuck you for it."

Onca leaned back in his chair and stared at her, un-blinking. "You'll *what*?"

With an upward glance, she heaved a sigh as though resigned to do something extremely distaste-ful. "I'll fuck you for more of this if I have to. I'm still hungry."

Onca didn't know whether to laugh, cry, or throw up.

"I don't really want to," she went on. "I mean, I've done it a few times. Never seen what there is to get so excited about. Men seem to like it, though."

For once in his life, Onca was speechless, which might have been due to the sharp pain near his heart.

"Of course, I've never met a Zetithian guy before. Maybe you don't like it any more than I do."

Onca had fucked over a thousand women—at a thou-sand credits a pop—and to the best of his recollection, he had enjoyed each and every moment. He cleared his throat. "We like it okay."

She simply nodded, eyeing him expectantly.

"You don't have to fuck me for food," he went on. "There's plenty more where that came from—or some-thing else if you'd prefer."

She cocked her head to one side, intensifying the elfin quality. "Why are you being so nice to me?"

That same pain knifed him in the chest again and his jaw dropped. "I—we Zetithians have to stick together. There aren't many of us left, you know."

She frowned, staring down at her empty bowl. "No, I didn't—at least not until you told me just now. All I knew was that my family was in danger. Even though we'd lived here all my life, I think my father intended for us to go someplace else—until those creeps killed them all." She was silent for a moment, and when she spoke again, her voice was a whisper. "I'm not even sure they ever saw me. My mother heard them coming. She told me to start running and never look back. I've been running ever since."

She had probably been too scared to trust anyone, and since people came and went so often on Rhylos, her family's disappearance might never have been questioned. Even if the Nedwut bounty hunters had been caught, one less child among the bodies could have easily gone unnoticed. What Onca couldn't figure was why no one had ever bothered to tell her what happened to Zetith, and that she had a guaranteed home on Terra Minor.

Then again, with her hair covering her ears so completely, she could easily have been mistaken for some other species. Even Onca hadn't realized what she was at first. All he had seen was a big ape trying to carry off a child.

What he'd *thought* was a child. Whereas her eyes had been pleading a moment before, he could see the age and the strain in them now. The life of a fugitive would age anyone beyond their years.

And make them hungry. He took her bowl, refilled it, and set it back down in front of her. "Do you want some bread and cheese with that?"

"Yes, please." She sighed with apparent relief. "Thanks for not making me fuck you for it. I'm sure you're a very nice man, but I'd rather not."

Onca burst out laughing. "A lot of women have paid good money for that privilege. I believe you're the first to show such a complete lack of enthusiasm."

"Really? Women actually *pay* for sex? I thought only men did that."

"Clearly you've never been to the brothel district."

She stared at him, aghast. "Why would I want to go *there*?"

She had a point. The fact that the men's brothels were on the other end of the district from the women's would make it a dangerous place for a young girl. Onca hadn't heard of anyone snatching ladies off the street, but there was a first time for everything.

Onca shrugged. "I don't know why you would. It's where I work, though—and there are some seriously hot guys working that area."

She snorted in a most unladylike manner. "I've seen males of lots of species, but none that I'd want to fuck."

"Really?" Onca knew Zetithian girls were hard to seduce, but surely she had a *few* sexual urges. He pulled out his comlink and flipped through the pictures. "Here, check out these guys—they're Statzeelian twins. And this one. He's *very* popular." Rashe had a sword tattooed on his chest that drew the eye downward to his impressive tool. Some women thought tattoos were hot. Onca had never seen the need for ink—not when he had clients booked two years in advance.

Curious, she took the link and flipped to another page. "Hmm...I kinda like the look of this one."

Onca peered at the display. *Great*. She'd found the photo taken when Jerden was voted the best fuck on Rhylos for the third year straight. "That's Jerden, my former partner. He's married now, so you can't have him." He shook his head wistfully. "He sure made us a ton of money—especially after the *Damenk Tribune* named him the Hottest Hunk in the Galaxy. Twice." At least she had good taste.

She paged through a few more pictures. "Is this you?"

"Um, yeah." He was beginning to regret showing her any pictures. It was embarrassing for some reason—which was strange because under ordinary circumstances, he would have been naked when he first met her. Although most of his clients were older, this girl wasn't exactly a blushing virgin. In typical Zetithian female fashion, she simply didn't like the idea of sex—and never would until she found the right man.

"You look pretty good," she said, rather grudgingly, he thought.

"I *am* good," Onca said, though without his usual conviction.

Nodding, she paged back to Jerden, studying the image closely. "Do all Zetithian guys have that little ruffle around the end of their penis?"

Definitely embarrassing. "Standard equipment."

"Hmm. Interesting." She handed the comlink back to him and went to work on the stew again.

So much for that. Maybe she would like one of Cat

and Jack's boys better. At eighteen, they were a little younger than she. Still, they were closer in age to her than he was.

What am I thinking?

In Jack's opinion, an unmated Zetithian man was an abomination, and she'd been after Onca to settle down for ages, telling him he was looking for trouble by keeping the Palace open. Given that their fluffer had been killed by a nutcase of a woman who wanted her job, Jack made a decent argument against continuing the brothel. Onca had told her he would quit when he was ready—though he'd neglected to tell her when he stopped booking appointments. He didn't need her help in trying to decide whether to pick up where he'd left off or retire permanently. Being told what to do went against Onca's nature in ways Jack didn't understand.

"Tell me again why you threw such a fit when I, um, rescued you?"

Despite their initial disparity, they had gotten along reasonably well since then—although he suspected that the offer of food might have had something to do with her level of cooperation.

And she'd thought she might have to fuck him for her dinner.

She really must've been hungry.

"My friends have been disappearing. I was trying to find out where they went."

"Admirable, but did you never suspect you might wind up facing the same fate?"

"Well, yes," she conceded. "But I knew what I was getting into and was prepared. They weren't."

"You *think* they weren't prepared. They might have

known exactly what was happening and it didn't do them any good."

"Possibly. I'm...well, I'm a little...*tougher* than they were."

Onca chuckled. "Tougher? You mean as in harder to chew?"

"Maybe." With a withering glance at him, she swallowed the last of her second bowl of *chupka* and wiped her mouth with a napkin. "Um, you *did* mention bread and cheese, didn't you?"

"Yes, I did. What'll you give me for it?"

Her eyes narrowed. "You said I wouldn't have to fuck you."

"That's right, and don't worry, you won't. I'm looking for information, not a good time."

Her snort left no doubt as to what she *didn't* consider to be a good time. "What kind of information?"

"Are any of your missing friends Zetithian, by any chance?"

"No," she replied. "Why do you ask?"

He shrugged. "Just a question. I never dreamed I'd find a Zetithian girl on the streets of Damenk. I mean, I've lived on this planet for ten years and I've never seen one before. For all I know, there might be more of you."

She shook her head. "Dalmet was Levitian, Cassie was Davordian, and I'm not sure *what* Peska was, but she didn't look anything like me."

That information shot down his original suspicion that the bounty was being paid on Zetithians again. "So it's just young girls going missing?"

"Young *street* girls. Don't know about any others."

And the man who'd attempted to carry her off was a

Herpatronian, which smacked of something really nasty. "Pretty girls?"

"Sort of—though I wouldn't have thought a Herpatronian would care."

He hesitated. "Maybe he wasn't taking them for himself."

"You mean he was stealing girls to sell as sex slaves? Yeah, that's what I've been thinking."

Onca had forgotten who he was talking to. This kid must have seen a lot of perverted behavior in her time. "Or worse."

Judging from the skeptical arch of her brow, she considered that particular fate to be the worst of all.

Onca disagreed. "I won't go into all the other possibilities, but if they were sold as slaves, they may at least still be alive."

She paled slightly. "I hope so. I mean, if someone only wanted to kill them, that Herpatronian would've killed me before you ever got there."

Apparently she hadn't run into many sadistic psychopaths. *Thank the gods*. Maybe she didn't even know there *was* such a thing as a serial killer.

But Onca knew. Their race had been the victim of perhaps the most notorious serial killer of all time. While others had only *attempted* genocide, Rutger Grekkor had nearly succeeded. His method of operation hadn't been to do all the killing himself. He had hired henchmen, and he'd had the wherewithal to do it on a massive scale.

Onca wanted to help this girl, but first, he had to get her off the street. If he let anything happen to her, Jack would have his hide. An additional bloodline added to the tiny Zetithian gene pool was worth more to the future of his race than the hundreds of children he had already sired. Thus far, Onca had only fathered crossbreeds. She had the potential to produce purebreds.

"I take it you're alone now? All your friends gone?"

"Bread and cheese?"

He blew out a breath. "There's at least one left, then."

She shot him a glare. "You're not dumb, are you?"

"Hey, I may *look* like a big, dumb stud, but I wasn't born yesterday—speaking of which, if you've been on the street all this time, how can you be sure about your age?"

"I was two years old at the start of the new millennium. And it's 3020, right?"

"Right." He certainly couldn't fault her math. "Okay, kid." He held out his hand. "My name is Onca, and I was born not long before Zetith got blown to bits in 2984. And your name is…?"

She stared at him for a long moment before she replied. "Kim."

"Pleasure to meet you, Kim. Now, where's this other friend of yours?"

"I wish I knew. She was following me. I hope that creep didn't catch her—though she isn't what you'd call…"

"Pretty?"

"Not unless you like Kitnocks."

In Onca's opinion, Kitnocks were even uglier than Norludians, but there was no accounting for taste. "Got a signal worked out?"

"Yeah. Been trying to decide whether to trust you or not."

"You can trust me," he said. "I'll even help you find your friends."

"How?"

Onca hadn't figured that out yet. "Dunno. Maybe we should call the police."

"No. Please don't. We've, I've—"

"Stolen lots of stuff?"

"Yeah. They'd probably throw us in jail until the *next* millennium."

"I doubt that. What's the Kitnock girl's name?"

"Jatki," she replied. "She's probably watching the house. Nice house, by the way."

Onca shrugged. "Nothing special. Just a house."

"More like a palace to me."

"You want to see a palace, you should see my brothel. It's pretty cool."

She frowned. "I'd rather not."

"Oh, come on. I said I wouldn't fuck you. Don't make such a big deal out of it." He pulled a wedge of cheese out of the stasis unit and handed her a loaf of bread. "Here, I'll even give you a knife."

"I've got one," she said.

He arched a brow. "Where?"

With a sly grin, she drew it out of one of the tails of the satin thing she was wearing.

"Not bad," he remarked. "Although I'm guessing that isn't your usual attire. Would you like something else to put on? One of my shirts would probably look like a dress on you."

She nodded. "I do feel sort of naked."

He wasn't about to tell her she *looked* naked—not after getting her to trust him this much. He waved a hand. "Eat up. I'll be right back."

Onca went into the bedroom and checked his closet.

He didn't have a whole lot of clothing himself, although he did find a tunic that Roncas had given him. As little as Kim was, she could probably borrow something from the tiny Zuteran. He pulled his comlink out of his pocket. "Oh, God. I can hear her now."

Roncas answered on the first ring, her bright pink face filling the viewscreen. "You couldn't have been home for ten minutes, and you're calling me *already*?"

"Yeah. I need to borrow some clothes. I found a girl on the way home."

The Zuteran's derisive laughter sounded like a bird twittering. "You are not serious!"

He rolled his eyes. "I know it sounds weird, but it's not like that. I rescued her from a Herpatronian."

Her teardrop-shaped eyes stared back at him in total disbelief. "You *rescued* someone?"

"Is that so impossible?"

"Don't make me answer that."

"Hey, just because I've never done it before doesn't mean I'm incapable."

Roncas didn't reply, mainly because she'd pressed her lips together as though trying not to laugh. Her silvery hair rippled.

"I do carry a gun, you know."

"You *shot* a Herpatronian?"

"Pinged him on the ass. He was assaulting a lady."

"A lady small enough to wear my clothes? How old is she? Seven or eight?"

"Twenty-two," he shot back. "And get this—she's Zetithian."

Roncas arched a brow. "Rather small for a Zetithian, wouldn't you say?"

"Been starved too much," Onca replied. "Must've stunted her growth."

"Okay. This I *have* to see. I'll be there shortly."

Although she had been hired to add a touch of class to the operation, Roncas had loosened up considerably during her time as the Palace receptionist. As a result, her once-formal speech patterns were now an odd mix of Stantongue and a variety of Earth-based idioms, liberally laced with Rhylosian slang. She still looked like a porcelain doll, though. Hopefully Kim wouldn't freak out when she saw her. Zuterans were about as rare on Rhylos as Zetithians.

Kim was nibbling on a piece of cheese when Onca returned to the kitchen, proving that her liking for cheddar was stronger than her need to escape. He tossed her the tunic. "A friend of mine is on her way over with some clothes. You can wear that in the meantime."

"Is she your girlfriend?"

"Nope. She's technically an employee, although sometimes she acts like she's my mother. Don't worry. She's harmless."

Kim slipped on the tunic, which, as Onca had suspected, hit her at mid-thigh. Reaching beneath it, she pulled out the strip of satin from where it had been tied around her breasts and used it as a belt.

"Not bad." Actually, she looked more like an elf than ever, but he thought it best not to say so.

"Onca." Something about the way she said it made it sound like a question. "That's not your full name, is it?"

"I was a baby when my parents put me on the refugee ship. They said my name was Onca. Fortunately, no one seems to care that I don't have a surname."

Except me. Although he would never admit it to anyone, it made him feel alone, disconnected.

"Kimcasha Shrovenach." She smiled wistfully. "I have to say it to myself every day so I don't forget it."

"Nice name," he said.

"Yeah." She glanced at the table. "I think I'm full now. Thank you."

"You're welcome." The atmosphere between them had changed. Onca couldn't put his finger on the how or the why, but something was different. Something that made him want to take her in his arms and never let go...

No need to get all mushy. His attempt to shake off the feeling failed. Maybe she should stay with Roncas.

Yeah, right. Two tiny little women against a Herpatronian?

Nope. Not gonna let it happen. No way.

Chapter 3

THE WHINE OF A SPEEDER, FOLLOWED BY A CHIME that seemed to reverberate throughout the house, broke the silence. Kim dove under the table. While she might feel foolish when Onca's visitor turned out to be harmless, looking stupid was infinitely preferable to being caught unawares.

"I'm sure it's only Roncas," Onca said. "Not the police or a gang of Herpatronians."

She drew in a shaky breath. "I'll believe that when I see it."

With reflexes honed by years of eluding anything and everything, Kim prided herself on her ability to keep herself safe. Letting that thug catch her had taken all the determination she possessed. She tightened her grip on her knife.

Onca gave her a grim smile. Shaking his head, he called out, "Let her in, Captain."

"Captain?" Kim echoed. "Have you got a-a servant?"

"No. Captain is the house computer. He likes to be called Captain."

"You're joking."

"Nope. Ain't that right, Captain?"

"It is," a deep, disembodied voice replied. "I shall allow the Zuteran to enter." The voice sounded reluctant, even weary.

Onca grimaced. "You needn't sound so damned sulky

about it." He glanced at Kim. "Captain doesn't care for Roncas. I've never understood why."

"She is…*peculiar*," the computer said in a haughty tone. "And she's much too pink."

Never having heard of Zuterans before, Kim suspected that perhaps the computer hadn't, either. "I bet you don't like her because her species wasn't in your database."

A rude buzz confirmed her suspicion.

Onca gaped at her. "Damn. I never thought of that." He aimed a scowl at the ceiling. "You stuck-up, holier-than-thou piece of shit—"

"Now, now," a tiny, silver-haired woman said as she entered the kitchen. "Don't go pissing off the computer."

"Should've replaced the fucker when I bought the house," Onca grumbled. "Never has behaved the way he should."

Kim thought it odd that a computer would even be capable of behavior, let alone be referred to by a mas-culine pronoun. "Maybe you should treat it more like a machine."

Onca arched a brow. "You've obviously never lived in a house run by one of *them* before. They have ways of retaliating."

Roncas giggled. "Like the time he started waking you up with an Erasic trumpet fanfare?"

With a nod, Onca darted a look at Kim. "Yeah. That's when I started sleeping at the Palace." He frowned. "Might have to get a new system now that I'll be spending more time here—or reprogram him." He held out a hand. "You can get up now, Kim. I think it's fairly obvious Roncas isn't here to rape or murder you."

Ignoring his offer of assistance, Kim crawled out from under the table and stood up.

Roncas aimed her huge, teardrop-shaped eyes at Kim and twittered. "Twenty-two years old, my grandmother's ass," she scoffed. "This kid has certainly pulled the wool over your kitty-cat eyes, Boss. Good thing you haven't tried to nail her. She's naught but jailbait."

Kim stared at the strange, birdlike woman whose skin was as intensely pink as Captain had described. "I'm not a kid," she insisted. "I'm taller than you are." An observation that, for once, was actually true. She had at least a centimeter on the Zuteran.

"Perhaps, but my species is naturally small," Roncas said. "Yours is not." The Zuteran continued to study her. "Wish I'd thought to bring my scanner. Then we'd know for sure."

"What difference does it make?" Onca said, clearly exasperated. "I'm not planning to fuck her. I just fed her and gave her a shirt. There's no crime in that." His eyes widened. "Is there?"

A weary sigh came from above. "If anyone cares to consult my superior skill and knowledge, Miss Shrovenach is indeed her stated chronological age, plus four point five months, and is precisely one hundred forty-eight centimeters in height. Shall I give you her weight as well?"

"No!" Kim knew she was undersized. She didn't need Onca's computer to tell her that the little birdwoman outweighed her.

"And providing her with food and clothing is not a crime on this or any other world," Captain continued. "With the possible exception of Zutera."

Roncas let out a cry like a bird of prey about to strike.

"Now, now," Onca said, echoing Roncas's earlier admonition. "Let's not get pissed off at the computer."

"Why not?" the Zuteran shot back. "You fuss about him all the time."

"It is impolite to refer to any sentient being in the third person when he or she is present in the room," Captain intoned.

"Sentient being?" Roncas echoed. "You think of yourself as *sentient*?"

"Although mechanical, I am possessed of senses and am conscious. Therefore, I am sentient."

Onca put up a hand, shaking his head. "Don't argue with him, Roncas. Trust me, you can't win."

Kim was beginning to believe she'd fallen in with a pair of lunatics who argued with computers and made a habit of handing out free food and clothing to street urchins. Of course, if that were true, she and her compatriots would have known about it and taken advantage of the service long ago. She still didn't trust him—or Roncas—enough to give Jatki the all-clear signal. Not yet, anyway.

Having shot a scathing glance at the ceiling, Roncas held out a bundle of clothing. "Here, Kim. These will probably fit you, that is, if they don't fall off. I must say, I've never seen a child so thin before."

Kim gritted her teeth. "I am not a child!"

"I believe we've established that." Onca nodded toward what she assumed was his bedroom. "Why don't you go try those on? If they don't fit, I'll take you shopping."

"Shopping? You mean with money?"

Onca stared at her as though she had sprouted wings. "Uh, yeah. I wasn't planning to steal anything for you."

Of *course* he meant with money. He'd probably never had to steal in his life—and he certainly wouldn't need to start now. Not when he could afford a computer-controlled house like this one. Without further comment, she took the clothes from Roncas and left the room.

As nice as the kitchen was—no matter what Onca thought, in her eyes, it was palatial—his bedroom could have belonged to a king. High-ceilinged and with a carpet so soft she might have been walking barefoot on a cloud, the walls were an iridescent greenish blue that changed color with every move she made. Multicolored ivy with huge heart-shaped leaves grew up the wall from an urn sitting in a corner, making a circuit of the room where the walls met the ceiling. The far wall was covered with the image of a deep green forest so lifelike that birds actually flitted from branch to branch and a waterfall cascaded from a crevice high up on a rocky cliff face. The round bed was set on a low dais with a gauzy drapery suspended above it that was studded with lights that twinkled like tiny stars.

Now that she had eaten, exhaustion overcame her wary nature, and at that moment, fucking Onca for the privilege of sleeping in his bed didn't seem like such a hardship.

He promised he wouldn't do that.

She glanced at her bare feet. They were filthy—and so was the rest of her. She couldn't climb into that bed without taking a bath first.

For as long as she could remember, her only baths involved sneaking down to the shore for a swim in the

ocean. Soap and fresh, clean water were amenities she
hadn't had since the murder of her family.

A footstep drew her attention as Onca stopped just
outside the open doorway. "If you want to get cleaned
up, the soap is there on the ledge." He pointed at the
forest-covered wall. "Just tell Captain when you're
ready to dry off."

Kim's jaw dropped as she realized that the "image"
of the forest was real. "Th-thank you."

He replied with a nod and left. The door slid shut in
his wake.

Kim stepped gingerly across the room to the edge of
the forest. A slight humming was the only clue that a
force field had parted to let her pass, which explained
why the birds were in the forest and not in the bedroom.
Onca might insist that this was "just a house," but the
enormity of his wealth stunned her like a pulse blast.

The trees were alive, as was the grass that covered the
ground. Looking up, she saw open sky where the ceiling
should have been and watched as several birds flitted in
and out of the trees. As she approached the waterfall,
she noted that the floor beneath it was actually a stone
catch basin, and the excess water drained away through
a notch near the cliff face to become a gurgling stream
that wound its way through the trees.

The forest was dimly lit by the morning sky above,
but the moment she gazed at the "shower," thinking she
needed more light, the catch basin and the rocky wall
behind the cascading water slowly illuminated. Putting
out a tentative hand, she tested the temperature of the
water, which was cold at first, then gradually became
warmer as it washed over her skin.

Kim could see the ledge Onca had referred to now—a shell-shaped depression held a bar of soap. Stripping off the tunic and the few scraps of satin that formed the rest of her attire, she stepped into the basin.

The closest she had come to taking a shower in many years involved standing out in the rain, and though the climate on Rhylos was warm as a rule, rainfall was infrequent and slightly chilly—something to be avoided rather than enjoyed. But now, as hot water deluged her body, plastering her curls to her head, Kim couldn't imagine a greater pleasure—although the meal she had just eaten came close.

She picked up the soap, which formed a thick, foamy lather at her slightest touch. Smoothing it over her skin was akin to washing herself with an addicting drug— soft, creamy, ecstatic...

Ecstasy. Although she had heard that term used in reference to sex and the effects of various drugs, she had never fully understood the meaning of the word until now. Kim had never taken any illegal street drugs—or any of the legal ones, for that matter—and sex had left her cold. Food and other essentials were far more important. Still, if she'd known soap could elicit this kind of response, she might have stolen some of it sooner. As it was, she considered taking this bar with her when she left—as she fully intended to do.

She couldn't stay here. Not when her friends were suffering. She almost despised herself for taking this time away from her search to indulge in something so blatantly selfish. Never mind that she probably wouldn't have any luck finding them during the daylight hours.

Well...perhaps a short nap would be okay. Even the

most dedicated detective had to sleep sometimes. Brains tended to work better when they weren't running on insufficient sleep. Not having spent much time in school, there were plenty of things Kim didn't know, but this was one lesson experience had taught her.

Rinsing off the last of the soap, she stepped out of the basin. "Um, Captain. I need to dry off now."

Half expecting a towel to drop from the sky, she was startled when a warm breeze wafted around her instead. Within a few seconds, she was completely dry. "Great. Could I borrow a comb?"

"Unnecessary," Captain said. "The dryer was already set for Zetithian hair."

Whatever *that* meant. Curious, she ran an experimental hand through her curls, amazed to find that her fingers met no tangled resistance whatsoever. Obviously there were advantages to being found by a rich Zetithian.

On the other hand, long spiral curls like Onca's were totally impractical for anyone living on the street— something she had discovered when hers had gotten caught on a street vendor's stall during her first attempt at thievery. She had escaped the encounter with a bleeding scalp, a Rhylosian sausage, and the intention of cutting her hair as soon as possible. The next thing she had stolen was a knife, which, despite its rather blunt edge, she'd used to hack off her waist-length tresses. Kim had learned a lot since then, not the least of which was how to put a razor-sharp edge on an old blade. She'd also discovered that shorter hair made her appear younger than her actual years. Onca and Roncas weren't the first to make the assumption that she was a child—a side effect she had frequently used to her advantage.

Looking like a kid hadn't helped her friends, though. Every one of them had been as undernourished as she, and they had still been snatched off the street. At least, Kim *thought* that was what had happened to them. She really didn't know.

As large cities went, Damenk was relatively safe, and since much of the wealth accumulated there relied on the tourist trade, the local government did as much as possible to maintain that illusion. However, the city had its seamier side, something Kim had seen firsthand.

The death of her family wasn't the only example. Jatki's father had sexually abused his daughter for most of her life until the poor girl finally ran away at the age of twelve. Kim had found her huddled in a corner on a dark backstreet, crying her eyes out. The other members of their gang all had similar stories and good reasons for not trusting anyone in authority.

Kim still wasn't sure Onca could be trusted. For all she knew, he and Roncas were behind the disappearances of the other girls. She doubted it, though. Onca might not mean any of that crap about never fucking her, but he didn't seem cruel.

Plus, he was Zetithian. Somehow she suspected that fact was more significant than his personality or even his line of work. He had a certain guilelessness about him that made her want to trust him. Glancing around the room once again, she realized this was probably the safest place she had ever been in her life.

Resisting the urge to dive into the bed for a nap, she snatched up the clothes Roncas had brought, donning a pair of slacks and a tunic. Like the shirt Onca had provided, they were made of exotically patterned silk and looked expensive. Unfortunately, the slacks kept sliding off her hips, necessitating the use of her "bra" as a belt again.

She approached the door with no idea how to open it. "Okay, Captain. Let me out."

"As you wish," Captain replied. "Although a simple wave of your hand is all that is required."

"Oh."

Onca and Roncas were still in the kitchen and had undoubtedly been discussing her, for their conversation ended abruptly as Kim entered.

"Don't you look cute," Onca said, although his smile seemed a little forced.

"I love what you've done with your hair," Roncas added. "It's much...smoother."

"I didn't do anything to it," Kim said. "The dryer did it. Or maybe it was the soap. I'm not sure." She drew in a deep breath. "I guess I'm all set for whatever nefarious plans you two have for me."

"Nefarious?" Onca echoed. "Dunno about that." He glanced at Roncas, then shifted his gaze back to Kim. "Did Captain say anything to you?"

She shrugged. "Just something about a Zetithian setting on the hair dryer and how to open the door."

"Good. I thought maybe he told you we were going to sell you into slavery or something equally *nefarious*."

Roncas twittered again, leading Kim to assume this was her way of laughing. "You can trust him, Kim. He hasn't got a mean bone in his body." She cast a snide look in his direction. "Not very smart, though."

"Hey, now," Onca said. "I'm plenty smart. Got good grades in science and math and all that crap."

"That isn't what I meant." Roncas gave Onca an indulgent smile and patted his hand, then leaned toward Kim and added in a confidential manner, "He's somewhat lacking in common sense."

Onca opened his mouth, presumably to protest, but Roncas wasn't finished.

"And he's not what you'd call tactful."

"What *is* this?" Onca demanded. "Pick on the boss day?"

Roncas tossed a lock of her silvery hair over her shoulder. "You aren't my boss anymore. I can be truthful."

"Maybe so, but you don't have to be nasty about it."

Roncas arched a brow at him. "I am *never* nasty."

"You two have been working together too long," Kim observed. "I think you *both* need a vacation."

"Yeah, well, that's *your* fault, sweetheart," Onca snapped. "I'd be starting my vacation right now if I hadn't had to rescue your skinny little butt from that Herpatronian."

Roncas shook her head sadly. "See what I mean? No tact whatsoever."

"But it's true!"

Kim certainly couldn't argue that point. "I'll just be going…" Sidling past the table, she headed for the front door.

"Oh, no you won't!" Onca jumped up from his chair. "If you leave now, I'll never find you again."

"I believe that's the general idea." Roncas got to her feet. "Come, child, I'll take you to my house."

"Lock the door, Captain!" Onca rounded on Kim with desperation in his eyes. "If you disappear, Jack will kill me."

"Oh, she will not," Roncas said. "You don't have

to keep Kim here against her will to protect yourself from Jack."

"Against her will? Mother of the gods! I rescued her, brought her home, gave her food, clothing, and a fuckin' *shower*, and now you're telling me I'm keeping her here against her will?"

"He's got a bit of a temper, too," Roncas said with a sniff.

When Kim and Jatki had made their plans to discover the fate of their missing friends, Jatki had insisted that Kim not give her the signal unless she was absolutely certain the coast was clear. She was sure now.

"Calm down, Onca. I won't leave—yet. But I need to let Jatki know I'm okay."

Onca landed in his chair with a thud. "Do whatever you want. God forbid I should be accused of holding you prisoner." He ran a hand through his hair, grumbling. "Last time *I* try to be a fuckin' hero."

Kim hesitated, biting her lip. "Jatki is probably hungry too."

"Sure. Bring her on in," Onca said with a sweeping gesture. "Feed her anything she wants. Clean out the stasis unit and rob me blind. I don't give a shit." Pushing his chair away from the table, he stood up and stalked off. "I'm going to bed. If you want anything, ask Captain. You obviously don't need *me*."

Kim watched the door slide shut behind him, feeling more bewildered than she had ever been in her life.

"Trust him now?" the Zuteran said with a smug smile.

"You did that on purpose, didn't you?"

Roncas shrugged. "Thought it might help you trust

him a little better." She cocked her head to one side, seeming more birdlike than ever. "Did it work?"

"Yes," Kim replied. "I believe it did."

Roncas nodded toward the door. "Go get your friend. I'll stick around for a while in case you and the boss need a referee."

"Thanks."

The main door slid open as Kim approached. Apparently Onca's last directive carried more weight than his order to lock her in.

Stepping out onto the porch, she gave the all-clear signal to Jatki.

And waited.

She gave the signal again.

And waited some more.

A few minutes later, Roncas came up behind her. "Where is she?"

"No clue," Kim replied. "I just hope she didn't do something stupid."

Roncas laid a hand on her shoulder. "Onca told me what you were trying to do when he found you. Sounds to me like you've already done something stupid."

"Maybe, maybe not." Kim scanned the street, alert to the slightest movement. All she saw was a yellow tabby slinking off between the two houses across the road. "Jatki and I have been together for a very long time. She'd better have a damn good reason for disappearing on me now."

"Perhaps she didn't see where you and Onca went," Roncas suggested. "Did you arrange a place to meet if you got separated?"

"Yeah. I'd better head over there. She'll be worried sick."

If she isn't dead.

"I'll come with you," Roncas volunteered. "We can take my speeder. If I let anything happen to you, Onca and Jack will *both* kill me."

"Something tells me this 'Jack' and I would get along pretty well."

"She's definitely a survivor," Roncas said. "Probably the toughest female I've ever met."

Kim smiled. "You're pretty tough yourself."

"True, but Jack is a lot taller." She pulled a tiny pulse pistol out of her pocket and checked the stun setting. "And she carries a bigger gun."

"Yeah, well, hopefully we won't need it." Patting her own pocket to reassure herself that her knife was secure, Kim nodded toward the speeder. "Let's go."

Chapter 4

WHAT A WAY TO START A VACATION.

Or his retirement. Onca still wasn't sure which it would turn out to be, but if this first day was any indication of what was to come, he probably ought to go back to the Palace and stand out on the street and solicit like all the other guys in the district.

Onca had never needed to do that before since he was only "seen" by appointment. Simply by soliciting, he could easily make five thousand credits a day. If he was diligent, he could probably do eight, even without Roncas. Too bad he didn't need the money.

Roncas had always handled the business end of things—booking appointments, scanning the clients, taking their money. Onca wasn't stupid. He could do all that shit. He didn't need her. Especially after she'd turned on him like that. Kim probably thought he was a complete asshole.

Not that it mattered what she thought of him, but he did want to make sure she got her fair share of the trust fund. He didn't fully understand why she wasn't jumping at the chance to become rich overnight. Being concerned about her friends was admirable. Surely she could understand that a rich woman had a better chance of finding them than a homeless waif.

Waif. She was a perfect example of that. Small, starved, no home, no family, and fewer friends now than she'd ever had before. Onca would be her friend if she would let him. But no, she had to go on being noble, dedicated, and trustworthy.

Yeah. All the things he wasn't—at least, according to Roncas. He'd never realized Roncas had such a low opinion of him. Paying someone a salary apparently made them blind—or at least mute—to your faults.

Stripping off his clothing, he stepped under the waterfall, letting the soap and warm water work their magic on him. He washed away the scent of his last client, trying to remember her name or her face.

He couldn't recall either of those things. She was simply the last in a long line of women he had slid his cock into and given joy. Would he miss the attention? The way women craved him, the way they gazed at him with adulation while in the throes of the orgasms triggered by his *snard* or later, when filled with *laetralant* delight?

Probably. Then again, if he missed all that, he only had to stand out on the street naked and say, *Come, mate with me, lovely lady, and I will give you joy unlike any you have ever known*.

Would that standard pickup line actually work with a real Zetithian girl? It hadn't worked very well on the refugee ship—not that those times counted for anything now. Outnumbered four to one, the girls on the ship could afford to be choosy. Back when he and his partners were working the brothel, many women had chosen Tarq or Jerden over him. The ladies on Rhylos had only had Onca for two years now.

Not that any of his clients ever complained. Maybe those others simply didn't like redheads.

Or maybe I really am *an asshole.*

Not that it mattered. Plenty of women would jump at the chance to mate with a Zetithian for life, whether they liked him or not. The fact that he was rich would just be icing on the cake.

"I don't care," he said aloud. "I'm ready to be alone for a while anyway."

"Shall I lock them out when they return?"

Onca should have known Captain would be listening. *Great*. He would live here until he was old and gray, bickering with his computer.

What a life.

"No, don't lock them out when they return," Onca grumbled. "I'm not *that* big of an asshole."

"I was unaware that you were *any* size of such a thing."

"Yeah, well, don't go spreading it around. Wouldn't want to ruin my reputation."

"I shall keep it to myself."

Onca hesitated, frowning. "Wait a minute. When they return? You mean they *left*?"

"They did. They are going to look for that Jatki person."

"Son of a bitch!" Onca exclaimed. He stepped out from under the waterfall. "Dry me. *Fast*."

"As you wish."

Shaking back his hair, Onca stood with his arms outstretched, allowing the dryer access to as much body surface area as possible. "Did they say where they were going?"

"No, but they were armed and took the speeder in which Roncas arrived."

Shit. Onca had a speeder too. However, having no idea which way they might have headed left him with no alternative but to wait for them. Roncas had her comlink, her speeder, and Onca had seen that little pistol of hers a thousand times. There was no need for him to try to be a hero again—especially since it didn't work out so well the last time. Kim would probably be pissed at him for following them anyway. "I might as well go to bed."

"Considering your current state of exhaustion, that is advisable."

"Wake me up when they come back." *If* they came back. Somehow, Onca wasn't sure they would. He could call Roncas later.

Oh, hell. He could call her *now*. Roncas had said he was lacking in common sense. Maybe she was right.

"Hey, Captain. Get Roncas on the house comlink, will you?"

Onca could've sworn he heard the computer snickering. "One moment."

He arched a brow at the nearest sensor. "Aren't you supposed to suggest shit like that whenever I'm acting like I'm too stupid to live?"

"Perhaps. But it is such a joy to watch you struggle."

"Thanks. I'll keep that in mind the next time I'm struggling."

Moments later, Roncas's huge eyes filled the view-screen on the wall in Onca's bedroom. "Not now, Boss. We're busy, I'm driving, and you're naked."

"I'm *always* naked," Onca retorted. "You've probably only seen me dressed eight or nine times in the past ten years."

"Yes, but the kid hasn't seen you undressed, and we must protect her innocence."

"My name is *Kim*." Onca couldn't see her, but Kim

was obviously in the speeder with Roncas. "And I'm not *that* innocent."

Especially since she'd at least seen a picture of him naked. "You tell her, Kim," Onca said. "Where are you?"

"On the way to the rendezvous point Jatki and Kim had arranged," Roncas replied. "She didn't come out when Kim gave her the all-clear signal."

"And you didn't bother to tell me this because…?"

The comlink sensor shifted to reveal Kim sitting in the passenger seat. "You didn't seem interested."

"That's because I didn't think you needed me. Do you?"

"Well…no. Not really."

"Fine. Call me back if you think my pathetic self can ever be of some use."

"You aren't pathetic," Kim said. "Just…unnecessary at the moment."

Onca sneered at her image on the viewscreen. "Didn't you ever hear the one about there being safety in numbers?"

"Not in so many words." Her eyes flicked sideways to Roncas. "Maybe he's right."

"Mother of the gods! For once in my life, I'm right. Maybe. Ha!"

Onca wasn't sure why all of this had him so irritated, but he couldn't deny that he was supremely annoyed.

Probably something I ate. Or didn't eat. Or lack of sleep. The latter being the most likely, he decided.

"If you want to come with us, we're at—no, wait! There she is!" Kim exclaimed, pointing straight ahead.

"See any Herpatronians around?" Onca asked.

"Nope. Don't see anyone but her." Kim's face fell. "She isn't giving me the signal. Something's wrong."

REBEL   45

Onca rolled his eyes. "Probably doesn't expect you to be in a speeder. Or it *could* be a trap. Do you have a signal for that?"

Kim nodded. "She isn't giving me either one."

"One Kitnock looks very much like another, you know," Onca said as he pulled on his pants. Stepping into his shoes, he headed for the back door. "Where are you?"

"The corner of Latreess and Mornil," Roncas replied. "On the edge of the commerce district. You know where that big red Wiklaraben statue is?"

"Yeah. I know it. Head two blocks east and wait for me. Do *not* go anywhere near that girl 'til I get there. Understood?"

"Bossy, isn't he?" Kim commented.

Roncas nodded. "You don't know the half of it."

"Nice," Onca snapped. Snatching up his tunic, he checked to make sure he had credits, his comlink, and his Nedwut pulse pistol. *At least one of us is prepared.*

"Sign me onto the speeder link, Captain," he called out as he darted out the back door.

Climbing into his speeder, he tried to remember the last time he'd used the damn thing. *At least a couple of months ago.* Fortunately it was protected by a light weather shield and wasn't covered with dust. Firing up the engine, he flew off toward the commerce district.

He glanced at the linkpad. "You two still there?"

"Yes," Kim replied.

"I've been thinking—"

"*That* sounds dangerous," Roncas said.

"Will you *stop*? I'm thinking maybe I should cruise by and give her your signal. I mean, the bad guys aren't out to get *me*. So it'd just look like I was picking her up."

"I'm presuming that would be for sex," Roncas twittered.

"Thought you were trying to protect the kid's innocence," Onca drawled. "Doesn't sound like it to me."

"Yeah, right," Kim said. "Like my innocence needs so much protecting. But a Zetithian picking up a Kitnock? Nobody would ever believe *that*."

Onca gritted his teeth so hard his fangs dug into his lip. "Will you two knock it off? I could be picking her up to take her to the space station to go visit her Great-Aunt Vlordkin for all anyone knows. It doesn't have to be for sex."

"True," Roncas admitted. "This isn't the brothel district."

"Why, thank you, Roncas," Onca said sweetly. "That wasn't so hard, was it? Can you still see her from where you are?"

"Just barely," Kim replied. "We'll keep an eye on her until you get here."

He flew on through the city, dodging slower traffic and a huge Darconian male who was lumbering across the street. His scaly tail swished back and forth in his wake, nearly flipping the speeder as Onca skimmed over it.

"Sorry!" he yelled as he flew past.

The Darconian thumped his tail on the street in reply. Onca wasn't completely sure what that meant and thought back to the last time he'd fucked one of the dinosaur-like lizards. As he recalled, sex had definitely involved tail thumping.

Must be a good thing, then.

Or at least the Darconian equivalent of *Hey, no problem, pal.*

Banking the speeder through a turn, he remembered he didn't have to worry about that sort of thing anymore. No more getting an erection from Audrey's scent in order to fuck what amounted to a snub-nosed *Tyrannosaurus rex*. Those days were over, whether he went back to work at the brothel or not. Fucking Darconians hadn't been possible for several years now, anyway. Not since Audrey was murdered by that crazy Davordian woman.

We were too greedy.

That was where they had gone wrong. Sex with females who aroused them naturally was the only way to go. Besides, Darconians never got their money's worth. The joy juice pumped out by the coronal serrations of a Zetithian penis didn't have the orgasmic effect on them that it had on, say, Terran females. The *snard* seemed to work, though. At least, they all said it did, and that reaction was tough to fake.

Audrey's death had affected Jerden the most, but Onca knew if they hadn't followed her suggestion to hire her so they could fuck anyone with a thousand credits to spare, she would probably still be alive today. Jerden wasn't the only one undone by the guilt. Onca had endured his fair share.

Not that feeling guilty would bring Audrey back. Nonetheless, as Onca saw it, his job was to keep Kim alive long enough to claim her portion of the trust fund. Perhaps it was his way of atoning for that other sin. He wasn't sure. He only knew he had to deliver her to Terra Minor alive and well. Then he could get on with his life.

Such as it was.

―✺―

Kim never took her eyes off Jatki as her friend stood next to the building they had picked for their meeting spot. They had chosen it because it was out in plain sight, making it difficult for an ambush or a kidnapping—all of which seemed less incredulous and more possible as the hours ticked by. The girls had always kept to the shadows, eluding the police, irate merchants, or males with nefarious intentions.

She liked that word, nefarious. There were lots of words she didn't understand the meaning of, much less how to spell them. Not that she needed to do much of that, but with her limited education, learning was a forbidden passion to her.

Kim didn't like feeling stupid, and being streetwise didn't count. She could read and write well enough to interpret signs and do basic math, but that was the extent of her knowledge. Any science had been learned through observation. Jatki had been in school longer and had taught her a few things, but what Onca said about Zetith left her stunned.

Her parents must have known at least some of Zetith's history, but they had never mentioned the destruction of their homeworld. Perhaps it was too painful for them to discuss or perhaps they thought their children were too young for such knowledge. Either way, history was a subject Kim knew very little about, and living on the fringes of society made it difficult to keep up with current events. Small wonder she hadn't heard about the destruction of Zetith or the man responsible for it. He must have been incredibly rich to wage a war against her people and still have enough money left to create a trust fund.

She hated to admit it, but she had never even heard of a trust fund before and had derived the meaning from the context of the conversation. Was there such a thing that could fill a person's head with knowledge without sitting through years of schooling? Maybe there was if you had enough to pay for it. Imagine waking up one day with a head full of facts and figures and the know-how to express artistic talent. Peska could draw well, not that the materials were readily available to them. She'd stolen a lump of something called clay once and had given it to Kim.

"You make things out of it," she had said. "Watch."

Peska had pressed and formed the ugly lump into the shape of a flower, then a dog, then a bird with outstretched wings. Kim had kept that clay for months, turning it into something different each day until it was no longer pliable. It remained in the shape of a fish until one day she realized it was no longer among her tiny cache of possessions. Ever since then, she imagined that happiness was a never-ending supply of clay or some other substance she could shape into whatever her heart desired.

Peska had called it sculpting. Funny word for something so marvelous. Kim hardly dared to hope that what Onca had told her was true. If so, the first thing she was going to buy with her money was a big hunk of clay and some drawing paper and pencils for Peska.

That is, if they ever found her.

She kept her eyes on Jatki, praying to any deity that would listen that her Kitnock friend didn't disappear right in front of her eyes. The others had gone missing during the night. Surely Jatki was safe on the street in broad daylight.

Onca's voice over the comlink broke the silence. "Okay. I see her now. What's the signal?"

Kim raised her hands in front of the comlink pad and cracked the knuckles on the index and ring fingers of her left hand.

Onca snickered. "That's it? My, how unique and imaginative. No one would ever accidentally duplicate such a gesture."

Obviously he was retaliating for the way she and Roncas had teased him. "It's Kitnock fingerspeak for 'All clear.'"

"You don't say."

"I *do* say," Kim retorted. "Haven't you ever noticed how Kitnocks crack their knuckles a lot when they get together?"

"I don't believe I have," Onca replied. "But then, I've always fucked them one at a time."

"Onca!" Roncas exclaimed. "Will you *please* watch your language?"

Kim had to bite her lip to keep from laughing. "Trust me. That's our signal."

"Not much of a signal unless the person you're signaling can *see* you, is it?"

"Better than yelling it out if there are nasty Herpatronian rapists hanging around, don't you think?"

"Maybe," he conceded. "Okay. I'll give it a try, but it's still a rotten signal."

Kim watched as he pulled over to the edge of the street and opened the canopy of the speeder. After waving at Jatki, he held up his hands and cracked the two knuckles.

Jatki shook her head and leaned back against the

building, her fingertips gripping the rough surface as though she was stuck to it.

"Dammit, Jatki, I'm not cracking my knuckles again," he yelled. "You get your ass in this speeder right *now*. Kim sent me."

Instantly, his speeder was surrounded by the nastiest-looking bunch of—to be honest, Kim didn't know *what* they were, but they didn't look friendly.

"Get in the speeder!" she screamed over the comlink, hoping Jatki could hear her.

The results were immediate. Jatki dove into the passenger seat, the canopy slid shut, and Onca's speeder screamed off down the street. The gang of thugs fired a couple of pulse blasts in their wake with no apparent effect.

"Great mother of the gods!" Onca swore. "Don't you girls *ever* go off without me again! Didn't I tell you it might be a trap? Didn't I?"

"Calm down, Boss," Roncas said. "We need to rendezvous somewhere other than your house in case we're followed."

"Your place?"

"Oh, hell no," Roncas said without the proper inflection to accompany her words. "I was thinking we should go to the Palace."

"Or maybe somewhere more neutral, like the restaurant district?" Onca suggested. "Jatki looks like she could use some lunch."

Although she hated to admit it, Kim was hungry again herself. She was used to the feeling, but if Onca was offering to buy lunch, she would definitely eat it. "Are you okay, Jatki?"

"Yes," her friend replied. "And you're right. It was a trap. I've got a tracking device on me."

"Must not be very smart crooks if you know it's on you. Get rid of it," Onca snapped. "Throw it out in the street."

"I can't," Jatki replied. "They, um, made me swallow it."

"Well, shit," Onca said. "What the fuck do we do now?"

Roncas was twittering so hard she was having trouble steering her speeder. "I think having lunch is actually the best thing for her to do."

"What? Oh, yeah, right." Onca chuckled. "Guess we really do need to feed her. A lot."

"Better make it someplace safe if they're tracking us," Kim said. She was about to suggest they head straight for a police station when Onca snapped his fingers.

"I know just the place," he declared. "Nobody will bother us there, and if we need to, we can shoot our way out."

"Oh, no," Roncas groaned. "Not Oswalak's. Their food always gives me the runs."

"That's the idea," Onca said. "And the guys that work there are bigger and meaner than any Rackenspries ever thought about being."

"Is *that* what those things were?" Kim asked. "I've never seen them before."

"Yeah. Nasty little shits. Easy to buy off, too, which probably means someone paid them to waylay us. The guys at Oswalak's will know what to do if any of them follow us."

Kim wasn't so sure about that. "Can you trust them?"

"Oh, yeah," Onca replied. "The cook owes me a favor."

"How come?"

"I fucked his sister for free. Don't give out many freebies, so technically, he owes me a thousand credits. This should make us even."

Chapter 5

SHEMLAK WASN'T QUITE AS ACCOMMODATING AS ONCA had hoped. After being shown to their table, a quick word to their waitress had brought the cook swaggering out of the kitchen. However, having heard Onca's request, he stared down at him with a level of intimidation that only a Darconian could achieve.

"Let me get this straight," Shemlak said. "You want protection from a bunch of Rackenspries?"

"Yeah," Onca replied. "Got a problem with that?"

"Not really, I'm just wondering why. What'd you do, refuse to fuck one of them?"

Roncas sat beside him, twittering her amusement. Onca attempted to silence her with a sharp look and a nudge, both of which were unsuccessful.

"Not exactly. Besides, I'm on leave. Or retired. Or something. Not sure."

Shemlak's huge, reptilian eyes narrowed. "You actually *quit*?" He glanced at Roncas for confirmation. "Really?"

Roncas nodded. "Paid me a parting bonus and everything."

"Um, yeah." Onca arched a brow. "Does it matter?"

Shemlak let out a howl. "Ganyn will be pleased. She's been hoping you'd retire ever since you gave her that shot of your *snard*."

Onca failed to see why Ganyn would care one way or the other, unless she thought he might be giving out more freebies now that he was no longer working at the Palace. For the record, he wasn't. "I don't do Darconians anymore. Not since Audrey's death. Scent's not right."

"You didn't have Audrey when you did Ganyn. Remember? She brought along that Terran friend of hers."

"Tell me about it," Onca said with a snort. "I wound up doing them both."

"To their collective delight," Shemlak said. "They *still* talk about it."

"Yeah, well, I only did it because Ganyn had an appointment scheduled with Jerden and he'd already gone off the deep end. I quit doing species that required a fluffer after that."

Although Onca had done his best to honor all of Jerden's commitments in the wake of Audrey's murder, the strain had nearly killed him. Jerden had taken a certain satisfaction in fucking Darconians, enjoying the way their scales changed color during orgasm. Onca had never seen the attraction. He hadn't charged Ganyn because, truth be told, he didn't think he could do it even with a fluffer. The fact that he had still astonished him.

"What's a fluffer?" Kim asked.

Roncas twittered. "Someone whose scent keeps the guys...interested. Audrey was the Palace's fluffer until a crazy Davordian woman killed her because she wanted her job."

"Which is why I stopped using a fluffer," Onca declared. "And it's also why I decided to retire. I didn't want anyone else getting killed." He nodded at Shemlak. "Tell Ganyn I'm sorry, but my working days are over— probably forever."

The Darconian's laughter was enough to jiggle

the glowstones hovering near the ceiling above them. "She'll be so disappointed." Shemlak thumped Onca on the back with enough force that he nearly smashed his face into the table—a reminder of how dangerous it was to hang out with Darconians.

Glancing around the restaurant, he noted that for a place that served what were essentially uncooked— although undoubtedly fresh—fruits and vegetables, Oswalak's was doing a thriving business. They hadn't had to wait for a table, but the spacious room was filled to near capacity with customers of a dozen different species. The decor, however, was pure Darconian, which meant carved stonework on the walls, stone tables, and stone benches. The furnishings had to be sturdy enough to serve the Darconian clientele, all of whom weighed in at about two thousand kilos.

He nodded toward Jatki. "The Rackenspries made this kid swallow a tracking beacon. Think you could dish up a bowl of *tholuka* berries for her?"

Shemlak laughed even harder. "You *know* what they'll do to her."

"Yes, and you needn't tease the poor girl. Trust me, she feels bad enough already."

One look at Jatki would have proven his point to just about anyone, including a Darconian. Her skin, which should have been greenish-brown, had a slight yellowish tint to it, and the corners of her enormous mouth had taken a decidedly downward turn. Onca had never been able to understand why a species with arms and legs that looked like sticks needed a mouth that big, and as narrow as her torso was, he doubted it would take more than one bowl of *tholuka* berries to completely expunge the contents of her digestive tract. Jack had expressed similar sentiments once, saying that Kitnocks reminded her of Beaker from *The Muppet Show*. Onca had no idea what she meant by that—but then, Jack had some rather antiquated tastes in entertainment.

Onca had tried doing a Kitnock after Audrey's death, but was forced to admit defeat. Their scent was as asexual as their appearance, and the only difference he had ever been able to discern between the sexes was that the males wore red body stockings while the females wore blue. Never having seen any of them dressed in any other colors or styles led him to believe that even *they* couldn't tell the difference.

Jatki, however, was unique, and Onca could understand why Kim had been convinced of her identity. The tufts of hair growing from the top of her cylindrical head were purple—a variation Onca had never seen before, and one that clashed horribly with the orange-green tint of Shemlak's scales.

Onca winced as Shemlak patted Jatki on the back— although he did seem gentler with the Kitnock girl than he'd been with him.

"Don't worry," Shemlak said. "We'll take care of you. If any Racks come around, I'll step on them."

That was the other reason for bringing the girls to Oswalak's. Darconians weren't impervious to pulse weaponry, but it took a really strong setting to stun one of them. Not that there were many who would even attempt it. Shemlak was big, even for a Darconian, and could probably take out a dozen Rackenspries with one swipe of his tail.

With a wink at Onca, Shemlak swung his head

toward the patio. "Hey, Ganyn! Get your scaly tail in here. We've got a customer you might want to see."

Oh, shit...

Moments later, Ganyn, a slightly smaller version of her brother with blue highlights to her otherwise green scales, came in from the patio where she had presumably been waiting tables. "Onca, *baby*. Come to Mama!"

Onca braced himself as Ganyn snatched him off the bench, giving him a hug that squeezed most of the breath from his lungs. "Hey, Ganyn," he gasped. "Long time, no see."

Roncas let out another twitter, Kim's smirk clearly displayed her amusement, while Jatki still seemed stunned by the entire scenario.

"Why don't you ever come to visit me?" Ganyn demanded. "You sweet, delicious little thing, you." She kissed him in true Darconian style, swiping her long tongue across his cheek. "I've missed you dreadfully."

Onca patted the top of her head, wishing he had never agreed to fuck a dinosaur woman, for free or otherwise. Then again, saying no to a Darconian wasn't easy. "Sorry. Been too busy."

Roncas grinned—a wicked, devious grin. "He's retired now, so he can see you more often."

After shooting his former receptionist a look that promised retribution, he gave Ganyn a quick kiss somewhere near her ear. "But only for lunch. Sorry."

"I understand," Ganyn said, although she didn't seem very happy about it. Setting him back on the bench, she nodded at Kim. "A Darconian couldn't hope to compete with a Zetithian girl, anyway."

Onca's mouth fell open. "We only met this

morning," he said after recovering his wits. "She isn't my mate or anything."

The moment the words were out of his mouth, Onca realized his mistake.

"Ah. So *that's* how it is!" With an exhale that sounded more like a hurricane than a sigh, Ganyn leaned down and licked his cheek again. "There's hope for me then."

Figuring he had nothing to lose, he aimed a beseeching look across the table at Kim.

She cleared her throat. "I, um, really like him, though. You never know how these things will turn out."

Onca felt slightly relieved until he noticed her peculiar expression—sort of like she'd been pinged with a pulse pistol.

"I mean, he *did* rescue me from that Herpatronian," she went on. "And he saved Jatki from the Rackenspries. He's promised to help me find my missing friends too."

"Maybe," Jatki said, speaking up for the first time since their arrival. "I still don't trust him."

"Mother of the gods," Onca muttered. "Here we go again. Why *wouldn't* you trust me?"

Jatki sat slumped on the bench, looking down at her hands, her slit-like eyes blinking rapidly. "We don't know anything about you. At least, *I* don't. I see no reason to trust you."

"But I *saved* your ass, didn't I?" he demanded. "Isn't that enough?"

"Not for me."

For the first time, it occurred to him that maybe the reason Jatki hadn't jumped into his speeder right away was because she feared *him* as much as the Racks. She had clung to her side of the speeder during

the entire ride to Oswalak's and was now seated on
the opposite side of the table as far away from him
as possible. He could understand why she might not
trust him, but that she seemed *afraid* had him bugged.
No one had ever been afraid of him before—or had
any reason to be.

"That's okay," Roncas said. "She missed the orienta-
tion lecture."

Turning slowly, he gave Roncas his version of the
evil eye. "And what *exactly* do you mean by that?"

Kim giggled. "Don't worry. I'll explain it to her later."

"He wouldn't hurt a fly," Ganyn said, stroking his
hair with a little more force than necessary. "Sweetest
man in the galaxy."

Shemlak let out a snort that made Jatki cringe. "Yeah.
Right. Better take their order, Ganyn. As far as you're
concerned, he's a lost cause."

———

That was weird.

For one brief moment, Kim wished she was the one
Onca had kissed. Not only that, she was a bit envious
that Ganyn could run her long, scaly fingers through his
hair and *she* couldn't.

Even weirder.

When it was her turn to order, not trusting herself to
look at Onca again, she focused on Roncas instead. "I
don't know what to ask for."

Onca handed her a menu. She took it without meeting
his eyes and glanced at it briefly. "I don't know what
any of this means."

"She'll have the fruit," he said to Ganyn. After the

waitress left, he added, "Trust me, you wouldn't like the vegetables. They're kinda bland and stringy."

Accustomed to eating whatever she could get her hands on, Kim wasn't that particular. She thought he would have figured that out by now, but apparently, he hadn't.

Another waitress brought their drinks and Kim focused on sipping hers—which wasn't difficult since it was sweet and frothy and probably the best thing she had ever tasted. Still keeping her eyes fixed on the table in front of her, she was nonetheless aware of Onca's scrutiny.

"You can't read very well, can you?" he finally asked.

"Is it that obvious?"

"It wouldn't be if I hadn't known Tarq. He had a helluva time learning to read, and he never did get good at it. Something about words being sort of jumbled up when he looked at them. Since you've been on the street since the age of ten, I'm guessing you didn't get to spend much time in school." He nodded at Jatki. "Or you, either."

"Jatki taught me some stuff," Kim said. "She went to school until she was almost thirteen."

If Onca thought it strange that she was speaking for her friend, he kept it to himself. "I'm not much of a teacher, but I bet Captain could pull up some educational programs. You two could learn all kinds of stuff from him."

"Great idea," Roncas said. "He could teach them to annoy the crap out of you."

"Okay. So maybe it *isn't* a good idea," Onca grumbled. "Forget I said anything."

Kim had just been offered the one thing she wanted

most of all, and he was letting it drop? "I think I'd like that. But we need to find our friends first."

Roncas gave Onca a nudge. "Looks like you'll be starting a school for street kids."

"There are already schools like that. I'm offering them a home."

Kim gaped at him in disbelief. "You'd let us live in your *house*?"

He shrugged. "Sure, why not?"

Kim could think of a hundred reasons why not. Not the least of which was the way Jatki was trembling.

He scares me, she said in fingerspeak.

"I'm pretty sure we can trust him," Kim said aloud. She could understand that language far better than she could speak it. Zetithian knuckles didn't crack quite as easily as those of Kitnocks.

"Yes, you can trust me," Onca said. "If nothing else, I have Ganyn to vouch for my character. That is, if you trust Darconian waitresses." He didn't wait for Jatki to reply before continuing. "So, Jatki. Why don't you tell us how those little pigs captured you and made you swallow a tracking beacon?"

Jatki reached for Kim's hand beneath the table, and Kim gave it a reassuring squeeze. Jatki had been so brave while making plans for this mission. Kim didn't fully understand what her problem was now, unless one of the Rackenspries had hurt her. Then again, they *had* made her swallow a beacon, and somehow Kim doubted Jatki had been very cooperative.

"I—I followed the Herpatronian," Jatki said. "I thought if I saw where he went, we would know more about where to look for the other girls."

"Good idea," Onca said with a nod. "What went wrong?"

"I'm not sure. I think he expected to be followed because he hadn't gone far when he turned down another street. By the time I got to the corner, he was gone. Then those creeps jumped out and grabbed me."

"The plot thickens," Roncas said. "So you never saw where any of them wound up?"

Jatki shook her head. "I was too scared to follow them after they let me go." She glanced at Kim. "And I had no idea where to find *you*. All I could do was go back to our meeting place." Her voice dropped to a whisper. "I think they're after you, Kim."

"That's not too surprising," Onca said. "She's the one that got away. She's a danger to them, and they know it."

"So what do we do now?" Kim asked.

"Hmm…well, they used Jatki as bait to try to get *you*. I guess we should use *her* as bait to catch *them*."

Jatki started cracking her knuckles again.

"Oh, I don't mean you, specifically," he said. "I mean the tracking beacon. We could put it on someone else, and they'd follow the signal right into our trap."

Kim tried to find a fault with this plan and couldn't do it. *Yet*. "But wouldn't we wind up just catching those Rackenspries?"

"Maybe. Maybe not. Might catch the ringleader, although I doubt it. That's the sort of thing flunkies usually do." He chewed thoughtfully on a fingertip. "I guess we could torture them and make them talk."

"You can't be serious," Roncas snapped. "That's, that's—"

"I believe the word you're looking for is inhumane,"

he said. "That is, if you happen to be Terran. Come to think of it, that's the Stantongue word for it too." He sat for a moment, staring off into space. Then his expression changed, becoming quite devious. "Aw...it couldn't be *that* easy."

"What?" Kim prompted.

"We'll *buy* them off," he announced. "I'm sure I can pay them more than those other thugs can. My business might be more legitimate than theirs, but I bet they don't charge as much per hour as I did."

Jatki stared at him. "Exactly what kind of business are you in?"

"Haven't figured that out yet, huh?" Roncas snickered. "He's a hooker."

"I am *not* a hooker!" Onca insisted. "Hookers stand out on street corners trolling for customers. I am a highly paid private entertainer seen by appointment only. Women waited *years* to spend an hour with me."

Roncas rolled her eyes. "He's a *hooker*."

"*Was*," Onca snapped. "I'm retired, remember?"

"Yeah, well, you might have to go back to work to pay off those Racks," Roncas said. "And don't even *think* about revoking my bonus or I'll sic the Brothel Guild on you."

Kim glanced at Jatki. "Can you tell they've been working together too long?"

Jatki replied with a weak smile, which was an improvement of sorts.

"How did they get you to swallow that beacon, anyway?" Kim asked.

"Said they'd kill me if I didn't," Jatki replied. "Besides, it was wrapped up in a piece of bread. I was hungry."

"Poor kid," Onca said. "And here we are making you eat *tholuka* berries."

"I don't mind," Jatki said. "I'd like to get that beacon out of me anyway. It's a creepy feeling, knowing I can be tracked."

"Better stay away from Terra Minor," he said with a chuckle. "Immigrants have a tracking implant inserted into the base of their skulls when they land there. Keeps the riffraff in line—or so they think. Doesn't always guarantee compliance with the rules, though."

Kim shuddered. "Sounds terrible."

"I'm told it's painless, although I don't see how it could be. By the way, that's where you'd have to go to collect your share of that trust fund I was telling you about."

"I'd rather not."

"Don't worry," he said. "Zetithians are exempt from the implants. And you don't have to stay there if you don't want to. But since it was designated as the new Zetithian homeworld, that's where everything's headquartered, including the database from the refugee ship, which has just about every scrap of data there is pertaining to Zetith. Amelyana lives there. I'm sure she'd love to meet you."

"Who's Amelyana?"

Onca grimaced. "Technically, she's the one who about got us all killed—but she *did* manage to save a few of us. She was Rutger Grekkor's wife. Took a Zetithian lover—the son of the Zetithian ambassador to some planet or other. Anyway, after Grekkor killed *that* guy, she went to Zetith to find another lover."

"You'd think she'd have learned from her first mistake," Kim said.

"Yeah, well, that's the problem, see? We're not only the best lovers in the galaxy, we're sort of addicting." He held up a hand as if to silence any protests she might have made. "Trust me, it's true. And I'm not the one who said it.

"Grekkor was so stinking rich, he paid an army of mercenaries to kill us off. As you might've guessed, he was a little nutso. After they blew up any means we had of getting off the planet, they diverted an asteroid to crash into Zetith. Then Grekkor put a bounty on any offworld survivors. Nedwut bounty hunters killed most of them—which I'm *sure* is what happened to your family. Before the asteroid hit, Amelyana stole one of her husband's starships and picked up about a hundred Zetithian kids, including me. We flew around in space for the next twenty-five years until another Zetithian, Trag Vladatonsk, finally killed Grekkor. With him dead, Amelyana inherited his wealth and set up the trust fund."

"I have to admit, I didn't believe you when you first told me that," Kim said. "It all sounds so...*crazy.*"

Onca shrugged. "You don't have to take my word for it. There's plenty of evidence to prove it's true." He glanced up as Ganyn returned with their food. She set the plates on the table and then pinched him on the cheek before swaggering back to the kitchen.

"That's gonna leave a mark," Roncas said.

"Probably." Onca rubbed his cheek for a second or two, then picked up a piece of fruit and bit into it. "Not too bad. Watch out for those yellow star-shaped things, though. They'll put a pucker in your mouth like you wouldn't believe."

He was quiet after that, leaving Kim to wonder if he

was simply hungry or if telling that story made him sad. It certainly made *her* feel that way. All those people killed because Amelyana fell in love with one man—or maybe it was two. Onca didn't say whether she had ever found another lover. Considering that part about Zetithian men being addicting, she probably had. But how could anyone become addicted to another person? It didn't make sense.

Although Kim had done her best to avoid looking at him earlier, now that he seemed preoccupied, she found it difficult to keep her eyes off him. Watching him made her feel strange, but it wasn't a *bad* feeling.

Maybe he really is addicting.

Kim tried one of the purple fruits. It tasted good but had a mealy texture. She liked the red, crunchy ones better.

"These berries are sweet, but kinda"—Jatki stopped in mid-sentence, her face turning even more yellow than it was before—"slimy."

Onca pointed to a sign in the corner. "Restroom is that way."

Chapter 6

ONCA COULD ALMOST FEEL KIM'S EYES ON HIM. THE chance to further her education seemed to have pleased her, but something in her gaze was a bit...unnerving. He had eaten half a *crafnet* before he realized what the problem was. Zetithian girls had always made him feel like he was lacking in some way, and a few of his clients at the Palace had done the same thing.

As Zetithians went, Onca was about average—not as handsome as Tarq or as big and muscular as Jerden. He'd never admitted it to anyone, but since none of the girls on the refugee ship would give him the time of day, he'd been a virgin when he started working at the brothel—a fact that his flirty, womanizing attitude had concealed reasonably well. His first client—a Terran woman in her fifties—had given him confidence, along with a few suggestions. Still, as blown away as she'd been by the joy juice, he doubted she'd noticed how nervous he was.

His performance had improved with practice, and he was now as skilled as any lover and more experienced than most. After Audrey's death, he'd done his best to pick up the slack rather than canceling Jerden's appointments. Onca had assumed that, as far as their clients were concerned, a Zetithian was a Zetithian and none of them would care one way or the other. Most didn't complain—at least, not afterward—but a few had been rather vocal about their disappointment when they got him instead of Jerden.

And now Roncas had called him a hooker in front of both of the girls. That it was essentially true didn't matter; it was still a less than glowing assessment of his character. He could've done without the hugs and kisses from Ganyn too. Sure, she was a nice enough woman and had a good opinion of him, but the fact that she was a lizard emphasized just how indiscriminate he'd been.

Not surprisingly, his offer to let the girls stay with him hadn't been met with much enthusiasm. No doubt they figured him for some kind of pervert. He wasn't, of course, but he *could* relate to a couple of homeless orphans—at least, he assumed Jatki was an orphan. As afraid of him as she was, he thought there might be more to her story—perhaps including someone who really *was* a pervert.

Jatki returned from the restroom a few minutes later, her color a little more normal as she slapped the tracking beacon down on the table beside his plate. "Don't worry. I washed it." She resumed her seat next to Kim. "Could I have some real food now?"

"Sure," Onca replied. "Anything you want."

"I'll have the vegetables," she said, rubbing her belly. "Not sure I could take any more fruit for a while."

Onca waved at Ganyn as she passed by and gave her Jatki's order.

"Sure thing, sweetie," the waitress replied. "Anything for *you*."

Well…at least Ganyn thought he was sweet. Perhaps she even thought enough of him to take the beacon and be the bait for their trap. He could just imagine the piggy faces of the Rackenspries when they tried to capture a Darconian. Then he realized he didn't have to give it to anyone. He could leave it right where it was. The little punks would come looking for it eventually. In fact, he was surprised they hadn't barged in on them before now.

Unless their boss was smarter than they were— although if the boss had any sense at all, he wouldn't have hired a bunch of Racks to do his dirty work.

Nor would Rutger Grekkor have hired Nedwuts to wipe out the remaining Zetithians. Nedwuts were good hunters, if somewhat lacking in intelligence. Still, when there was dirty work to be done, an instigator couldn't always be choosy when it came to hiring henchmen.

Henchmen... "Say, you girls don't know any other street kids, do you? I mean, the sort you'd trust?"

"Sure," Kim replied. "There are a lot of us—more than you might think."

"What if we got all the kids together and organized them—you know, provide them with food and shelter so they wouldn't have to steal? We could use them to search the city and try to find your friends. Think they'd go for it?"

Kim hesitated. "Some of them might. I'm sure they would all want the food and a place to stay, but there are some who actually *enjoy* stealing."

"Those aren't the kind we'd want," Onca said. "I'm talking about the sort that wouldn't steal unless they were forced to—who would jump at the chance for a more normal life."

"Like me and Jatki, you mean," Kim said. "Yeah, there are a few like us. Unfortunately, three of them are already missing."

"There aren't any others you'd trust?"

She chewed her lip as though pondering his question. "Yes, but finding them will be the hard part. We tend to hide from the other gangs—some of them are real creeps. There are a few that aren't *too* bad, but none of us stay in the same place for long."

"Yeah," Jatki said. "It's not like we have an official headquarters or a clubhouse."

Onca nodded. "But you're bound to have some hide-outs you've used more than once. You know…the really good nooks where no one has ever found you?"

Fangs sinking into her lower lip, Kim looked at Jatki with such an unreadable expression, he half expected the Kitnock girl to start cracking her knuckles.

Once again, Onca felt his irritation rising. "You don't need to tell *me* where it is. You can show Roncas if you don't trust me."

"It isn't that we don't trust you," Kim said. "We're not used to trusting *anybody*." She glanced at Roncas. "Sorry, but that's how it is."

"Which makes it real hard for us to help you," Onca said. "Every now and then, you have to take a leap of faith."

Astonishingly enough, Jatki was the one who spoke. "There's an empty warehouse on the north end of the commerce district. It was supposed to be torn down, but the owners are in a dispute with the city over how much the land is worth. We have a place on the upper floor. It's a long way up and there isn't much of an escape route, but at least the street sweepers can't see us."

"And neither can anyone else," Onca concluded. He understood the need to avoid the sweepers. The flatbed

droids roamed the city gathering up anyone they found
sleeping in the street and carried them off to the city's
drunk tank. Onca had never been picked up, but he knew
a few guys who had. Some of them had given up booze
altogether as a result of the experience, and those who
hadn't made a point of staying off the street. *Nobody*
wanted to get stuck spending the night with a bunch of
drunken Drells. They were annoying enough when they
were sober.

"Yeah," Jatki said. "Hardly anyone else ever goes
up there."

"Maybe we should check it out," Roncas suggested.

Kim shook her head. "Wouldn't be anyone up there
during the day, and we do our best not to leave any evidence that we were ever there."

"So where did you leave your clothes?" Onca was
fairly certain that Kim had never been one to wander the
streets nearly naked—not that anyone would remark on
it, but she didn't strike him as the type.

"I had them," Jatki said. She glanced at Kim. "Lost
them. Sorry."

"No worries," Onca said. "Just a question." Still, if anyone looking for Kim had found her clothing, there were
plenty of species on Rhylos that could use them to follow
her scent trail. "The bad guys didn't get them, did they?"

Jatki winced. "Maybe. I'm really not sure."

"Great," Onca said with a roll of his eyes. If that was
the case, the Racks could've already tracked Kim to his
house—which meant he and the girls really had nothing
to lose by going back there, whether they were followed
or not. No matter what happened, he wasn't about to let
a bunch of fuckin' Racks run him out of his house.

Shemlak swaggered over to their table with Jatki's veggies. He was moving as nonchalantly as possible for a Darconian, but Onca caught the high sign he was giving him—not to mention the fact that her lunch was in a box.

"One of the guys spotted a bunch of Racks hanging out in the bar across the street. You might want to head out through the kitchen entrance," Shemlak suggested. "We moved your speeders around back." He glanced at the beacon lying on the table. "Leave that here. I'll hang it on Draddut after a while. They'll get a real surprise if they try to jump *him*."

Since Draddut was even bigger than Shemlak, this was an excellent plan. "Ask him to squeeze some information out of them while he's at it, will you? I'd rather do that than pay them off. Goes against my principles to throw money away like that."

"Principles?" Roncas echoed. "Didn't know you had any."

Onca slammed his palms on the table. "Roncas, if you dislike me so damn much, why the hell did you ever come to work at the Palace?"

"Jerden hired me, remember? I hadn't met you when I took the job."

"I tell you *what*," Onca grumbled. "You give your receptionist a big bonus and she turns on you."

Roncas patted his hand. "I'm not turning on you. I'm speaking my mind."

"Same difference," Onca said, snarling. "Let us know what you find out, Shemlak, and tell Draddut not to lose that beacon. We may decide we want to use it to trap those punks ourselves at some point, but right

now, we have another strategy in mind." He got up from
the table. "Kim, you're riding with me—seeing as how
Roncas can't stand me and Jatki doesn't trust me."

Shemlak chuckled. "Just take it slow and easy
and maybe no one will notice you're going out the
wrong door."

Roncas led the way with Onca bringing up the rear.
Their escape would've been perfect if Onca hadn't yelped
when Ganyn pinched his ass as he tried to slip past her.

"You come back and see me again sometime, sweet
thing, and I'll bring my friend Judie along for the ride.
She misses you too."

Which meant that at least *one* woman who didn't
have scales and a tail liked him. With a quick wave at
Ganyn, he climbed into his speeder. The fact that Kim
got in beside him without any hesitation made him feel a
little better. "Let's split up and take the long way back,"
he said to Roncas.

"What if they're waiting for us?" she asked.

"With Captain on guard duty, they'll be sorry if they
do—which reminds me, I'd better give him a call."

"Right," Roncas said. "See you there." The canopy
slid shut as she turned her speeder toward the east and
took off down the alley.

Onca fired up his speeder and headed in the opposite
direction. Closing the canopy, he activated the cloaking
mechanism. "We're, um, invisible now. So if you see
anything about to hit us, give a yell."

"Invisible?" Kim echoed. "Really?"

"Yeah. I bought this speeder from a Nerik who swore
that feature would be the most useful thing ever. This is
the first time I've actually used it."

"Seems like it'd be kinda dangerous when there's much traffic."

"It is. Which is why it's illegal—and also why I need you to keep a lookout. All speeders have anti-collision sensors on them, but they don't work when we're cloaked, and neither does the navigator function. I have to fly it manually." He tapped the comlink pad. "Ahoy, Captain. Seen any strangers hanging around the house?"

"Not at this time," the computer replied. "Shall I activate the defense mode?"

"Yeah, but let Roncas and Jatki in if they get there ahead of us."

"And who, pray tell, is Jatki?"

"A Kitnock girl with purple hair. Trust me, you'll know her when you see her."

"I am certain of it," Captain said.

"Okay. Call me if you notice anything weird going on in the neighborhood."

"I shall comply. Captain out."

Terminating the link, Onca turned to Kim. "So, you want to tell me why Jatki thinks I'm worse than a Herpatronian rapist?"

"She doesn't think that. Really. Don't feel bad. It's more *what* you are than *who* you are. Men terrify her."

"I noticed that. I'm guessing some guy roughed her up?"

"Yeah. Her father used to molest her, and when he got tired of that, he liked to beat her up."

Expecting to hear almost anything but that, Onca felt like he'd been punched in the gut by a Darconian. "That's—that's...*horrible*. She's a runaway then?"

"Yeah. Which is why she *really* doesn't want anyone to know where she is. Especially her family."

Onca had never known his family and would have given his entire fortune to see them alive and well again. He couldn't imagine not wanting his family to find him. But then, he'd never been abused.

"Look out!" Kim shouted.

Onca halted the speeder just shy of another vehicle that was cutting through the alley. As inattentive as he was in the wake of Kim's revelation, he considered it best to stop for a moment. Easing the speeder closer to one of the buildings, he lowered the parking struts.

"Why are we stopping?"

"Because I'm too freaked out to drive. Mother of the gods! How can a father *do* that to his own child? I don't get it."

"Yeah, well, he's probably not the only one. Even on a nice, clean, happy planet like Rhylos."

Damenk prided itself on being the cleanest city in the galaxy. Everything—buildings, streets, and especially the landscape—was scrupulously maintained. Even the alleys were pristine. Flowers bloomed from planters behind each building and trailed from balconies above. Litter simply didn't exist, and the trash receptacles were works of art. And yet, heinous crimes still occurred—even in private homes like Jatki's. Onca shivered. No wonder these girls felt safer on the street than they would in his house.

Until now, when someone was apparently hunting them down like vermin. "Look, Kim. I know you girls have no reason to trust me, but I swear on the crumbling dust that was once my planet, I will not hurt you or any of your friends."

Onca had been trying not to look at her too much, but

he couldn't help it now—not when she sat with him in such a small, enclosed space. Nor could he ignore her scent. She had washed with the same soap he always used, and yet she smelled completely different—sweet, feminine, and something else he couldn't identify. Swirling in the air between them, her aroma kept his gaze riveted on her, drinking in her deep brown eyes and shining curls. The curve of her cheek. The upward slant of her brow. She wasn't just cute. She was *adorable*.

Allowing himself to be alone with her in a cloaked speeder was a mistake. Having Jatki cowering away from him would have been better than this. No one could see them here. No witnesses. No protection.

"I believe you," she whispered.

A heartbeat later, she hitched in her seat, leaning toward him until her lips touched his cheek. Strange new sensations flowed from the point of contact, weakening his resolve.

"You didn't have to do that."

"I know, but I wanted to." Her curious gaze roamed over his face. "Your cheek is so smooth." She traced the line of his jaw with a fingertip, setting off a renewed surge of astonishing tingles. "I never realized Zetithian men didn't have facial hair. My father never grew a beard, but I didn't know it was because he *couldn't*."

"None of us can." Onca was surprised he could even speak. She was so close; the air was thick with her unique essence.

"But you have hair in…*other* places."

She had obviously been paying attention to the pictures. "Yes." Until he heard the vibration in his reply, he wasn't aware he was purring.

I have to stop that.

Unfortunately, he had to hold his breath to do it.

"Ganyn seems very fond of you."

He shrugged. "Maybe. But it doesn't mean anything. She'd have been just as fond of Jerden if he'd been there for her appointment."

Kim sat back in her seat. With the increased distance between them, Onca breathed a little easier, but her scent was still incredibly powerful—mesmerizing, intoxicating.

"Would you kiss me?" she asked.

His eyes widened. "I shouldn't do that."

"Why not?"

"Because I—I'm too—" He managed to stop himself before he blurted out that he was too old for her, too used. She was young and fresh. She deserved a man like that—an untarnished youth closer to her own age. "I'm supposed to be protecting you from the bad guys and helping you find your friends. Stuff like that. Not kissing you."

"Oh." She glanced away, frowning. "Sorry. I just wanted to know what was so special about Zetithian guys."

"You'll find out someday. I have a friend whose sons are about your age." He forced out a chuckle, pleased to find that he was no longer purring. "There are three of them. You can afford to be choosy."

Pain seared his heart as he thought about how many times he had been passed over by "choosy" girls. Even after all this time and so many different women, the memory still hurt.

"You don't like me, do you?"

He gaped at her. "What? Of course I like you. I mean, we only met this morning, but I—"

"Then it's too soon for you to kiss me?"

"Well, no, it isn't that." Onca had kissed about a bajillion women after having only met them moments before. Granted, the circumstances were completely different, but—

"Then what is it?"

"Oh, hell, I don't know…"

Seemingly of its own accord, his hand shot out and cupped the back of her neck, pulling her close, his lips parting when they met hers. Completely unprepared for the explosion of flavor and scent, his shocked mind barely registered her arms encircling his neck, the tentative swipe of her tongue over his lips, and the press of her body against his.

Sweet and intoxicating, her aroma curled its way through him until it reached his groin, pumping heat into his cock for an erection so swift and painful he nearly screamed. He knew how to suppress that reaction—he was one of the few males of any species who could—but Kim had somehow managed to strip away that control with one kiss. She might not have enjoyed her previous attempts at sex, but someone had definitely taught her how to kiss. Her tongue slipped past his lips and into his mouth, teasing him until he was nearly insane with the need to rip her clothes off with his fangs.

He was purring again, and he couldn't stop that any more than he could suppress his erection.

I will not fuck her. I can't do that. I can't…

To his great relief and infinite disappointment, she drew away from him, her fingers pressed to her swollen lips. "Did I do that right?"

Onca was purring so hard he could scarcely draw a breath. All he could do was nod.

"That sound you're making. Is that normal?"

He nodded again. "Zetithian males purr to entice females, and females purr—" He stopped as words deserted him. He couldn't tell her that. He was supposed to be looking out for her, not corrupting her. She wasn't a client. She was his... His *what*?

Mate.

The word pounded in his brain like a drum.

No. It can't be. Not now. Not like this...

"Are you okay?" she asked.

He barely trusted himself to look at her. She gazed at him with eyes that were even more beautiful than they'd been mere moments before. Although her scent had undergone a subtle change, the fragrance of her desire lingered.

And she was still absolutely adorable.

"Not really."

Chapter 7

THE KISS HAD AFFECTED KIM IN WAYS SHE HAD NEVER expected, leaving her with the most peculiar urge to bite him. Then there was the desire to see him naked—for real this time rather than a picture. Unfortunately, the fact that kissing him had made him look sort of sick made her hesitant to try it again.

Still, there was that purring thing he did, and that part about doing it to entice females. He'd said it was normal, but did he have control over it? Was he trying to entice her? She racked her brain trying to recall how her parents had acted toward one another. Maybe once a Zetithian couple was married, purring became less important—either that or they only did it in private. Onca had stopped before telling her why a female would purr. The fact that she never had must mean it involved something she'd never done.

A heavy ache settled in the juncture of her thighs along with a strange, slippery wetness—something that had been noticeably lacking during her two previous sexual encounters. The first boy had actually stopped when he realized how much pain he was inflicting. He'd never made another attempt, implying that there was something wrong with her. The other had withdrawn prior to his climax—to prevent pregnancy, he said, although she suspected he was as uncomfortable as she had been.

Her mouth was watering so much she had to swallow before she spoke. "I'm sorry. I didn't mean to make you sick." She swallowed again, but for a different reason this time. Sitting back in her seat, she stared out the window. A tiny *sereta* crept out from under one of the flowering shrubs planted by the rear door of the nearby building, its long ears and droopy eyes reflecting her own dismal mood.

Kissing Ganyn hadn't made Onca sick. Not like *her* kiss had done. Maybe he didn't like kissing. Maybe he never kissed his clients. It was, after all, an excellent means of transmitting disease.

Or maybe it's me *that makes him sick.*

That was certainly a lowering thought. She'd kissed those other boys. They'd seemed okay afterward, even if sex had been a total failure.

"I'm not sick," he finally said. "I'm just…tired."

She'd forgotten he had been up all night. He should have been in bed hours ago. But, of course, that was her fault too.

"Don't worry," she said. "I won't ask you to kiss me again." She glanced behind them, then nodded at the alley up ahead. "You can probably uncloak us now. I don't think we're being followed."

He sat staring at her for a long moment, his expression somewhere between bewilderment and regret. "Uh, yeah. Might be best if we take the scenic route, though."

Without another word, Onca retracted the parking struts and took off down the alley, uncloaking the speeder just prior to reaching the main street. Turning right, he merged with the traffic, flying past places Kim had never seen before. Beautiful, intricate designs adorned the polished surfaces of the buildings—each one constructed in a different style. Beings from all over the galaxy mingled on the sidewalks, some dressed in outrageous clothing while others wore nothing at all. Vines covered with vivid blossoms climbed up the lampposts, and the pavement styles changed with each block they encountered—some paved with simple stone bricks while others were done in colorful mosaics.

"Where are we?" she asked.

"Upscale restaurant district," Onca replied. "Some of these places charge you fifty credits just to walk through the door." He shrugged. "It's pretty ridiculous, really. The food isn't *that* good."

"So you've been in some of them?"

"A few. But like I said, it really isn't worth the money."

Kim wasn't so sure about that. Opportunities to feast her eyes on such beauty were rare.

"This area is dazzling at night." He pointed at a street lamp. "Those lights are docked on posts during the day, but at night, they detach and hover." Slowing down, he nodded toward a large open space to the right. "Speeders aren't allowed in those squares. The restaurants and bars there never close, and they have live bands playing music all the time. Some are paved, but others are more like parks, with trees and plants from all over the galaxy."

Kim could only nod and stare. She'd never dreamed Damenk was this big—or this beautiful.

"Ever been through the government district?"

She shook her head. "We try to stay away from those places."

"I can understand that," he said. "The buildings there aren't as pretty as these, but some of them are huge."

He sounded more normal now; that strange, purring note had vanished from his voice. She stole a glance at him, only to realize that the most beautiful thing she had ever seen was sitting right next to her.

And I make him sick.

"Maybe we should go back to your house now," she said. "You need to get some sleep."

He nodded. "What about you?"

"Me? I haven't slept since…" She paused, trying to recall the last time she'd curled up in a quiet corner for a few hours. "Night before last."

"Then we'd better cut the tour short." He banked the speeder into a turn. "We'll both think more clearly after a nap."

"Yeah. It's funny, but anytime I feel bad, I go to sleep and wake up feeling fine. I'm hardly ever sick, and my cuts and bruises usually heal overnight. Weird, huh?"

"Not for a Zetithian. Those are some of our more useful characteristics. Good thing, seeing as how half the galaxy seems to want to bump us off."

And the other half wants to have sex with our men. He didn't say that, although he was probably thinking it. Strange how he was willing to fuck a Darconian but had such an aversion to kissing *her*. He said he wasn't sick, but it sure took him long enough to say it.

That kiss certainly hadn't made her feel bad—strange, perhaps, but not bad. In fact, she wanted to do it again.

Yet another thing in this life I can't have. Crap. She felt like crying, and she never cried. Well…hardly ever. She'd cried a lot when she was younger, especially during those first few nights on the street when she was terrified and starving. She was a lot tougher now and tried not to think about those times. Something about Onca made her think back to when she was a child and part of a family—back when she'd had parents and sisters. Onca had been a baby when he was rescued from Zetith. He wouldn't have known his family at all.

She turned toward him but quickly averted her gaze. That one glimpse made tears sting her eyes—and not only because she wanted to kiss him. He'd said she and Jatki could stay with him. Maybe he wanted a family as much as she did. She had already decided she would stay with him and accept his help. However, she had no intention of becoming his adopted daughter. Not when kissing him only made her want to kiss him again.

"We'll take a loop through the commerce district and then back to my house," Onca said. "Ahoy, Captain. How are things on the home front?"

"All is quiet," the computer replied.

"Any sign of Jatki and Roncas?"

"I believe they are arriving at this very moment," Captain said.

"Alone?"

"They do not appear to have been followed."

"Good. Let them in and then lock the place down tight. We'll be there in about ten minutes."

"I shall comply. Captain out."

He hadn't tapped the comlink. Apparently the link was also voice activated. Did that mean Captain could have eavesdropped on their conversation, including the part where she'd asked for a kiss? Kim sank into her seat, wishing she could disappear. Sure, Captain was only a computer, but he'd claimed to be sentient and definitely had a personality. She could only imagine what it would be like to have the house controlled by an entity that was privy to her secrets.

Creepy.

Kim had done a lot of things she wasn't proud of, and she had secrets she'd never shared with anyone. She would have to keep those thoughts to herself—no audible soul-searching, even in the middle of the night.

"Um...can he still hear us?"

"Not unless I call him, specifically."

"But he could listen to us if he wanted to, couldn't he? I mean, how would you know whether he did or not?"

He pointed at the linkpad. "That lights up when he's online."

She was somewhat reassured until she remembered simply talking to Captain while she was in the shower. She hadn't noticed any linkpads there. "How can you tell if he's on when you're in the house?"

"He hears and sees everything in the house," Onca replied. "Unless you give him a direct order for privacy. Not that I've ever needed to do that. Although there've been plenty of times when I had to tell him to shut up."

"Oh." *Even creepier.* She hadn't thought about a computer being able to see. He was probably still laughing at how skinny she was. Then again, there would always be someone to talk to. "Do you ever talk to him simply because you're lonely?"

"Who says I'm lonely?" He sounded defensive, almost angry.

"No one. I just wondered." He would be telling her to shut up before long, and he was probably regretting half the stuff he'd offered her. Still, she'd already asked a lot of questions, and as touchy as he was, keeping quiet might be a good idea.

Unfortunately, her brain was buzzing with queries— most of them about being Zetithian. Here she was, sitting next to one of her own kind for the first time in twelve years, and he didn't seem to want to talk to her.

I should never have asked him to kiss me. He'd been okay before that. Considering what he used to do for a living, she wouldn't have thought it was too much to ask. Then again, perhaps it was. Maybe he had to be paid to kiss people.

Too bad I don't have any money.

———

Onca toyed with the idea of engaging the navigator function—with the cloaking device off, it would work now—but decided it was best to keep his eyes on the road. Inhaling Kim's scent already had him primed; if he looked at her again, he would be purring in no time.

Since he and Kim obviously needed a chaperone, he hoped he could convince Roncas to stay at his house while the girls were there. Not that he would ever tell her the real reason. He would never hear the end of it, and after that discussion about Captain, he didn't want the computer to know why Roncas was there, either.

Roncas might see the need and choose to stick around herself. As jumpy as Jatki was, she might be begging the Zuteran to do just that. He could only hope.

Kim was right about one thing; he *was* lonely. Or at least he would be once he was home by himself all the time. He'd thought about planning a real vacation, getting Dax to take him from planet to planet, but he was looking forward to doing nothing for a while. He had never allowed himself to just *be*, and he wasn't sure why that was. The closest he'd come to it was hanging out at the ranch after Jerden's wedding. Terra Minor hadn't appealed to him in the beginning—it was too tame a place for a bunch of guys who'd been cooped up on a starship all their lives. It wasn't until he was lying on a chaise lounge by the lake that he truly began to appreciate the quiet, peaceful nature of that world.

Rhylos was a busy, heavily populated planet. There were areas devoted to food production, but they weren't anything like the wide-open spaces on Terra Minor. That brief respite proved how much he needed some down time, and the pleasant feeling he'd had while sitting around the campfire had been the primary reason he'd stopped booking appointments.

But he had a mission now. A purpose. He would help Kim find her friends, then he would take her to Terra Minor to claim her portion of the trust fund. When she no longer needed his help, he could relax and enjoy his retirement.

Until he got bored and lonely.

No. He would fill up the days somehow. He could go for walks on the beach, swim in the ocean, stop by and see the guys in the brothel district now and then. Invite them to lunch. Talk over old times.

And live in the past.

Was that really what he'd thought about doing the whole time he was growing up on that starship? *Again, no.* He'd wanted to go places, do things, be…adventurous.

Okay. So he also wanted to find a mate.

Onca had kidded himself for years. *Women don't*

want me, so I don't need them had been his mantra for
the longest time. Every girl he'd ever taken an interest in had ignored him. He had even gone into the sex
business to keep from getting attached to one woman
in particular.

Was working at the brothel his revenge? He couldn't
give it away, so he made them pay for it? And what was
the "it" he was referring to?

Sex?

Love?

Him?

Maybe all three. He glanced at Kim before he remembered his determination not to look at her. She wasn't
crying, but he had obviously hurt her feelings.

And I promised never to do that. Poor kid. He knew
exactly how it felt to be rejected. Sure, she acted tough—
she wasn't defenseless by any means—but she was so
tiny, so thin. Even Roncas's silky tunic and slacks were
too big for her.

He had to make it up to her somehow. With any other
woman, one good fuck would be enough to make her
forgive him. This time, he had to come up with something else—and he'd better do it quick. They were almost home. If she walked in with that hurt look on her
face, Roncas would have his hide. He didn't have time
to buy her a new dress, and all he had in his pockets were
a few credits, a comlink, and a pulse pistol. She would
probably appreciate any one of those things, but—

"I'm sorry." The words were out before he even knew
why he said them. "I shouldn't have snapped at you like
that. I didn't mean to. I'm just…"

"Tired. Yeah. So am I."

Somehow he doubted that exhaustion was the only reason for her silence. "I'm really not as big a jerk as you probably think I am. This hasn't been—"

"Your typical day?"

He blew out a breath. "You got *that* right."

"Mine, either."

Taking her hand, he gave it a squeeze, stopping himself microseconds before raising it to his lips. *Better not.* That other kiss had caused enough trouble.

Onca certainly couldn't argue the fact that he'd been the one to do the actual kissing, either. Kim had only asked.

Well…maybe that wasn't all she'd done. But he could've resisted. *Should've* resisted.

"Thanks for the kiss."

His jaw dropped. "Uh, you're welcome." *I think.*

"For what it's worth, you Zetithian guys kiss a lot better than Terrans. I'm not sure if it's the fangs or the purring, but it was a good kiss."

Slightly stunned, Onca had no idea what to say. "I'm…glad you enjoyed it."

"I think I need more practice, though. Who was it you said had three sons about my age?"

Onca glanced at her, half expecting her to have morphed into someone else. She was still the same girl, however, her expression every bit as guileless as her tone.

"Uh…Cat and Jack Tshevnoe," he replied. "You'll probably meet them once you get to Terra Minor. Or maybe even along the way. My friend Dax has a ship, and he usually takes me anywhere I need to go. But if he isn't available, I'm sure Jack will jump at the chance to be the one to bring you in. Speaking of which, I need to send out deep space coms to her and several other people. They'll all be very happy to know you've been found."

"Didn't know I was missing," she drawled.

Once again, Onca had to reassure himself that Kim still sat beside him rather than some imposter. He cleared his throat. "I guess that depends on how you look at it."

"Fair enough," she said with a nonchalant shrug. "Do you get a finder's fee?"

He frowned. "No. What makes you think that?"

"No reason." She shrugged again. "Just a question."

Reaching the turnoff, Onca flew the speeder down the street toward his house. "Heads up, now. If you see any Racks or Herps, give a yell."

"Don't worry. I will."

Two of Onca's neighbors were out watering their flowers, but he saw nothing to arouse suspicion. Flying around to the back, Onca parked the speeder and popped the canopy.

Kim's gaze drifted up the side of the house, coming to rest on the third-story balcony. "If you're the only one living here, how come you have such a big house?"

"I dunno. Look around. See any smaller ones?"

"Well, no," she admitted. "But it seems like an awful waste of space."

He grinned. "Not anymore. I've got plenty of room for you and your gang—three bedrooms and a bathroom on each of the upper floors."

"Do all the bathrooms have waterfalls like yours? That was pretty cool."

"No. I had that one put in when I bought the place.

I wanted something a little more Zetithian. The brothel has the same design." Jerden and Tarq had come up with the idea of making the Palace as much like their homeworld as possible. Onca couldn't remember Zetith at all, but he still felt more comfortable among the trees and waterfalls.

Kim climbed out of the speeder. After giving the hem of her tunic a tug, she combed back her hair with her fingers. "Aren't Zetithians always born in litters of three?"

"Yeah. Your point?"

She nodded at the house. "You've got enough room there for a wife and two litters." With a wink, she added, "You've been planning ahead, haven't you?"

Chapter 8

PLANNING AHEAD? FOR A WIFE AND TWO LITTERS? This time Onca caught his jaw before it dropped. He'd been gaping at her like an idiot enough as it was. "Not intentionally."

Kim nodded, but her sly smile suggested she didn't believe him. She pointed to the far side of the house. "What's that over there?"

"A pond," he replied. "The waterfall runoff goes through a purifier, then out to the pond, and then through another purifier before coming back in to the waterfall."

"So the pond is clean enough to swim in?"

"As long as you don't mind swimming with a giant turtle and some really big fish." He chuckled. "The turtle loves company. If you tell Captain to stop up the drain under the waterfall, he'll come inside and swim with you."

She cast furtive glances in all directions. "Do you think it's safe for me to take a look at it now?"

After conducting his own visual scan of the area, he nodded. "Sure, go ahead. I'll, um, keep you covered."

Onca led the way with his pistol drawn, unsure whether to stick close to her or stay back so he could keep a lookout. The latter was probably the best option, but for some reason, he was reluctant to do so.

The pond was shaded by a huge *linwayla* tree with trailing branches that nearly reached the water, its purple flowers interspersed with palmate leaves. The grassy bank sloped down to the water's edge from the ring of closely planted *tantuth* shrubs. Onca opened the gate and ushered her inside. "The shrubs keep the turtle from getting out, and they're a lot more attractive than a fence."

Kim touched the shimmering leaves with a tentative fingertip. "I've never seen anything like these before. They look like they're made of glass."

Recalling that same delicate touch on his face, Onca felt his throat tighten. "Yeah. They come from Edraitia. Pretty, aren't they?"

"Edraitia?" she echoed. "Never heard of it."

"Really? I bet you've seen some of the natives. Blue skin and bushy red hair?"

"So *that's* what Peska was! She never told me— wouldn't say why she was living on the street, either. She liked to draw—that is, when she could find something to do it with. She gave me some clay once. I made all kinds of shapes out of it until it was too dry to play with anymore." With a wistful smile, she cupped a leaf in her palm. "I really miss her."

"Hopefully we'll find her soon." If Kim kept saying things like that, Onca wouldn't wait until she received her share of the trust. He would give her everything he had. In fact, he wanted to do it right now.

What is wrong with me?

Shrugging off the odd feeling, he opened the automatic feeder and gave her a handful of fish food. "Here. Toss this in the water."

On cue, the fish surfaced and gobbled up every bit of it.

"Wow. I see what you mean. They're huge! Can you really swim with them?"

"Yeah. They nibble at your toes a little, but they don't actually bite. The pond's not very deep—you'd be able to touch the bottom."

Laughing, she looked up at him, her eyes brimming with mischief. "See? You even have pets for your children."

"That's funny. I thought they were *my* pets." Her laughter triggered a slight pang in his chest as he tapped the dispenser for more of the food. "The turtle's behind you."

To her credit, she didn't scream when she turned around. The turtle crawling up the bank toward her was easily as big as she was and probably outweighed her. "I thought turtles were green, not orange."

"Most of them are. This one's Delfian. They've got a lot of weird stuff there." Not the least of which were the native humanoid females who had eight breasts. "He'll eat right out of your hand, and he likes having his neck rubbed."

Kim held out her hand, and the turtle scooped the food from her palm. "Does he have a name?"

Onca shrugged. "Not really. I just call him Turtle. The fish are called *kalifins*."

"Are they Delfian too?"

"No. They're a species of goldfish from a lake about two hundred kilometers south of here." He nodded toward the pond. "Check it out."

She watched, openmouthed, as the *kalifins* swam together in perfect unison. After performing several spectacular leaps, they cut through the water with their golden tails fanned out above the surface, then turned on their sides and waved their long pectoral fins. "Did you teach them to do that?"

"No. That's something they do after you feed them. No idea why. Watch what they do next."

On the word, the fish flipped over onto their backs and skimmed across the pond with their bellies exposed and their tail fins cocked straight up in the air. Then they dove downward, disappearing into the water with one last wave of their showy tails.

"That is *so* cool!" Kim's delighted smile made Onca long to take her on a tour of the wonders of the galaxy. He'd seen a lot of them himself. Some close up, but most from pictures or holographic videos.

With little else to do aboard the refugee ship, Amelyana had filled the heads of her collection of orphans with all the knowledge she could pack into them— those that were capable of learning, that is. She hadn't been overly successful with Tarq, but he'd done okay for himself anyway. Onca still hadn't figured out that "lacking in common sense" remark Roncas had made. Given enough time to figure things out, he considered himself to be quite practical. Then again, in view of what he'd been doing ever since meeting the tiny Zuteran, he couldn't blame her for underestimating his abilities.

He gestured toward the gate. "We'd better get inside now."

"Yeah." She gave the turtle another pat on the head, then turned to go. "Thanks for showing me your pets." Her expression grew wistful again. "Cassie had a pet *trelink* once. She said it came from a place called Talus Five. It was little and furry and had big eyes and a long bushy tail."

"What happened to it?"

"Some of the boys from another gang stole it. I think they probably ate it."

"That's terrible!" Onca protested.

She shrugged. "They were hungry."

They passed through the gate, and Onca closed it behind them. "Cassie...she's Davordian, you said?"

"Yeah. She's very pretty. They have nice eyes, you know."

Over the years, Onca had serviced hundreds of Davordians and nearly all of them were beautiful, their electric-blue eyes being their most fascinating characteristic. He hated to generalize, but most of them were sluts too. The brothels were full of them—males and females—both as clients and as providers. They didn't mind being thought of as oversexed, either. Most of them seemed quite proud of that fact.

"Why was she in a street gang?"

"I've never been sure. She just showed up one day and asked if she could join up with us. I don't know if she'd gotten lost or if she was an orphan or what." She paused, frowning as she walked over to the house with him. "She liked boys a lot—she was also the first one of us to disappear. We all figured she found a guy she liked and went off with him. It wasn't until Dalmet vanished that we started getting suspicious." Her voice dropped to a whisper. "Peska went looking for them and never came back."

"Good thing you and Jatki were working together. Even so, the same thing could've happened to you."

"I know. But it was a chance we had to take." Kim paused at the back door, glancing up at him with a mixture of fear and anger in her eyes. "It scares me to death to think of them being…hurt."

Onca knew exactly what she was thinking, and also why she hesitated. Becoming a prostitute out of necessity was one thing. Being forced into it was quite another. Aside from that, the possibility that her friends had been murdered was very real. He would never have thought of that before what happened to Audrey. He knew crime existed on Rhylos, but that experience brought him closer to it than he'd ever been—or ever wanted to be.

"Yeah. I hope you never try that again. We'll do our best to find them or at least figure out what happened to them. But you do realize, we may never know."

She nodded. "That's what scares me the most."

Her subsequent shudder aroused instincts Onca had never given himself credit for having. Protective, possessive instincts. He wanted to take her in his arms and hold her until she stopped shivering. The whole "mate" issue crept back into his thoughts. Getting closer to her was wrong, and he knew it.

"Open the door, Captain." As the door slid back, he waved her inside. "After you."

He followed Kim into the kitchen, where Roncas and Jatki sat waiting at the table. "Took you two long enough to get here. Were you followed?"

"I don't think so. I used the cloak on the speeder for a while. Then we took the scenic route the rest of the way."

Onca expected her to make some snide remark, but Roncas seemed content to leave it at that. Following a brief nod, she yawned, her pearly teeth catching the light. "I don't know about the rest of you, but I'm beat. Mind if I crash here for a while?"

He nearly sighed with relief. "Not at all. We're probably safer here than almost anyplace else—and so are you."

"Yeah. That's what I thought." She got up from the table and motioned for the girls to follow her. "The spare bedrooms are upstairs."

Jatki stared at Onca with frank disbelief. "You have extra rooms?"

"Six of them," Roncas said. "And don't worry. They're fully furnished." With a wink, she added, "I did the decorating myself."

Jatki still seemed puzzled. "How come you have so many?"

"I have friends who stay here once in a while," Onca replied. He glanced at Kim. *So much for planning ahead.* "When a family of Zetithians comes for a visit, you need lots of room for all the kids."

He pictured Kim coming back to see him someday, with whichever of Cat and Jack's boys she wound up marrying. He guessed it would be Larry rather than Moe or Curly, although any of them would make her a good husband. Of course, they would have a litter of adorable children and—

"Onca!" Roncas said sharply. "Stop that."

"Stop what?"

"You were growling."

"I was not!"

"Yes, you were. Come on, girls. Let's let the beast get some sleep." Without a backward glance, Roncas led the way to the stairs, followed closely by Jatki.

Kim, however, hesitated. "Thank you for letting us stay here. I haven't felt safe in a very long time." The gratitude shining from her deep brown eyes was unquestionably sincere. "Come to think of it, I'm not sure I ever have."

"And you feel safe now?"

She nodded. "Ever since I first saw you. Weird, isn't it?"

"Yeah. Very weird." Like the way he had felt so... protective. *Best not to dwell on it.* "Captain will keep the place locked down tight and alert me if anyone comes snooping around." He gestured toward his bedroom. "If you need anything, I'll be right here."

Her brief nod was followed by a deliberate swallow. Moistening her lips with her tongue, she drew a breath as though about to say something but, instead, gave her head an infinitesimal shake and turned away.

As he watched her go, a sense of profound loss swept through him. A moment later, he realized he was purring.

At least she isn't around to hear me this time.

Nevertheless, as he stripped off his clothes and climbed into bed, he couldn't help wondering when he'd *started* purring. Was it before or after she left him? Purring was supposed to entice females, but she'd gone upstairs without saying a word. If she *had* heard him purring, would she have stayed?

I have absolutely no idea.

He was still trying to sort it all out when he finally fell asleep.

Kim, Jatki, and Roncas each took a different room on the second floor. Onca's bed had tempted her earlier, but Kim gave in to this one without a fight.

Her body did, anyway. Her brain had other plans.

Sleeping in a real bed for the first time in years should have had her nodding off instantly. However, Onca's expression when she left him standing there in the kitchen kept her awake for a very long time—not to mention the fact that he'd been purring.

If he didn't want her kissing him again, he damn well better stop doing that. Too bad his words were so completely at odds with the way he looked and acted. Except that last thing he'd said.

"If you need anything, I'll be right here."

He should have known better than to say such things. Kim wasn't exactly well-versed in courtship rituals, but that sounded like an open invitation to join him in his bed. He hadn't meant it that way, of course. He'd meant other stuff, like…

Like what? She'd been living on the streets of Damenk for years, and now she was safe inside his house, snug and warm in an actual bed. There was food in the kitchen if she got hungry, and drinking water was readily available. All she had to do was ask Captain if she had any questions. What could she possibly need from Onca aside from himself?

He made her drool. Every time she laid eyes on him or thought about him, she felt…hungry—and not the kind of hunger caused by an empty stomach. She wanted to bite *him*, especially when he purred. The feeling was disturbing, to say the least.

She shouldn't stay here. Just as soon as they found the missing girls, she would go to Terra Minor and claim her money.

Yeah, right. And throughout all that time, Onca

would be with her. She was stuck with him for now—and who knew how long it would take to do all of those things? She certainly didn't. Finding her friends might prove to be impossible, which meant that at some point, they would have to admit defeat and call off the hunt.

But how long would it take to reach that point?

A month? A year?

She never wanted to stop searching until she discovered the truth.

Maybe he was right. If she had more money and a home of her own, she would be better able to enlist the aid of the proper authorities to find them. Maybe after a few fruitless months, she could go to Terra Minor and then return to Damenk to resume her quest.

But what if the girls weren't there anymore? What if she had to go to another world to find them?

Somewhere in the midst of her conundrum, she fell asleep. However, she didn't dream about her lost friends. Her dreams were scattered and incoherent. One minute she was with Onca in his speeder, and the next, she was swimming in a lake with small children and giant turtles. Large, glossy animals with long noses nibbled on the grass nearby. Snowcapped mountains reared up beyond the lake. Kim didn't have to be awake to know she had never seen such a place with her own eyes. Then she realized she *was* awake, and her stomach was growling.

How many times had she simply ignored that gnawing ache and gone back to sleep? She had no idea, but this didn't have to be one of those times.

Tossing back the covers, she sat up on the side of the bed. The room was dark, but her night vision was sufficient for her to see the silky tunic Onca had given her lying at the foot of the bed. Strange she hadn't noticed it before.

Getting up from the bed, she donned the tunic and padded across the room in her bare feet. The door slid back, hardly making a sound. She crept out into the dark hallway toward the stairs, noticing a light blinking above another door just beyond the stairwell. As she approached, the door seemed to part in the center.

A lift. Of course a house as big as this would have one. She walked onto it and the doors closed with a barely audible *snick.* The dimly lit interior had no obvious buttons to push.

"Down," she whispered.

"Acknowledged," Captain whispered back. "Hungry?"

She replied with a nod, which he apparently saw.

"There is fruit, cheese, and bread in the stasis unit. The stew, alas, is all gone. With three more mouths to feed, Onca clearly needs to go to the market."

Kim hated knowing how much it would cost Onca to look after her and Jatki, and she fully intended to pay him back as soon as she got her money from the trust fund. "Thank you."

"You're welcome." The doors opened out onto an area between the kitchen and a room she hadn't seen before. Empty except for a large table and chairs, even her breathing seemed to echo as she peered into it. Moving soundlessly into the kitchen, she saw she wasn't the only one who'd gotten hungry. Onca was there ahead of her.

Not only that, he was naked.

Chapter 9

ONCA HAD JUST SUNK HIS FANGS INTO A COOKIE OR HE probably would have screamed. As it was, he nearly choked on the crumbs.

"Captain didn't say anything about cookies," Kim said as she came toward him in the darkness. "He only told me about the bread, fruit, and cheese."

"Maybe he doesn't think you should be eating sweet stuff in the middle of the night." Holding his breath, he waited for Captain's inevitable retort, but for once, the meddling computer held his peace. He held out the bag. "Want one? They're from the Twilanan bakery on Sixth Street."

She reached into the bag and took two. "I'm really hungry."

"I'll bet you are. We sort of missed dinner tonight."

What a stupid thing to say. She probably missed more meals in a typical week than he had in his entire life. "Want some milk?"

"Yes, please."

He got another glass out of the cabinet and filled it from the jug on the table, thankful he hadn't bothered to turn on the light—which might have made a difference with any other woman. However, being Zetithian, Kim's night vision was undoubtedly as good as his.

Great.

At least one of them was dressed—sort of.

Unfortunately, her shimmering garment only heightened his awareness of what she might or might not have on underneath it.

He handed her the glass, not trusting himself to speak.

She took a bite of her cookie and chewed it slowly before swallowing in a manner that was simultaneously innocent and sensuous. "These are really good. What kind are they?"

"Um…pumpkin spice."

Obviously she could ignore his nudity. Either that or she was punishing him for hurting her.

No, that wasn't it. She hadn't come downstairs with any motive beyond finding something to eat. She couldn't have known he would be down here stuffing cookies in his face trying to stifle his—his *what*?

Lust?

No. It wasn't that simple. If it had been, he could've ignored it—could have tamped down the urge quite easily. She'd done something to him. He could defy the attraction to other females if he put his mind to it. Kim, however, was impossible to resist.

She glanced at the cookie he had all but forgotten he held in his hand. "Aren't you going to eat that?"

"What? Oh…yeah."

Taking a bite, he fought the urge to stuff the whole thing in his mouth so he couldn't kiss her.

She had said she wouldn't kiss him again—which meant he probably *should* wolf down his midnight snack and get his ass back in bed. In the morning, he would head over to the Palace to see if there were any likely clients hanging around. Maybe after he'd fucked eight or nine of them, he might be able to look at Kim without wanting to tear off that tunic he had so thoughtfully given her and fuck her until she screamed.

But of course, he couldn't do any of those things. Not now. He closed his eyes, as if that action might banish the image of her lying naked in his arms.

It didn't. If anything, the vision was even clearer with his eyes shut.

Then he remembered something—something highly significant. She said she wouldn't *ask* him to kiss her again. She never said she wouldn't kiss him or that he couldn't kiss *her*.

There was a difference.

She wasn't the one resisting.

I am.

The rules governing the behavior of Zetithian females didn't seem to apply to Kim. Onca should have had to purr and tease and do everything in his power to seduce her. She wasn't playing by the rules, and if her scent meant anything at all, she was the one doing the enticing. The only problem was, she didn't seem to know how.

Thank the gods for that.

He ate another cookie while mentally reviewing the reasons why he couldn't let any of that happen. Onca had already fathered a bajillion kids. Jack's sons hadn't found mates yet, and they were only half-breeds. Crossing any of them with a pure Zetithian female would strengthen that bloodline—would strengthen any of the hybrids, for that matter. In the interest of continuing the species, she should have several litters by several different men.

She isn't a broodmare. She wasn't that strong. She

was tiny and fragile, and he needed to stop thinking about all this before he went insane.

After gulping down the last of his milk, he stuck his hand in the bag of cookies only to discover it was empty. "Sorry. Didn't mean to be such a pig."

"No problem. Thanks for sharing."

My, she's a forgiving soul… "Think you can go back to sleep now?"

Her gaze drifted to his groin. "Maybe."

Oh, no…

One swift, downward glance was enough to assure him that while his brain had been occupied with all the reasons why he shouldn't fuck her, his dick had found enough of her scent to remind him why he *should*. It wasn't in full bloom yet, but it was getting there.

"Tell me something." She pointed at his cock. "Why does seeing *that* make me want to bite you?"

Onca couldn't find the words to reply. He sucked in a breath so laden with her scent, his cock reacted instantly, and he exhaled with a purr.

"Wow." She took a step toward him and then another. She wasn't touching him, but as close as she was, she might as well have grabbed him by the balls.

Her intoxicating aroma rooted his feet to the floor, eliminating the possibility of putting more space between them. As he drew in another deep, purring breath, blood surged into his groin, forcing orgasmic secretions to flow from the coronal ridge of his penis.

Kim's eyes were like two glowing embers, her voice a hoarse whisper. "I *really* need to bite you now."

"Kim…*please*…"

Onca caught a glimpse of her gleaming fangs just

before she launched herself at him, gripping his shoulders and wrapping her legs around his waist. A snarl exploded from his throat as her teeth sank into the muscle at the base of his neck.

She was already in his arms, and within a few swift strides, she was on her back in his bed. A voice inside his head told him to be careful, to take it slow. But as her nails raked the length of his arms, he lost any semblance of control and plunged his cock into her.

Nothing in all his years at the brothel could have prepared him for this. Being with Kim went so far beyond mere sex, he didn't even know how to think about it, let alone know what to call it. She felt like no one else ever had. Hot and wet, yes, but there was more to it than that. She…fit him. Perfectly. He held nothing back, and she took it all, urging him for more.

When her first orgasm sucked him in even farther, her eyes rolled back in her head. "Holy Maloney, this is good."

A laugh spilled out of him. "Just good?"

"Oh, maybe better than that. I can't…think right now."

Onca wanted to do things she would use even more superlatives to describe, but at the moment, he couldn't think very well himself. All he could manage was a straight in and out, stretch-her-to-the-limit fuck. He couldn't even make himself slow down. The longer he went, the more climaxes she reached and the closer together they came. By the time his balls clenched and his *snard* shot into her, her pussy gripped his dick in one continuous orgasm.

Her pupils dilated, and the glow from within surged then ebbed as her lips formed a soundless O.

Unblinking, his enraptured gaze held hers like a lifeline. *Beautiful*.

Her body relaxed beneath him, her soft, purring sighs playing in his heart like a song. He might regret this later, but at that moment, regret and Kim didn't belong in the same thought.

A deep breath expanded her lungs, pressing her chest tightly against his, the fabric of her tunic the only thing between them. "I'm actually purring. *Way cool*..." Her eyelids drifted downward as though she savored the vibrations. "Is it always like that with Zetithian guys?"

"Well...yeah. I guess." To be honest, he wasn't sure. Onca had given joy to hundreds of women, but none of them had ever lit up quite the way she had. Perhaps it was always that good for Zetithian women. Never having been with one, he didn't know.

Her slow nod was almost as mesmerizing as her eyes. "I figured it had to be pretty awesome to arouse so much jealousy." She frowned. "It's funny, but I can feel something moving inside me, even though you're holding still."

"It's that, um, ruffle thing. It sort of...waves afterward."

"Feels fabulous." Her yawn increased the contact between them again, making Onca wish he'd taken the time to yank off her tunic.

At least I know she isn't wearing anything underneath it.

"I think I could probably sleep for a week."

"That's the *snard* effect," he said. "Causes what we Zetithians call *laetralance*."

"I'm guessing *snard* is the Zetithian word for semen?"

He nodded. "*Laetralance* doesn't translate into Stantongue—or any other language for that matter."

"Yeah. I can see why." She smiled briefly, then her eyes narrowed as her expression grew thoughtful. "Which explains why Ganyn was so glad to see you."

He grinned. "Our coronal secretions don't have any effect on Darconians, but the *snard* seems to work just fine."

"I'm surprised *any* of it works," she said. "I mean, I can see how it would affect other mammals, but a lizard?" She paused, frowning. "I'm trying to imagine you doing this with her. I can't picture it."

"Yeah, well, it wasn't what you'd call pretty. She nearly squashed me with her tail. Jerden used to do Darconians all the time. Dunno how he survived."

Kim pressed her fingers to her lips as though trying to stifle her giggles and failed miserably. Her whole body shook with laughter, giving his cock little squeezes that made him want to purr again.

He was pleased she could appreciate the humor—lightening the mood when it could have gotten uncomfortably deep. That whole mating thing he'd thought about earlier...he was probably wrong about that. Sex with Kim was better than it had ever been with anyone else, but that didn't mean they had to be mates. He hadn't mated with any of his clients. She could still wind up with one of Jack's boys.

Onca was simply her instructor—a coach to teach her the procedure. Plenty of cultures did that. In a way, he'd had that experience himself. His first client had been older, and she'd taught him quite a bit. He wasn't doing anything wrong by being here with Kim. He could stand back and proudly watch her marry someone closer to her own age.

He should have been able to do that. But why was it so hard? Why couldn't he picture her standing beside anyone but himself?

Infatuation. Lust. Proximity. Any of those things could explain what happened tonight. Hell, exhaustion could even justify it.

That's right. I was too tired to think straight. The previous day's events were enough to wear anyone to the bone, making him less wary, more susceptible to her intoxicating aroma. Besides, her scent *should* affect him more than those of other alien females. They were the same species. Oh, yes. It all made perfect sense.

But when she fisted her hands in his hair and pulled him down for a toe-curling, heart-stopping kiss, those arguments lost most of their impact—perhaps all of it.

———

I'm keeping him.

As she kissed her way from his lips to his cheek, Kim knew the best way to do that wasn't to beg or cling. He had to *want* to stay with her. She wasn't sure how she knew that.

Or maybe she *did* know the reason. Cassie's *tre-link* had stayed, not because it was caged or leashed, but because it was treated with kindness, affection, and respect.

And love.

Perhaps the most frightening emotion of all. Cassie had cried for days after those boys had stolen her pet—which she wouldn't have done if she hadn't loved the furry little beast. Kim's reaction to the disappearance of her friends was similar, but Cassie had at least known what happened to the *trelink*. The fate of the three girls remained a mystery—one Kim had to solve before she could give any thought to her own happiness.

Unfortunately, at that precise moment, she didn't even want to move, let alone set out on a quest of such magnitude.

Still, it probably behooved her to get back to her own bed. The trick would be to strengthen her resolve enough to ask Onca to let her up. Succumbing to the desire to kiss his lips off probably wasn't the best way to do that.

Biting him had been a satisfying event in and of itself. He was still bleeding from the place she'd bitten him. She kissed him there, then licked the wound, surprised that it seemed to close up almost immediately.

That was probably normal too. His wound, her saliva... Probably some time-honored method of healing among Zetithians.

Clearing her throat only made her purr louder. "Guess I should go back upstairs now."

"Yeah. Right." With a quick nod, he rose up on his hands and knees and rolled over onto his back, taking his body heat with him.

The loss of contact was shocking—like some vital organ had been ripped out of her. How long would it be before she got it back? A day, a month? She was ignorant of so many things. But she could learn.

Despite the protests of every part of her body, she was able to sit up on the side of the bed. Breathing harder than normal, she noted she was still purring, though the vibrations had grown very faint.

"Do you need me to help you?"

He didn't sound anxious or solicitous. He was simply offering his help—something he probably knew she would need.

"No, I think I can make it." Through sheer force of will, she stood up. Her knees were weak, but their strength increased with each passing moment. "I probably got your bed wet there. Sorry."

"That's okay. Really. No worries."

She hesitated, gnawing at her lower lip. "I—I'm not sure what I should say to you. Thank you, maybe?"

To her relief, he didn't laugh. "That'll do."

"Yeah. At least I don't make you sick anymore."

"You never made me sick, Kim. I'm sorry you thought that." Glancing downward, he plucked idly at the sheets. "I think I've reacted differently to you because you *are* different. I've never been this close to a Zetithian girl before. Not even when I was a kid on the starship." Rising up on his elbow, he tossed his hair back over his shoulder. "Those girls were...well, let's just say they didn't like me very much."

As Kim drank in the sight of him, she couldn't imagine any girl not liking him—Zetithian or otherwise. He was astonishingly attractive, especially stretched out naked on his bed. She liked him that way, enjoyed looking at him, touching him. He smelled good too.

I bet he even tastes good.

Beyond kissing—and biting—him, she hadn't really done that yet. But she would...eventually. "Well, just so you know, *I* like you."

A hint of a smile quirked the corner of his mouth. "I like you too, Kim."

"Good night, then," she whispered. "I'll see you in the morning."

He moved slightly as though about to get up. "Sure you can make it upstairs okay? We used to let our clients sleep it off before they left the Palace."

"Don't worry. I'll use the lift. I'm fine." She wasn't, of course. In fact, she had a sneaking suspicion she would never be quite the same again.

Which isn't necessarily a bad thing.

"Good night, Kim. Sleep well."

"I'm sure I will." With yet another gargantuan effort, she left the room. Making her way through the kitchen to the lift, she only had to wait a second or two before the doors slid open.

Kim half expected Captain to make a comment of some kind, but silence reigned as the doors closed behind her. As the lift hummed its way to the second floor, she had to steady herself with a hand placed on the wall. No, she would never be the same again. Not after the delights she had enjoyed that night. Her ecstasy might have been even greater than Onca's. After all, for him, sex was a job.

Still, he had admitted that his response to her was different from his reactions to other females. But was that purely because she was his first Zetithian?

Maybe. She preferred to believe there was more to it than that.

And she definitely intended to find out.

Chapter 10

ONCA KNEW THEY COULDN'T WASTE TIME TRYING TO locate Kim's friends, not only because she was worried about them, but because if they didn't hurry, there might not be anyone to find. He awoke early and did some digging of his own, ending with a call to Rashe, the bronze-skinned star attraction of a brothel near the Palace. According to Rashe, there were far more questionable brothels in the sector catering to male clients than Onca had ever suspected.

"I don't get that," Onca declared. "None of the guys in our sector are working there against their will. You're saying there are women who *are*?"

"Of course there are. Lots of men like the idea of fucking helpless, terrified females." Rashe let out a derisive snort. "You Zetithian guys always were kinda naive."

"It's got nothing to do with being naive," Onca insisted. "It's about having respect for the people you stick your dick into—whether they're male *or* female. Using kidnapped girls for sex slaves is one of the more horrific things I can think of. I don't see how they can get away with it."

"A few credits dropped into the right pockets can make all the difference in the world." Rashe snickered. "And don't sound so sanctimonious. There are plenty of guys who like it when a woman takes a strap to them—and women who enjoy doing it."

Onca couldn't suppress a shudder. Jerden might have enjoyed the occasional smack on the ass, but Onca never had, nor had *inflicting* pain ever turned him on. The mere thought of hurting a woman would have made his dick soft, whether her scent aroused him or not. "Maybe, but those dominatrix types don't do it because they've been forced to."

"True, but some of the girls in the rougher brothels are there because they enjoy being mistreated." With a knowing smirk, he added, "Or they get paid a bundle for *pretending* to enjoy it."

"I doubt if the girls I'm talking about are getting paid—and I certainly don't believe they volunteered."

Rashe shrugged, tossing a lock of jet-black hair over his shoulder. "Depends on how hungry they were. Sometimes a full stomach is worth getting roughed up a little."

Onca didn't have to think very hard to be reminded how thin Kim was and just how hungry she'd been when he found her.

"I'll fuck you for it if I have to."

That he hadn't taken her up on it didn't matter. She'd been hungry enough to make the offer. Still, getting something in return for being fucked was one thing. Being taken off the street and enslaved was something else altogether. And that Herp hadn't exactly been making Kim an offer she couldn't refuse when Onca had pinged the fuckwad on the ass. He'd been about to drag her off somewhere and—

I can't think about that.

He cleared his throat as though it might also clear his mind. "The last I heard, kidnapping was still illegal, even on this fucked-up planet."

"Yes, but if those girls were already living on the street, who would notice they were missing? And for that matter, who would care?"

That was precisely the problem Kim had faced. Small wonder she and Jatki had concocted such a dangerous scheme. "And the local government doesn't want to admit there are street people to begin with."

Rashe nodded. "Bad for tourism."

Onca wondered how many "tourists" were there to take advantage of the sex trade—a business he had once been an integral part of. He and his partners had done their best to make it as legitimate an operation as they possibly could. They had booked appointments, screened their clients for disease, and insisted that any children conceived be reported to the Zetithian Birth Registry. No one had ever been forced to do anything. They were simply offering a luxury service at a very high price.

The price alone meant that most of their clients were rich women, and wealth didn't necessarily guarantee honesty and integrity—or even mental stability. Onca didn't have to think hard to recall one ridiculously wealthy man who had been in a position to not only kill his wife's lover and get away with it, but to destroy an entire planet and most of its people. And then Chantal Benzowitz had killed Audrey to take her job. The woman was a total nutcase, but she'd had enough money to book an appointment with Jerden.

But how many of his clients had sold everything they possessed—or committed highway robbery—to pay for an hour with a Zetithian? That idea had never occurred to him.

"Once these atrocities are made public, what do you think *that* will do for tourism?"

"Public?" Rashe echoed. "Take my advice and keep your head down and your mouth shut. There are some very powerful people in this city who don't want you or anyone else fucking with their livelihood. You step on the wrong toes and you could wind up dead."

Rashe had already hinted at corruption among the brothel owners, and possibly law enforcement, but this sounded bigger than that. "What are you saying, Rashe? That the city government is corrupt, or simply its employees?"

"I'm saying you might want to let this one drop. And if you don't, you'd better watch your back."

"I'll do that," Onca said.

Rashe arched a brow. "What? Let it drop or watch your back?"

"Let's just say I'm not gonna let it drop."

"It's your funeral, dude. Don't count on much help from this sector. You start some kind of crusade, and we might all wind up on the street."

"Not if we work together. If you put the word out in the district—among people you trust—we might get something done about it. Shit like that puts us all in a bad light. Getting rid of the taint will make the legitimate brothels seem a bit more...respectable."

Onca wasn't sure Rashe cared what anyone thought of him, except his clients. He was in the sex business because it allowed him to fuck as many women as he liked. And being Terran, he didn't need a fluffer to fuck a Darconian. Onca had yet to decide whether that was an advantage.

Rashe chuckled. "Not sure I actually trust *any* of these

guys, but I'll give it some thought. The Statzeelians are probably out, seeing as how they walk around with their women on leashes."

That was another custom Onca had never understood. In fact, it tended to piss him off. "Then again, they're pretty easy to rile up. Get them mad enough and they might be willing to knock some heads together."

Roncas strolled into the kitchen. "Morning, Rashe," she said with a wave at the viewscreen. "I'm surprised you're still up."

"I'm always *up*," Rashe said with a wink. "But I'd probably be asleep by now if your boss hadn't called me."

"He's not my boss anymore."

"Yeah. I heard. Hey, if you're looking for a job, you could work for me."

"Don't need to." Roncas covered a yawn. "Besides, I'm playing chaperone for him and his new friends." The smirk she shot at Onca suggested she knew something about Kim's late night visit to his room.

Oh, shit.

Then again, Onca hadn't said anything about needing a chaperone. Roncas had simply opted to spend the night. *Maybe.* No telling what she and Jatki had talked about on the way back from Oswalak's. Perhaps Roncas's remark didn't mean what he thought it did.

Yet another instance where it might be best to keep my mouth shut.

"Sounds more like you'll be helping him hide out from the bad guys." Rashe laughed. "Or maybe you'll be the one watching his back."

"Clearly I've missed something," Roncas said, helping herself to a cup of coffee.

"I'll let him tell you," Rashe said with a yawn of his own. "I'm beat. I had to fuck a bunch of ladies celebrating their class reunion."

Roncas took a seat at the table and blew on her coffee before taking a sip. "Really? What year?"

"2970," Rashe replied. "The old girls about wore me out."

Onca grinned. "Wuss."

"Bet I had more fun than you did last night," Rashe retorted.

"I'm sure you did." Onca was lying through his fangs, of course. That one round with Kim topped anything else he'd ever done. "Get some sleep. I'll check back with you later." His expression sobered. "We really need to do this, Rashe. It isn't something we can ignore."

"I've ignored it for a long time," Rashe admitted. "Shit, maybe I *am* a wuss."

"A lover, not a fighter?" Onca said. "There's no law against being both, you know."

"Yeah. I know." He blew out a breath. "And that whole warrior thing *is* in my blood."

"I can't say it's in *my* blood. We were a peaceful race until the war began. From what I hear, we put up a pretty good fight, though. Too bad the odds were stacked against us."

"Yeah. Kinda like what happened to my people—but that was a very long time ago."

"I'm sure you've still got some grit left in you," Onca said. "Meanwhile, see if you can drum up some support in the neighborhood. I'm going to try to find a few more recruits."

"Onca's Army?"

"Something like that." Onca chuckled. "Street kids and hookers going up against—just what *are* we up against, Rashe?"

"I'm not sure," Rashe replied. "But whatever or who-ever it is, I'm guessing it's big."

"Couldn't be any bigger than Rutger Grekkor, and it only took one Zetithian and a few friends to take him down. The trick is finding out who's in charge."

"Something tells me that knowledge alone might be enough to get you killed. Be careful."

Onca glanced up as Kim and Jatki wandered into the kitchen. "Don't worry. I will." If for no other rea-son than to see Kim safely delivered to Terra Minor. After that, he had an idea his own life wouldn't matter very much.

———ᴡᴡ———

Kim's heart nearly stopped. "What's going to get you killed?"

Onca flipped off the comlink. "Nothing," he replied. "At least, not yet."

Kim wanted him to live for at least another seventy or eighty years. By that time, she might actually be tired of looking at him. She'd thought he was handsome before, but today…

Wow.

She opted for a seat across from him, rather than the one beside him. Biting him at the breakfast table seemed inappropriate somehow. Besides, sitting on the opposite side of the table gave her a better view.

"I ordered some groceries," Onca said. "Should be here any minute."

"Who'd you order from?" Roncas asked. "Karkun's?"

"Yeah. Right now, the Norludians are about the only ones I'd trust aside from Shemlak's gang." Frowning, he added, "Gotta remember to send those hails out to Jack and Dax."

A chime sounded. "Your deliveries have arrived," Captain intoned. "Shall I admit them?"

"Not yet." Onca got up from the table with a pistol in his hand. "Wait 'til I get there."

Kim let her gaze follow him to the door. His only visible fault was that he was wearing jeans—although she had to admit, they looked damn good on him.

"Why would he only trust Norludians?" Jatki asked.

"Because they're almost impossible to buy off or corrupt in any way," Roncas replied.

"Really?" Kim had learned early on that Norludian merchants seemed to have a sixth sense about the wares they sold, which made it tough to steal from them. "I never knew that."

Roncas twittered. "They're too outspoken—can't keep secrets about anything, whether you pay them or not."

"Yeah, real blabbermouths," Onca said with a wink. "The only reason I'm concerned is that they may have been overheard talking about delivering food to us and been followed."

Jatki's skin turned yellow. "You didn't tell them *we* were here, did you?"

Onca shook his head. "Why don't you ladies wait in my room until they're gone? The less they know, the better."

"But we can't cover you from in there," Kim said.

"Right," Roncas agreed, drawing her pistol. "I'll stay here. You girls go hide."

Kim was about to protest when she caught a glimpse of Onca's concerned expression. He hadn't given an order. He'd simply made a request—and a reasonable one at that. "Okay." She nodded toward the bedroom. "Let's go, Jatki."

She might not have liked the idea, but next to stealing, her ability to know when to disappear ranked among her most useful talents.

Now, there's something to be proud of. Stealing and hiding. And yet, those traits had kept her alive for a long time. Hopefully that trend would continue. "How about we leave this door open and just get out of sight?"

"Sounds good. Looks less suspicious that way." Onca glanced up at a sensor. "Okay, Cap. How many are out there?"

"Only two," Captain said. "Both Norludians." Judging from his haughty tone, Captain didn't approve of Norludians any more than he did Roncas's species. And he probably didn't like being called "Cap," either.

Onca tucked his pistol behind his back. "Open the door."

Kim couldn't see a thing, but she heard every sound.

"Hey, man. You throwing a party or what?" one of the Norludians asked. "Never known you to buy so much stuff before."

"Oh, you know how it is," Onca drawled. "I'm retired now, so I'd rather stay home and cook. Got some friends coming in a week or so. Thought I'd better be prepared."

"You should be able to feed a small army with all this."

Onca chuckled. "Obviously you've never been visited by Zetithians. *Lots* of kids."

"So I've heard. Now that you're retired, you gonna have some kids of your own?"

"Have to find a mate first," Onca replied.

"Yes, but who would want him?" Roncas asked.

The other Norludian laughed. "No accounting for taste, is there?"

Onca's growl sounded reasonably authentic. "Yeah. Right. See you guys later."

The front door closed behind them. "Engage the defenses again, Captain," Onca said. "Okay, girls. The coast is clear."

Kim and Jatki went back into the kitchen to find Onca peering out the window facing the street.

"See anything?" Kim asked.

"No, but that doesn't mean someone won't jump them once they're out of sight." With a wag of his head, he added, "Maybe we're blowing this way out of proportion. Yes, they could have tracked you here, but it doesn't seem like it."

"Better play it safe though," Roncas said. "After all that stuff Rashe was going on about, even *I'm* worried now."

"You mean you weren't before?"

"Not particularly. Never thought about this being some huge conspiracy. Scary, isn't it?"

Onca nodded. "If we weren't trying to find those missing girls, I'd say it was time to get the heck out of Dodge."

"Dodge?" Kim echoed.

"One of Jack's favorite expressions," Onca said with a dismissive wave. "Really old and really obscure, like most of the stuff she says. She's a little hard to follow sometimes—although you can usually catch her drift."

Kim giggled. "Is that another one of them?"

Onca's brow rose. "Yeah. I guess it is." He set his pistol on the table. "So, what would you ladies like for breakfast?"

Kim would've liked another kiss or two from their host but refrained from saying so. Onca didn't seem interested in letting Roncas and Jatki know about their... whatever you called it when two people got together in the middle of the night for sex.

"Good question," Roncas said. "I'm usually having supper this time of the morning."

"Trust me, we are *not* particular," Kim said.

Jatki stared at the sacks of groceries as though they were made of gold. "I will eat anything you give me."

"Over your bellyache now?" Onca asked.

"Oh, yeah."

He tossed her a muffin. "Then dig in."

Kim didn't know the name of half the stuff she ate that morning, but she didn't give a damn. It all tasted great and her stomach was full—not to mention the delight she derived from watching Onca. Something was different about him. His smile was sweeter, he laughed more readily, and he didn't even seem irritated when Roncas picked on him.

After a while, she finally had to admit that this was probably his typical personality—when he wasn't exhausted, pissed off, hungry, or—

No. The change she saw in him couldn't have anything to do with sex or the fact that she had been the one he'd done it with. A more probable cause was the *lack* of sex. Fucking several women a day was bound to get old after a while.

It wasn't until he smiled at Jatki and offered her another muffin that Kim realized what the difference was. He was feeding the hungry, giving shelter to the homeless, giving hope where there had previously been none.

And he felt good about it.

While this was understandable, Kim couldn't quash the notion that what he'd done with her the night before was simply another means of helping the needy.

I certainly was in need.

Was that all she was to him? A charity case? If so, that was quite a donation considering what he'd said about Shemlak owing him a thousand credits for his session with Ganyn. Kim wondered why it was Shemlak who would have been indebted to him anyway. Had he given the time with Onca to his sister as a gift? If so, Kim could think of a lot better ways to spend that much money.

Or could she? If she were offered a similar sum versus an hour with Onca, which would she choose?

She was still contemplating this dilemma when Captain interrupted her thoughts.

"Sir, I believe you have a visitor."

"Who is it?"

"A tall, dark-skinned Terran with long black braids and a sword hilt tattooed on his chest."

"On his *chest*?" Onca echoed. "Damn. You mean he's actually wearing pants?"

"I believe so."

"That's a first. Didn't think he owned any clothes at all. Is he alone?"

"So it would seem," Captain replied. "However, he does appear to be armed."

"With what?"

"A bow, a quiver full of arrows, and some sort of hatchet."

Onca looked out the window. "I think that's called a tomahawk. Better let him in."

Chapter 11

ONCA HAD NEVER SEEN RASHE IN FULL REGALIA BE-
fore, but standing on the doorstep in buckskin breeches
and beaded moccasins, he appeared to be ready for
battle. In addition to the weapons Captain had described, a knife dangled from a loop on his belt and—
thankfully—he also carried a pulse pistol in a shoulder
holster. If the bad guys were watching the house, the
mere sight of him probably had them shaking in their
boots. He even had feathers in his hair.

"War paint and all, huh?" Onca observed. "What
made you change your mind?"

He shrugged. "Dunno. Woke up from a dream about
a helpless young girl being pounded by a couple of
Herps and couldn't go back to sleep."

"That'll do it," Onca agreed. "Come on in."

Onca stepped aside while Rashe entered, then led the
way into the kitchen.

"Nice house, dude."

"Yeah, yeah…" Onca waved a hand at the two girls.
"Kim and Jatki, I'd like you to meet Rashe. He works
out of a brothel down the street from the Palace called
the Pow Wow."

Kim appeared undaunted by Rashe's painted visage,
merely eyeing him with curious interest. Jatki, however,
turned slightly yellow and hid behind her friend.

"Shit, you didn't tell me she was Zetithian." Rashe
held out a hand. "Nice to meet you, Kim, Jatki."

Kim gave him a firm handshake. Jatki barely touched his fingers.

Onca chuckled. "I didn't tell them you were Comanche, either. Then again, I didn't expect you to show up."

"Comanche?" Kim echoed.

"Yeah," Onca replied. "Native American tribe from Earth. Nearly wiped out at one time, but they were able to make a comeback." He shot Rashe a wry smile. "Sort of like Zetithians that way."

"Never thought about it like that," Rashe said. "But you're right. I guess there's hope for you guys yet— although there were a lot more of us back then than there are of you."

"Yes, but Terrans don't have children in litters of three."

"Good point." Rashe nodded at Kim. "So is she your new mate?"

Onca didn't know how to answer that without getting into trouble. "Uh...I'm not... That is, *we're* not..."

Rashe snickered, shaking his head. "Suit yourself, dude. She's damn cute. Better not let her get away. I have a feeling she could keep you warm in spite of your *retirement*." His gaze swept Kim from head to toe. "Not sure about having triplets, though. She's kinda small."

"But she's tough." Onca nearly bit his tongue to keep from adding that he had already proven what a pounding her pussy could take.

Rashe grinned. "I'm sure she is."

Damn. Onca had forgotten how much charisma Rashe could pack into a smile. He was a lot like Jerden that way. Similar type, too—tall, muscular, exotically handsome. At least he wasn't Zetithian. Otherwise, Onca wouldn't have stood a chance with Kim.

Wait a minute. What am I thinking?

Not that it mattered. Kim wouldn't go for a Terran, no matter how sexy he was. She needed a Zetithian—a point Onca had already proven beyond a shadow of a doubt.

Roncas cleared her throat. "You guys might want to stop talking about Kim like she isn't here."

"Oh, yeah. Sorry, Kim," Onca said. *Time to change the subject.* "So, Rashe. Did you sign up any more recruits?"

"Nope. The Statzeelians thought about it, but then a bunch of Davordians showed up and were willing to pay extra to watch the twins suck each other's dicks." Frowning, he added, "Never have understood why some women like that."

Roncas twittered. "Don't men like seeing two women together?"

"Yes, but that's different."

"And why is that?" Roncas asked.

Rashe gave his chin a thoughtful scratch. "I'm not sure. Maybe it's because if two women get each other off, a man can still fuck them. Once two guys have sucked each other's dicks dry, there's nothing left for the woman."

Onca snickered. "Speak for yourself."

Rashe stared at him, round-eyed. "What? You mean you do other men?"

"No, I don't do other men," Onca grumbled. "But coming once doesn't mean I have to stop. My turn-around time is maybe twenty seconds, so I can do a group of women one right after the other."

"Hmph. Guess I should've sent that class reunion to you."

"I'm *retired*," Onca said, gritting his teeth. "Can we talk about something else, like how we're going to rid this city of kidnapping and corruption?"

"Dunno how we're gonna do that," Rashe said. "Sounds like we'll need a fuckin' miracle."

"Well, start praying to the Great Sun God or whoever it is you worship and see if you can get us one," Onca snapped. "In the meantime, are you hungry?"

Rashe rubbed his stomach. "I'm always hungry."

"Great. Sit down and—take the fuckin' quiver off first."

"Oh, right," he said with a sheepish grin. "Not used to wearing anything. These buckskins are killing my dick. Dunno how you stand those jeans."

Kim burst out laughing. "I can tell we're going to have fun with him."

Onca's smile was probably weak and pathetic, but at the moment, he didn't give a damn. "I don't suppose you actually know how to *use* those weapons, do you? Don't they take a lot of practice?"

"I practice," Rashe said around a mouthful of a *craf-net* muffin. "Sometimes."

"Oh, joy. Any idea what the twins can do?"

"No clue. But I'd be willing to bet they've got pulse rifles. Probably aren't any good, though. Their women won't let them near anything with a kill setting on it. Too dangerous. That's how their species nearly wiped itself out."

"Didn't know those two had women—of their own, I mean."

"Didn't until recently. I have a feeling they're about

to retire too." Rashe heaved a sigh. "All the good ones are quitting. Means more business for me, of course, but I can only do so much."

"I know the feeling," Onca said. "I didn't realize how tired I'd been until I woke up this morning feeling... good." He was trying his best not to, but he couldn't help stealing a glance at Kim.

She was the reason he felt like a million credits, but she obviously wasn't going to rub it in—or even acknowledge it. He couldn't figure her out. She should have at least met his eyes with a conspiratorial smile. A nod. A little wave. Even a smirk.

Nothing.

Damn. She was playing it so cool, it might never have happened. He knew he hadn't dreamed it. No possible way. If nothing else, there were the white stains on his sheets. He couldn't have done that without her.

Wait a minute. He didn't want her to want him. Did he? Wasn't she supposed to hold out for someone younger?

Still, he'd like to think he'd made some sort of impression on her. It was, after all, a matter of pride.

But she thought Rashe was fun. And there was that killer smile of his...

He watched helplessly as Kim poured a glass of *moeshi* juice and gave it to Rashe. And smiled at him. Sat down in the chair right next to him. Not across the table from him.

Like she did with me.

He needed to focus on the mission, not her. He'd only fucked her the one time, like he'd done with so many others. Obviously he meant no more to her than his clients had meant to him.

Crap.

She gazed at Rashe with undisguised interest. "Did you really come all the way from Earth?"

"Yeah," Rashe replied. "Been on Rhylos about fifteen years now."

"What made you come here?"

Rashe shrugged. "I was working my way across the galaxy, picking up jobs on starships to pay my passage, and I wound up here."

"Yes, but why would you want to work in a brothel?" She passed him another muffin, along with butter and a knife before he even asked for them. "Did you need money that badly?"

"I sort of got drafted," he said with a chuckle. "I was wandering around the city and wound up in the brothel district. The pheromones they pump into the air down there gave me the biggest boner I'd ever had in my life, and before I knew it, I had three women hanging all over me. After I'd fucked all three of them, they paid *me*." He popped a *sporak* in his mouth and chewed it slowly. "Freaked me out a little." He winked at her. "But I got over it."

"Where all did you go before that?" she asked, clearly fascinated.

Rashe slathered the muffin with butter and took a bite. "Rutara, Derivia, Darconia—the usual trade routes—and a dozen other planets I can't remember. I liked it here, I definitely enjoyed the work, and the money was good, so I stayed."

Kim sat there hanging on his every word, her eyes glued to his face.

Must be the war paint. Or maybe it was the tattoo.

Onca had never seen the need for ink. Maybe he'd been wrong about that.

Maybe he'd been wrong about a lot of things.

A glance at Roncas proved she knew exactly what Kim was doing—or at least suspected it. Either way, she certainly wasn't interfering. Rashe seemed to appreciate the attention, although he was undoubtedly accustomed to being the object of feminine adoration. Onca probably was too. The fact that Kim was ignoring him had to be driving him nuts.

Good. A little jealousy might be the best thing for him. Might make him reconsider pawning her off on one of Jack's boys.

Better not push my luck. She shifted her attention to Onca. "So, what do we do now? Go out and try to find more recruits for the army? Or are we ready to attack?"

His befuddled expression was priceless. She couldn't have gotten to him more if she'd hit him right between the eyes with Rashe's tomahawk. "Uh...I don't know. What do you think, Rashe?"

"I think we're gonna get ourselves killed is what I think. But what choice do we have?"

"We need more information," Roncas said. "Run down the list, Rashe. Which brothels have you heard the most about?"

Rashe drummed his fingertips on the table. "Only a few, but supposedly the worst one is called the Den."

"Short for Den of Iniquity, I suppose?" Roncas said. "Hmm...never heard of that one, which doesn't necessarily mean anything. Not exactly my end of town—or what I'm interested in."

Rashe grinned. "What *are* you interested in, Roncas?" He nodded at Onca. "Ever do *him*?"

Kim felt her heart slip to her navel. She'd never thought of that. Maybe he was in love with Roncas. Maybe that was why he—

Roncas squeaked like a bird that had just been pounced on by a cat. "Absolutely *not*. I was an employee, not a client."

"Shouldn't stop you now, though," Rashe said. "I would think you'd be, you know, curious."

If looks could kill...

"In a word, no. I'm only here because Onca asked me to bring over some clothes for Kim, and then Jatki asked me to stay." She arched a brow at Onca. "She was afraid he might get...horny."

"If she didn't want me, it wouldn't matter whether I was horny or not," Onca insisted. "Really, Jatki, I wouldn't do anything like that to you. Honest."

Roncas sniffed. "And he *is* honest. Can't fault him there."

"I know that," Jatki said, her voice so soft Kim barely heard her. "And I'm sorry for not trusting you. I do have a suggestion, though." She glanced up, looking Onca straight in the eyes—possibly for the first time. "Follow the money."

Onca's gaze narrowed. "What do you mean by that?"

"Whoever winds up with the money is the one you need to go after."

Onca nodded slowly. "You're right. With Grekkor, it was a matter of where the money was coming *from*. It's the other way around this time, but I see what you mean. The Herps and Racks are just the minions of someone higher up."

"But do we really have time to do all that?" Kim asked. "Our friends need rescuing *now*."

"What we need is a hacker," Rashe said. "Someone who can get into their system and dig up the dirt."

"Val," Onca said with a nod. "Best hacker there is, and he can provide aerial reconnaissance too." He glanced at Roncas. "*Now* she'll get excited."

He wasn't kidding. Roncas's eyes lit up like twin suns.

"Okay," Kim said. "I'll bite. Who's Val?"

Onca grinned like she'd just offered to bite *him*. Rashe might be a handsome devil, but Onca was...delicious. Kim moistened her lips with a slow, sensuous sweep of her tongue.

Onca's eyes widened and his gulp was such that he had to clear his throat before replying. "The name's short for Valkyrie. Some woman hacked into our scheduling computer and substituted her name for someone else's. Val traced it back and found out who did it and how. Then he firewalled our system until even *he* couldn't tap into it. Considering his background, he'd probably be happy to help out on a mission like this."

"What's his story?" Jatki asked. "Why would he help us?"

"He's a clone," Onca replied. "A *genetically manipulated* clone. There are a few others like him. Call themselves Avians."

Roncas sighed.

"Oh, here we go again..." Onca muttered. "Calm down, Roncas. It's embarrassing the way you start tweeting whenever he comes around. I'm surprised you don't melt whenever you see him."

"Which isn't nearly often enough," Roncas said fervently. "Wish *he* needed a receptionist."

"But why would he want to help us?" Kim asked. "And why would his being a clone matter to anyone?"

"Because he's not a real person," Onca said. "At least, that's what a lot of people think. Cloning is illegal, so he shouldn't exist, but your basic mad scientist—I forget the guy's name." He glanced at Roncas.

"Ilya Zolo," Roncas said. "Nasty piece of work."

"Anyway, Zolo had this lab out in the middle of nowhere on Orpheseus Prime where he was putting together all sorts of weird combinations. The Avians are one of his later creations—apparently a lot of his earlier efforts failed once he started doing more than just cloning people. Anyway, the Avians are Terran clones, so they're basically human, but they've got wings and a few other birdlike traits. Incredible eyesight, for one."

Kim couldn't believe it. "You mean they can actually fly?"

"Oh, *yeah*." Roncas shivered, letting out a musical twitter. "They're the hottest things on wings."

Onca rolled his eyes. "She practically has orgasms from watching Val swoop around."

"The takeoffs are the best," Roncas said. "*Incredible* wings."

"I still don't get the part about him not being a real person," Kim said. "Just because he's a clone… I mean, it isn't *his* fault he was created."

"That attitude is slowly changing, thanks to Anara Threlkind," Onca said. "She's a lawyer who found two of Zolo's clones working in a hotel and sort of fell for them. With a little detective work, she discovered the lab and got Zolo thrown in jail. She freed the clones who were being held there and has been fighting for their rights as individuals ever since."

"So Val was being held captive?" Kim had been hiding out and practically starving for most of her life, but at least she'd been free.

Onca nodded. "Apparently it was pretty horrible—cages and such." He shuddered. "He kept the Avians chained up. And that's not the worst of it."

"I think we can skip that part," Roncas said. "I can't stand to think about it."

"Me, either," Onca said. "Anyway, you can see why he'd be willing to help rescue your friends and anyone else we find there."

"I just hope we don't find *another* crazy dude at the end of this," Rashe said.

"He—or she—probably won't be crazy this time," Onca said. "Just exceptionally greedy and heartless."

"I dunno," Rashe said. "Sounds a little nutso to me."

Kim nodded her agreement. Only a soulless person could do some of the things she'd witnessed. As far as she was concerned, that made them less than human—or inhumane, as Onca had said—and she wanted no part of them.

Unfortunately, those were the kinds of beings she'd often had to deal with.

Or run from.

Unlike Onca. Roncas had mentioned his honesty—and that was part of it—but he had a certain sweetness to him, as well. He might not like to show it, but it was there. He even seemed to be winning Jatki over.

Onca had a warm heart and a kind soul. She suspected

he had been wounded in the past, which might be why he tried to hide what he probably saw as a weakness, but his true nature was clearly evident in everything he did.

Even in what he'd done with her the night before.

Perhaps she was wrong to feign interest in Rashe. She hadn't done anything as blatant as sitting in his lap or telling him how wonderful he was, but the very last thing she wanted to do was to hurt Onca. He'd been so kind to her. He deserved nothing less in return.

Onca leaned back against the kitchen cabinet, chewing a thumbnail. "I'm thinking maybe we *do* need to move faster. Breaking into one of the brothels would be tough, but I could pretend to be a client and see what's going on in there. I could specify I wanted someone like one of your friends. That way we'd at least have some idea of what we're up against."

Roncas laughed. "I can see it now. You'd get in there, and those girls would probably want to make you *their* prisoner."

He smiled, showing his fangs. "Why, Roncas, I do believe that's the nicest thing you've ever said to me."

"Don't let it go to your head, Boss. You're cocky enough as it is."

It was now or never.

"Maybe a *little* cocky." Kim ran her eyes from his groin to his chest before finally allowing them to come to rest on his face. "But it works for him."

Onca's expression shifted from pleasantly surprised to something slightly more secretive as a tiny smile lifted the corner of his mouth.

Holding his gaze, she gave him a slow, subtle wink.

Chapter 12

IF ONCA HAD BEEN COMANCHE RATHER THAN Zetithian, he would have let out a war whoop loud enough to curdle the blood of any foe. Instead, he opted to wink back at her. "Why, thank you, Kim." His smile stretched into a full grin. "You don't know how much that means to me."

"She's really cute, dude," Rashe said. "Don't fuck it up."

"Oh, Kim, say it isn't so," Roncas lamented.

"Say *what* isn't so?" Kim shot back. "I only said he was a little cocky. And he *did* save my life—or at least my freedom." Her chin dropped and her voice grew soft. "I realize that now."

She seemed so tiny sitting there next to Rashe, who was easily twice her size, perhaps more. Onca wanted to take her in his arms and kiss her like there was no tomorrow—the way he'd kissed her last night and yesterday in the speeder. His heart gave a little twist as the realization struck.

This is happening whether I like it or not.

The scariest part of it was, he was rapidly approaching the point that he *did* like it. And she obviously liked him. Too bad he was the only Zetithian she'd run across since she lost her family. She might not think he was so hot when she had other options. Still, saving her life and freedom had to count for something.

"We'll do our best to get to the bottom of this, Kim," Onca said. "I can't promise you more than that."

Roncas tapped an imperative fingernail on the comlink pad. "We need Jack. Call her. Now."

Onca couldn't think of many people he would rather have on his side in a fight than Jack Tshevnoe. Tough as nails, she came with a lot of firepower and some damn fine warriors. Unfortunately, she was also the one who ragged on him the most about settling down and starting a family. No doubt she would scare poor Kim to death with all of her talk about Zetithian procreation. And then there were her sons. Those boys would give Onca some serious competition. He wasn't sure he was ready for that, whether it was in Kim's best interest or not.

I'm so fuckin' confused... "What's the matter, Roncas? Don't you think our best will be good enough?"

"I'm saying we need help. I don't want any of us to get caught or killed." Her lips formed a moue of distaste. "And I especially don't want anything to happen to *you*."

Momentarily stunned, Onca gaped at her. "Who are you and what've you done with Roncas?"

Her lips thinned into a sardonic smile. "Very funny. It's just that I'm seeing something I should've seen when I walked in here yesterday."

"I'm not even going to ask what that is," Onca said— although he suspected it had something to do with his lack of tact and common sense or his volatile temper, none of which he would admit to.

Well...maybe a *tiny* bit of a temper, and he did have a tendency to be blunt, but that remark about lacking common sense was uncalled for. After all, *he* hadn't been the one to go haring off after Jatki without backup.

"I'm gonna tell you anyway," Roncas said. "You and Kim are members of an endangered species. Risking your lives unnecessarily is fucking stupid."

Rashe chuckled. "Don't mince words, Roncas. Tell them what you *really* think."

Favoring Rashe with a withering glance, Roncas went on, "Remember what you said about how pissed Jack would be if you let Kim get away? Well, she'd skin me alive for letting you get yourself killed."

"I have no intention of getting killed."

"Famous last words," Roncas said. "Call Jack. If she can't get here soon enough, we'll take it from there. But at least try."

Onca hadn't planned on asking for Jack's help in finding the girls. All he really wanted from her was a ride to Terra Minor. And if she wasn't available, he could always take Kim there on some other ship. "Okay. But if she can't get here in a day or two, we're going ahead without her. Agreed?"

"That's easy for you to say," Roncas drawled. "I mean, what're the odds she'll be that close?"

"Astronomical. But Jack isn't our only hope. There's Val and I know some other guys we could ask. Shemlak for one. Having a Darconian army might even be better than Jack." He knew his argument was weak. What they needed was— "What about Leroy?"

"Now you're talking," Roncas said with a nod. "Call him."

Onca sent out the same message to all three. *Needed on Rhylos ASAP for rescue mission involving a Zetithian girl.* It wasn't strictly the truth, but it *would* get their attention.

Kim heaved a weary sigh. "Okay. Who's Leroy?"

"Lerotan Kanotay," Onca replied. "Arms dealer."

Kim nodded. "'Nuff said."

Shemlak and a few of his friends promised to lend a hand, but by the time his fourth attempt finally got through to Val, Onca's temper was obviously beginning to fray. Kim felt like she was about to come unglued. She sat at the table with her chin on her folded hands, her tapping foot reflecting her impatience. Rashe gripped his tomahawk as though considering the best way to smash the comlink.

"Where the hell you been, Wings?" Onca snapped. "Don't you ever answer your fuckin' comlink?"

"Hello to you too, Fangs." Kim couldn't see the viewscreen from where she sat, but Val sounded annoyed.

"Mr. Tactful strikes again," Roncas murmured. She stood behind Onca, waving at the viewscreen. "Hi, Val."

"Hello, Roncas." Val sounded only slightly less irritated. "I see you're still hanging out with this loser."

"Not really," Roncas replied. "He retired, so I'm out of a job."

"Congratulations."

Onca rolled his eyes and visibly counted to three before he spoke again. "We need some help."

"More challenging than the last time, I hope."

"Maybe. We need you to hack into the computer system of a place called the Den."

"Sounds interesting," Val said. "Mind telling me why?"

"We think there are some friends of ours—wait a minute." He beckoned to Kim. "C'mere, Kim. You tell him."

Onca rose from his seat in front of the comlink, and Kim took his place. Her first glimpse of the Avian made her glad she was sitting down.

Roncas had drastically understated the man's attraction. Light brown hair shot with gold fell in gentle waves to his shoulders, and though his full lips, cleft chin, and firm jaw would've turned the heads of most women, his eyes were what made her stare. Crystalline blue and slightly larger and rounder than a human's should have been, they had no whites whatsoever.

Kim had never seen eyes like that on anything.

"Some friends of mine disappeared," she finally said. "We think they were kidnapped."

He blinked, his huge, round pupils reacting dramatically to the light. "What makes you think that?"

"Someone tried to take me too. Onca shot him."

His eyes narrowed. "Really? *Onca* rescued you?"

"Yes, he did," she snapped. "Why is everyone always so surprised when I tell them that?"

"Because it's completely out of character for him," Val explained. "You obviously haven't known him very long."

"Well, no, I haven't. But that's not important right now. I need to find my friends. I-I just know something terrible happened to them. Rashe thinks they might be in a place called the Den to be used or sold as..." She stopped there, hating to even say it aloud. "S-sex slaves."

Val's eyes flashed like blue ice. "Imprisoned?"

She nodded. "That's our guess."

His gaze slid past her. "You aren't at the Palace, are you?"

"No. We're at Onca's house."

"Be right there."

The screen went dark.

"That's Val for you," Onca said. "He always was a bit theatrical."

"Oh, he is *not*," Roncas twittered. "You're just jealous because he's better-looking than you are."

Onca glanced at Kim. "Should I be jealous?"

"That's probably the most loaded question I've ever heard," Rashe said. "But I think we should *all* be jealous of Val. I mean, the dude can fuckin' *fly*."

"Yeah, well, so can Scorillians," Onca snapped. "But wings aren't everything." He kept his gaze focused on Kim, obviously expecting an answer.

Having already decided that what little flirting she'd done with Rashe had hurt Onca's feelings, Kim wasn't sure what to say. How much teasing was too much? She didn't know Onca well enough to judge, and her own inexperience wasn't helping. Still, Roncas picked on him constantly, and she didn't want him lumping her into the same category as the Zuteran. "Jealousy is a wasted emotion," she said, doing her best to seem unbiased. "Everyone has their good points."

"But you've got to admit, he's gorgeous," Roncas insisted. "Those incredible eyes, those fabulous *wings*."

"Yeah." Kim shrugged. "If you like birds."

Onca's lips twitched. "And you're a cat."

"Yeah." Deeming it best to drop that subject before she leaped into his arms and sank her teeth into him again, she shifted her attention to Roncas. "Are any of those Avian clones female?"

"No," Roncas replied, her entire body aflutter. "None of them are married, either. Val won't say why."

"Maybe it's because they don't have dicks," Rashe suggested. "Or they might've been castrated."

Roncas let out a screech that nearly split Kim's eardrums. "You don't know what you're talking about!"

"More likely it's because they're afraid to breed," Onca said. "Some hybrids can't reproduce, and even if they can, there's no telling how their children would turn out."

Roncas sighed. "I'd be happy to volunteer for the experiment."

Onca shook his head, frowning. "Since they were cloned from humans, I'm guessing they might cross better with Terran females."

"May I remind you that Valkyrie has extremely acute hearing," Captain said from above. "And since he is currently on approach, you might wish to end this discussion before he lands."

"Good idea," Onca said. "See anyone else around?"

"No," Captain replied. "I believe the coast is clear. Shall I let him in through the cupola?"

"Yeah. You know Val. He never comes through the front door if he can help it."

"I do hope he doesn't attempt to enter through your bathroom again," Captain said. "That was most embarrassing."

Onca shrugged. "Not really. Wasn't the first time he'd seen me naked."

Jatki clapped a hand over her mouth but failed to stifle her laughter.

"Go ahead and laugh, Jatki." Onca chuckled. "It *was* pretty funny. If you'd seen the look on his face…"

Kim stared at her friend, openmouthed with astonishment. There were *two* men in the room, and Jatki was actually giggling. When Valkyrie entered the kitchen with rustling wings and fire in his eyes, she lost her composure entirely and howled with glee.

Val came to an abrupt halt. Standing with his feet apart, arms crossed, and wings unfurled, he glared at Jatki. "You find my appearance amusing?"

Nearly convulsing with helpless laughter, Jatki simply shook her head and pointed at Roncas. The Zuteran's skin, which had been a rather shocking pink to begin with, was now a brilliant shade of lavender.

Appearing not to notice this change in hue, Val merely said, "Good morning, Roncas," in a manner that led Kim to suspect that his presence always made the Zuteran turn purple. Following another brief, puzzled glance at Jatki, he aimed his piercing gaze at Kim. "You are only a child."

Kim blew out an exasperated breath and got up from her seat. "Tell him, Captain."

"Miss Kimcasha Shrovenach is twenty-two years and four point five months of age," Captain droned. Apparently Kim wasn't the only one getting tired of having to vouch for her age. "She is not a child."

"And Jatki wasn't laughing at you," Kim went on. "She was laughing at something Onca said before you got here." She stole a peek at Roncas.

Still purple.

"Lighten up, Wings," Onca said. "You're too sensitive for your own damn good."

Val responded with a slight ruffling of his feathers.

"Nice wings," Kim commented. Composed of

feathers that were the same golden brown as his hair, his huge wings arched from his upper back before tapering to tips that nearly touched the floor. His broad chest was bare, displaying well-developed pectoral muscles.

"Thank you." Shaking back his hair, Val spread his wings slightly before folding them against his back. Even barefoot, he was slightly taller than Onca, and a pair of shiny brown pants fit him like a second skin, disproving both of Rashe's suggestions regarding his genitalia.

After exchanging a speaking glance with Roncas, Kim continued. "Will you help us find my friends?"

"I will." Val's voice was deep and solemn. "I cannot bear the thought of innocents being caged."

While she could understand this sentiment, Kim wasn't completely sure where he'd gotten the idea. "Caged? Who said anything about cages?"

Rashe shoved the tomahawk's handle through the loop in his belt, focusing on the task as though unwilling to look Kim in the eyes. "He's probably right about that. I've never actually seen it myself, but the girls in those places are usually kept in cages when they aren't being…used."

Kim's head swam as every drop of her blood seemed to pool in her feet, leaving her legs wavering.

Onca spun a chair around and helped her to sit. "Dammit, Rashe! Couldn't you have phrased that a little differently?"

"There isn't any other way to say it," Jatki said. "My father used to do the same thing to me." She looked up at Val with eyes filled with complete understanding. "We both know what that's like, don't we?"

"Yes, we do," Val replied. "And we must do whatever we can to keep it from happening to anyone else."

Kim felt like she was going to throw up and *then* pass out. Onca's warm hand on her back steadied her, but her voice was a rough whisper. "Oh, Jatki, I'm so sorry."

"It's over now," Jatki said. "But the thought of going through it again terrifies me. I believe I'd rather die."

"We'll do our best to make sure that doesn't happen," Onca said. "There are enough of us here now to go after these thugs." He aimed a glare at Roncas. "We don't need to wait for Jack."

"We should," the Zuteran insisted. "And you know it."

Kim knew Roncas was right on several points, but the sense of foreboding and urgency was becoming more overwhelming by the second. "I can't stand the thought of my friends being held in cages. We've got to save them."

Jatki nodded her agreement. "We shouldn't wait."

"If they're still there to save." Val arched his wings before settling them against his back again. "They may have been sold."

"That's where you come in," Onca said. "You can hack into their system and find out where they were taken. We also want to find out where the money's going. There has to be some kind of corruption or pay-offs, otherwise places like that would've been shut down a long time ago."

"Do you really believe they'd keep records like that?" Rashe scoffed.

"Not out in the open," Onca said. "Which is why we need Val's expertise."

Jatki gasped. "I hadn't thought about them being sold. They could be anywhere in the galaxy! No telling how long it might take us to find them."

"That's why we need Jack," Roncas said. "She tracked her sister for six years before she finally found her."

"And by the time Jack gets here, we'll know where to look," Onca argued. "We should go now—tomorrow at the latest."

"I just thought of something," Kim said. "What if they aren't there at all? What if they never were? I mean, we're guessing, aren't we?"

Chapter 13

ONCA HAD NEVER HAD ONE OF THE PRESCIENT VISIONS that visited Zetithians on occasion—possibly because nothing of any significance had ever happened to him before—but now would have been a good time to start. Practically everyone he knew had experienced at least one vision, and Jack's husband, Cat, always knew when the mate of a Zetithian friend conceived. He even knew the sex of the children—not to mention the fact that he had been the one to envision the Nedwuts redirecting the asteroid that obliterated their planet.

"But it's a pretty good guess, don't you think?" he asked. "I mean, we all seem to agree on the likelihood—don't we?"

Rashe nodded. "I'd bet almost anything that's where they are."

Or where they were. Onca hated to think they might already be too late, which was why he'd disagreed with Roncas. If some patron took a shine to one of the girls and had the money, she was as good as gone.

Judging from Kim's anxiety level, if she hadn't had a vision, she was at least having some serious intuitive feelings—feelings he saw no reason to ignore.

"We'll give it until tomorrow morning. That'll give Val some time to hack into their system."

"It would be best to do it on-site," Val said. "But from here, I can tell how deeply encoded their records are. If they're buried as deeply as I think they'll be, that's a good indication they've got something to hide."

Onca gestured toward the comlink. "You can access Captain's link to the Web from there."

Val glanced at the chair, arching a brow. "I don't suppose you still have that barstool, do you?"

Kim giggled. "I wondered how you were going to sit down without smashing your feathers."

"I can do it," Val said with a shrug of his wings. "But it's more comfortable to perch."

"Should've guessed that," she muttered.

"Hold on. It's around here somewhere." As Onca started toward the pantry, the door swung open.

"Valkyrie's preferred seat is behind the stepladder," Captain said.

"Where—oh, yeah. Here it is." He pulled out the tall wooden stool and set it next to the kitchen cabinets before moving the comlink to the countertop. "There you go, Wings. Have at it."

Onca had seen Val do it a hundred times, but noting the way Kim's eyes never left the Avian made him wary. That wink she'd given him seemed almost flirtatious, and she'd indicated that she preferred cats to birds. But Roncas had been drooling over Val—and turning purple—ever since they were first introduced. The guy definitely appealed to women.

I need to stop worrying so much. Having already been intimate with Kim gave him an advantage over anyone else. She would have that experience to compare with any others that came after.

His thoughts stopped there as his heart took a dive. The very idea that she might have any kind of sexual relations with anyone but him made him feel downright murderous. He couldn't sit still and think about it. He had to do something. But what? Haul her off to his bed and fuck her again? Bake her a cake?

Hmm...I could do that. It wasn't as if he didn't know how. She probably hadn't had cake in her life. The cookies were good, but—

Yeah, right. I'll bake her a cake while Val sits at the computer hacking into a file that might help us find her friends.

Cake baker...computer hacker... Which would she choose? He guessed her choice would depend on how hungry she was.

I'm losing my fuckin' mind.

That was the problem. He wasn't fucking anymore. Since that had been his primary occupation for the past ten years, he had no idea what to do with himself.

Why the hell did I retire?

Upon further reflection, he was forced to admit that, along with the desire for a more normal life, he'd mainly done it to shut Jack up—which wasn't a particularly good reason, whether she was right about the perils of the sale of Zetithian sex or not.

A flutter of Val's feathers drew his eye. "Sorry, Val. Forgot you don't like having an audience." He nodded toward the living room. "We need to get out of here and let him work." Onca wasn't sure why Val disliked being observed so much, but he suspected it was from having spent the greater part of his youth locked up in a cage while whatshisname studied him.

"And what, pray tell, will we do in there?" Roncas asked. "Sit and talk?"

Onca glared at her. "Got a problem with that? I mean, that's all we've been doing so far." He raked a hand through his hair. "Watch a movie, read a book, play a game or something. Geez, Roncas. Don't you have a life, either?"

Roncas cocked her head, considering his question. "Do you know, I actually don't? Seems like all I've ever done is eat, sleep, and work."

Rashe snickered. "Sounds like my life." His expression sobered. "Guess we all needed a good adventure to liven things up."

Kim's eyes darted back and forth between him and Rashe. "Didn't any of you go to school?"

"Well, yeah, when we were kids, but—" Onca stopped as he remembered the one thing Kim had seemed interested in during that first conversation he'd had with her.

"I wasn't in school very long," Kim said. "I've learned a few things since then, but not a whole lot. Sometimes I feel really stupid."

Onca smiled. "If you were stupid, you wouldn't have stayed alive this long. But I'd be happy to teach you anything you'd like to learn."

Roncas twittered. "Better let Captain be your teacher, Kim. I can only imagine what you'd learn from *him*."

"Oh, for heaven's sake, Roncas," Onca snapped. "I've probably had more education than anyone on the planet. What do you think we did on that ship for all those years? Amelyana taught us tons of stuff."

"I'd like that," Kim said. "Could we start right now?"

Her eyes were aglow with eagerness. A man made of sterner stuff might have been able to ignore her request. Onca wasn't one of those men. "Sure. Can you read?"

"A little," she replied. "Enough to get by, but not enough to read a book."

He glanced at Jatki. "What about you?"

"A little more than that," Jatki said. "I'm out of practice, though."

Teaching both of them wouldn't allow him to get as close to Kim as he would have liked. He was in the process of resigning himself to that fact when Jatki surprised him.

She pointed at Rashe. "Can he be my teacher?"

Rashe's astonished expression was so much at odds with his war paint as to be downright comical. "I-I suppose so."

"Great," Onca said, pleased to have at least one problem solved. "Roncas, you go ahead and do whatever you like, and Rashe and I will find out how well these ladies can read."

Roncas glanced at Val, whose intense gaze appeared to be glued to the viewscreen. "Maybe I'll, um, fix lunch. Something complicated."

Yet another problem solved. "Go for it." Hanging out in the kitchen with Val would keep her out of Onca's hair, although he knew her ruse was pointless. As absorbed as Val normally was while he worked, he probably wouldn't notice much else—not even Roncas flitting around the kitchen.

She sidled up to Val, eyeing his wings with fascination. "What would you like for lunch?"

Val jumped as though the Zuteran had yanked out a handful of his feathers. "I am not hungry."

"It's not lunchtime yet," Roncas cooed. "I'm just asking."

Onca couldn't recall ever having seen Val eat

anything, although he knew he had to in order to maintain a body like that.

"Fruit and nuts," Val replied.

Kim giggled. "Sounds really complicated, Roncas. Should take you at least a couple of hours to get it ready."

Onca held his breath waiting for Val to retort, but once again, the Avian was focused on his task to the exclusion of everything else. "What was that stuff you brought to the Palace last month?"

"Paemayan stew," Roncas replied.

"Think you could make some of that?"

"Yes, but it takes hours to cook," Roncas protested. "I'd be in here all—"

Onca arched a brow so high it hurt.

Roncas frowned. "What—oh, yeah. Sure. Paemayan stew." Glancing at the clock, she let out a peculiar-sounding twitter. "No problem."

———

If Onca was trying to play matchmaker between Roncas and Val, Kim suspected he wouldn't have much luck. Sure, Val was a handsome fellow, but he seemed a bit… stuffy. Onca was much friendlier.

Maybe it's a clone thing.

Or maybe she simply preferred Zetithians in general—and Onca specifically.

Nothing wrong with that. She felt sorry for Val. Sure, he could fly, but he seemed intent on cutting himself off from other people. Maybe that was a clone thing too.

All she knew was that she would much rather have Onca teach her how to read than anyone else. They could spend lots of time sitting side by side. She would get to listen to him purring, which would undoubtedly cut their lesson time short if they wound up doing what they'd done the night before.

Something told her she wouldn't find him in the kitchen eating cookies in the middle of the night again. And if they ate supper before they went to bed, she might not wake up at all.

Perhaps I should have Captain wake me up anytime Onca has a midnight snack.

Captain didn't have to know why he was getting her up—at least, not for anything other than food.

She followed Onca into the main room, her eyes immediately drawn to the artwork attached to the walls. Cushioned sofas and chairs lined the perimeter, and an enormous sculpture with a trickling fountain stood near a picture window that faced the street. The rear window looked out onto the hillside behind the house where flowers grew in profusion and another sculpture stood like a tall metallic plant, its leaves waving in the breeze.

"Have a seat there by the window," he said, indicating the couch next to the fountain. "Jatki and Rashe can sit at the other end so we won't disturb each other too much."

She looked down into the pool at the base of the waterfall. It, too, was filled with goldfish, but of a different species with amazingly long, delicate fins. She sat there for a moment, enjoying the peaceful setting, just as she had done with the pond outside. The water flowing down over rocks and pebbles soothed as well as fascinated. If ever she wasn't able to sleep, this place would lull her to sleep faster than anything she'd ever known—except for Zetithian sex.

Onca had nearly knocked her out the night before. Granted she'd been tired and more comfortable than ever before, but what he'd done to her went beyond that. She doubted she could resist him if they were ever alone together again. Not that she wanted to resist him. She was unsure of how fast she should move, how intimate they could become before he considered her to be his mate and an essential part of his life.

Would she have to conceive his children before that happened? Or did that come afterward? She wasn't even sure it mattered. Perhaps she could ask Captain for more information when she was alone in her bedroom.

Right now, however, she was anxious to learn what Onca had to teach—and not with regard to love, either in the physical or mental sense.

Onca gave a small, flat device to Rashe, then came over and sat down beside Kim, holding a similar object. "You can access any book ever written on this thing, so I'm sure we can find some stuff for beginners." He tapped the screen on the pad, and pictures popped up, images that moved so swiftly, they seemed to merge into one another. Eventually, the mass of color settled into what she recognized as printed words.

He handed her the pad. "Here. Take a look at this. Can you read any of it?"

Most of what she'd read involved the names of streets and businesses. These words meant nothing to her at all. She shook her head.

"Okay, then. Let's take a step back." He tapped the screen again, and single letters formed. He named them each in turn for her. "Do you remember any of that from when you were in school?"

"Yeah. I think so. There was a song we used to sing."
She sang the first part of it, stopping when he nodded.

"Good. We'll start from there."

As she sat there beside him, absorbing letters and
sounds like a sponge, old lessons came back to her. She
also soaked up his essence—that scent or aura surrounding him. Her mind became more acute, more honed and
attentive, rather than drifting away. Simply sitting next
to him cleared her thoughts and calmed her fears. The
very air around him spoke of warmth, protection, and
more. She barely heard the soft voices of Rashe and
Jatki at the other end of the room. Val and Roncas might
have been in another city rather than the same house.

Isolated from the others and completely engrossed,
she let him fill her head with new words and meanings.
He taught her to spell her own name, to arrange the letters in such a way that they meant her and only her. He
showed her his name, then the written names of Jatki,
Roncas, and Rashe.

She studied them side by side. "Did you know your
name is a part of hers?"

"What?"

"Look," she said. "If you write the name Roncas and
erase the *R* and the *S*, you get Onca."

He stared at the pad. "Well, I'll be damned. You're
right." Grimacing, he went on, "Don't tell her that. She's
bound to use it against me somehow, like she's two letters better than I am or some such nonsense."

Kim laughed. "Or you could argue that for you,
only four letters are necessary to make you unique
and special."

"Yeah, right. It's only a coincidence, but I'm sure

Roncas will find some way to rub my nose in it. Don't give her any ideas."

"No worries. I'll find something else to embarrass you."

"Like what?"

"Oh, you know, like naming the turtle after you or something."

His eyes lit up. "I've got a better idea. Why don't we name it Roncas?"

"Or how about just Ron?"

"Perfect."

Giggling, she slid sideways, leaning against him as he laughed along with her. Dropping an arm around her shoulders in a move so natural she almost didn't notice it, he gave her a quick hug and kissed the top of her head.

He was purring.

Snuggling closer, she tapped *I lik that* into the pad.

He corrected the spelling, and then wrote, *like my purring?*

She studied the words he'd written, nodding when she'd finally made sense of them. *u r swet*, she wrote.

"None of that, now," he admonished. "You need to spell the words correctly, not just the way they sound. Like this." *You are sweet*. Then he changed it to read, *So are you*.

Kim was entranced. She could communicate with him silently, say whatever she wanted, and no one else could hear her. It was like the Kitnock fingerspeak, only better.

He tapped in more words. *Kiss me*.

She glanced at Jatki, who stared at the pad she held while sounding out the words as she read. Rashe had his eyes closed, but frowned occasionally as though listening. She was almost afraid to look up at Onca.

She didn't have to. His purring grew louder as he traced the line of her shoulder with his fingertips.

Please?

Reaching across him, she grasped a lock of his hair and pulled him around to face her, blocking her view of Rashe and Jatki. His glowing eyes met hers and he exhaled softly, licking his lips.

Kim knew how tasty those lips were, how wonderful they felt when pressed against hers, and how they could make her forget her own name, let alone how to spell it. He was only a breath away, and she leaned closer until their lips touched. His purr became a groan as she nipped his lower lip and then sucked it into her mouth. Heat flooded her core, and she deepened the kiss, tasting him fully, wishing she could do so much more than kiss him.

I want to devour him.

If only they were alone in his bed where she could lick and savor each and every bit of him. She longed to learn his flavor and scent so well she would never forget them and would be capable of following his trail through space and time. Those boys of Jack's would have to be incredibly special to make her forget Onca. Whether they arrived on Rhylos in one day or a thousand didn't matter now. They were already too late—and had been from the moment she'd laid eyes on this man.

She didn't care who knew how she felt or who saw her kissing him. Roncas could fuss as much as she liked. She could keep her Avian clone. Kim didn't want him. She wanted Onca.

He's mine.

Chapter 14

KIM WAS A QUICK STUDY—AND NOT ONLY WHEN IT came to reading and spelling. Her kiss was sweeter every time their lips touched. How was that possible? Beyond that, how was he supposed to kiss her and not fuck her? Especially now when her scent was driving him insane with need?

The only time he'd ever had to be satisfied with a mere kiss was when he'd been with Kim in the speeder. His ability to stifle an erection was only useful in non-sexual situations. It didn't work with Kim. The gods knew he'd tried, but he simply couldn't do it.

"Kim," he whispered against her lips. "Please..." He was begging again. Except this time, he wasn't sure what he was begging her for. Was he asking her to stop or was he asking for more?

Even knowing that Jatki and Rashe were only a few meters away didn't deter him the way it should have. Considering the things Jatki's father had done to her, he knew he should back away from Kim right now. To any casual observer, Onca would appear no better than—

No. He was making love with Kim, and she was a willing participant. There was a huge difference, although perhaps not in Jatki's eyes.

He drew back, the strain of separation nearly splitting his mind apart. He was purring so hard, he didn't have enough breath left to speak. He tapped in a message on the pad.

Sorry. My bad. Jatki can see us.

Kim studied the words as though she had no idea he itched to dive into her, dick first. He would never be able to understand the way women could simply turn off their desire whenever they needed to.

Well, no. She hadn't turned it off. He could still smell it. Women could control their reactions better. That was the difference.

After a few moments, she nodded as though she understood and then wrote *tonit?*

Staring at that word was like a splash of cold water in his face. Tonit? What the devil did *that* mean? Then he realized he wasn't thinking phonetically.

Tonight.

Tonight. All night. Every night.

Oh, yeah…

Onca corrected her spelling and wrote *yes.*

Her slow smile convinced him she had read the word correctly.

Pulling up an easy story for her to read, he went on with the lesson. As she read the simple words and phrases aloud, the mere sound of her voice captivated him. Completely unable to resist her, he gave up trying not to purr.

His friends had been so sure this would happen to him someday. But unlike the gradual process he had expected, his feelings for Kim had crashed into him like the asteroid that destroyed Zetith.

He glanced over at Rashe and Jatki. The Kitnock girl appeared to be reading, occasionally tapping the pad for the audio function. Rashe was snoring—completely exhausted after a night spent servicing his clients.

Onca knew the feeling. It boggled the mind to think how many women he'd slid his cock into.

And now I only want the one.

Considering his retirement, this was probably a good thing. However, he should have been able to make it through at least *one* night without sex. Sitting next to Kim had him so hard his balls were numb. He wouldn't get erections like that if she didn't want him.

Damn. She must be as anxious as I am.

Kim's voice startled him out of his reverie. "Looks like everyone else decided to take a nap."

Rashe wasn't the only one who'd fallen asleep in class. Leaning sideways, Jatki's tall, cylindrical head now rested on the arm of the sofa.

"Do you want to go upstairs and lie down for a while?" he asked.

"Only if you go with me."

"You're killing me. You know that, don't you?"

"Really? You're the one who's purring."

"Yeah, well, that's your fault, sweetheart," he argued. "If you weren't so damned cute, I wouldn't be purring, you wouldn't be interested, and my dick wouldn't feel like it's about to explode."

"And if you weren't so irresistible, your purring wouldn't affect me."

"Where'd you hear that?"

"I, um, asked Captain for some information on Zetithian biology."

"I see." Onca knew the computer wouldn't deliberately lie to Kim, but given Captain's attitude, he might have put his own spin on the details. "Want to, um, practice what you learned?"

"Absolutely." She glanced at the clock on the wall. "I think we'll have time before lunch. Roncas said that stuff she was making would take hours. We've only been sitting here for an hour and a half at the most."

Placing a finger to his lips, he nodded toward Rashe and Jatki. "Let's see if we can sneak upstairs without waking them."

"Dunno about Rashe, but Jatki is a fairly light sleeper."

"And we're both cats." With a wink, he pointed toward the rear hallway. "We can get to the lift from here." He didn't have to ask if she was sure.

Her scent told him everything he needed to know.

As she tiptoed out of the living room, Kim fought the urge to run. The idea of being chased by Onca was exciting somehow. Nevertheless, the moment the lift doors closed behind them, he pounced on her like a tiger on its prey. Turning in his embrace, she flung her arms around his neck as he picked her up, pinning her against the wall of the lift.

A snarling purr rose up from the depths of his chest. "Forgive me if this isn't gentle and romantic, Kim. But I want to fuck you so bad, I can't see straight."

Her response was to bite him in the same place she'd bitten him the night before, although those teeth marks were now completely gone.

Good. I like that place.

Last night, she had been the aggressor, but this time, he was all over her, pulling at her clothes in his haste to bare her body to his eyes and his touch. Kim had never liked the idea of surrendering herself to a man. Now, she wanted to be naked in his arms as much as he seemed to want it. The doors opened and he swept her from the lift, carrying her across the hall and into her room.

Falling onto the bed with her, he raised his head. "Shut the door, Captain, and don't let anyone in unless I say so. Just let us know when lunch is almost ready."

"Understood."

Kim dragged his tunic over his head and made a dive for his chest, her fangs bared. The bite she left on his pectoral muscle bled until she licked the wound. The bleeding stopped almost instantly.

With a growl, he pulled off her slacks and spread her legs apart, pressing his face into the apex of her thighs. For a second, she feared he would bite her, but his growls gave way to a low-pitched purr as he licked her painfully engorged clitoris. His tongue rasped against the tight bud, sensitizing it until she had to cover her mouth to stifle her scream.

Captain's crash course in Zetithian sexual practices had warned her that taste was as important as sight and smell for the people of their race. But he hadn't in any way prepared her for how it would *feel*.

At the moment, she couldn't taste Onca's orgasmic fluids, and Captain hadn't said a thing about male saliva doing the same thing as the delicious juice from the penis. She wanted some of that—tried to sit up and reach for him—but he pushed her back down, refusing to let her go. Reaching for his hair, she gave it a yank. It was too intense, too harsh, too...*fabulous*.

Pulling his hair only made him suck harder. He

stopped long enough to slide his tongue inside her, teasing her from within as he purred. Her eyes squeezed shut as every muscle in her body clenched, thrusting her upward to force him more deeply inside her. Withdrawing, he latched on to her clit again until her orgasm detonated. The climaxes she had reached while his cock was inside her were different. Those triggered by his fluids were more of the mind. This pinnacle was reached by her body, reducing her to a gasping, shuddering heap.

He had his jeans off in an instant.

"No, not yet," she pleaded. "Wait…"

Gulping in breaths of air, she shuddered as the contractions of her body forced them back out.

"I need you, Kim."

"I know. Hold on. I want to do that to you."

With strength she hadn't known she possessed, she pushed him onto his back. She gazed at his meaty cock for one fleeting moment before sucking it into her mouth.

Sweet. Salty. Hot. Delicious. His cock tasted like *him*. Breathless, she sucked him hard, licking his dick while running her greedy hands over his nude body.

He's mine.

They had parted too soon last night. She knew that now. He could do more—a *lot* more. Moistening her fingers with his cock syrup, she squeezed and pumped her hands up and down on his rod. She wanted to taste his cum—the cream that was supposed to be deliciously orgasmic in its sweetness.

"Kim…" His voice held a note of warning. Seconds later, he gasped as his cock spewed out a blast of semen for her to savor. Sweet didn't begin to describe the flavor—creamy, delightful. Heat filled her lower back and blood sang through her vessels, flooding her with sensations so profound, she was surprised her toenails didn't curl. She held on to him as his ruffled cockhead began its sweeping wave, tickling her tongue.

"Sit on it." His voice was so thick with his purr and some unfathomable emotion, she barely understood him, nor could she find the strength to follow his command.

She hated to let go, but she only knew one way to scratch that internal itch. Her head swam as she tried to raise herself. A moment later, Onca grasped her beneath her arms and dragged her onto his prick. Kim sighed with relief as he filled her with his cock. She could feel it moving, swirling—even drumming inside her. Collapsing on his chest, she lay there, helpless and completely unable to move.

Onca was motionless, as well—except for the movement of his penis deep inside her. Slowly regaining her senses, she rose up from his chest. Onca gripped her hips, lifting her up and then slamming her back down with a satisfying smack. She still couldn't believe he fit into her so easily when she should have felt as though she'd been impaled with a spike. He *belonged* inside her, almost as though they'd been made for each other.

Perhaps they were.

She had no other explanation for the way he had altered her perception so quickly. Little more than a day before, she'd had no use for any male on the planet and held none of them in affection. For the most part, she dismissed them as troublemakers, the bane of feminine existence. There had been so few she could even

stand, let alone fall in love with—and she certainly
hadn't enjoyed those few attempts at greater intimacy
with one of them. Not like this. Not like Onca. He was
uniquely wonderful.

And to think, she hadn't liked him at first.

Would she retain this opinion of him? Or would he
disappoint her, let her down in some way as the others
had done?

Was he truly that different? Would she feel the same
about any other Zetithian, or was this feeling unique?
Was she in love or in lust? Was it purely chemical or
physical with no meeting of the spirit?

Kim had never had these sorts of questions in her
mind before and didn't know the answers to any of
them. But as she gazed down at his fiery hair and shining eyes, the bond between them became more powerful, even as she grew stronger herself. Rocking forward,
she took control, doing her best to keep moving despite
the orgasms induced by his coronal fluid.

Although often referred to as cock syrup or joy
juice, that fluid had no official name, not like *snard* or
laetralance—at least, not according to Captain's accumulated data. Those nicknames were in the Standard
Tongue rather than the language of Zetith. She found
it most peculiar that Zetithians hadn't bothered to give
something so remarkable its own title.

Later, she intended to give more thought to its name.
Right now, she simply enjoyed its effects and the wondrous feel of his thick cock inside her.

Onca gazed up at her, his lips curling into a smile. "Good?"

"Incredibly good." Her eyes drifted shut as she savored the slow penetration and withdrawal. Pressing her

weight down on his groin, she moved her hips sideways, then shifted into a circular pattern.

Were those her groans or his?

Doesn't matter.

"Ohhh…" That was definitely him.

She echoed his sigh as her head fell back. After matching her movements for a few moments, he took up an opposite spin with his cock, stirring inside her like a spoon in a bowl of soup. Another climax seized her, tightening her grip on his dick, sucking him ever deeper into her core. His balls pressed against her bottom as he thrust up into her, his short, growling breaths signaling his own pinnacle of ecstasy. His slick sauce filled her, then spilled down over his groin, making her circular motions even smoother and more delectable. His semen had such a powerful effect, her muscles weakened until she seemed to melt, her body sinking down to flow over him like butter.

Somewhere in the distance, a gong sounded.

"I believe Roncas is nearly finished with the preparations for the noon meal." Captain's voice was hushed, as though even he was unwilling to break the spell.

"Be there in a minute." If the lazy, drawling note in Onca's voice was any indication, Kim suspected it might take longer than that.

She had returned to her room under her own power the night before. However, after a double dose of *snard*, she could scarcely raise her head.

Onca gave her a nudge. "Need help this time?"

"I think so. Although a nap sounds better than lunch right now."

"Nope. You need to eat." Cupping her head in his hands, he aimed her face toward his. "Gotta keep up your strength." With a wink, he gathered her into his arms and sat up. Swinging his legs over the edge of the bed, he stood, his cock still firmly wedged inside her.

She giggled. "Think we should go down to lunch like this?"

His chuckle made his cock quiver delightfully. "Roncas would probably spill the stew." He gave her a quick kiss. "I really hate to do this, but—" Hugging her against his chest, he lifted her off his cock.

The loss was such a shock to her system, she almost cried out in protest.

Turning around, he sat her on the side of the bed. "Be right back."

She watched him walk to the door, thinking that a picture of his perfect ass belonged in a museum somewhere. He returned a few moments later with a wet washcloth and a towel. Pushing her onto her back, he parted her thighs and wiped her clean, then dried her with the towel. He helped her put on her slacks, then sat her up and dropped her tunic over her head. After donning his own clothing, he scooped her up in his arms and carried her to the lift. The doors closed and their descent began.

"D'you suppose anyone missed us?" she asked.

He shook his head, smiling. "I doubt it. Roncas wouldn't leave Wings for a second, and Rashe and Jatki are probably still asleep."

"They might wonder if they see you carrying me, though."

"Oh, I'll put you down, but not before I have to." His expression sobered. "I'm so glad I found you—for so many reasons."

"Me too."

For so many more.

Chapter 15

"I'VE GOT GOOD NEWS AND BAD NEWS," VAL SAID AS Onca and Kim entered the kitchen.

Jatki and Rashe were already seated at the table. Roncas flitted around the stove like a frantic moth.

So much for keeping our little tryst a secret.

Rashe's bland expression gave nothing away, but Onca knew better. Noting Kim's wobbly gait, he put a hand on her back to steady her. "Let's hear it."

Val spun around on his barstool to face the others. "The good news is—I couldn't find any indication that any girls have been sold recently."

"And...?"

"The bad news is—I couldn't find any evidence that they weren't."

Kim's mouth flew open. "What? I don't get it."

Damn. "He means he couldn't hack into the system at all."

Val nodded. "Which proves they definitely have something to hide."

Onca pulled out a chair for Kim and helped her to sit before scooting it up to the table. "So we can assume the girls are there?"

"Maybe not those *particular* girls," Val said. "But with firewalls like these, I'm guessing they've got a whole bunch of ladies who need rescuing."

Roncas ladled out a bowlful of stew from the smaller

of the two pots sitting on the stove. "Are you sure all that security isn't there simply to protect the identity of their customers? Plenty of our clients at the Palace didn't want anyone to know they'd been there."

Rashe snickered. "Didn't want their *husbands* to know, you mean. This place could be locked down for that same reason."

"The original system at the Palace was adequate defense against all but a determined search," Val said. "This goes way beyond what I set up for your scheduling logs."

Roncas set the bowl on the counter next to Val and gazed up at him with adoring eyes. "And we never had another problem after that."

She was practically cooing. Unfortunately, Val didn't appear to notice she had served him first.

"Do you think you could hack into the system using their equipment?" Onca asked.

"Not sure," Val replied. "The trick would be catching them with their files open."

"Yeah. That would be a trick, all right." Rashe shook his head. "Especially since we may have to risk crashing the gates."

"We *do* have the Darconians on our side," Onca pointed out. "But I still think I could get in as a client. At least we'd have some idea what was going on."

Roncas twittered right on cue.

Onca held up a hand. "I know what you're going to say, Roncas. We've been through this before, and it won't happen. I have no intention of fucking a bunch of helpless women—whether they want me to or not."

"Yes, but if you're inside and there's a raid, you'd

look just as guilty as the other clients—and being a brothel owner yourself kinda destroys your credibility as an upstanding citizen."

"Maybe, but the odds the cops would raid the place on the same night we're there are astronomical—and even if they did, they certainly wouldn't catch me in the act."

To be honest, he had an idea he might never be capable of offering sex on demand again—at least, not without Kim nearby. For Jerden to imprint on Audrey's scent had taken years of intimate contact. Kim's potent aroma had done it to Onca in a matter of hours. He could have pinpointed her precise location in the room with his eyes closed.

Had Kim been anything other than Zetithian that wouldn't pose a problem—at least, not for her. She could have gone her merry way and perhaps fallen for one of Jack's boys while Onca ran the risk of never being aroused by another female again.

But she *was* Zetithian, and if they remained together much longer, neither of them would ever respond to the scent of anyone else. Would she resent the fact that she had become mated to him before she met another Zetithian male? With his education, Onca should have had a clearer understanding of the biology involved, but he'd never dreamed the bond could develop so quickly. Would Kim accuse him of taking advantage of her ignorance?

Maybe. Although there was some consolation in knowing she couldn't be stolen from him by Larry, Moe, or Curly.

Deeming it best to move on to another topic, he asked, "I don't suppose we've received any replies to the deep space coms I sent out?"

"Only one," Val replied. "Lerotan Kanotay says he'll get here as soon as he can, but he's a long way off."

"Which means that Jack and Dax are even farther away or they would've responded by now." Onca glanced at Rashe. "Sure we can't recruit the twins? We could confuse the hell out of the enemy with them."

"I dunno," Rashe said. "They're real wusses when it comes to laying their lives on the line. Not sure we could trust them not to turn tail and run."

"Okay then. I'll go in as a client—they take walk-ins, don't they?"

Rashe chuckled. "Yeah, dude. They aren't quite the high-class place yours was."

"I'd like to see this brothel of yours sometime," Kim said. "You say it's full of trees like your bathroom?"

"Yeah, only a lot bigger, with sections of the floor that float up into the trees. I still haven't decided whether to sell it or lease it. Considering its location, a brothel is about all it could ever be. This district isn't exactly the greatest spot for a home for street kids."

Not unless he wanted a business as shady as the Den. Besides, the pheromones in the air down there would have the kids fucking each other in a heartbeat—not exactly a huge drawing card. Well…it might be for some, but certainly not all of them. Kim and Jatki had good reasons for avoiding that region in favor of the lower-end commerce district. The subliminal advertising there only made you want to buy the cheap stuff, not fuck anyone in sight.

Roncas gave him a push toward the table. "Sit down, Boss. Your soup's getting cold."

Seeming to take this as a hint, Val picked up his spoon. "Smells great, Roncas."

"Thanks," Roncas snapped. "I made yours with nuts instead of meat." Apparently Val was a tad late with his compliment. Even her subsequent coo held a trace of annoyance.

Onca knew the feeling. Nothing was quite as frustrating as unrequited love—unless it was not knowing what was going on in the mind of the object of your affections.

Right now, Kim was simply eating her lunch. Was she thinking about how much taller she might have been if she'd had sufficient food while growing up? Or was she still lost in the afterglow of sex? He knew a couple of Mordrials who could tell him precisely what her thoughts were— not that he would ever have the guts to take that route.

Talk about something that would piss her off…

He picked up his spoon and tasted the stew, which was almost as good as what he made himself. "This is really good, Roncas. Thanks."

"My, my," she drawled. "For once, you're displaying a tiny smidgen of tact."

A retort had almost reached his lips when he turned it into a grin. "Amazing, isn't it?"

———ᨆ———

Kim let the banter between Onca and Roncas pass by without comment, enjoying the hum of the voices around her. So far, this had been one of the best days of her life. She had already learned to read a little better, she'd had a marvelous time with Onca, and the stew was filling her stomach quite nicely.

If she hadn't been so worried about her friends she would have said she was…

Happy.

Most people took that kind of happiness for granted. Kim savored every moment of it. Her only regret was not fucking Onca for the stew he'd given her yesterday, which would have made her even happier.

Maybe. A lot had happened since then. She had even eaten enough to make the distinction between Roncas's cooking and Onca's. His stew had tasted better. She would never tell Roncas that, of course. She was a little surprised Onca hadn't.

He seemed to have mellowed—more so than a good night's sleep could explain. Jatki seemed different too. She was acting, well...*normal*—like she'd grown up in a home where she felt safe and protected and had never lived on the street.

Kim studied Onca out of the corner of her eye. His hair was beautiful and he was very handsome, but even that didn't explain why watching him chew and swallow was so fascinating or why simply sitting beside him made her feel so good. She longed to put down her spoon and smother him with kisses.

Am I in love with him?

That was one explanation. Two days ago, she wouldn't have given up food for anything, especially a kiss.

But two days ago, she hadn't met Onca. He hadn't rescued her—or Jatki—yet, and sex with anyone was something to avoid rather than crave.

And she did crave him. Too bad she had to be content to sit beside him instead of sitting *on* him with his lovely ruffled penis buried deep inside her. The stew was tasty, but Onca was better.

The comlink dinged and Val spun around to check it. "Looks like a hail from the *Jolly Roger*."

"Thank God," Roncas said. "Now we'll get some decent help."

"You keep saying that like the rest of us are completely worthless," Onca said. "Rashe, Wings, and I could probably handle this by ourselves."

The look Roncas gave him said otherwise. "Before you guys go off half-cocked, let's hear what Jack has to say, shall we?"

Val tapped the link. "They must be closer than we thought. It's a video com."

Onca shot Roncas a quelling look. "Do not say *anything*." He was practically growling at her. Kim couldn't blame him for that. Roncas picked on him every chance she got. Clearly, she had never fucked him or she wouldn't feel that way.

Val passed the link over to Onca, which at least gave Kim a better vantage point.

A woman with short dark hair appeared on the viewscreen. "Hey, bucko, how's it hanging?"

Onca chuckled. "Just fine, Jack. We weren't expecting to get more than a text message from you."

"You reckoned without Larry," Jack said with undisguised pride. "That boy's a whiz with a comlink. So, what's all this about a rescue mission involving a Zetithian girl? Have you found her yet?"

"Yeah. Actually, her friends are the ones we need to rescue."

Jack scowled. "You lied to me, bucko. You know how much I hate that."

"Would you have come if I'd said we were trying to find a Levitian, a Davordian, and an Edraitian?"

"Maybe. What happened to them?"

"Kidnapped and sold into slavery," Onca replied. "At least, that's what we think."

"I'd have come anyway," Jack declared. "Can't stand that shit. So where *is* this Zetithian girl?"

"She's here at my house." Onca angled the viewscreen slightly—away from Kim.

That gesture along with his tone of voice put Kim on the alert. He seemed evasive for some reason.

"Glad you're keeping her safe," Jack said. "Makes you wonder how many others are out there, doesn't it?"

"Sure does."

"I hear you gave up the sex business."

Narrowing his eyes, Onca lifted his chin. "That's right."

Definitely defensive.

"Glad to hear it. You'll live longer. So tell me about this girl—or let her tell me about herself."

Onca hesitated, his posture becoming more rigid by the second. Taking in a deep breath, he blew it out slowly as his gaze slid toward Kim. "She's right here. Talk to her." He tilted the viewscreen again, this time in the other direction.

Kim's first direct view of Jack caught her just as her jaw dropped.

"Well, I'll be a monkey's uncle," she exclaimed. "You really *are* just a kid."

Kim was about to call on Captain to vouch for her again, but Onca spoke first. "She's small for her age."

Jack snorted. "Small for what, a fifteen-year-old?"

"She's twenty-two," Onca snapped. "And I can prove it."

Onca only *sounded* pissed. Kim's blood was beginning to boil. "I can't help it if I'm small."

"Maybe not," Jack conceded. "But that's unusual for a Zetithian. Might be a genetic defect of some kind. We'll have to get that checked out before we pair you off with anyone."

Kim was really ticked now and would have shouted a retort if Onca hadn't intervened.

"Aw, lighten up, Jack," he drawled. "She's had a tough time of it—not enough food or anything else for most of her life. I'm sure her genes are perfectly normal."

Jack shifted her focus back to Kim without missing a beat. "Twenty-two, huh? Good age for my older guys—or even Tisana's. Hers are sixteen and mine are eighteen. I'm sure you'll like one of them."

Kim was prepared to hate them on sight. "We'll see about that. I mean, I *do* have a choice, don't I?"

"Of course you do," Jack said. "We aren't talking about arranged marriages. That shit doesn't work with Zetithians anyway. I just want you to know you have options."

A young Zetithian male with long black hair appeared behind Jack and peered at the viewscreen. "Don't make her mad, Mom. She's really cute."

Rashe laughed. "That's what I told Onca."

"Onca?" Jack's eyes widened in frank disbelief. "He's too old for you, kiddo—aside from the fact that he probably won't ever settle down. You'd be better off with someone else."

"I'm not *that* old," Onca protested.

Apparently Jack disagreed. "Onca, *sweetheart*—you might not be too old for a twenty-two-year-old Terran, but in case you hadn't noticed, Kim isn't human, and you've got fourteen years on her."

"Have I missed something?" Kim asked.

"Humans age faster than Zetithians," Jack explained. "Do you really want to hook up with a guy old enough to be your father?"

Kim barked out a laugh. "Beats having a fourteen-year-old father. But enough about that. We need help finding my friends. We think they've been kidnapped and taken to a brothel called the Den where they're either being used or sold as sex slaves. Will you help us?"

Jack nodded her approval. "I'll say this much for you, kid, you've got your priorities straight. And yes, we'll help you. But I can't fold space or alter time. We're about three days from Rhylos."

"Leroy's coming too," Roncas put in. "He didn't say where he was, though."

Jack scowled. "That's because he doesn't want to admit he's been selling guns to the Luxarians—and if that's where he is, we'll get to Rhylos ahead of him. I doubt if you'll need his kind of firepower anyway." She winked at Kim. "Situations like this require a more subtle approach."

Kim doubted that Jack had ever taken the subtle approach to anything in her life. "I don't think we should wait that long. My friends might be sold offworld by then—if they haven't already."

"She has a point," Onca said. "We'd already decided that if you weren't close by, we'd go ahead without you."

Jack ran a hand through her hair, shaking her head. "I can't argue with your logic, but damn, I wish you'd wait for us. If you let anything happen to that kid, your ass is grass."

"Don't you think I know that?" Onca practically spat the words at the viewscreen. "I've got a plan that won't put her at any risk."

"Mind telling me who *will* be at risk?"

"Me," Onca replied. "I'll—"

"And how is that better?" Jack demanded.

Onca sighed. "Look, Jack. I've sired a bajillion kids. No one needs me anymore."

Kim's mouth fell open. "That's not true. No one is expendable—and siring children is *not* the only thing you're good for."

"Really? As I see it, that's all *any* of us are good for," Onca said. "That's why we need to keep you safe until you've had a few litters. Preferably with several different men."

"Are you crazy? I don't want anyone but—" Kim caught herself before finishing that declaration. Something had changed—and not for the better.

Jack cleared her throat. "Not sure that's possible with a Zetithian girl. You *know* how they are."

"Yeah, but I'll bet you can find a way around that, Jack. Right now, we've got bigger fish to fry. If you can't get here, we're going ahead as planned. Tonight."

"Didn't give me much leeway, did you?" Jack said with a sardonic smile. "Makes me wonder why you even bothered to send out the com."

Onca nodded toward Kim. "She needs a ride to Terra Minor. You can pick her up when you get here."

A sharp pang pierced Kim's chest. Onca sounded so cold and abrupt. To hear him talk, he had never given a thought to loving her and didn't care if he ever saw her again. He'd made no promises about staying together forever, but surely he wouldn't hand her over to Jack without a backward glance. Not after making love with her.

Would he?

One call from this Jack person, and the happiness Kim had so recently discovered evaporated. *Poof*. Gone in an instant.

Like my family. Swallowing back the lump in her throat, she barely heard the rest of the conversation between Jack and Onca. She didn't care what happened now.

I should've known better. Nothing lasted forever, but was he truly that heartless? Could he make her feel that kind of joy without forming any kind of attachment to her?

Of course he could. For him, sex was simply his livelihood, his trade, his occupation. He was used to fucking women once and never seeing them again.

Too bad Kim wasn't used to being one of those women.

"I'll get there as quick as I can," Jack was saying. "In the meantime, you all be careful."

"We will." Onca's finger was poised to terminate the link.

"Hold on a second." Grabbing the comlink, Kim angled it toward her. "That boy of yours. What did you say his name was?"

"Larry." Jack grinned. "Handsome fellow, isn't he?"

Chapter 16

ONCA FELT LIKE HE HAD JUST SIGNED HIS OWN DEATH warrant. The one girl he had ever felt anything for, and he'd tossed her to someone else.

She probably hates me now.

Jack was right, of course. He was too old for Kim. Teaching her was okay, but that happily-ever-after shit wasn't gonna happen. Not for him. Kim seemed to have received the message, loud and clear.

Switching off the link, he stared at it as though it were the source of his woes. Perhaps it was. Damn that Larry for getting a message through—and a video, no less. The kid was a real whiz. Onca had to give him credit for that much.

But could Larry love Kim the way she should be loved? Would he see her for the miracle she was? Perhaps not. But that didn't mean he couldn't make her happy.

Shoving the comlink aside, Onca hung his head over his half-eaten stew. Roncas chirped away at Val. Rashe said something that actually made Jatki laugh. Kim didn't say a word.

Jack had never been the voice of reason before. Why the hell did she have to make so much sense now? Picking up his spoon, Onca mechanically ate the remainder of the stew. The condemned always got a last meal, didn't they?

Not that he was truly condemned. Once they freed

those girls from the Den, his life would have more meaning than ever before. He would see to it that they were educated, had plenty to eat, and a place to call home. He would get over Kim. Whether or not he ever recovered sexually didn't matter. What he'd told Jack was the truth. He had already done his part to save the Zetithian race. Now he could save someone else.

Strange how everyone seemed to think it was funny that he would help anyone aside from himself. Was he really that selfish? Maybe. Or maybe he'd changed.

Rashe gave him a nudge. "Tonight, huh?"

"Yeah. Might as well."

"Without a plan?"

"We've *got* a plan. I'll knock on the damned door, ask if they've got a Levitian girl I can fuck, and go from there."

"You're sure no one will recognize you?" Rashe asked.

Jatki nodded. "Yeah, what about those Racks that came after us when you picked me up?"

"We were moving pretty fast—and Racks aren't very bright," Onca said. "The only one who *might* recognize me is the Herp who tried to kidnap Kim."

"I doubt it," Kim said. "You may be the only Zetithian man on the planet, but they don't know that, and from a distance in the dark, you could pass for a Terran or even a Davordian. I mean, you didn't even realize *I* was Zetithian right away. Besides, Herps have crappy night vision."

"True," Onca agreed. "And it's not like I've ever spent any time in that end of the brothel district."

"What about weapons?" Roncas asked.

Val shook his head. "With all that security on their

computer system, I'm guessing they've got a weapons sensor. He'll have to go in unarmed."

"We have Shemlak and his gang for backup," Onca said. "Communication will be the tough part. If I get in trouble, the first thing they're gonna do is cut the signal to my portable link—or confiscate it. A few Darconian comstones would come in real handy."

"I dunno," Rashe said. "Those stones are awfully expensive. Not sure a bunch of cooks and waitresses could afford one—and we'd need at least two of them."

Jack had plenty of the stones, and their use had gotten her and her crew out of several tight spots.

Yet another reason to wait for her.

He couldn't do that. They had already wasted enough time. Reminding himself that he had only found Kim the previous morning didn't help a whole lot because it seemed so much longer than that.

After all, it wasn't every day a guy found his perfect mate and then realized it would be wrong of him to keep her.

———

Kim listened to the discussion with half an ear. If she was to be kept "safe," she wouldn't be taking part in the rescue—a circumstance she didn't like one little bit.

She had always been the strong, resourceful one. Relying on others to take charge was out of character for her. She should be the one risking her life to save her friends, not Onca.

And he was *definitely* taking a risk.

Granted, he had several buddies to help him, but he

would be the one going inside. What if the girls weren't there? What if he risked his life for nothing?

At the moment, she felt more like sacrificing herself than ever. If Onca didn't want to be the one to father her litters, what was the point in having any? She didn't want to have children with several other men. She wanted to have Onca's babies, not Larry's or anyone else's.

Why didn't *she* get to choose? After all, she was the one who would be giving birth to all of those children. She had a right to say who their father would be.

The more she thought about it, the angrier she became. She didn't care if she came across as a sullen, pouting child. This just wasn't right.

"I'll go in the front," Onca said. "The Darconians can patrol the street, and Rashe, you can watch the main entrance."

"While I circle above the building to make sure no one tries to escape from another exit." Val didn't seem to smile very often, but he was smiling now—albeit a bit grimly. "I can't wait to hack into their system and put a stop to these atrocities."

"I hope you get the chance," Onca said. "This may end up being more of a fact-finding mission than an all-out rescue. Still, a little aerial reconnaissance would be useful beforehand."

Roncas twittered. "And I'll be standing by to call the cops when all hell breaks loose."

Kim had heard enough. "I'm going with you."

Onca's expression darkened, but before he had a chance to protest, she continued, "I'll stick close to Rashe or Shemlak, but I'm going to be there. Jack doesn't know all there is to know about what we're dealing with. You don't have to tell her we didn't follow her orders."

"But she's right." Except for a few giggles, Jatki had barely made a sound during lunch and the ensuing conversation. Clearly she had been paying attention. "You *should* stay here where it's safe. I'll go. The girls will know me, if that's what you're worried about."

It wasn't—although it was an excellent argument. "The girls in the brothel have no reason to believe you guys are trying to rescue them," Kim pointed out. "Having me and Jatki on hand would help gain their trust."

Rashe nodded. "She's got a point, dude. If you were one of those girls, would you trust us?"

Onca glanced at Val before giving Rashe the once-over. "I'd probably trust me and Val. We look pretty tame. Not so sure about you, what with the war paint and all."

"Tame? I can wash off the war paint, but you've got fangs and he's got wings and the craziest eyes I've ever seen—and then there are the Darconians, who scare the living shit out of most people. If we let those girls out, they'll probably take off running and wind up right back where they were in no time."

"Not if we shut down that place and any others like it."

Rashe folded his arms, aiming a scowl at Onca. "Do you really think we'll be able to do that? I warned you to keep your head down and your mouth shut, didn't I? We're playing with fire here."

"So you say," Onca drawled. "You were kinda cryptic before. What exactly have you heard?"

"No names, if that's what you mean. Just that they're people you don't want to mess with."

"Told you we should wait for Jack and Leroy," Roncas muttered.

Onca slammed his palms on the table. "Whether we wait for Jack, Leroy, or a miracle, we still need to get inside to gather some evidence. Right now, all we've got is conjecture."

"Some damned good conjecture, though," Rashe said in an undertone.

"If nothing else, we might be able to give those girls a little hope," Jatki said.

Val nodded. "Very true. Sometimes that's all the oppressed need to find the courage to start an uprising."

"Uprising?" Onca snorted in disgust. "What can they do? Refuse to put out? The guys who go there probably love raping helpless girls."

Kim nearly fainted at the thought, but his harsh words had the desired effect.

"Okay. Let's do it," Rashe said. "I can't stand shit like that. Just flat, fuckin' can't stand it."

The doorman at the Den certainly looked wicked enough to kidnap young girls, but then, Cylopeans were among the more hideous creatures in the galaxy.

"What the devil do you want?" he snarled.

"I should've thought that was obvious," Onca replied. "This is a brothel, isn't it?"

"That depends on the color of your credits."

"Don't worry, asshole. I've got money." The last thing Onca wanted was to have to talk his way inside. He already felt queasy and having an extended conversation with a Cylopean wouldn't improve his condition.

The guy stunk to high heaven. "Do I get to play with some girls, or do I have to nail your bony ass out here in the street?"

The doorman snickered, sounding even more sinister than a Nedwut. "You need more than one?"

Onca shrugged. "On a given day, I've been known to do eight or nine. But I'm feeling less interested all the time. If the girls are as ugly as you, I'm not sure I'll be able to get it up."

"Our girls are among the loveliest in the district." The man licked his lips. "Young and fresh."

Onca could barely suppress his shudder of revulsion. "You sound like you're selling Mondavian chickens."

"Funny fellow, aren't you?"

"I'm glad you find me so amusing." Not bothering to rein in the sarcasm, he continued. "How much to get past your ugly mug and see some of these *lovely* girls?"

"Fifty credits. Right here, right now."

"How much more when I get inside?"

With a sly smile, the Cylopean rubbed his thin snout with a bony finger. "The price depends on how many of our ladies want you."

That didn't sound right. "You mean they have a *choice*?"

"Why, of course they do. This is a high-class establishment. Or were you unaware of that fact?"

Onca's gaze swept the exterior of the building, ending with the doorman's tattered robes. "Doesn't look like it from here."

"Fifty credits."

Onca slapped the money on the man's outstretched palm, hating to have even that much contact with him.

"You may fuck as many of our ladies as you

desire—as long as *they* desire *you*." The crackling hum of a deactivating force field sounded as the door swung open. With a bow, the Cylopean waved him through.

Not good. They should've guessed there would be more than a simple lock on the door. Unfortunately, at the moment, Onca had no way of reporting this to any of his comrades.

The stench of unwashed bodies assailed his nostrils as he stepped inside. He was met by a Herpatronian who betrayed no sign of recognition, although he did seem vaguely familiar.

Probably the one I pinged in the ass.

"This way, please," the Herp said, sounding far more polite than was typical of his kind. "We'll let the ladies have a look at you."

Onca followed him down a narrow hallway and into a large, circular room where the worst of his fears were realized. The dimly lit space was lined with rows of cages filled with females from practically every planet in the known galaxy. As soon as he entered, they all began screaming at once.

A moment later Onca realized they weren't screaming in terror.

They were *volunteering*.

Most of the girls were naked, and those who were clothed immediately struck provocative poses, doing their best to catch his eye. Their apparent interest baffled him completely.

Was Roncas right? Had they actually heard about Zetithians?

Somehow he doubted it, but he was still at a loss to explain their excitement. As thin and pale as they all were, a little food and sunshine would have been far more beneficial than sex—even with a Zetithian. The few Kitnocks he saw were even skinnier than Jatki.

He stared at them in dismay. Kim had done her best to drum her friends' names and descriptions into his head, but when faced with so many clamoring women, Onca doubted he would recognize any of them.

Cassie is a Davordian with short blond hair. Peska is Edraitian and has a scar on her left forearm. Dalmet is a Levitian with dark brown hair and a crooked nose.

Since Davordians were fairly common on Rhylos, Onca figured he would have better luck singling out Dalmet or Peska than he would Cassie. "Got any Levitians?"

"A few," the Herp replied. "But they don't seem to want you."

Strike one. "How about that Edraitian over there? I love red hair."

"She's not asking, either." The Herp slapped his hairy thigh and let out an annoying guffaw. "Guess she's not hungry enough yet."

Holy shit.

The girls probably didn't get fed unless they volunteered.

I'm really *gonna hurl now.* The Edraitian sat in her cage with her back to him. *Not hungry enough…* The girls who weren't vying for his attention probably hadn't been there as long as the others.

Therefore, those who ignored him might be the ones he was looking for.

Forcing himself to focus on his task, he studied each girl until at last, he spotted a blond Davordian who wasn't issuing a blatant come-on. She sat quietly, occasionally stealing a covert glance at him.

He pointed at the girl he hoped was Cassie. "What about that one?"

The Herp shook his head. "She's not behaving tonight. Pick someone else."

Onca took a few steps closer to the Davordian's cage. How could he possibly gain her trust without giving himself away?

Then again, he *was* Zetithian...

Drawing in a breath, he blew it out as a purr, doing his best to sound seductive *and* trustworthy. "Come, mate with me, my love, and I will give you joy unlike any you have ever known."

He had never used that line before, but just this once he prayed it would work. Then he remembered something else. If this was indeed Cassie, having known a Zetithian girl, she might feel some degree of trust for a male of the same species.

Still purring, Onca swept his hair behind his ears. A smile revealed his fangs as he casually scratched one ear, drawing attention to the pointed tip.

The Davordian girl's luminous blue eyes widened, and she lunged at the bars of her cage. "Pick me, please!"

Chapter 17

KIM STOOD IN SHEMLAK'S SHADOW, WATCHING ONCA haggle with the doorman across the street, praying to every deity she had ever heard of that her friends—and Onca—would soon be safe.

She didn't really expect him to simply march out of the place with the three girls in tow—unless he bought them. They hadn't discussed that possibility. If caught in the act, it would be tough to prove he intended to free them, which meant he was at risk no matter what he did. He hadn't been kidding about sacrificing himself, and her heart pounded harder than ever with the fear that she might never see him again. She was about to rush toward him and beg him to forget all of it when Shemlak touched her arm.

"He's in." The Darconian shifted his weight from one massive foot to the other. "And there's a force field on the door."

"Great," she muttered. "So we can't go in after him?"

"Not unless we can disable the field. I can take out that Cylopean without any trouble, but we may need Val to get us past the barrier."

At least they had a means of communicating with Val directly. Onca also had a link on him, and they had set it up with a panic button that would send out a signal to everyone on their team. But as he'd said before, if he was in trouble, that would be the first thing they would dispose of.

Unless they got rid of him first.

That thought sent a chill through her, making her shiver in spite of the warm night. If Rashe was right about there being some big bad conspiracy behind brothels like this one, they could all wind up deported or imprisoned.

Or dead.

Why had Onca suddenly changed from the man whose company she had enjoyed so much that morning to a grim, self-sacrificing martyr? The best she could come up with was that he believed Jack's assessment—that he was too old for Kim, and that she would be better off marrying one of Jack's sons.

She'd been too hasty in showing interest in Larry. She knew that now and wished she could tell Onca the truth—that she had been so hurt and stunned, she'd reacted before giving herself time to consider the situation in a rational manner.

Obviously no one expected her to be rational. True, she was young, but life on the street had taught her that allowing emotions to dictate her actions wasn't always the best policy. She had been firm in her determination to take an active part in this mission, and she'd given valid reasons to support her decision—particularly the idea of having someone there that the other girls would trust. Jatki alone might not be enough. Unfortunately, even Captain seemed to think she should keep out of the line of fire.

Damned computer thinks he knows everything.

Well, actually, he probably *did* know everything—most facts, anyway.

Onca and his friends had spent the afternoon

discussing strategy, ultimately reaching the conclusion that they were simply going to have to wing it. She wished they could've hired some henchman to actually go inside, or simply watch the door and interrogate the customers as they left—taking an exit poll, as Roncas suggested.

Kim had no idea what they were talking about most of the time. Instead of interrupting their planning session, she spent a few hours in her room, listening to Captain drone on about the Rhylosian government and its legal procedures. Having to stop him frequently to define various terms slowed her progress, but she now had a better understanding of how such processes worked, all of which made her fear for Onca's safety even more.

They couldn't even call the police. Roncas was right. In a raid, Onca and every other customer would be arrested and possibly imprisoned along with the proprietors. No one would believe he was there on a rescue mission—especially with only a few of his buddies and people like her and Jatki to vouch for him. If her friends weren't in there, he wouldn't have a leg to stand on. Then there was the possibility that even the police were in on it—or being paid to look the other way.

All of which pointed to the need to avoid involving anyone in authority.

What was the word they'd used? *Vigilante?* She had never heard it before, but apparently the cops took a dim view of anyone taking the law into their own hands— which was exactly what they would be doing.

Still, Jack was on her way and, if Roncas's opinion meant anything, she was a force to be reckoned with and so was the arms dealer, Lerotan Kanotay. Kim didn't

know much about Onca's friend Dax, aside from the
fact that he had a nice ship and could take her to Terra
Minor in style if Jack wasn't available. At least Dax was
married and didn't have any sons of marriageable age.
Getting a ride with him would protect her from match-
making plots to keep her and Onca apart.

Maybe.

Many of these same thoughts would have been buzzing around in her head even if she'd stayed behind.
Unfortunately, getting a firsthand look at what they were
up against hadn't done a thing to calm her fears. This
wasn't some cheap-ass operation. Force fields were expensive. Even street urchins knew that. Most businesses
relied on locked doors and iron bars for security. There
was money behind this place—and lots of it.

She focused her attention on the door as the Cylopean
admitted another customer—a big, mean-looking Terran
with tattoos and a bald head. The horror of Peska or
Dalmet being at the mercy of such a man made her
shudder. Cassie could probably take it. Davordians were
among some of the more sexually uninhibited species in
the galaxy, and Cassie liked boys. Still, the thought of
being taken by force was enough to chill Kim's bones.
Sex with guys she liked had been bad enough.

Nothing like being with Onca at all.

The minutes ticked slowly by. A few men came
out, but no one else went in. They were giving him an
hour—which, according to Rashe, was the standard time
allotment in a brothel of this type.

Yet another thing I didn't know.

A steady stream of foot traffic trickled along the
street, most of the passersby seeming to ignore the

Den's existence. She spotted the occasional Darconian among them, knowing that they were some of Shemlak's friends and relatives—Draddut being the largest of them all. Kim had barely contained her laughter earlier that evening when Onca was seized and ruthlessly hugged by Ganyn, who was among those patrolling the area. Kim was glad she had come along. If anyone could bull her way past the doorman and his force field to rescue Onca, it was Ganyn. Even with a running start, Kim would probably bounce right off the barrier.

Although Rashe still considered this particular brothel to be the most likely, he knew of at least three others with questionable reputations. What if they had to check out those places, too? What if her friends weren't in any of them? They could be dead or even on other planets by now.

What had seemed so simple in the beginning when Kim and Jatki had formed their own plans had somehow become a monstrous, terrifying undertaking.

"We need to go after him now," Kim said. "I can't wait the full hour."

Shemlak chuckled. "That's why Onca wanted you to stay behind. He knew you wouldn't be able to sit still and let him do what he has to do. And it's also why he stationed you here with me. Not many people are willing to take on a Darconian."

"I don't see why—"

"He knows you care about him, Kim." He nodded toward the brothel. "And he also knows women don't like to see their men walk into places like that, whether it's for a good cause or not."

Their men? When had Onca become her man—at

least, in the eyes of others? She felt very strongly about him, but she had kept those feelings to herself. She didn't understand how anyone else could know about them, especially Shemlak.

"He's doing this for you," Shemlak went on. "Not for himself."

"How could he possibly think that getting himself killed is something I would ever want him to do?"

"You were willing to risk your life to discover what happened to your friends, weren't you?"

"Well, yes, but that's different."

"Not really," Shemlak said. "Discovering the fate of these girls is important to you. Therefore, it's important to him."

Kim couldn't see the connection. At least, not unless— "He doesn't love me, if that's what you're getting at."

"You think not? I believe he does. Enough to risk his life to keep you safe. Enough to let you go if it's in your best interest."

"That's ridiculous. We only met yesterday. How could he possibly know what's best for me?"

"He sees the bigger picture, Kim." The Darconian paused, shaking his ponderous head. "I never would've given Onca credit for thinking on that scale, but apparently he can. You won't leave this world to collect your share of the trust fund and go on with your life without first rescuing your friends—or at least doing everything you can to discover their fate. He knows that and sees this as the only way to get you to go willingly."

"What if we succeed? What if we find my friends and no one gets killed? Will he still send me away?"

"Probably. Either that, or he'll go someplace where you can't find him."

Kim refused to accept—or believe—any of it. "How do you know so much?"

"Rashe filled me in on the details, and I know Zetithians. I knew Jerden and Tarq, and both of them would've done exactly what Onca's doing now. Nobody ever thought he was the type to care much about anything or anybody, but I've never known a species whose men worshipped women as much as those cats do. Well…maybe worship is the wrong word. But I can tell you this much—Zetithian men are too damned noble for their own good."

On that point, she and Shemlak were in complete agreement. She blew out a breath. "How much longer do we have to wait?"

With a rumbling chuckle, he patted her head, nearly driving her feet into the pavement. "Don't worry. We'll get him out of there. Then you can tell him what a fool he was to risk his life for you and your gang."

"He's a fool for a couple of other reasons, too," Kim said. "I just hope I get the chance to tell him that."

"So do I."

———— ⁓ ————

Given the sexual nature most Davordians possessed, Onca should have been able to do this one with both hands tied behind his back.

Nothing.

Not so much as a quiver of interest from his cock. This circumstance—though highly inconvenient at the moment—illustrated all that had occurred since his last night in the Palace.

Oh, yes. He was mated to Kim. Body, mind, and soul.

Not that he needed proof. He had known it with that first kiss. Jack would have laughed her ass off if she'd known the truth. He, of course, had no intention of telling her anything about it.

He'd had a tiny bit of difficulty convincing the Herp that he wanted this particular girl, but now that he stood facing her from the doorway of the small room to which they had been taken, he was at a loss as to how to proceed. The room was surprisingly clean, and the bed appeared comfortable enough to lure any of the girls from their cages—if for no other reason than to lie down in a soft place for the half-second before some man jumped on them and did his worst.

Onca shook off the shudder and got down to business. "What's your name?"

The Davordian girl's eyes filled with tears as she gazed up at him. "We aren't supposed to tell anyone our names."

"Hmm. Too bad about that. Mind if I call you Cassie?"

Her startled reaction was more than enough to confirm her identity. "I-If you wish."

"You girls don't get fed unless you beg the customers to fuck you. Am I right?"

"I wouldn't know."

Clearly she wasn't going to make this easy. "Are these rooms bugged?"

Her puzzled frown and her reluctance to answer his questions spoke volumes. What a client did with these girls was his own choice, but the girls' behavior had to be monitored—and their adherence to the rules enforced.

Something else we didn't think about—along with the force field on the door.

Crap. He was going to have to at least *pretend* to fuck this girl.

With a limp dick? *Yeah, right*.

This was *such* a bad idea.

"I'm guessing they are—especially if you're afraid to tell me your name." He held out a hand. "My name is Onca. I'm Zetithian. Perhaps you've seen others like me before?"

She didn't take his hand, merely shaking her head as she stared down at the thickly carpeted floor.

To pull off this charade, he should throw her down, rip off what little clothing she had on, and nail her to the bed. Then perhaps he could whisper in her ear, telling her he was there to rescue her and all the others. He should be able to do that. After all, she was a pretty, blond Davordian. He'd done a hundred others just like her—perhaps even more than that.

The trouble was, he had never needed to be forceful with any of them. Hell, he'd barely even had to purr. Most Davordians threw their arms around his neck and pulled *him* down. Being the aggressor wasn't in his nature. At all. Even Kim had made the first move with him—asking him to kiss her and then leaping into his arms and biting him. Granted, he'd taken it from there, but right now, he had absolutely no idea how to even make this farce look good.

Reconnaissance mission, hell. I am so screwed.

If he didn't leave the building in an hour, the others would know something had gone wrong, and hopefully, come after him and the girls. Rashe could have done this much better. At least *he* could have managed an erection.

As Onca made a move toward her, the girl cringed away from him. He didn't understand why she wouldn't trust him at all, especially since he knew her name.

"Um…Kim sent me."

When she still refused to respond, he hesitated, re-thinking his tactics. Should he ask for another girl or keep trying to wear this one down until she talked? Clearly, she was more afraid of her captors than she was of him. As far as she was concerned, he was just another dumb john.

He swallowed hard and tried again.

"Tell me how you got here. Were you kidnapped?" He knew someone was listening, but at this point, he wasn't sure it mattered.

Bad plan.

He threw up his hands. "Okay, Jack. You were right."

The girl stared up at him with yet another puzzled frown. "You're calling me Jack now?"

"No. Just talking to myself. No use pretending. I'm only here to find out if Kim's friends are in this place. If you're one of them, great. We're here to rescue you. If not, we're both fucked." Not expecting much to come of it, he tried the door, which was, of course, securely locked.

"You're more fucked than you think, pretty boy." The Herpatronian's voice came from a speaker located somewhere in the room.

"Yeah. I figured that. But I do have friends."

The man's laughter curdled Onca's blood and out-raged him at the same time. "For your sake, I hope you brought along an army. Not that there'll be much left of you to find when I'm finished with you."

Onca let out a sigh. "Yeah. I figured that too."

Hoping the signal wasn't blocked, he hit the panic button on his comlink.

"You're right," the girl blurted out. "My name is Cassie. Is Kim safe?"

"Yeah, she and Jatki are outside with the rest of my gang. I hope to hell they can get through that force field or we're gonna be in for a rough night."

"It might be rougher than you think," Cassie said. "That Herp likes boys."

"Oh, joy."

Chapter 18

KIM'S HEART PLUNGED TO HER FEET, TAKING ALL THE blood in her head with it as the panic signal sounded from Shemlak's comlink.

"Time for plan B." Shemlak stepped out of the shadows just as Val swooped down from the sky, landing lightly in front of him. "I'll take out the Cylopean. You work on that force field."

Shemlak swaggered up to the doorman with his pistol drawn, which, as Kim noted a moment later, was probably a mistake. The force field flickered, extending to include the station by the entrance.

"Great mother of the desert!" Shemlak thundered. "If you want to live to see tomorrow, you'll drop that field."

"Not likely," the Cylopean sneered. "We know how to deal with troublemakers."

What was left of Kim's circulating blood froze in her veins at the thought of how such people would "deal" with Onca. If he lived through this fiasco, Jack would kill him. And if Jack didn't kill him, Kim would be tempted to do the honors herself. "This was a *terrible* idea. I told him that, didn't I?"

"Maybe," Shemlak said. "Can't remember."

Val launched himself at the force field in full flight and ricocheted off it, flying up into the air before landing on his feet. Obviously he had no more super powers than any other large bird. Against a force field of that

strength, his only use would be his ability to disable it—
from the inside.

Shemlak tried next, aiming his pistol at the field,
turning the setting to kill.

"No, wait!" Kim yelled. "Let's all fire at once to
weaken the field. And Draddut, you get ready to ram
through it."

Clearly unafraid and perhaps even anxious to do
battle, Draddut scraped his enormous feet on the pavement as he leaned forward, positioning himself for the
charge. Ganyn, Rashe, Val, Shemlak, and Roncas aimed
their weapons at the door along with Kim and Jatki.

"Ready, aim, fire!" Kim shouted. The force field crack-
led where their pulse beams converged. "Now, Draddut!"

For a creature so large and cumbersome in appearance, the huge Darconian took off running at a surprising speed. Aiming for what was undoubtedly the
weakest spot, he barreled past the beams just as Kim
gave the order to cease fire. Hitting the field with an
impact that was probably audible three blocks away,
Draddut bounced off the barrier and landed with a thud.

The Cylopean cackled with laughter. "Your pathetic
attempts are no match for our equipment."

Kim glanced around in desperation. Most of the prudent passersby had fled, but a surprisingly large number
of onlookers remained. Some of them were even cheering.

"Don't just stand there gawking," Kim screeched.
"Do something!"

Nobody moved. Spotting a group of police officers in
the crowd, she fired a couple of shots over their heads.
"You guys have been chasing me for years. Now's your
chance to come and get me."

Ignoring her taunts, the police stood their ground. One of them laughed.

Kim stood there, gaping at them. "Rashe was right. They really *are* in on it."

———

The door slid open and two Herpatronians shouldered their way inside.

Onca pulled Cassie behind him. "Getting kinda crowded in here, don't you think?"

"You could say that," the Herp on the left snarled. "Get her out of here."

Grinning, the other Herp shoved Onca aside. "Hunard's gonna have some fun with you, pretty boy." Grabbing Cassie by the arm, he dragged her away. The door slid shut.

Onca studied his opponent. He was no match for a full-grown Herp, and he knew it. The simian race was known for its belligerence, strength, and, unfortunately, its agility. Onca had nowhere to run or hide. Not that he had any intention of giving up without a fight.

"I've wanted to get my dick into one of you cat boys for a long time," the Herp said.

Onca flicked a particle of fluff from his sleeve. "Well now—Hunard, is it? You should've booked an appointment while the Palace was still open. My ass isn't for sale anymore."

"I'm not buying," Hunard shot back. "I'm *taking*."

"And I'm not offering."

"Even better," Hunard snorted. "I'm getting hard just thinking about ripping your pants off and fucking your pretty little ass." Parting the front of the peculiar diaper-like garment that most Herps favored, he whipped out a dick the size of Onca's forearm. "Think you can take it?"

Onca shrugged. "I've seen bigger. And you know what they say—it's not the meat, it's the motion."

"I'm gonna love making you scream."

"Promises, promises…"

Agile and strong they might be, but Herps were also predictable. Onca sidestepped the first lunge with an ease that drew a growl from the outraged ape. "You might as well give up and bare your ass for me right now, *Onca*. Or did you give the girl a fake name?"

"No need for me to lie," Onca replied. "All of my clients knew my name. Not that many of them cared, but I did at least introduce myself."

"Bet you never bothered to dress, either."

"Generally not. This was different." Onca edged away from him again. Reaching the door would serve no purpose. The best he could do was to keep moving and pray his friends got to him in time. "I wasn't actually planning to get laid. I was here on a rescue mission."

Hunard snorted. "Some rescue."

"Call it a reconnaissance mission, then. Either way, my friends know what's going on in here, and they'll break in eventually. Then we're going to shut this place down for good. You know, kidnapping young girls— even the kind who live on the street—isn't very nice, aside from being illegal."

"No one cares about that shit. Not when we've got so many customers willing to pay."

"By the way, how much *do* you charge?"

"Five hundred a fuck," Hunard replied. "Big bucks no matter how you cut it."

Onca laughed. "I got a thousand per session—but then, my clients had more discriminating tastes, and some people thought I wasn't charging enough. I hated to seem greedy, though, and since the Palace was a legitimate business, I didn't have to 'cut it' with anyone. Especially not to keep them quiet."

Hunard's eyes narrowed, seeming to disappear beneath his prominent brow. "What makes you think we have to do that?"

"What part of 'kidnapping is illegal' don't you understand?" Slowly slipping his hand into his pocket, Onca pressed the panic button again, then tried to open a channel to Val. He might not make it out of the Den to tell the story, but if someone else were to hear this—

Hunard wasn't quite as stupid as he looked. Taking advantage of Onca's momentary distraction, he made a grab for him.

This time, he didn't miss. Within seconds, Onca's shirt lay shredded on the floor, and searing pain shot through his chest as the Herp's huge paw scored his skin. Onca knew he had at least one advantage over a Herp. Sure, they had claws, but they also possessed the flat teeth of a herbivore. Zetithians had fangs. Onca hoped he wouldn't have to use them. The thought of sinking his teeth into any part of a Herp made him sick. Then again, when fighting to literally save one's ass, some sacrifices must be made.

"So, you can bleed," Hunard said with a satisfied smirk. "I like that."

"You would," Onca retorted. "Never cared for it

myself. But then, I'm guessing your blood isn't as pretty and red as mine—probably a disgusting muddy brown."

"My blood is as red as yours, cat boy. Not that you'll be seeing any of it."

Onca shrugged. "My loss."

"You won't be making jokes once I've split your butt apart with my dick."

"Probably not," Onca agreed. "But in the meantime, I mean to get in as many digs as I can, starting with how fucking ugly you are. I mean, you're so ugly, you probably have to blindfold your boyfriends before they'll let you near them." He glanced downward. The Herp's dick was not only hard, it was dripping. Obviously drawing blood appealed to him. "Ugly cock too. You ought to keep it in your diaper until you're ready to use it."

"I'm ready to use it, all right. You just wait until I ram it in your ass. I'll *really* make you bleed." His lips curled into a diabolical grin. "Then I'll rip your nuts off so you'll be more docile—although I do like boys with some fight in them."

Onca had hoped the diaper jibe would piss the dude off. Obviously, he'd heard that one before—or, more likely, didn't know what a diaper was. On the other hand, Onca understood the nut-ripping comment perfectly and doubted it was an idle threat. "Guess you ought to let me keep my balls then." Seeing no further need for secrecy, he pulled the comlink out of his pocket.

"Toss me that comlink, and I'll be gentle with you."

"Nah. I think I'll keep it. Might want to call the police or my friends."

"You won't have the chance."

"No? I think—that is, I'm pretty sure Val has heard every word of our conversation. Isn't that right, Val?"

Onca waited.

Val never said a thing and neither did anyone else.

He hadn't really expected a call to go through, but had the panic signal worked? If not, he had a good forty-five minutes before anyone even *tried* to rescue him.

Clearly, setting the time limit at an hour was a mistake.

———

"My friends are in there," Kim yelled at the crowd. "They were kidnapped and enslaved. Forced into sex slavery—in horrible places like this."

The populace was unmoved, although she did get a few versions of "Hey, baby, you're really hot" from several of the men. Moments later, a group of Terran males began to advance toward her, licking their lips in a highly lascivious manner.

Then she remembered where she was. The brothel district—where the very air they breathed was laced with powerful sex pheromones. She wasn't sure about the Darconians, but Val and Rashe should have been affected. A glance at the two men proved this supposition to be correct. Dressed in leather, Rashe's erection wasn't as obvious, but Val sported a remarkable bulge in the crotch of his stretchy leggings. Roncas was still purple.

Far from recruiting anyone to help, Kim was more likely to be raped in the middle of the street. If their behavior to this point was any indication, the police wouldn't intervene. Thankfully, Shemlak and his crew were on her side.

There had to be a way to use this to her advantage. Somehow.

The Terrans were closing in. Shemlak started toward her, but Kim put up a hand to warn him off. "Anybody who wants to get into my pants has to catch me first."

With that, the Terrans and every other male in the horde surged forward. Kim took off toward the brothel, hoping the Cylopean might see her as a potential inmate and actually let them in.

She hit the force field running, bouncing back like a rubber ball. "Fuck!"

On the word, the field dissolved and the door swung open.

"The password is *fuck*?"

How obvious is that? Scrambling to her feet, she ran through the door, hitting the astonished Cylopean with a stun beam as she passed by.

The door and the force field closed behind her. Hoping the others had heard her expletive, she kept on going down the dark hallway.

And ran straight into a Herpatronian.

Her pistol was only set on stun, but with the business end of it rammed into the Herp's belly, the pulse knocked him back at least two meters.

Continuing on, she came to a large room lined with cages filled with girls. Momentarily horror-struck, she couldn't even form a word until she heard her name called. Cassie and Peska were both screaming at her, rattling their cages.

"Thank the gods!" Kim shouted. "Have you seen a Zetithian guy in here?"

Cassie pointed at an arched doorway. "Down that hall, third door on the left."

She hadn't seen Dalmet. Was she in that room with Onca? Surely he wouldn't have hit the panic button if she'd been with him. He'd have taken advantage of the time to gather information from her first.

Unless he really was fucking her and had hit the panic button by mistake.

Without stopping to consider this possibility or how Cassie had known where he was, she sped down the hall, coming to a halt at the designated door, which was, of course, locked.

Electronically. With no handle or knob to jiggle or force open.

And no control panel beside it, either.

She needed Draddut, and she needed him *now*.

Onca was quick on his feet, but he'd underestimated the determination of a horny, homosexual Herp.

Following five minutes of circling the room exchanging insults, the Herp caught him by the belt.

"I see you finally learned how to feint," Onca gasped as with one hand, Hunard sliced through his belt and shredded his trousers.

Taking advantage of the Herp's tenuous grip, Onca spun away, yelping as Hunard's claws laid open his flank.

Snarling, Hunard threw Onca's pants against the wall. The comlink cracked and fell to the floor in pieces.

"Dammit, that link was *guaranteed* not to break. I want my money back."

"Very funny," Hunard sneered.

Now completely naked, Onca bared his fangs and
fisted his hands. "Come a little closer, big guy, and
you'll see how funny I can be."

"Don't worry. I will. You know, you really are a
pretty fellow," Hunard drawled. "Love the curly hair."

Onca rolled his eyes. "Wish I could say the same for
you, Ape Dick."

Never having faced down a rapist, Onca suspected
that Hunard's every thought and sense must've been
focused on nailing his ass. He wasn't even rising to the
taunts anymore, and nothing seemed to faze that boner.

Discounting the possibility of divine intervention, Onca
had two options left. He could take the offensive or ease off
and lure the Herp into a trap. What would happen after that
was anyone's guess. Thus far, he'd only seen two Herps
and a Cylopean. There were bound to be others, particularly in light of that *you and what army* remark. He might
eliminate this one only to have six more take his place.

Then again, Hunard could've been bluffing. With the
girls in cages, keeping them in line required very little
manpower, and their care and feeding was probably automated. Obviously no one cared what the customers did
to the girls. The two Herps could handle any fights that
might arise between the men.

The men... Hunard might not be the only one who
liked to fuck other males. "Got another room where you
keep the slave *boys*?"

"Not yet, but we're working on it. You may have the
honor of being the first."

"Guess you'd better not kill me then, huh?"

The Herp barked out a nasty laugh. "I might keep you
for my own personal use."

Onca had been debating whether to kill Hunard or not. What he and the others had done to the girls was certainly enough to warrant it, but it was bad karma to kill—aside from the fact that he would prefer not to bring the law down on himself any more than necessary. This revelation, however, made him feel a bit murderous. Still, it wouldn't do to appear to be too accommodating…

He glanced at the remnants of his clothing piled up against the opposite wall. The belt might be useful as a weapon and so might the sharp edges of a broken comlink. Taking a deep breath, he made a run for them.

Hunard grabbed him by the hair as he flew past. Yanking him off his feet, he snaked his sinewy arm around Onca's waist, pinning his arms to his sides. His breath was hot on Onca's neck, and the stench would've disgusted a Drell.

"But that's only if I don't fuck you to death right now."

Chapter 19

KIM HAMMERED AT THE DOOR WITH HER FISTS. IT WAS so solid she doubted anyone on the other side could even hear her.

Was there a password for this door as well? She tried every word she could think of starting with "fuck" and ending with "done." Nothing worked. There had to be a way to open it in case of emergency—unless it was all controlled from a central location. She'd taken out the Herp and the Cylopean. She hadn't seen anyone else. What if those were the only two working here?

Impossible. All those girls? *No way.*

She ran back down the corridor to where the stunned Herp lay sprawled in the floor. Keys were rather old-fashioned, thumbprints and palm locks being the more common means of security. And that door didn't appear to have a visible lock...

The Herp didn't have anything on him but a pulse pistol, which she confiscated, and a small medallion on a chain around his neck.

Surely it wouldn't be that easy. It couldn't be.

Then again, these were fuckin' Herps. How smart could they be?

Yanking the chain from the Herp's neck, she leaped to her feet. A moment later, she heard voices. Familiar ones.

"Thank the gods!"

Rashe came charging down the hallway, brandishing his tomahawk. "Wish we'd known the password was 'fuck' to begin with. Would've saved us a lot of trouble. Are you okay?"

"Yeah, but he's not." Kim held up the medallion. "I think this may be the key. It was all he had on him."

"Don't suppose you checked inside his undies, did you?"

Kim shuddered. "I'll leave that to you. I'm going to test my theory." She took off running. The girls were screaming as she passed by the room where they were caged. Skidding to a halt, she ran over to Cassie and held up the medallion. "Is this the key?"

Cassie nodded. "That's what they use to open everything. Not sure how it works, though. They always press them and sort of mumble something. I've never been able to catch what it is they say."

"Another freakin' password." This time, Kim was certain it wouldn't be as easy as saying the *F* word. The security on the main door was one thing—regular customers probably knew what to say and passed through without question—but letting girls in and out of their cages was another. Stepping back from Cassie's cage, she shouted to the room at large. "Do any of you know the passwords?"

Several of the girls volunteered suggestions, but none worked when Kim tried them, despite pressing the stone center of the medallion until her fingers ached.

Rashe appeared at her side. "We broke into the control room and took out another Cylopean, two Racks, and a Terran. Val's hacking into the system now. Turns out that Herp you stunned wasn't the only one they've got."

"Herp?" Cassie exclaimed. "Holy shit! That guy, Onca, is trapped in a room with him."

"Why the hell didn't you say so before?" Kim shot back. "Here we are, wasting time when Onca's probably getting the shit kicked out of him."

Rashe chuckled. "Dunno about that. Zetithians can be pretty tough when you corner them." Grinning, he tapped his teeth. "Fangs. Remember?"

Kim found this only mildly reassuring. Using his fangs would require Onca to actually *bite* that Herp— the mere thought of which made her gag.

"Oh, and by the way, thanks for taking out that Cylopean on your way in. Made it a lot easier—that and the fact that Roncas has a real nasty mouth on her these days. You should've heard her screeching at the Cylopean dude in the control room." He paused, shuddering. "Scary little woman."

"You broke into the control room? How?"

He shrugged. "The door was open."

"Are you sure the doors to the, um, *other* rooms aren't controlled from there?"

"They probably are—in some way or other—but we haven't figured it out yet. Val's good, but the control panels are labeled in Cylopean. He can't read them."

"I take it the Cylopean in the control room wasn't being very cooperative?"

"Stunned, actually." Rashe grimaced. "We should be able to squeeze some information out of him when he comes around."

"And in the meantime, Onca is stuck in a room with a Herp—and we have no idea how to get him out."

"A *homosexual* Herp," Cassie put in. "A real mean one too."

"Okay, that's it," Kim growled. "Where's Draddut?"

"He and Shemlak are holding off the cops and everyone else at the main entrance," Rashe replied. "Not sure we want them to leave their posts."

Kim scowled. "Maybe we need more than a password and the medallions. Maybe we need the Herp, too—or at least his fingerprints." She glanced at Rashe. "Think you could drag him in here?"

"No problem. Be easier to just bring his hand, though."

Kim arched a brow. "Bloodthirsty, aren't you?"

"A bit," Rashe admitted. "Seeing all these girls in cages kinda brings out the savage in me. Val didn't even want to come in here. Said it would mess with his concentration too much." His gaze swept the perimeter where the girls now sat quietly in their cages. "It's kinda fucking me up too."

Kim felt the same way, but she couldn't allow her empathy to impair her determination to find Onca. Right now, the girls were safe. *He* was the one in danger. "Grab that Herp and let's get going."

Rashe stroked the edge of his tomahawk with a loving caress. "Sure you don't just want his hand?"

"No. I want the whole Herp. If he wakes up, you can threaten to chop off his balls to get him to cooperate."

Rashe nodded. "That'd do it."

Racing back to the fallen Herp, Rashe grabbed a foot while Kim took the other.

"Damn, this dude's heavy," Rashe complained.

"We are *not* chopping off his hand." Then again, if that other Herp had actually raped Onca, she might be tempted to use Rashe's tomahawk to do a bit of castrating herself.

They finally made it to the third door on the left.

Assuming that the thumb and forefinger were the required digits, Kim pressed the unconscious Herp's fingers to the center stone of the medallion. Before she'd had the chance to try any passwords, the door slid open.

The first thing she saw was blood.

Everywhere.

Onca didn't have to open his eyes to know Kim was there with him. Her sweet fragrance overpowered the stink of Herpatronian sweat and the metallic tang of his own blood. Her touch on his face flooded him with warmth.

She loved him. Her emotions flavored her scent, and he breathed it in, reveling in the joy of it. That love was wrong, and he knew it—but just this once, he let himself bask in the glow of her affection and her caring touch. The hint of sadness in her scent forced his lids to rise and his eyes to focus on her beautiful face—to behold the sorrow and relief in her gaze, the gentle curve of her cheek, and the fullness of her softly parted lips.

"Oh, Onca…" she whispered as she knelt beside him. "I'm so sorry. This was all my fault. I should never have let anything happen to you."

He gave her a weak smile. "Jack will be so pissed."

"No, she won't. You're alive and appear to be all in one piece."

"Almost wasn't," he admitted. "Damned Herp was determined to fuck me to death."

Her breath caught in her throat. "He didn't—"

An attempt to shake his head failed. "Wasn't for lack of trying. Never saw such a horny bastard in my life."

She paused. "You're both…naked."

"Yeah, well, Herps prefer their men undressed. Didn't you know?" He nodded at the pile of useless clothing. "Looks like I'll have to walk out of here that way too." He blinked as his vision clouded again. "That is, if I *can* walk out of here. Not sure about that."

"But how—?"

His chuckle was undoubtedly as pathetic as his smile had been. "Sonofabitch couldn't handle the *snard*."

"You—you *didn't*." A groan from the Herpatronian heap by the bed drew her attention. "I can't believe *snard* had anything to do with his condition. You couldn't respond to his scent." She wrinkled her nose. "Could you?"

"No, but he sure seemed to like mine. His dick was like a steel pipe. Had the devil of a time putting a bend in it."

"You *bent* his dick?"

"Twisted his balls too. I thought about ripping his throat out, but this seemed more appropriate. Don't think any of his junk will ever work the way it's supposed to again." Wincing, he raised a hand to his ear. "My hearing may never be the same, either. Never heard anyone scream like that." He ran a knuckle over his jawbone and winced again. "A Herp can pack quite a punch when he's trying to get you to let go of the goods." Reaching up, he touched her cheek. Still lovely. Still the most beautiful sight he'd ever seen. "Good thing he passed out before I did."

"You look like you're about to do that now, dude," Rashe said.

Roncas stuck her head in the door. "Val figured out the release sequence based on something you all did. Any idea what it was?"

"Herp fingerprints on a medallion," Kim replied.
"I don't think there was a password, other than for the
Herp to identify himself to the controller."

"Must be a sensor above each door," Rashe said.
"Not sure how they would distinguish among the
cages, though."

"Probably a number," Onca suggested. "At least, that's
what it sounded like when he got Cassie out for me—
although it might've been spoken in a different language."

"Makes sense," Rashe agreed.

"Think we can find him some clothes?"

Onca was momentarily puzzled until he realized Kim
had been referring to him. "Wouldn't be the first time I
walked through this district barefoot and naked. I'm more
concerned about the girls. With all the sex pheromones
floating around out there, if we let all of those ladies loose
at once, there's liable to be a mass gang rape in the streets."

"Crikey, I hadn't thought of that," Rashe said. He
glanced at Roncas. "How far would you say we were
from the Palace?"

"Too far," Roncas replied. "Aside from the fact that
this place is, well…under siege."

"You're shittin' me, right?" Rashe said.

Roncas shook her head. "I wish I was. There's a mob out
front—including the police—and according to the external
sensors, Val says they've also got the rear exit covered."

"Hmm," said Kim. "Considering the type of business
this is, seems like these guys would've built in some sort
of escape route."

"Do you *really* think they're that smart?" Roncas
snapped.

Kim flapped a hand toward the unconscious Herp.

"You mean this bunch or the ones behind it all? I'd say someone somewhere had some brains. The equipment here doesn't strike me as being cheap—or easy to install."

Onca smiled at her. "You obviously have brains. Not so sure about mine anymore. Think they're sort of… scrambled." The room seemed to be getting darker.

Or was it his eyes?

—⁓—

Rashe sighed. "He'll be out for a couple of days."

"Might give us enough time to figure out what to do next." Kim knew from her own experience that Onca would wake up feeling perfectly well, but having him out cold for however long it took for his body to heal itself was inconvenient, to say the least. She glanced up as a ponderous tread sounded from the hallway.

Shemlak stopped at the door. "Damn, these rooms are small. Obviously they don't cater to Darconians."

"Not many brothels do," Rashe said. "I think the Palace was the only one with enough space."

Shemlak nodded. "Onca let me take my wife in there once. Awesome place to fuck—whether you're a Darconian or not."

Kim thought it best to let that pass. "Hey, how come you're not guarding the door anymore?"

"Val changed the password on the force field. It's kinda funny seeing all those guys out there bouncing off the field yelling 'fuck' at the top of their lungs." Shemlak let out a low, rumbling chortle. "Almost hated to leave, it was so entertaining."

"What's the new password?"

"'Wings.'"

Rashe rolled his eyes. "Should've guessed that."

"Yeah. But those idiots will never think of it." Shemlak nodded at Onca. "Want me to put him to bed?"

"Yes, but get that Herp out of here first," Kim said. "He's polluting the air."

Shemlak took Onca's attacker by the foot and dragged him to the door. "How about I find some empty cages to put these guys in?"

"Perfect." Kim couldn't imagine a better punishment than to have each of the perpetrators wake up in a cage. "Put them all in cages. Naked."

"Great idea—" Shemlak began, then shook his head. "Not sure I want to see a naked Cylopean. Herps are bad enough."

Rashe grimaced. "I fucked a female Cylopean once—or tried to. Had to give her money back."

Kim didn't have to ask why. "What about the one I stunned?"

"Still right where you left him," Shemlak reported. "He's inside the field, though. Guess we'd better lock him up before he wakes up and tries to fuck with the computer."

"Not likely—at least, not anytime soon," Roncas said. "I stunned him again before I came down here to make sure he'd stay put."

"You're one helluva henchman, Roncas," Rashe said. "Ever done this kind of thing before?"

"I used to work for a chocolatier. Damn stuff is almost as addictive as *snard*, and much easier to steal."

"Ah. That explains it."

Only Shemlak's upper body fit through the narrow door. Fortunately, he had relatively long arms. Scooping Onca up from the floor, the Darconian laid him gently on the bed. Kim pulled the covers up over him and tucked them in. She smoothed his blood-matted hair back from his bruised face. He had been so brave to venture in here alone. True, he had found her friends, but look what that sacrifice had cost him—beaten to a pulp and nearly raped by a Herp.

Shemlak was right. Onca *did* love her.

Now all Kim had to do was keep him alive long enough to get him to admit it.

Chapter 20

"Before we open the cages, we need to check these other rooms," Kim said. "We saw a nasty-looking Terran come in here while we were watching the door. The gods only know what he's up to."

"He's out cold in the control room," Roncas said. "Apparently he was an employee, not a customer."

Kim had an idea he was both, but at least he was accounted for.

"Can you hear me?" Val's voice seemed to come out of the walls.

"Sure can," Rashe replied. "I see you're getting a feel for their com system."

"That and other things," Val said. "I've checked the other rooms on that hall, and they're all empty."

Roncas frowned. "Not much going on here tonight. Makes you wonder how the place stays in business."

"I'm still trying to figure out how to open the cages," Val went on. "But it would help to have someone to go down *there* to see."

The hesitation in his voice suggested that Val was still shaken by the fact that the girls truly were caged.

Like he had once been.

Although Kim had seen some terrible things during her life on the street, she had been spared the part about being locked up. Val had started his life as a prisoner. He had an incredible amount of freedom now—could actually spread his wings and fly—but anyone could understand the horror he felt upon encountering a situation such as this.

Kim's own sense of duty had grown far beyond the desire to rescue her buddies. There were at least thirty girls trapped in this horrid place.

And so far, she hadn't seen Dalmet.

"We should probably talk to them before we let them out," Kim said. "We've got to assure them that they're safe now, and beg them not to go haring off into the street only to be captured again."

"Good idea," Roncas said. "I'll go with you. Jatki's already down there doing her best to keep them calm." The Zuteran's normally smooth brow was furrowed with concern. "What are we going to *do* with all of those girls? Onca's house isn't big enough, and even if we could get them there safely, what's to stop these thugs from finding us? Onca isn't exactly inconspicuous, you know. He's the only Zetithian man on the planet—and if we can't even trust the cops…"

"There's always the Palace," Rashe said. "If it's supposed to be closed, maybe they won't look for us there."

"Yes, but Onca owns that building," Roncas pointed out. "If the higher-ups really are involved in this scheme, we wouldn't be safe there, either."

Kim understood the problem. However, if there was one thing she knew about, it was how not to be caught or found. "Abandoned buildings have sheltered us before."

"But the Palace isn't abandoned—" Rashe stopped as his lips stretched into a diabolical grin. "We could hide them at the Pow Wow and every other legitimate brothel in the southern district. Val could fly them out one at a time."

"Or we could shuttle them over in Onca's speeder,"

Kim said. "It's got a cloaking device. Val could fly one of us out to get it."

Roncas put up a hand. "What's to stop anyone from shooting him out of the sky?"

She had a point. "We'd need a diversion," Kim said with a nod. "We could boot all the bad guys out the front door. That might help."

"Don't forget you've got a gang of Darconians on your side," Shemlak said. "A bunch of us storming out of here would scatter the crowd enough that no one would notice Val flying off the roof."

Rashe frowned. "Have we got any way to *access* the roof?"

"If we don't, we can create one." Shemlak smacked his fist into his palm as though itching to tear the whole place apart. "We could also carry the creeps who work here and pitch them into the crowd."

"That is, if there still *is* a crowd," Kim said. "There might not be if we wait until morning. I'm guessing the potential customers and anyone else who joined in the mob would've given up and gone home by then, and we'd only have the police to deal with."

Shemlak nodded. "True. If we sit tight long enough, we might be able to simply walk out of here."

"And go *where*?" Roncas reiterated.

"No, wait! I've got it!"

All eyes turned to Rashe. "The Statzeelians! They walk around with women chained to them all the time. Who would recognize most of these girls anyway? Val could fly them out one at a time, drop them off with one of the twins, and they could go strolling down the street without attracting any attention at all."

"Might take a couple of weeks to do that," Roncas said.

"You got anywhere you need to be?" Rashe countered. "I mean, what with you and Onca being retired and all."

"We'd have to get the girls in better shape and pretty them up a bit to pass for a Statzeelian's woman," Roncas said. "They'd also need the proper clothes, and I don't know if you noticed, but there weren't any Statzeelian girls in those cages."

"Speaking of which, we've got to get them out of there," Kim said. "C'mon, Shemlak. Drag those Herps into the—what would you even call a room like that? The living room?"

"How about the prison?" Once again, Val's voice seemed to come out of nowhere. "I've figured out the release command for all of the cages. Better get down there."

Kim was torn between freeing her friends and remaining with Onca. All he needed was to sleep, but *still...*

Ganyn came stomping down the corridor. "Where's my sweet Onca?"

"In here," Shemlak said. "This Herp tried to bugger him." The culprit dangled from the Darconian's grasp like a plucked chicken.

"You bastard!" Drawing back a fist, Ganyn gave the Herp a kidney punch that he would undoubtedly feel for the rest of his life. "Out of my way." Shoving her brother and the groaning Herp aside, Ganyn wiggled through the narrow doorway. "My poor Onca," she crooned, running a surprisingly gentle hand over his forehead. She glanced up at Kim. "You all go on and take care of those girls. I will guard him with my life."

Kim didn't doubt that for a moment. As bodyguards went, no one could possibly be a better protector than a love-struck Darconian. She leaned over and kissed Onca's cheek. "Be right back."

Throughout this entire evening, Kim had known she might never see Onca alive again. Her most sincere wish had been granted. Now it was time to grant the wishes of thirty slave girls whose fate might very well have been her own had Onca not intervened.

This rescue wouldn't have been possible without him. His courage, his sacrifice, and his pigheaded determination to go in alone... She owed him and his friends so much. Unfortunately, their battle wasn't over yet. Squaring her shoulders, Kim led the way down the corridor.

Kim had seldom seen so many smiling faces when she joined Jatki, but a deafening cheer went up when Shemlak and Draddut swaggered into the cavernous space dragging the unconscious thugs behind them.

Cassie raised her voice above the din. "Is Onca okay?"

Kim nodded. "He just needs to rest for a while, and he'll be fine."

"I certainly hope so," Cassie said. "He's our hero!"

Kim wasn't sure what to make of that. Would being the hero of so many adoring ladies make Onca forget her? Possibly. Then again, being the only Zetithian among them gave her a decided advantage. Shaking off that momentary doubt, she focused on a more pertinent detail. "Where's Dalmet? I haven't seen her."

Cassie's electric-blue eyes filled with tears. "Peska and I are the only new ones. We don't think Dalmet was ever brought here."

Barely suppressing a groan, Kim stiffened her spine. "There are supposed to be other brothels like this in the city. Don't worry, we'll find her—even if we have to tear down every last one of them."

"Trust me, those girls will be grateful, whether Dalmet is with them or not." Cassie's voice sank to a whisper. "This is the most horrible place you can imagine, Kim. And to think, I used to *like* sex. Not sure I ever will again."

Kim didn't know how to respond to that—aside from the fact that she knew of at least *one* man who could change the mind of every inmate in the building without breaking a sweat. Onca would only have to purr to have them all clamoring for his attention.

Well…maybe not *all* of them. There were a few species represented there that Kim had never even seen before. One girl looked more like a bug than a humanoid. She even had wings.

"We'll do our best to free all of them," Kim said. "Onca plans to establish a home for street kids—that is, if we don't wind up in jail. The police are either in on this racket or they're being paid to look the other way. None of us will be able to rest easy until we figure out who's behind this—and we're guessing it's someone with a great deal of power."

"Onca's idea sounds really nice, but I'd like to get the hell off this planet," Cassie confided. "I've always heard that anything goes on Rhylos, and you can see where that got us."

"We might get some things changed eventually."

"Shed enough light into the darkness and it loses its power to frighten?" Cassie's words held a ray of hope.

Unfortunately, the skeptical manner in which they were uttered diminished them a bit.

"Something like that," Kim agreed. "I—"

She was interrupted by Val's voice over the com-speaker. "Get ready, everyone. I'm going to disable the locks."

The cage doors swung open and the girls all ran from their prison cells with shouts of triumph.

Kim was hugging an ecstatic Cassie when the entire room plunged into darkness.

As screams rang out around her, her first thought was of Onca. Ganyn may have sworn to protect him with her life, but had they left the door to his room open or was he trapped inside? She was about to dash off to check on him when Shemlak's rumbling tones stopped her.

"No worries," he said. "We've got glowstones."

Kim's excellent night vision enabled her to see better than most of those present. Even so, she was heartened as a small stone in Shemlak's palm began to glow, its radiance growing in strength until the entire room was filled with light.

Draddut winked at Kim, holding up another glow-stone. "Thought they might be useful on a night raid."

"No shit, dude," Rashe said. "We might have to fight our way out of here after all. This isn't a matter of the lights simply going out for the night." He glanced at Cassie. "Is it?"

She shook her head. "It never gets that dark in here."

Kim groaned. "They've cut the power to the building, haven't they?"

"Yes, and with the force field disabled, they'll be breaking down the doors soon," Shemlak said. "We'd better set up an ambush and be ready for them."

Draddut nodded his agreement. "That main corridor is fairly narrow with the access halls to the control room and the cell block branching off from it. Positioning ourselves there would be useful—although we've already seen how easy it was to take out the control room."

Rashe scratched his chin, smearing his war paint. "You know, for a bunch of cooks and waiters, you guys seem pretty well-versed in warfare."

Shemlak shrugged. "On Darconia, most males are trained for battle. Our females say we're too volatile to be good for much else." With a swipe of his heavy tail, he slammed the two Herps against the wall. "Perhaps they're right."

A blast from the main entrance shook the building, drawing screams from the girls and a growl from Rashe.

"I suppose claiming to have taken the employees hostage would be useless at this point?" Roncas ventured.

Draddut rolled his huge eyes, their normally cavernous pupils constricted by the light from the glowstone he still held in his hand. "Would *you* trade their safety for thirty girls?"

"Well, no…" Roncas admitted. "Just a thought."

Val came running in from the control room. "There's a lot of debris by the main door. Might take them a little while to clear it."

"They may not even bother with that," Shemlak said. "With the main entrance blocked, they'll probably focus their attention on the rear exit, expecting us to escape that way."

Jatki moaned, cracking her knuckles in patent despair. "Trapped like rats."

Shemlak patted the top of her head, flattening the

Kitnock's bushy purple hair. "Not entirely. As many of us as there are, we can shoot our way out the back. A wide stun beam would take out most of the crowd."

"Unless they do the same thing to us," Kim pointed out.

"True," Shemlak admitted. "They might stop some of us, but with the girls scattering in every direction, they'll probably aim at me and Draddut." He paused, grinning. "Larger, slower-moving targets, you know."

"Can you guys actually be stunned?" Roncas asked. "I mean, do pulse weapons even *work* on you guys?"

"Not unless it's a heavy stun or the kill setting at point-blank range. The lighter stuns barely slow us down. The police know that, of course. Lucky for us, their standard-issue pistols don't have the kill setting on them. Now, if they're carrying illegal laser weapons, that's another matter altogether."

Kim didn't like the idea of the girls scattering and said so. "We need to arrange a place to meet up with them."

Rashe shrugged. "The Palace and the Pow Wow are still our best bets. They're close and large enough to conceal everyone—for a while, at least."

"I can fly on ahead to the Palace and make sure it's open." Val glanced at Roncas. "I don't suppose you have the key, do you?"

She shook her head, her silvery hair reflecting the light from the glowstones like a faceted gem. "It's a palm lock. Onca or I would have to open it."

Val's extraordinary eyes swept the Zuteran from head to toe. "You are small. I could easily carry you there. However, it would be best if we departed from the rooftop."

Kim had to stifle a laugh as Roncas turned the deepest shade of purple yet. "Is there a way out onto the roof?"

Val nodded. "I spotted it from the air before we came inside. I doubt we'll have any difficulty escaping through it. Most roof access points are left unlocked."

"Which you would know," Kim muttered. "One of the girls has wings. She should go with you."

"The Scorillian, you mean?" Rashe said. "She might be able to fly out one of the smaller girls—the Rutaran, perhaps."

Kim gasped as an idea occurred to her. "What if you fired a wide stun beam from the roof?"

"Excellent strategy!" Shemlak said. "I doubt any of my crew could climb up there, but Val and Roncas could provide enough cover to give us time to escape."

Roncas checked her comlink. "We'll call you when we get there." She nodded at Val. "Let's go." He and Roncas darted off. Jatki sent the Scorillian and Rutaran girls after them.

Rashe addressed the room at large. "The Zetithian Palace and the Pow Wow are in the southern section of the brothel district. Do any of you know where they are?"

Several of the girls raised their hands.

"Good," he said. "You will be the group leaders. Everyone pick a leader and stay with your group if you possibly can."

Another blast shook the building. Dust and smoke billowed in from the main corridor.

"Move out!" Shemlak shouted. "Rashe, you and Kim lead the girls to the exit. Take this." He slapped the glowstone in Kim's hand. "We'll hold them off here."

"What about Ganyn and Onca?"

"We'll get them," Draddut yelled. "Go now!"

The girls didn't need a leader. As Shemlak and Draddut headed out the door and up the corridor toward the enemy, the newly freed slaves fled the room in the opposite direction like a herd of frightened beasts.

Passing Rashe in the hall, Kim handed off the glow-stone. "Take it! I can see in the dark."

This was one job she couldn't trust to anyone else. She ran down the dark side hall, screaming for Ganyn.

Light from the doorway ahead proved that Ganyn had also brought along a glowstone—perhaps one of the many beads in the necklaces she wore. The blast had weakened that section of the building, buckling the doorways.

"I can't fit through!" Ganyn yelled.

Kim stared at the crumbling lintel above the door with horror. "Lay Onca on a sheet and slide him out here. Then you can use the bed to smash through the wall."

Moments later, the corner of a sheet and Onca's feet appeared. Kim grabbed both and tugged with all her might. "Push him!"

Ganyn must have given it her all because Onca shot across the floor, knocking Kim flat on her back.

"Great mother of the desert!" Ganyn screamed as yet another blast shook the walls. "They'd better stop that shit or I'm gonna pound *somebody* into dust."

"Hurry!" Kim yelled. "The walls are giving way!"

Using her entire body as a battering ram, after two attempts, Ganyn burst through the doorway in a shower of dust and plaster.

Ganyn snatched Onca from the floor. Kim took off down the corridor with Ganyn in close pursuit.

Kim didn't even slow down when they reached the

exit. The door was already open wide, and she ran through it, firing pulse blasts to clear the path ahead. Once outside, she leaped over the stunned bodies of their opponents. Apparently Roncas and Val had succeeded. There wasn't a slave girl in sight.

Shemlak and Draddut came pounding up behind them. "Didn't trust us to get him, huh?"

"You don't know the half of it," Kim growled.

Dashing off in the direction of Onca's speeder, she motioned for the others to follow just as several Rackenspries and two hulking Terrans in police uniforms came around the corner of the building. Shemlak fired first and dropped the Terrans. The Racks scattered.

Kim leaped into the pilot's seat while Ganyn settled Onca in the passenger side.

"Good luck!" Ganyn called as she and the other Darconians took off running in different directions. Kim found the canopy button just as more Racks converged on the vehicle.

"Captain," Kim yelled. "How the hell do I fly this thing?"

"I shall engage the autopilot," Captain said with unperturbed calm. "Where do you wish to go?"

"Anywhere!"

Chapter 21

"AND MAKE IT FAST," KIM TOLD THE COMPUTER. "Engage that cloaking device while you're at it."

"May I remind you that the cloaking feature and the autopilot will not function simultaneously?" Captain sounded almost apologetic.

"What? Oh, yeah. Right. Forgot about that." For Kim to fly the speeder manually was almost as dangerous as being shot at by a gang of Racks. "Can you add in some evasive maneuvers?"

"I shall attempt to do so."

The first move slammed them sideways into one of the Racks, who was hammering at the canopy with a steel pipe. "Ooh, I like that. Keep it up."

Captain replied with a grunt that could've meant almost anything. The speeder shot forward, pinning Kim against the seat back. Not having to fly the speeder herself meant she could tend to Onca. However, aside from tucking the sheet in around him, there wasn't much else she could do. The speeder's restraints held him in the seat, but his head lolled sideways in the banking turns. They might escape their pursuers only to have Onca wind up with a broken neck.

"Is there anything to hold his head?" she asked after another evasive move slung her against the door.

A padded loop slid out of the seat and curved over Onca's forehead. "Better?"

"Much." She glanced at the rearview screen. "Shit. They've got speeders."

"Did you really think they wouldn't?"

"Well, no—but then, we didn't reckon on the police being involved to begin with."

"Bad planning." Captain sniffed. "In order to keep from leading them to wherever you intend to go, you will have to fly manually and engage the cloak."

How hard could it be? "Tell me how."

"The speed bar on the dashboard responds to the touch of a fingertip. Slide up the bar to increase the speed. I believe the steering apparatus is self-explanatory."

"Got it." She took a deep breath. "Turn off the auto-pilot and give me the controls."

The speeder lurched sideways, narrowly missing the police speeder drawing up alongside them.

"Can I ram them?"

"You may if you like," Captain replied. "However, this speeder is equipped with a cloaking mechanism, not armor."

"Seems like a cloak would give us *some* protection," Kim grumbled.

"No more so than any standard type of outer covering. The police speeders, however, probably *do* have armor. Ramming them is inadvisable."

As if to prove the computer's assessment, the police speeder veered sideways. Kim's peripheral vision caught the movement, enabling her to dodge the blow. "I think I'm getting the hang of this."

"I am pleased to hear it."

Kim would've been more pleased if Onca were to suddenly awaken and take over the controls.

However, that was an event she couldn't count on anytime soon. Considering his injuries, he would be out at least until morning.

"Shall I engage the cloak?"

"Not yet," Kim said. "I want to lead them in the wrong direction first."

"If you live long enough," Captain murmured.

"Give me a little credit," Kim snapped. "I'm a fast learner."

Captain sighed. "You are, indeed. I shall refrain from any further detrimental comments."

"Thanks." Kim had never moved so quickly through the streets in the dark. As a result, she was a tiny bit disoriented. "Which way to the commerce district?"

"Take a right at the next corner and proceed east."

Traffic was crossing in front of them. The police sirens wailed from behind, and Kim had no idea where she was going.

Think.

She would have to turn and engage the cloak where it was safe or someone would ram into them—which was the main reason such devices were illegal, especially for use by those with nefarious intentions. In fact, she was surprised the people chasing them didn't have that capability.

Flying on, she dodged through the traffic, doing her best to avoid the pedestrians while keeping her attention focused on the road ahead. Could a speeder be affected by a pulse weapon? Somehow, she thought not. Especially this one. She didn't have to be a rich girl to know it was a higher-priced model—and the cloaking device only added to its value. A man like Onca wouldn't own a crappy speeder. She hoped it was better than what the police were flying.

A narrow miss of an oncoming vehicle brought her brain back where it belonged. She got into a rhythm after a bit, pleased to see that she was actually putting some distance between them and the police.

At last, she saw her chance. Ignoring the traffic signals, she sped through an intersection just as the cross-traffic began to move. As they crossed behind her, cutting off her pursuers, she took a sharp right at the next block.

"Cloak us...*now*!"

Recalling how dangerous it was to fly while cloaked, she opted to do what she and Onca had done when they left the Darconian restaurant. Pulling in behind another parked speeder, she waited.

One by one, the police speeders whipped by.

Four of them.

"Seems a bit much, doesn't it?" Now that she had time to think, the whole thing seemed like overkill. Cutting the power to the building, setting off explosives, armed men storming in like they were going to war... She glanced at Onca. He was only one man—and he had gone in unarmed.

Perhaps it *was* a war.

Kim mulled over the chain of events. The police in the crowd could have stopped all of them—including Onca—from getting inside if they'd really wanted to. Jatki's comment about being trapped like rats seemed truer than ever. Having seen other Kitnock girls in the brothel made Jatki's capture and subsequent release even more peculiar. She hadn't been rejected because she wasn't attractive enough—unless purple hair was considered a serious fault in a female Kitnock. She had been bait for a trap and she knew it.

"We're in deep shit, aren't we, Captain?"

"I'm sure I couldn't say," the computer replied.

Kim snorted. "I *know* you have an opinion. Why are you being so diplomatic now? Afraid Onca will hear you?"

"I believe him to be in the restorative sleep common to injured Zetithians. So no, I do not expect he can hear me. I am hesitant to speak because I am uncertain of the truth of what I suspect."

"Faulty data?"

"Conjecture. My programming isn't terribly good at it."

"Try me."

"You're in deep shit."

"Yeah." She stroked Onca's arm, drawing comfort from his warmth. "We can't say we weren't warned. Rashe told Onca what he suspected. We went ahead with it anyway."

"A noble undertaking, to be sure."

"Risky, though. Then again, I haven't been safe since I was ten years old. You'd think I'd be used to it by now." She stared out at the lights, the people walking the streets, other speeders as they cruised past—all completely oblivious of the dangers lurking nearby. "For once in my life, I had a chance to truly be safe. Onca would've protected me—would've protected all of us. Too bad there isn't anyone to protect *him*."

"I disagree," Captain said. "He has you."

Kim smiled. "Thanks, Captain. I needed that."

A police speeder passed by in no particular hurry—merely out on patrol. She waited until it disappeared from view.

Time passed and traffic thinned to a trickle.

"I think we've waited long enough," she said. "We should head on before someone else tries to park here." Easing away from the curb, she flew the cloaked speeder slowly along the street, dodging pedestrians and other vehicles.

"No wonder this cloaking device is illegal! It's downright suicidal. I don't think we're being followed now. Uncloak us and set the autopilot for the Palace—no, wait. Rashe's brothel would be better. Someone might recognize this as being Onca's speeder."

"Agreed," Captain said. "Engaging autopilot."

Kim took the opportunity to keep an eye out for other police vehicles, but didn't see anything suspicious. Still, after all they had been through that evening, she had no desire to take unnecessary risks. "Plot an indirect route and bring us in the back way—if there is one."

"Understood."

Even Captain seemed subdued during the journey. What he was thinking about was anyone's guess. He had claimed to be sentient, but did computers actually *think* when they weren't interacting with others? She had no clue about that, but her own thoughts were so disturbing she wished she could turn them off.

Onca was safe for the moment, but Kim shuddered to think what could have happened if they hadn't been able to get him and Ganyn out. Would they have been captured or crushed under the rubble? As a captive, she couldn't begin to guess what Ganyn's fate might have

been, but she suspected Onca would've been subjected
to even harsher treatment than the girls had endured.

If only Dalmet had been among the slaves they'd
freed! Then Kim could have gone on to Terra Minor
with a reasonably clear conscience. As things stood,
however, their task was incomplete, their adventure
only beginning.

If adventure was even the right word. Crusade might
be more appropriate—and crusaders didn't always live
to tell tales of their daring deeds. She couldn't imagine the reaction of the general public if the details of
their quest were to become widely known. Hookers and
homeless street people working to free kidnapped sex
slaves? If the news media were also being manipulated,
their story might never be told.

"That's what we need now," she murmured aloud.
"Publicity—and lots of it. I don't suppose Onca knows
any famous people, does he?"

"Jerden, his former partner, was reasonably famous,"
Captain said. "He was named the hottest hunk in the
galaxy, and was voted the best—if you'll pardon the
expression—fuck on Rhylos for three years in a row.
Perhaps if he were to be contacted…"

"That's a thought." She wondered where Onca had
ranked in that poll—probably a close second or third,
considering he was one of the three Zetithians who had
worked in the Palace. "Anyone else?"

"Not that I'm aware of. There may have been some
famous ladies among his clients, but I don't have access
to that information."

"Hmm… Maybe if we checked into the Palace computer we could find someone."

"Possibly. But may I remind you that any famous ladies might have used a false name to avoid any unpleasant repercussions?"

Kim sighed. "Yeah. It's not like he was an artist or a hotshot dress designer. He was selling sex. Right now the only people who would vouch for him are hookers, homeless kids, and sex slaves. Not much of a recommendation, is it?"

"You are forgetting Roncas, Valkyrie, and the Darconians."

"True, but Roncas worked for Onca, and Val's not only a clone, he's a computer hacker. Last I heard that wasn't considered a respectable occupation. The Darconians are legitimate businesspeople, but who knows what kind of connections they have, if any." She hitched in her seat. "Bad idea, I guess. Are we getting close yet?"

"We will be arriving in two point six minutes," Captain replied. "See anything suspicious?"

Kim shook her head. "Seems pretty quiet—which doesn't mean a thing." Sighing, she glanced at Onca. "Sure hope someone's there to help me. I don't think I can carry him."

"They have had sufficient time to arrive here on foot. Shall I call them?"

Kim chuckled. "Funny thing about living most of your life without any communication devices whatsoever. You tend to forget to use them."

"Quite understandable."

"Makes me wonder why no one has tried to call us, though."

"Perhaps they are concerned that this speeder might

have fallen into the hands of your pursuers. In which case, communication would be inadvisable."

"Yeah. Call Rashe."

Seconds later, Rashe's image popped onto the viewscreen. "You know, for a bunch of cooks and hookers, we didn't do too badly. If you've got Onca, that's almost everyone accounted for."

"Yeah. I've got him," Kim said. "Who's missing?"

"Shemlak and Draddut haven't checked in and neither has Jatki. The rest of the girls are in the Palace with Roncas and Val. Ganyn and I are here at my place. You haven't heard from anybody, have you?"

Kim's heart skipped a beat upon hearing of their missing friends. The Darconians were armed and could undoubtedly take care of themselves, and Jatki did have a pistol…

Now I've lost her too. She fought down the rise of bile in her throat at the thought of what might have happened to the Kitnock girl. "No. You're the first we've tried to call. I, um, kinda forgot I could do that. We're almost there. I'll need help with Onca."

"We'll be waiting."

—∿∿—

Since Rashe worked alone, his brothel was small compared to the others on the street. Built in a conical shape, it gave the outward appearance of having been constructed from leather and long poles. The decor was quite rustic, seeming to match his buckskin breeches and primitive weapons.

"You really believe in roughing it, don't you?" Kim asked as Ganyn carried Onca inside.

Rashe shrugged. "The ladies seem to like it. I went for as much authenticity as possible without going overboard on the price." He nodded at one of the pictures hanging on the leather interior. "That's a replica of an actual museum piece by a Native American painter from the twenty-first century."

Done in black ink, it reminded Kim of Peska's drawings, although the subject was an unfamiliar four-legged creature. "What is that?"

"An Earth animal called a horse. Beautiful, isn't it?"

Kim nodded as she studied the animal's high arched neck and plumed tail. "I've never seen anything like it."

"Jerden and his wife raise them on Terra Minor. You can ride them if they're trained. They run very fast."

"Something else to look forward to when I get there."

If I get there. Then she remembered she *had* seen those creatures before. In a dream—or was it a vision? Perhaps it was.

I might never know.

Her gaze swept the dim interior with its rough-hewn furniture and padded leather cushions. Fully half the floor was a bed made of colorful blankets. "This is a lot different from that *other* place."

Rashe cleared his throat. "The southern section caters to a totally different clientele."

"Meaning women. Yeah. I suppose men don't care as much about such things."

"Not *all* men like what goes on in there, Kim. You know that, don't you?"

She nodded. "It's sad to think that *anyone* likes it."

He didn't disagree. "There are other brothels like that one, and since we didn't find Dalmet—"

"We'll have to do this again? Yeah. I figured that. Did Jatki ever turn up?"

His solemn expression never changed. "Not yet."

She blew out a breath and gave him a weak smile. "Well…thanks for your help." She glanced at Ganyn who still held Onca cradled in her arms as though reluctant to put him down. "You too, Ganyn. I couldn't have done this without you."

"No problem, sweetheart," Ganyn said. She nodded at Onca. "Want me to take him upstairs?"

Shaking his head, Rashe held out his arms. "I'd better do it. That doorway wasn't built with Darconians in mind."

Kim didn't see anything remotely resembling stairs. "What doorway? Where are you taking him?"

"Oh, I don't live in here," Rashe said. "I've got a house out back. You'll be safer there."

"But I didn't see a house…"

"You wouldn't." Rashe grinned. "That's why it's so safe."

Having just gotten out of an invisible speeder, Kim shouldn't have been surprised. "It's cloaked?"

He nodded. "Lift that flap over there and you'll see what I mean."

Kim found a break in the leather and pushed it aside to reveal a standard-sized door that certainly wouldn't have admitted a Darconian.

"I'll let you in the other way, Ganyn," he said. "Just don't let anyone see you. We need to get that speeder inside too."

Kim had no idea how he planned to do that and didn't bother to ask. "This is getting weirder all the time."

"Nothing weird about it. The same Nerik who sold Onca that speeder convinced me that my business would improve if I appeared to actually live in a teepee, and he sold me the tiles to cloak my house." Rashe paused as the door swung open. "Not sure if he was right about that, but I'll say this much for him, the dude was a damn good salesman."

Chapter 22

KIM FOLLOWED RASHE THROUGH THE DOOR INTO A home even more luxurious than Onca's. Clearly his business had done well, whether the ruse of living in a teepee had anything to do with it or not. Thick carpeting covered the floors, and the furnishings all looked expensive and relatively new—not to mention scrupulously clean. The reason for which was immediately apparent as a dome-shaped housekeeping droid hovered in from the next room.

"See what I mean? Nobody expects a wild Comanche to live in a place like this. Doesn't fit the character at all."

"I suppose not." Kim was having some difficulty reconciling the two widely divergent lifestyles herself. The colors and designs were similar, but that was about it.

Ganyn peeped through the doorway, which was too narrow to admit much more than her head. "What about Onca's speeder?"

"Oh, yeah. Hang on while I put him down and I'll let you in the back way." Rashe laid Onca on a sofa that appeared to be softer than most beds Kim had seen. "See if you can sneak it into the garage."

The speeder wouldn't pose a problem since it could be cloaked. On the other hand, Kim couldn't help giggling at the thought of a Darconian *sneaking* anywhere.

"Sure thing." Ganyn winked at Kim. "After all, we

wouldn't want anyone to steal our baby's speeder, would we?"

"Our *baby*?" Kim echoed.

"You know what I mean," Ganyn said with a lift of her brow. "You don't hold all the rest of us against him, do you?"

Once again, Kim was mystified that anyone else could possibly know the depth of her feelings for Onca. "Um…no. I don't. Why should I?"

"Oh, puh-*lease*," Rashe begged. "Don't start with that crap. And don't tell me you aren't gonna sleep with him, either."

"He seemed a little gruff this afternoon," Kim said. "I'm not sure he's very happy with me right now."

"Right now?" Rashe fingered the handle of his toma-hawk as though itching to throw it at her. "You saved his sorry Zetithian ass back there. Of course he'll be happy with you."

"Maybe. But that doesn't mean he'll want me to sleep with him." She frowned. "Does it?"

Rashe blew out an exasperated breath. "This could take *days*. Ganyn, let's get that damned speeder put away before anyone sees it."

Kim stared after him as he stalked off toward the rear of the house. Onca was right where he left him, barely covered by the sheet. It struck her then that this was the first time she had ever seen his penis in its flaccid state. Anytime he was awake, he had been affected by her scent.

That had to count for something.

Rashe's insistence that saving his life might influence Onca's attitude wasn't a very good argument. If it hadn't been for Kim, he wouldn't have needed rescuing in the first place. He would be safe and sound in his own bed with no one chasing him except for the hordes of women who were hot after his adorable ass—which probably included any female who had ever laid eyes on him and quite a few who hadn't.

How would he have dealt with that? Tell Captain to lock the doors and have food delivered by the Norludians? He would have been better off leaving Rhylos and going to Terra Minor. At least there he wouldn't have the distinction of being the only Zetithian man on the planet.

Unless adulation appealed to him—although he didn't strike her as the type to enjoy being hounded wherever he went. Nor would he care for staying holed up in his house all the time. No, the way he'd been strolling home the morning he rescued her indicated a desire for a simpler, more normal life.

Fat lot of good I've *done him.*

At least she could keep him warm. She found another of those colorful blankets and spread it over him. If Rashe intended for her to sleep with Onca, there was more than enough room on that couch, even though she would have preferred a bed—particularly one on the second floor. She wasn't sure where Ganyn would stay—that is, if she stayed at all. Kim doubted she would be recognized as one of Onca's gang, unless anyone who worked at Oswalak's was suspected on general principles. Darconians weren't quite as rare on Rhylos as Zetithians. Then again, few species were.

As if he'd read her thoughts, Rashe returned, saying,

"Don't worry. I'll put him upstairs. He owes me for this one."

Scooping Onca up from the couch, Rashe headed for what Kim assumed, correctly as it turned out, was a lift. Kim followed him to an upstairs bedroom, pulling back the covers on the bed.

"You'll both be comfortable here," he said as he put Onca down for the second time. "The bathrooms don't have waterfalls, but they're adequate."

"I'm sure they are." Covering Onca with the blankets, she tucked him in as carefully as she had at the Den, then sat down on the side of the bed.

Rashe gave her a nudge. "Hungry?"

Had she ever said no to that question before in her life? Probably not. Nonetheless, she hated to leave Onca, even though she knew him to be safe. "If it's okay with you, I think I'll stay with him for a while."

"No worries." He patted her hand. "Take your time and come downstairs whenever you're ready."

She thanked him, and he left her alone with Onca. Left her free to stroke his cheek and comb the tangles from his hair with her fingers. She should bathe him too. The stench of that Herp still lingered, fouling the normally sweet air that surrounded him.

Funny how these men who sold themselves for women's pleasure could be such decent, honorable men. Rashe was as good a man as Onca in that respect. She wouldn't have thought it of them. Selling sex had never been a truly respectable occupation on this world or any other—at least, not as far as she knew. According to Captain, there had never been *any* brothels on Zetith.

Given the degree of bonding between a mated pair

of Zetithians, she hadn't been surprised to hear that. Although poorly versed in the ways of her own kind, she suspected that she was already mated to Onca. Finding him there in the Den had solidified her belief that he was the only man for her. Jack's boys might be attractive, but they weren't Onca. They wouldn't talk like him, smell like him, or kiss like him, and she didn't even want to know whether they could make love as well as he did. Considering his previous occupation, she doubted they could come anywhere near his level of expertise— although that wasn't the only consideration or even the most important.

Apparently Rashe thought she needed to eat, for the little droid hovered in with a tray and set it on the bed in front of her. Reluctant to look away from Onca even for a moment, Kim ate sparingly, barely tasting the food. She had the strangest feeling that if she stopped watching him, he might disappear.

Or die.

Finally convincing herself that her gaze couldn't prevent either of those things, she found what she needed in the bathroom and washed him, doing her best to expunge every trace of the evening's ordeal. The angry cuts on his side seemed to be healing right before her eyes—a phenomenon she had never witnessed before. She had always been the one who recovered in her sleep.

Despite her exhaustion, Kim remained awake, wanting only to cleanse the blood from his skin and hair and watch over him while he slept. Her pistol was still in the holster at her hip, and she had no desire to remove it.

Just as Ganyn had done, she would guard him with her life.

Considering where he'd been when he conked out, Onca expected to wake up in a strange place, but never in as nice a bed as this with Kim's scent filling his head.

He was already drunk on her scent when he rolled over and found her, right there within arm's reach. As her lips parted to receive his kiss, he didn't think. Didn't hesitate.

She was his mate. He could deny it all he liked, but her enticing aroma said otherwise. He should let her go—should let Larry or one of the other boys have her. He knew that—was convinced it was the best choice— but right now, she belonged to him.

Kim tasted spicy and exotic—like something Rashe might've fed her.

That's where we are. Rashe's house.

A safe place. Were the girls all free and accounted for? He didn't know, and may the gods have mercy on his soul, at that moment, he didn't care.

"Kim." Her name was barely a whisper as he pulled her into his arms. There were worse things than waking up beside the tiny Zetithian girl who had stolen his heart. Her small body nestled against his, her lips warm where they touched him.

By the gods above and beyond, she was sweet. Intoxicating. Luscious. He couldn't even speak. He knew he'd been hurt. Badly. But he was better now, and she was soft and warm and whole and he wanted her.

No. That wasn't it. He *needed* her. Like he had never needed anything before. They had come through an in- credible adventure. Ordeal. Misadventure? Perhaps all

three. He didn't know and didn't care. He could hand
her over to Larry another day. On this night—or was it
morning already?—she was his.

Somewhere, somehow, her clothing was gone. She
lay naked in his arms, her lips seeking his. She wanted
him too. Perhaps she also needed to affirm that they
were both still alive and whole—their hearts still beating, their lungs still breathing, their loins still lusting.

"I want you."

Had he said the words or only felt them in his heart?

Words didn't matter. He only wanted to dive into her
and taste the sweet warmth of her essence. Filling him
with need, with joy, with love...

What the hell happened to me? He could admit it to
himself if no one else. After all the women he had been
with—all the protestations of love he had heard them
utter—none of that mattered now. Kim was in his arms,
and he was dying for the need of her.

She was like wine, filling all of his senses with delight. Her hair soft beneath his fingers. Her lips warm
against his own. By all the gods, no one could fault him
for this. No one could blame him. Those other women
meant nothing to him now. This slip of a girl tied him up
in knots, filling him with lust and want.

In another moment, his cock found her entrance.
Instinctively, his shaft sought her like the beacon of light
and hope that she was. No one could stop this. Ever.

She slid onto him like a warm glove.

Perfect. Soft. Wet. Utterly delightful. He was inside
her, filling her body, hearing her sighs, her moans, her
gasps of pleasure. Had he ever experienced anything to
compare? He thought not. Cared not.

"Oh, Kim…" No other name touched his mind or his lips.

Great mother of the gods. This was the most astonishing moment of his life. His mind opened, letting the visions fill it until he could no longer see the present at all.

Time raced ahead to reveal shady trees, open fields, blooming flowers, and laughing children. And in there somewhere was Kim. Holding him, caressing his face, climbing inside his soul like the elfin sprite she was.

He smelled sweat and desire, hers and his combined. The sweet nectar of her essence, the thick syrup from his cock. Her body tightened around him, and her purr heightened his yearning. Stopping now would have meant his death. But she wasn't asking him to stop. Urging him on, she pleaded with him to give her joy, now and forever.

She felt so right. Her arms, her legs, her tight sheath gripping his cock as though she never intended to let him go. Her desire for him made her joy his only goal and her wishes the only ones he needed to fulfill.

Her fingers threaded though his hair, pulling him down for kiss after kiss. He had lost control before, but not like this. Not this engulfing, swamping feeling. He had taught her the ways of love. Now she was teaching him. Teaching him the things that made her sigh and moan and beg for more.

Tears poured from his eyes at the thought that someone else should have her—should be her mate and grow old with her. Poor Kim. He didn't want her to mate with a man whom she might outlive. Better for her to have a younger man—one who could be there for her for the rest of her life and mourn her loss when she was gone. Onca didn't want her to have to lose a mate. What a terrible ordeal that must be. Jerden had been all but destroyed when Audrey was killed. He had found another love, but the loss, the awful, irreplaceable loss...

He was selfish, hoarding Kim for himself. But he'd been through pain and hell for her. Wanted only to do her bidding, to make her happy, to satisfy her cravings and needs. That ought to be worth something.

She should have a man to be proud of—one who could love her as she deserved to be loved. His dear, sweet Kim...

Another man might be a better mate, a better husband, a better companion for the remainder of her life, but no one could love her more.

Her gaze locked onto his, her warm brown eyes drawing him in like a beckoning hand. "Look at you," she whispered. "I didn't think you would—"

"I shouldn't. I should stop right now. But I can't. I simply can't do it."

Her body tightened around his cock as her orgasm took flight. He could see it in her eyes. He was sobering now, though he hated the thought. Rocking into her, he watched her soar. Other men could do this to her. Other Zetithian men, that is.

No. No one could do what he could do. Not Larry, Moe, or Curly. He was damn good at what he did. Those boys were amateurs—virgins, perhaps—and they were only eighteen. Onca had been a virgin until he was twenty-six. But then, their situations differed. They were free—as free as any sons of Jack Tshevnoe could ever be.

He laughed aloud, but his thoughts remained unspoken. *Kim. You are such a delight. They can't know what they're missing. I won't let them.*

She wasn't fertile. He knew that—somehow. He wasn't sure how he knew it. There were…symptoms. She hadn't had them. He had only been with her for two days. Or was it three? He wasn't sure. With his cock inside her warmth, his brain might not be working at full capacity.

Oh, hell…

Rising up, he arched above her as his body emptied its seed into her waiting womb. He should have withdrawn, eliminating the chance for further entwining of their minds and bodies. But he wanted to see the joy in her eyes one more time. He could give it all up after that.

Or could he? Maybe, maybe not, but as her pupils dilated, opening her soul to his view, he knew he would never see a more beautiful sight than this. Not if he lived a thousand years and spent all that time giving himself to every woman in the galaxy.

Joy…

———

Kim knew her scent was to blame for what Onca had done. But as someone once told her, all was fair in love and war.

This, apparently, was both.

She'd stayed right there beside him, propped up against the headboard watching the door to keep from looking at him—a tactic that had worked for perhaps five minutes. The rest of the night had been spent letting her eyes and hands roam over his nude body.

The fact that she was taking advantage of his helpless state weighed on her conscience only briefly. From the very beginning, she knew she would have to play dirty to keep him. After all, he was attracted to her against his will, his better judgment, and the pressure from his peers.

As if any of those things could possibly be stronger than the sexual urges of an adult male—particularly a Zetithian with a good sense of smell. All she had to do was maintain her desire for him—whether he purred or not—and nature, as the saying went, would take its course.

Her sigh was one of deep contentment. For once, she had nature on her side. Onca's cock deep within her felt absolutely right—the perfect melding of male and female. He didn't stand a chance.

All too soon, he rolled onto his back, not even trying to take her with him. He was thinking too much already—thinking about all that crap Jack had thrown at him about Kim's defective genes and the fact that he was too old and wasn't the type to settle down with one woman.

Jack should have known better. She had a Zetithian husband who would've slit his own throat rather than leave her. Kim didn't have to meet them to know that. Shemlak was right about Zetithian men. Onca was no different from the others.

Pulling the covers up over them both, Kim snuggled in beside him, her hand resting on his penis, then slipping lower to caress his balls. He was still wet, still hard, still delicious.

Ducking under the blankets, she sucked his cock into

her mouth, savoring the sweet mingling of flavors. The smooth, blunt head pressed against her cheek felt marvelous, and she sighed with delight knowing she had succeeded in capturing his full attention. As it moved over her skin, the creamy sauce coated her face and his intoxicating essence filled her senses with a need that could never be completely satisfied. She would always want more of him. Each orgasm was the stimulus for the next—on and on into infinity.

He was the most addicting form of man candy in existence. How could he possibly be so stupid as to think he could simply hand her off to Larry? He certainly wasn't pushing her away now. His fingers tangled in her curls, holding her firmly against his cockhead while the ruffled corona bathed her skin with his deliciously orgasmic nectar. Such actions only intensified her need for him.

Silly man. He could protest all he liked, but she wasn't going anywhere. Larry, Moe, and Curly could find their own damn women.

She was already taken.

Chapter 23

WHOA SHIT. I DID IT AGAIN.

Onca glanced at the tray on the nightstand. She must have kept watch over him during the night. He couldn't help but be touched. "You had dinner up here?"

Kim nodded. "Yeah. Um…a lot happened after you passed out."

"I'll bet it did. Thanks for getting me out of there. Did you have any trouble?"

Her snicker suggested there had been plenty of that. "I'll fill you in on the details over breakfast."

He sat up and looked around the room. Kim at least had a shirt and pants to put on. He didn't have anything. Then he remembered what that Herp had done to his clothes. "Guess I'll have to wear a towel unless Rashe can lend me a loincloth. This *is* his house, isn't it?"

"Yeah. Nice place, huh?"

The old-fashioned clock ticked on the wall above them. Having just fucked himself—and presumably Kim—into a stupor, he wasn't sure how to play this. He certainly couldn't claim not to have known what he was doing. Therefore, he opted for the casual approach, meaning he didn't mention it at all. "Sure is. I thought about cloaking my place, but since it's obvious there has to be a house on that spot, I didn't see the point."

"Good thing Rashe did," Kim said.

As quickly as she threw on her clothes, he suspected

she was feeling every bit as awkward as he was. There would be no hiding any of it from Rashe now.

Not that he had anything to hide. People who had been through life-and-death ordeals always fucked each other senseless afterward. At least, he thought they did. Never having been in a situation of that type before, he wasn't sure.

"Are you, um, okay this morning?" he asked. "I was kinda disoriented when I first woke up."

"Oh, really?" She sounded pissed.

Wrong thing to say.

"Well, yeah. I mean, I passed out at the Den last night and woke up this morning with no idea how I got here."

"Ganyn carried you out of there, and I brought you here in your speeder." Oh, yes, she was pissed all right. Her clipped words and abrupt tone proved it.

"Were you followed?"

She shook her head. "I flew it cloaked for a while."

Considering her lack of experience with automated flight, let alone the manual variety, it was a wonder they had both survived. However, in light of his previous faux pas, he thought it best to keep that opinion to himself, opting for a mild form of praise instead. "That's not easy to do."

"Captain told me how to fly it. I got the hang of it after a while."

"I'll bet you did." He smiled at her, hoping she would take the hint and lighten up a little. Unfortunately, if her tight-lipped expression was anything to go by, even getting her to smile would be tough. Funny how everything seemed so different in the full light of day.

I never should've touched her.

"Did you get the other girls out?"

She nodded. "Just one problem."

"Oh?"

"Dalmet wasn't there."

His heart sank. They would have to do it all over again. "I was afraid of that. The Levitian I saw didn't fit her description."

"Peska and Cassie were there, though."

"I don't suppose they know where Dalmet is?"

"Nope. And we didn't have time to extract that information from anyone else, either. Val had barely figured out how to work their comsystem when they started bombing the place."

Onca's eyes widened. "Bombs? You're shittin' me, right?"

"I wish I was," she replied. "It got pretty wild. They blew up the main entrance after we were all inside. If Val and Roncas hadn't gone up on the roof and fired on the crowd at the back door, we probably wouldn't have gotten out of there alive. As far as I know we still haven't heard from Shemlak or Draddut. Val and Roncas are at the Palace with the girls."

"All of them?"

Closing her eyes, she sank her fangs into her lower lip. "All but Jatki."

"Oh, no," Onca groaned.

"I know she got out of the building—and she knew where we were meeting up, but no one seems to know which way she went."

"She could be with the Darconians," he suggested. "If anyone could protect her, they could."

"I hope you're right." She paused, shivering. "Being in one of those brothels would absolutely kill her."

Onca had an idea she was right about that, but chose to remain optimistic. "She had a pistol, didn't she?"

Kim nodded, but tears leaked from the corners of her eyes.

"I'm sure she'll turn up. She might have decided to lay low until the heat dies down. Even if they caught her—"

Kim put up a hand, cutting him off. "I don't even want to think about it right now. She might have come in during the night—along with the Darconians."

"Right." He couldn't blame her for not wanting to dwell on the subject. The reality of the night before had been bad enough. Still, the amount of firepower puzzled him. "Bombs." He glanced up at her. "Doesn't that seem a little *excessive* to you?"

"Yeah. We were all kinda freaked out. I mean, you went in unarmed. What happened?"

"By the time I got Cassie alone in that room, it was fairly obvious the girls were being monitored. I couldn't even get her to tell me her name. Then I realized I was screwed no matter what I said to her."

"So you just up and admitted the truth?"

"Yeah. Stupid, huh?"

"Not really. It got them to show their true colors. Funny thing, though. They seemed to have been expecting us. You were the only customer in the whole place."

"That's interesting." With no other choice, Onca finally got up and draped a sheet over his shoulder just as Rashe's droid floated in with a pair of pants. "Thanks, pal."

The droid beeped and floated out.

"Guess this means we won't be getting breakfast in bed." She said it with a trace of regret. Perhaps she wasn't too mad at him after all.

"That's okay. Besides, we need to have another strategy meeting if we're going to find Dalmet. We only *think* they planned an ambush for us this time. The next place we hit will probably be locked down so tight we'll have to fight our way in."

Kim chuckled for the first time. "Yeah. Did you notice the password for the Den was 'fuck'?"

"No, but it's certainly appropriate." He laughed along with her even though he still wasn't sure she was very happy with him.

"That's about the only thing funny about it," she said, sobering quickly. "The police definitely seemed to be involved in some way. Four of them chased us—and by that I mean you and me, specifically. Hardly anyone went after the girls."

"Too many, I guess—aside from the fact that they weren't much of a threat."

"Yeah. No one would believe their story, even if they knew who to take it to." She hesitated. "I was talking with Captain on the way back here last night, and I think that's what we should do next."

"Go public, you mean?"

"Yeah. I know we're not very important people, but if enough of us spoke up…"

"The right people might hear about it? Yeah. We can do that now that we have witnesses and actually know what's going on in those places." He shrugged. "Guess that's something else we need to discuss over breakfast."

Stepping into the pants the droid brought him, he tucked his still-hard cock into them as best he could, bringing to mind Rashe's comment that his buckskins had been hurting his dick. If asked, he would have said he and Rashe were about the same size, but these were tight to the point he wasn't sure he could sit down in them. Assuming that Ganyn was there, he hated to go down to breakfast naked—especially considering the way Kim's scent affected him. She might *act* like she was annoyed with him, but her scent couldn't lie to his dick.

—◆◆◆—

Rashe already had Roncas on his comlink when they came downstairs. The back door must've been a lot bigger than the front because Ganyn was there in the kitchen with him, although she did take up a considerable amount of space. Even sitting on the floor, her head nearly touched the ceiling. She gave Kim an I-know-what-you've-been-up-to grin that Kim chose not to return. She still wasn't sure exactly *what* she'd been up to. One minute Onca seemed like he was about to declare his undying love, and the next, he slipped right back into the role of emotionally detached coconspirator. She couldn't decide whether to kiss him or strangle him.

"We've got the girls settled in," Roncas reported as Kim took a seat at the breakfast table. "Val flew out to get some supplies. We've never had so many mouths to feed before. I don't know if the stasis unit can hold enough to keep them fed for more than a day, but we'll figure that out at some point. What about you, Boss? Feeling better?"

"Good as new," Onca replied. "Kim had an idea about getting the news media in on this. You know—to create sympathy for our cause and get the public on our side?"

Roncas grimaced. "Sorry to be the one to break it to you, but the bad guys beat us to it." She tapped her linkpad and a headline popped up on the viewscreen.

"*Local Brothel Owner Incites Riot*," Onca read aloud. There was even a picture of him. "Oh, joy."

"You're really screwed now, dude," Rashe said.

"Thanks, pal," Onca said with a sneer. "It's so nice to have optimistic friends."

The link chimed and Draddut's image popped up on the viewscreen next to Roncas.

"Dude!" Rashe exclaimed. "Where are you?"

"Oswalak's," Draddut replied. "Figured it would be best if at least one of us came back here. The boss is having a shit fit as it is. Have you heard from Shemlak and Ganyn?"

"Nothing from Shemlak yet," Rashe said. "Ganyn is here with us. Roncas and Val are at the Palace with the girls. Don't suppose you've seen anything of Jatki, have you?"

"Wasn't she with the rest of the girls?"

"Apparently not."

Staring at the comlink, Onca let out a gasp that made Kim's blood run cold. "Mother of the gods! How long have you been wearing *that*?"

"What are you talking about?" Draddut hooked his thumbs under the strips of leather around his chest and shoulders that constituted typical Darconian male attire. "I've been wearing this for years."

"Not the harness. *That*." Onca pointed to a small decoration on the shoulder strap.

Draddut gave it a brief glance and then shrugged. "Shemlak gave it to me. Said to wear it."

Onca gritted his teeth until his neck veins popped up. "No wonder those guys knew we were coming. Didn't it strike you as odd that they'd have that much firepower waiting for us? And that there were no other customers? That's the tracking device those Rackenspries made Jatki swallow."

"Really?" Draddut frowned. "Shemlak never said what it was. Just told me not to lose it."

Kim had never seen a Darconian appear to be at such a loss—or a disadvantage. She almost felt sorry for him. "They probably think it's still in Jatki," she said. "I bet it freaked them out when they started following the signal and all they ever saw were Darconians."

"And yet they still followed it." Onca shook his head. "Damn. I thought Shemlak was a better soldier than that."

Draddut looked like he was about to cry—that is, if Darconians were even capable of shedding tears. "Sorry. Guess he forgot about it."

"Not his fault—or yours. I should've noticed it before *and* remembered what he'd said about hanging it on you." Onca's exhale came out as a growl. "Maybe we can still use it to our advantage. Who could we put it on that would draw them away from us?" He glanced at the others. "Any ideas?"

Kim shrugged. "A random person on the street?"

Rashe threw up his hands. "I still don't get why anyone would be following that signal. They have to have figured out it isn't in Jatki anymore." He glanced at the comlink. "What about you? Were you followed?"

"Well…yeah." Draddut sounded slightly embarrassed. "A couple of Racks tailed me for a while. I, um, let them catch up and then I sort of knocked their heads together. Haven't seen them since."

"Most of the police chased Kim and Onca," Ganyn said. "Hardly anyone came after the rest of us."

"Yeah, well, they almost got us." Onca was growling again. "With Draddut patrolling the street, they had to know whoever had that device was in the area. You notice they didn't bring out the big guns until *after* he was inside—and I'd admitted to being there to find Kim's friends."

"Okay, so don't blame it all on Shemlak," Draddut said. "We still don't know where he wound up. He could even be dead by now."

"Surely to goodness they didn't catch him," Kim said. "They only sent Racks after you, which was kinda stupid. Who would they have that could take down a Darconian?"

"Another Darconian, maybe?" Rashe suggested. "Who knows? All we know is that he isn't here or at the Palace—or Oswalak's. Beyond that, he could be anywhere."

"Or he was on their side." Kim hated to even say the words but she figured someone had to do it.

"That's my brother you're talking about!" Ganyn roared. "He isn't that kind of man. Something happened to him."

"So we've got someone else to rescue?" Rashe plopped down in a worn leather chair that looked out of place in the gleaming kitchen but suited him better than anything else in the house. "Maybe they're holding him hostage—you know, so they can catch us when we go looking for him?"

Onca scowled. "Would *you* try to keep a Darconian hostage?"

"Maybe—if that was my only option." Rashe shrugged. "They could've stunned him. It isn't impossible, you know."

"And we all ran in different directions." Ganyn twisted her beads with trembling fingers. "Maybe he's the one they decided to follow."

"He could've lost his comlink," Kim suggested.

"Which is the most reasonable explanation yet," Onca said. "Either that or he got chased so far he didn't know the way back."

"I can relate to that," Kim admitted. "If Captain hadn't been there to give me directions, I'd have been hopelessly lost, and the same thing could've happened to Jatki. The brothel district isn't our usual territory."

"Mine, either," Ganyn said. "But I got here."

Rashe snorted. "Yeah, with me riding piggyback and telling you which way to go."

Kim barely covered her mouth in time to stifle her giggle. Ganyn already seemed a bit testy. Getting a Darconian truly angry seemed like a very bad idea.

Onca put up a hand. "Okay. Tell you what, Draddut. Take that tracking beacon off and throw it as far as you can."

"Sure we won't need it to lure them into a trap?" Rashe asked.

"Why bother? Obviously they know who we are— well, me, anyway. With my picture smeared all over the *Damenk Tribune*, we hardly need it. Seems to me the best thing to do is to give myself up."

"You're kidding, right?" Rashe said.

Onca grimaced. "No. Think about it. With me giving statements to the press and making a big stink, they'll do anything to make themselves look innocent. They might even close the other brothels and turn the girls loose. It won't totally eliminate the problem, but it *will* draw attention to what's been going on."

"And if they've got Shemlak," Ganyn said, "they might let him go too."

Onca tapped his chin. "We need to find ourselves a gutsy reporter who'll make sure what we have to say doesn't get hushed up."

Roncas's sudden burst of laughter sounded like a flock of angry birds, and tears streamed from her china blue eyes.

Onca glared at the viewscreen. "What's so damn funny?"

"Boss, you've probably fucked enough reporters to fill a space cruiser. I'm sure one of them would be willing to listen to your story."

"Tell you what, then," he said. "You and Val go through our records and find some likely candidates. In the meantime, keep those girls happy and do *not* let them out of the Palace. They're the only evidence we have."

"What are you planning to do?" Roncas asked.

"Read that article and figure out how to refute it."

"Good luck," Roncas said. "You were a customer at the Den. How are you going to avoid *that* rap?"

"That's where the girls come in," Onca replied. "I never touched a single one of them."

"Maybe not, but you did rough up that Herp." Roncas snickered. "He's charging you with assault."

Onca rolled his eyes, grumbling. "Great. And I

don't have any visible injuries to prove he did anything to me. First time being a Zetithian has ever put me at a disadvantage."

"Guess we should've taken pictures," Rashe said. "Right now, it's your word against his."

"I'm guessing most people would believe me over a Herp, but you never know how public opinion will go."

Kim knew which one she would believe.

Even if she *was* a bit miffed with him.

Chapter 24

ONCA WATCHED AS KIM TOYED WITH HER FORK, HER eyes never meeting his. "I can see talking to a reporter," she said. "But turning yourself in? When the police are apparently as corrupt as the people running that brothel? Seems like an unnecessary risk to me."

"Going public first will help," Onca insisted. "That way they can't stash me in a jail cell and forget about me."

"We won't let it drop, either," Rashe said. "We'll keep hounding them. They can't ignore a revolution."

"Revolution?" Onca repeated the word, wondering where in the world all this had come from. He had planned his retirement with the prospect of leading a more normal life. And now he was spearheading a revolution? It was out of character for him—so much so that the authorities would have a field day with the idea. Not that he'd ever broken any laws, but he had never cared much about anything or anyone. He had friends, of course, but he was by no means a crusader.

Nor had he ever been in love. Something had happened to him the moment he laid eyes on Kim. Something deep and everlasting. Life changing. And for the first time ever, meaningful.

Maybe that was it. His life heretofore had lacked meaning. For the first twenty-five years of it, he'd simply been biding his time until Rutger Grekkor's death would set him and his fellow refugees free. After that, he had used that freedom to enter into a highly paid, intensely pleasurable career. Even so, it was a lifestyle that didn't provide him with much in the way of freedom or purpose—or credibility.

Not long ago, he would have said that a life didn't need to have a purpose other than to survive and reproduce. Those were the basics. Anything else was gravy. Truth be told, he hadn't seen his life as meaning anything—aside from the reproduction part—and he'd said as much when questioned as to why he was so willing to risk it. Perhaps risking his life was what made it worthwhile. Or was he risking it because of his feelings for Kim? Did he have to prove himself to her by possibly winding up in prison for the rest of his—

No. Even beating up a Herp wouldn't get him imprisoned forever. He would be released at some point. But without Kim waiting for him, why would it matter?

"Dude, are you okay?" Rashe asked. "Scared, freaked out, or what?"

Onca shook his head. "No. None of those things. Just…thinking."

Thinking about the loneliness that had crept into his soul over the past two years. He knew it had been that long because he could pinpoint the precise moment it began. That moment in the aftermath of Jerden's wedding when their Davordian neighbor, Salan, had abandoned her attempts to seduce Onca and had gone off to fuck Dax's Norludian navigator, Waroun. She even ended up marrying the guy.

Salan had given up on a Zetithian and taken a Norludian. Onca had never understood why until now. She had done it because she didn't want to spend the rest of her life alone—taking affection where it was offered rather than pursuing a man who rejected her.

That vision he'd had earlier—and he knew that was what it had been—unnerved him when it should have given him hope. The setting of that vision had to be Terra Minor. To his knowledge, there were no wilderness areas on Rhylos. The entire planet was either cultivated or populated. Sure, he'd enjoyed spending time at Jerden's ranch, but he'd never seen himself as the type to live in the country.

He could have said the same for Jerden prior to Audrey's murder. Jerden had returned to Terra Minor mainly because it had been designated as the new Zetithian homeworld. Onca was beginning to question why he'd ever left it himself. He had a guaranteed place there—a home among his own kind. Trading that security for the brash, anything-goes life on Rhylos had been sheer stupidity.

But if he hadn't gone to Rhylos, he never would have met Kim or Rashe or any of the people who surrounded him now.

Rashe set a plate of food in front of him, and Onca ate it without hesitation. He wasn't terribly hungry, but it gave him something to do. A glance at Ganyn revealed the concern in her eyes.

"No one will think any less of you for not turning yourself in," Ganyn said. "We all know you acted in self-defense. I'm sure an honest judge would agree, but—"

"It's not that," Onca said. "I'm thinking about something else entirely." He didn't elaborate—wasn't even sure he could without sounding like a fool.

Kim's plate was empty long before his. "I'm going to go get cleaned up a little, if that's okay with you."

Why would it matter to me? Then he realized she
hadn't been speaking to him, but had spoken to Rashe.

"No problem," Rashe said. "Ask Tom-tom if you
need anything."

She gave Rashe a quizzical look at first, then comprehension struck, showing plainly in her face. "Oh, right.
You mean the droid."

Kim pushed her chair back and left the kitchen. Onca
listened as her footsteps faded. Until three days ago,
the only footsteps he'd ever heard in his house were his
own. The silence was deafening at times.

Rashe poured himself another cup of coffee. "Dude,
you're playing with that girl like a fuckin' yo-yo. And
trust me, she'll only take it for so long before she rips
you a new one worse than that Herp would've done if
he'd gotten hold of you."

Onca couldn't help wincing. "What makes you think—?"

"I know when a woman's been fucked. Especially
a woman fucked by one of you cat boys. I watched
plenty of them wandering past my place after you
nailed them. Most of 'em could hardly walk, and they
ignored me completely."

"But Jack said—"

"Since when have you ever listened to Jack?"

Onca hated to admit it, but he had probably paid more
attention to Jack's admonitions than anyone gave him
credit for. Following her advice went against his nature.
However, Jack had begged him to close the Palace—and
had cited some damn good reasons for doing so. The
fact that he had stopped taking appointments right after
their last meeting was solid evidence that he'd heard at
least part of her rant.

"Yeah, well, on rare occasions, she's right. This is one of them."

"Correct me if I'm wrong, but I don't see how this is any of Jack's business. Strikes me that this ought to be between you and Kim and no one else."

"Me and Kim and the whole fuckin' universe." Onca wanted to slam his plate against the wall, leave, and never come back. Walk out into the street and let them take him. He didn't want to care anymore. Life had been so much easier when he didn't give a shit. That was what was wrong with him. He *cared* now. He never had before.

He wasn't the only one orphaned by the destruction of Zetith. Yet the others seemed to have coped with it better. They all shared the same values and beliefs. He didn't value much and didn't believe in anything. He swore at the gods because everyone else did it, blaming them for the evils that befell him—which was pointless because for him, those gods didn't exist. He had no faith. No foundation upon which to base his life. The life he should have had was stolen from him, obliterated along with his homeworld, by a man who was already dead.

Anger welled up inside him until he could no longer contain it. Leaping to his feet, he strode to the door. All his hatred and righteous indignation came to a head. No one should have the right to dictate the life of another—especially to end it. *That* was what made his blood boil. That and the horrors those girls had endured in the brothels.

For the first time in his life, Onca was truly angry. Not irritated, not mildly annoyed.

Furious.

Angry people didn't accumulate friends or followers. Anger only begat more anger. He knew that. But at
the moment, he didn't care. He wanted to lash out and
punish, which would make him no better than any of
the others.

But there *was* such a thing as justice. And accusing
him of inciting a fuckin' riot was a blatant injustice if
he'd ever heard one, if not a flat-out lie.

Was this their intent? To make him mad enough to
show his face? If so, their plan was about to bear fruit.
But perhaps not the way they expected.

"Get on the link to Roncas and tell her I'm on my
way over there," he said. "I assume my speeder is
still here?"

Rashe nodded. "In the garage."

"Good. I need to talk to those girls. I might be back,
and then again, I might not."

Kim stood beneath the spray of hot water, remembering
the shower she had taken under the waterfall at Onca's
house. So much had happened since then; she had a
hard time wrapping her head around it. Perhaps when
the drama was over she would be able to sort it all out
and determine why Onca was so changeable. She knew
exactly how she felt about him, but he seemed to vacil-
late an awful lot.

Maybe that was simply a man thing. A *Zetithian*
man thing—although she couldn't recall her father
ever being afflicted by indecision. Then again, she
hadn't known him for very long, nor had she been
privy to his thoughts.

Not that she was privy to Onca's. He might simply be trying to maintain his focus on the job of rescuing slave girls and saw her as a distraction. She didn't like to think of herself in those terms, but it was beginning to seem that way. Shivering despite the warmth of the water, she tried to imagine going on through life without him.

She reminded herself that she was young. Many would have teased her about her first love, her first crush... He was more than that, wasn't he? Was she truly acting like a foolish, lovesick teen? His experience went so far beyond hers there could be no comparison. But to behave the way he did when they were caught up in the throes of passion and not feel *any* of it? She didn't understand that. Not even for a man who fucked for a living.

After rinsing off and drying herself—with an actual towel, rather than the breeze that surrounded her in Onca's bathroom—she discovered that Tom-tom had replaced the clothing Roncas had loaned her with something more suitable. Plain underwear, jeans, a pink T-shirt, and a pair of white running shoes. She wouldn't fool anyone into thinking she was older than her years in that kind of garb. There was nothing sophisticated about it at all. It was simply the sort of clothes a humanoid girl of her age would normally wear.

A glance at the mirror proved it. She looked like a typical teenager—perhaps even younger.

It's because of my hair. That mop of curls made her look closer to twelve than twenty-two. Perhaps she should let it grow longer so it would be more like Onca's. His was beautiful—its rich, auburn shade so much more interesting than her plain brown locks—and it didn't look as though it had ever been cut.

She gave herself a mental slap. Dalmet was the one she should be thinking of, not herself. Who knew what torment she was enduring at the moment? And now Jatki was missing. Kim had never felt quite so conflicted before. For the first time ever, she had a future. Money and a home awaited her on Terra Minor. She could have stayed at Onca's house until Jack picked her up and skipped all of this. If she went to Terra Minor and actually met other Zetithians, would she still feel the same way about Onca?

Maybe. That might be what was holding him back. He knew a lot more than she did about how Zetithians mated. He'd grown up among them. She hadn't. However, he hadn't said a damn thing, which meant the inner workings of his mind were as much of a mystery as they'd ever been.

She went downstairs to rejoin the others only to discover another problem. "Where's Onca?"

Rashe shrugged. "He took the speeder and went over to the Palace. Said he needed to talk to those girls."

Kim's jaw dropped. "But why now?"

"He's acting damn strange if you ask me," Ganyn said. "He tore out of here with a look on his face I've never seen before."

Kim wasn't sure how well Ganyn knew Onca. Beyond having sex with him at least once, she doubted he had spent much time with her. "Tell me he's at least flying it cloaked."

Rashe nodded. "I didn't see him leave, so he must have."

Kim's heart settled back into its normal pace—for about a second. "Seems like the Palace would be the most risky place for him to be right now. Wouldn't the police be watching it?"

"Probably."

The fact that Rashe didn't elaborate beyond agreeing with her made her even more wary. "Can he get inside without getting caught?"

Rashe nodded. "Security's pretty tight on that building. It'd have to be, what with all the women who would kill to get access to him. He can go in the back way without ever getting out of the speeder."

Considering what had happened to Audrey, Kim knew he wasn't exaggerating the dangers. "How long has he been gone? Would he be there yet? Can we call Roncas?"

"She was supposed to call us when he got there."

"And…?"

"Haven't heard a word yet."

"How far—?"

"Not very."

"Which means?"

"Either he's taking the scenic route or he's done something really stupid."

───

Onca flew into the open garage at the rear of the Palace, keeping the cloak engaged until the door closed behind him. He hadn't detected any sign of a surveillance team watching the place, but he was taking no chances—aside from the fact that if they were any good at their work at all, he *wouldn't* see them. Captain had tried to contact him, but he refused to acknowledge the hail. The more he thought about it, the more he realized how dangerous it was to call anyone at that point, particularly on personal comlinks. Shemlak might have been careless enough to forget about Jatki's tracking beacon, but he also might have realized how dangerous it was for them to contact each other now. Links could be tapped, and with Onca's involvement made public, the cloaking capabilities of his speeder and Rashe's house were the only advantages they had.

Popping the canopy, he climbed out and went in through the employees' entrance, something he hadn't expected to do quite so soon after his retirement. Already, the place looked different. The trees were still standing and the birds and butterflies still fluttered about, but it had never been so crowded before. Girls of all ages sat in small groups on the grassy banks of the creek that wound its way across the earthen floor from the waterfall.

He spotted Roncas behind a table where she was serving up bowls of soup to a line of the thinnest, most ragged bunch of waifs he'd ever seen—quite a few of which weren't female. The moment she waved at him, a cheer went up from the crowd. He made his way through the throng, receiving everything from pats on the back to kisses on his cheeks.

"Where did all these other kids come from?"

"Beats the shit outta me," Roncas replied. "They started showing up right after I talked to you. Said they'd heard we needed help and that this was a safe place."

Onca wasn't sure how safe it was, but obviously stealth hadn't been required for him to enter. He only needed to look hungry and wander in with the rest of them. "You didn't lock the doors? I wouldn't have thought—"

"Val spotted them out front the last time he flew in. Said we should feed them along with the others."

"That wasn't very smart," Onca remarked. "They

could be undercover agents trying to infiltrate our gang and uncover incriminating evidence."

Roncas twittered. "Point out anyone who doesn't look the part, and we'll dunk them in the creek."

He glanced at the smiling faces, wondering which ones the cops had sent and which were truly homeless and found he couldn't make any distinctions. "They could've been paid to do this."

"Oh, no, we weren't," a small boy said. "This big scaly guy told us you needed help, and that we should spread the word."

"A big *orange* scaly guy?"

The boy nodded vigorously. "He had one of my friends with him. She said she'd been trapped in a nasty fuck house and that you helped to set her and her friends free." He grinned, showing several gaps in his teeth. "You're her hero."

Onca stared at the boy, who couldn't have been more than seven or eight—no matter what species he happened to be—and for the record, Onca wasn't sure what species that was. With blue skin and a small tusk on the end of his snout, he looked like a cross between a Twilanan and an Edraitian. "Fuck house?"

The boy stomped his foot. "You know what I mean."

"Yeah. Just never heard it called that before." He cleared his throat. "This orange scaly guy...did he have a name?"

"Shemlak," the boy replied. "He said he owed you something."

"Yeah. An apology," Onca muttered. He glanced at Roncas. "Where's Val?"

"Gone to get more food."

Onca shook his head. "We might as well call the Norludians and have it delivered. Don't suppose you've come up with any reporters on the client list, have you?"

Roncas stomped her foot in a reasonable imitation of the child's indignation. "When would I have had the time?"

He frowned again as something else occurred to him. "I thought you said you had all the girls here with you. One of them obviously must've wound up with Shemlak."

"Yeah. Like I had the chance to do a head count while we were under attack. I had to take their word that they were all accounted for."

"Guess they must've missed one." He looked at the boy. "Who was with Shemlak? Anyone I might know?"

Onca wouldn't have thought a child so young would be capable of sarcasm. Clearly, he was wrong. The kid snorted loud enough that several of the others turned to stare at him. "I doubt it."

"Try me," Onca said. "I know more kids than you might think."

"A Kitnock girl named Jatki."

Chapter 25

"OBVIOUSLY JATKI EXAGGERATED THE PART ABOUT being one of the slaves," Onca muttered. "But at least we know she and Shemlak are okay. What's your name, kid?"

"Han," the boy replied.

"Han? That's all? It isn't short for something else?"

One of the other girls laughed. "Short for Handsome."

"Really?" Onca studied the boy for a moment before deciding that, whether it was true or not, the girl had meant it as a joke. He chose not to treat it as such. "I've only got the one name myself. Onca." He held out a hand. "Pleased to meet you, Han."

Han bobbed his head. "Same here. Can I have some soup now?"

"Sure thing. Just tell me where you saw Jatki."

He shot a surreptitious glance at the other children. "We have this place in the commerce district where we hide. Jatki knows about it. We don't tell anyone else."

"But the orange scaly guy was with her?"

"No. He was waiting for her a few blocks away. She told him we might be too afraid to talk if he was with her."

Onca chuckled. "Smart girl. Do you know where she is now?"

"She said she was going to try to find more of us. Shemlak said he would stick with her."

"Wish they'd bothered to tell *us* what they were up to," Onca grumbled. "We've been worried sick about them."

"Shemlak said he lost his comlink when he was fighting off the Herps who were chasing Jatki."

"Makes sense—certainly more than him getting captured or stunned. He's one tough dude." Giving Han a pat on the head, he aimed him toward the serving line. "Thanks for the information, Han. Go ahead and have some soup. Eat all you want."

The boy's eyes widened, taking on a dreamy glow. "All I want? I've never had all I want before in my life."

"You can now, kid. Chow down."

Onca went over to give Roncas a hand with the serving duties. Pretty soon, the Palace was filled with the boisterous laughter of children with full stomachs— which was as good a way as any to keep the kids off the street so they couldn't be nabbed by the bad guys.

Whoever they are.

Onca would've given a lot to be able to interrogate one of the Herps who'd chased Jatki. Unfortunately, with Jatki to protect, he doubted Shemlak had bothered to capture any of them. Pulling up a chair, he sat down at the link station in the office, hoping to glean something about the *real* perpetrators from the news article.

As luck would have it, however, Onca's was the only name mentioned except for the Den's owner, who reportedly resided offworld. Was that the only reason for the corruption? An absentee business owner whose employees had run amok simply because they lacked supervision? He doubted it, although the article seemed to lean in that direction—which was about the only good spin anyone could have put on the matter. The

undercurrent that Onca might turn out to be the hero of
the day was in there, but hadn't been embellished upon.
The fact that the girls "working" in the brothel had fled
didn't mean a damn thing. In a riot, any prudent prostitute would make herself scarce whether she was there
against her will or not.

Still, a good reporter with a photographer in tow
could've had a field day with all the empty cages. There
was no way to spin *that* story without the truth coming
to light.

Onca still hadn't figured out how all these kids were
going to help—except for the girls who'd been in the
Den. The only thing the rest of them could say was that
he'd fed them.

Perhaps the fact that they required feeding was
enough to shed some light on the need for better facili-
ties for Damenk's orphans. Onca never dreamed there
would be so many. There had to be at least a hundred or
more—and he doubted more than a third of the actual
number had shown up. As time passed, more trickled
in, but there was still no sign of Jatki or Shemlak and no
word from them, either.

When he called Rashe to report the news Han had
given him, he came very close to begging Kim to come
to the Palace but somehow managed to hold his tongue.
The less he saw of her the better. Rashe was right. His
on-again off-again attitude was bound to piss her off
eventually—if it hadn't already. Better to keep away
than to mess with her mind any further.

All he had to do was to get through this mess, find
Dalmet, and send Kim to Terra Minor. He didn't have
to go with her. Jack could handle the details, and Kim

wasn't a child. She could give her own account of who she was and where she came from.

And if she isn't here, I can't smell her—or see her or taste her or hold her while she sleeps. He tasted blood before he realized his fangs had penetrated his lower lip. He couldn't regret rescuing Kim, but he regretted just about everything else he'd done with her. From the very beginning, he'd known that getting involved with her was wrong. He was too old for her. If he turned himself in, he would at least be spared having to face her again.

Maybe. Then again, the case might be so open and shut, he would never serve any jail time at all. What he needed now was a good lawyer—one that hadn't already been bought off by whoever was behind this conspiracy.

Unfortunately, the only one who flew in was Val.

"Hey, Wings," Onca said as Val landed lightly beside him, despite being laden with several bags of groceries. "Roncas said you'd gone out for more food."

Val nodded. "I see we have already acquired more mouths to feed."

"Apparently Jatki and Shemlak sent them, so we know *they're* okay—at least they were the last time any of these kids saw them."

"I am pleased to hear it." Val handed the bags to Roncas, whose pink skin was already tending toward purple. "We feared the worst."

"Yeah, well, I guess you've seen the headlines. Think you could take a look through my files and see if you can find any reporters or lawyers?" Onca paused, frowning. "They would have to be cross-referenced against employment records or some such thing. It's not like we ever asked anyone to list their occupation when they scheduled an appointment."

"You astonish me," Val said with the barest hint of a smile. "I'm surprised you don't have their credit ratings and health records dating from birth."

"Be nice, now," Onca cautioned. "All we did was scan them for disease and fuck them—and tell them to register any babies with the Zetithian Birth Registry. The fees were usually paid in cash."

Val ruffled his feathers. "Too bad yours was such a shady business. I would imagine any reporters or lawyers booked their appointments under false names. I doubt I'll find anyone among your clients who'll be able to help you."

Onca let out a growl. "I hate it when you're right."

"You've got plenty of money, Boss," Roncas said. "You could probably buy off the jury—or the judge."

"But I'm *innocent*," Onca protested. "I shouldn't have to buy off anyone."

"Well, you did rough up that Herp," she reminded him. "They've got you there."

"I didn't lock those girls in cages, which should be the issue, not whether I let a randy Herp fuck me or not. *They're* the guilty ones, not me." Onca gritted his teeth in frustration. "Sure wish I knew who to trust—I mean, corruption isn't something you can see just by looking at a person." Onca heaved a sigh. "This could really get ugly."

"You knew that going into this," Val pointed out. "It is an evil business run by wicked people. You cannot expect to remain unsullied by the taint."

Onca ran a hand through his hair, shaking his head.

"What my partners and I did here at the Palace wasn't anything like that. What I saw in the Den was incomprehensible to me." He didn't have to ask Val's opinion. His quivering wings said it all.

"Then we must end it." Val glanced up at the sunlight pouring in through the open roof, triggering a dramatic pupillary response in his ice-blue eyes. "What you said about corruption isn't entirely true. My eyesight is far more acute than that of anyone else on the planet, and my memory is superior." His pupils dilated as he shifted his gaze back to Onca. "I can identify the police officers involved—*and* I know a good lawyer."

—⁓—

Kim sat in Rashe's living room, watching Tom-tom dust the furniture, feeling as though she would jump out of her skin at any moment. "This is worse than twiddling my thumbs at Onca's house." At least there she could have talked with Captain and perhaps learned something while she waited.

Rashe didn't have a house computer. He only had the droid and what were essentially manual controls. Tom-tom's repertoire of beeps and buzzes didn't make for very stimulating conversation—although he *was* a good cook.

Ganyn had already left to go back to work at Oswalak's, and Rashe was in the teepee with…someone. She understood their reasons for maintaining the illusion of innocence by going on with their normal routines—after all, no one had identified *them* as being involved in the "riot" at the Den. Onca was the only one who truly needed to hide, and he was essentially hiding in plain sight himself. Anyone who knew who he was would have to assume he was either at his home or at the Palace. What was odd was that no one had come looking for him—at least, not that she knew of. Surely someone would tell her if they'd heard anything.

On the other hand, there was no reason for her not to stick her nose out, was there? She was just another street urchin to anyone but the villains at the Den. No one else would know who she was if she wandered out. After all, *she* hadn't swallowed a tracking beacon, and she didn't necessarily have to carry a comlink. She could disguise herself as…

As what? A street walker? She reminded herself that she was in the brothel district. The air outside was laced with sex pheromones to the point that any man she passed by would see her as fair game.

Wait a second…

She was in the portion of the district that catered to females. *She* would be more apt to be overcome with the need for sex than the men would. But were the scents truly that specific? She thought perhaps they might be. Rashe and Onca hadn't seemed to be affected. Then again, they had been inside the house or the speeder, not walking around outside. And Ganyn was a lizard. Pheromones that would affect mammals might not do anything to a Darconian at all.

Hmm…

Rashe would freak out if he came back in the house and found her gone. And she wasn't about to stop by the teepee to advise him of her plans. She knew she was better off staying put, but the need to see Onca was overwhelming.

Perhaps the pheromones were affecting her after all. She was sort of…dizzy, for want of a better term. She'd never felt that way before—at least, not that she could recall. But then, she hadn't spent any time on this end of the brothel district. She and her pals had learned long ago that they were better off in the commerce regions where food and clothing were more readily available—and more easily stolen. The subliminal advertising there had ceased to affect them long ago.

Deciding she couldn't sit still another moment, she stood up and nearly fell back down.

Tom-tom beeped once and floated out of the room, returning a few minutes later with a delicately fluted cup filled with a hot beverage of some sort in one of his many "hands."

"Thanks, Tom-tom," she said, taking the cup. "I think."

After giving it a sniff, she took a cautious sip. She had no idea what it was, but it tasted good.

Rashe stuck his head in a few minutes later. "You doing okay?" he asked. "This has got to be boring as hell for you."

"Sort of," she admitted. "Do you think anyone would mind if I went over to the Palace to see Cassie and Peska?" The fact that Onca was also there was such a minor detail she saw no need to mention it.

Yeah, right.

Rashe wasn't fooled. "Onca, too?"

"Well, yeah. Onca too."

He strolled across the room and plopped down beside her on the couch, seemingly oblivious to the fact that he was completely naked.

"Nice tattoo," she said.

"What? Oh, yeah." Grabbing a pillow, he used it to cover his groin. "Forgive me. I know you aren't used to it, but I spend most of my time in the altogether." Heaving a sigh, he leaned back against the cushions. "I need to rest for a little bit. That last one was kinda energetic."

"You don't schedule appointments the way Onca did, do you?"

"No. Since I don't have a receptionist, if I'm standing outside, I'll do anyone who wanders by."

"How do you keep anyone else from walking in on you?"

"I have a busy sign I put up. Every now and then someone barges in on me when I'm with a client, but lots of ladies like the threesome thing, so it usually works out okay. Now, if I had *Onca* in there with me, we'd probably have women lined up halfway down the street."

"Business at the Palace was that good?"

Rashe snorted. "Come on now, kiddo. You've done him, so you know the sort of chaos those dudes would cause if they weren't seen by appointment only."

"How do you know—?"

He snorted again. "Don't make me laugh. You're already hooked on him, aren't you?"

"Hooked on him?" Kim knew he was right—whether she was willing to admit it or not.

"Sex with a Zetithian is dangerous, Kim—and he knows it. You'll get so attached to him you won't want anyone else."

"And that's a *problem*?"

Rashe didn't answer right away but sat chewing thoughtfully on his lower lip. "Probably not. *He* thinks it is, but I'm not so sure myself. Jack somehow managed to get his conscience working overtime." Chuckling, he added, "Never knew he *had* a conscience."

"I almost wish he didn't have one now." She took a deep breath and plunged ahead. "I'd really like to, you know…keep him."

"Interesting way of putting it." Wrinkling his nose, he sniffed the air and glanced at her cup. "Are you sick?"

"What makes you say that?"

"I smell chamomile. Tom-tom always gives it to me when I don't feel well."

"I *am* kinda dizzy," she admitted. "Not sure why that is."

Kim was glad Rashe hadn't just taken a sip of the tea himself or he probably would've sprayed it all over the sofa.

"No shit?"

She nodded. "I started feeling that way a little while ago. I figure it must be something in the air around here."

Clearing his throat in a rather ominous manner, he sat up. "Maybe." He scratched his head, messing up one of his braids. "I don't know jack shit about Zetithian women, but if you were human, I'd say you were pregnant."

Chapter 26

RASHE WASN'T THE ONLY ONE WHO DIDN'T KNOW JACK shit about Zetithian women. Kim was at something of a disadvantage herself. But she did know one thing. "I'm not human. Apparently we don't do the whole monthly cycle thing—at least, I never have."

"No PMS, huh? Damn. That alone is reason enough for Onca to snap you up." He gave himself an admonitory smack on the cheek. "Sorry. That was tacky of me. But there has to be *some* way for you to identify fertile periods. What I mean is, even animals go into heat and behave differently..." He tipped his head to the side as his eyes took on an introspective cast. "Then again, maybe that dizzy feeling is it. Be easy enough to find out. I'm sure that information is *somewhere* on the Net."

"Captain told me lots of things, but that wasn't one of them."

"Makes sense, though. You've only been hanging around with Onca for a couple of days. Even if you were pregnant, you wouldn't be having symptoms yet. At least, I don't *think* you would." He shrugged. "But what do I know?"

"Maybe more than I do—and I'll bet you're right." She wasn't sure whether to feel relieved or disappointed. Nevertheless, being in heat might explain why, despite her dizziness, she could hardly sit still. The urge to go dashing over to the Palace to find Onca was becoming stronger by the second. In fact, if Rashe hadn't come in when he had, she'd probably be on her way over there already. Too bad she wasn't sure where it was.

"Why do I get the feeling that pregnant is exactly what you'd like to be?" He heaved a sigh. "Don't bother answering that. Guess you want me to take you to the Palace, huh?"

"If you wouldn't mind."

"I'm not the one you need to worry about, sweetheart. Onca's gonna be pissed at me, no doubt about it." He chuckled. "I'm also guessing the bad guys are kinda freaked out by all the kids showing up over there. They made a mistake before. If they'd been a little less noisy, no one would've reported a riot, and they could've kept it out of the news. Now that the Palace is full of kids, they'll have a tough time explaining a show of force—which is probably what Shemlak had in mind when he told them to head over there. If Onca's surrounded by a bunch of kids, only a lunatic would use the kind of firepower they used at the Den."

"I'd like to believe we could depend on that, but villains aren't always that smart."

"Maybe not, but if this goes as high up in the government as I suspect, they've got to consider public opinion. Elected officials have to at least *pretend* to be decent, law-abiding citizens. Allowing the police to open fire—even with stun weaponry—on a bunch of homeless orphans will get a politician hounded out of office quicker than he can zip his pants."

Kim bit back a laugh. "I hope you're right about that."

Rashe patted the pillow in his lap. "Speaking of which, guess I'd better put on a pair and take you to the

Palace. If I let anything happen to you now, my goose would be cooked for sure."

Whether she'd ever heard that expression before didn't matter. The meaning was quite clear. "You think Onca really cares?"

"Oh, hell yes. He's *crazy* about you—just don't tell him I told you so. But I'm not talking about Onca. Jack's the one who'll kill me."

"You know Jack, too?"

He nodded. "Everybody knows Jack."

Kim didn't but suspected she would before long. "I'm beginning to believe we really should've waited for her. The way everyone talks, she could've solved this mystery single-handedly."

"Nah. Where's the fun in that? We may be glad she's on her way in case someone needs to save our asses, but with any luck, we'll have it all sorted out before she gets here."

"But what happens if Onca gets arrested? If the corruption is as bad as you say, how will he ever get a fair trial?"

With a wink, he stood and tossed the pillow on the couch. "Don't worry. Onca can take care of himself. He'll land on his feet. He always does."

Kim suspected this was the first time Onca had been in trouble of any kind, let alone something of this magnitude. "What makes you think that?"

Rashe shrugged. "He's a cat."

———

Onca had completely forgotten Val's connection to Anara Threlkind, the lawyer advocate for clone rights who had freed Val and his fellow Avians. "Does Anara live here on Rhylos?"

Val nodded. "I am certain she would take your case."

"How come you didn't mention her before?" Roncas demanded. "Seems to me she should've been the first one we called."

"Perhaps," Val admitted. "But we had very little to go on until we actually got inside the Den. Now we have proof."

Onca nodded. "He's right. We went in and got those girls out last night. The legal process would've taken forever, and with at least part of the police force on the take, there'd be no way to stop the proprietors from moving the girls somewhere else. No. We did the right thing going in the way we did, and if that Herp hadn't filed charges against me, I wouldn't have *needed* a lawyer."

By this time, Peska and Cassie and several of the other girls had drifted over to listen in on the meeting.

"What can we do to help?" Peska asked.

Onca thought for a moment. "Think you can look after the kids for a while?"

"Sure," Cassie said. "Shouldn't be too hard. After all the food they ate, I'm surprised any of them are still awake." With a shy smile, she added, "We owe you a lot, Onca. If there's ever anything we can do for you, all you have to do is ask."

"You don't owe me anything," he said, surprised to find tears stinging his eyes. "Just don't let anyone near the controls for the risers. Actually, it might be better if I disabled them."

"Risers?" Peska echoed.

"Sections of the floor that float up into the trees," he

replied. "They're the, um, bedrooms. They've got force fields on them so no one can fall off, but I'd rather the kids didn't know about them." Childproofing the Palace was a thought that had never occurred to him—or any of his partners. "This was a brothel, you know."

Cassie giggled. "I might've actually enjoyed working in a place like this."

At least she could laugh. "Our clients seemed to like it," he said. "We made it look as much like the forests of Zetith as possible. I don't remember them myself, but Tarq and Jerden do."

"I've never seen Davordia, either," Cassie said. "I guess most of us on Rhylos are transplants. One thing I've always wondered about, though. Are there any natives of this world?"

"If there are, I've never heard of them," Onca said. "I seem to recall hearing that there were no indigenous intelligent life forms here when it was first colonized. But then, the conquerors are the ones who write the history books."

"Probably similar to what happened to my people," Rashe said as he sauntered through the arched doorway from the reception area. "War, disease, famine—stuff like that." He glanced around at the "forest" and its new inhabitants. "If Jerden could see you now…"

Onca's retort died on his lips as Kim came in behind him.

One glimpse of her had Onca purring so hard he could scarcely control it. Not only did she look absolutely adorable in her pink shirt and jeans, as she approached her scent slammed into his groin like a quadruple dose of the most powerful aphrodisiac in existence.

He had to do something.

Now.

"Okay, then," he said, doing his best to speak without purring. "Here's what we're gonna do. Val, you contact Anara, and I'll run a search for investigative reporters. There are bound to be a few hard-nosed types who dearly love digging up dirt on politicians—maybe even some who are former clients of ours." He glanced at Roncas. "Can you think of any names?"

"Not really," she replied. "I don't watch the news much."

Onca gaped at her. "But you said I'd fucked enough reporters to fill a space cruiser! You mean you didn't recognize any of them?"

"That was more of an assumption than a statement of fact," Roncas admitted. "Besides, I think it's best if we keep this impartial. Getting someone you fucked to report the story might be seen as a conflict of interest. Stuff like that can come back to bite you in the butt."

"Yes, but if no one knows they were ever here—"

Rashe snorted. "Do you really think they wouldn't have told anyone about their visit to the Palace? Hell, I'm surprised your clients don't run around in *I fucked a Zetithian* T-shirts."

"Now, now, Rashe," Roncas admonished. "No need to be jealous just because women don't say the same things about fucking *you*."

"Some may have boasted about having been a client," Val said. "But certainly none who could help us now. Anyone with any power at all would have been more discreet."

"True, but there's bound to be *someone* willing to report the story." Onca blew out a breath. He hadn't

exercised his brain to this extent since he left the
refugee ship, and even then the problems he'd solved
were hypothetical. This was real life-and-death stuff.
He couldn't afford to let Kim's scent cloud his brain.
"Roncas, I want you to work on advertising. The public
needs to know the truth about what's going on here. We
ran ads for the Palace in the *Tribune* and on several other
sites. I never canceled those accounts because I wasn't
sure whether my vacation was going to turn out to be
an actual retirement. See if you can use them to drum
up support.

"After we've done all that and we know the reporters
are on the way, we're gonna call the damn cops and tell
them to get their asses over here." He glanced at Rashe,
carefully avoiding Kim's alluring eyes. "Val says he can
identify the policemen who were at the Den last night. If
any of them show up, he can point them out. With that
many witnesses, we should at least be able to undermine
their credibility."

"They've certainly done their damnedest to undermine yours," Rashe said. "Not sure what we can do to
combat that."

Onca didn't, either. "If anyone as any ideas, now's
the time to speak up."

Now that Onca was near enough for her to inhale his
scent, Kim knew Rashe's theory was correct. If she
wasn't in the throes of the first fertile period of her
life, she was definitely ill. Without Rashe's support-
ing arm, she probably would have fallen on her ass.
Unfortunately, the cure for her condition was busy.

"You've got us," Cassie said. "Everyone who was locked up in the Den owes you her life and her freedom."

"You saved me, too," Kim said. "And Jatki. You saved us *all*." She drew in a shaky breath, hoping it might clear her head. It didn't. In fact, that extra whiff of Onca made her feel even worse. "I know we're only a bunch of homeless orphans, but we'll find out who's behind this racket, and we'll make them pay. We won't let anything happen to you."

"I can't let you risk your lives for me," Onca protested. "I'm not worth—"

Kim let out a growl. "Don't you dare say that! You're worth more to us than any man on the planet. We won't let you sacrifice your life or your freedom for us again. We're your army now. We're here to protect *you*."

As woozy as she felt, she hoped the others would agree, although considering the horrors they had endured as slaves, she couldn't be sure. But as she glanced at the group that surrounded Onca, she saw raw courage and grim determination written on the faces of every one of them.

"They can't silence all of us," Peska declared. "And do we *ever* have stories to tell."

Onca nodded slowly. "If you can bring yourselves to talk about it, I'll do my best to find someone who'll listen."

Kim couldn't help noticing he avoided her gaze, which was probably just as well. She ached for him in ways she couldn't express aloud, nor could she hurl herself into his arms the way she longed to do.

We have to get through this first. Then, we'll see.

Knocking up a girl he had known for less than three days certainly wouldn't improve his public image. She had to be strong. Too bad she was weaker now than she'd ever been. She wanted nothing more than to lie down on one of those grassy "bedrooms" and float up into the trees with him while he worked his magic on her, body and soul. Her knees buckled at the mere thought of making love with Onca one more time…

"Kim!" Roncas said sharply. "Are you okay?"

Kim nodded. At least she thought she had. As dizzy as she was, she wasn't sure she had even moved her head.

"She's a little off-kilter today," Rashe explained. "Think you ought to sit down?"

Kim squeezed her eyes shut. "Yeah. Maybe over there by the waterfall. Might be…cooler." *And the air might carry less of Onca's scent.*

"I think the pheromones are affecting her," Rashe said. "You have them turned off in here, don't you?"

Kim had no idea who he had asked the question of, but Roncas replied. "That feature has *always* been turned off in here." She seemed rather huffy. "My Zetithians never needed any help getting women to desire them."

Onca's laugh sounded…strange. "Why, Roncas. That's the nicest thing you've said since I fired you."

"You didn't fire me," Roncas retorted. "You pensioned me off."

Kim didn't care if he'd cast the Zuteran out without a reference or a credit to her name. All she knew was that if she didn't put some distance between her and Onca, she was going to pass out. "Can you help—?"

She staggered against Rashe, who immediately scooped her up in his arms. "Sure thing. Over by the waterfall, you said?"

This time she didn't even try to nod. "Yeah."

"Hold on a second," Roncas said. "Let's run you through the medscanner and see what's wrong with you."

"Scanner?" Kim didn't know whether to agree or not. However, Rashe didn't give her the option and carried her back out to the reception area.

Kim wanted to run, but her legs wouldn't obey her brain. She was barely able to stumble through the scanner without falling as it was.

"Mother of the gods," Roncas whispered. "She's off the *scale*…"

"What's the matter?" Onca sounded very far away.

"Nothing that a little rest won't fix," Roncas said briskly. "She can lie down here on one of the daybeds."

Roncas helped her over to a nearby couch. Since this was undoubtedly where Onca's clients had slept off the effects of his *snard*, it was only fitting that she do the same. *Maybe*. Her own weakness annoyed her. Kim had scarcely been sick a day in her life, and now when Onca needed all the help he could get, she couldn't do a damn thing. The brief speech she'd made had sapped what strength she had left.

"Kim's sick?" Cassie said. "Really? She's *never* sick."

"She isn't sick now," Roncas said. "Just exhausted. It's been a tough couple of days."

"Her whole life has been tough," Peska argued. "I don't understand what could possibly be wrong with her now."

Kim wished they would all be quiet and go away.
All of them except Onca.

"Kim?"

He was purring. She felt it more than heard it. He was

too close—his fingers stroked her cheek, sending tendrils of warmth curling over her skin. She wanted him so very badly. Even though she knew she needed to be far away from him—so far away she wouldn't distract him from what needed to be done. That way her own head would be clearer, and so would his.

"Are you sure you're okay?" His tone was gentle but anxious.

"I think so." She was surprised he couldn't tell what the problem was by her scent alone. Perhaps he could. The question was, did he care? Would it matter to him? She touched his face, his hair. "I'll be all right after a nap."

She wouldn't, of course. Not unless he was there beside her, filling her with his body, his passion, his love.

And his children.

Chapter 27

ONCA HAD BEEN SURE IT WAS SAFE TO FUCK KIM before—and it *had* been safe then. He didn't need to see the results of the scan Roncas had run on her to know the truth. He could smell it. Fortunately, the pants Tom-tom had given him had his dick snugged up against his belly well enough that no one would notice it was the size of a Rutaran salami.

Maybe.

Zetithian women didn't experience the same cyclic periods of fertility that humans did. They only went into heat after sleeping with the man destined to become their mate. Closing his eyes, he kissed her cheek.

Jack is gonna kill me.

To mate with Kim now would be dangerous. They were in the middle of a war. Conceiving babies at such a time was—well…what people usually did in times of war. Throughout the ages, warriors on every world had left pregnant wives behind when they went off to battle. If the men didn't return, their women still carried their offspring.

Onca couldn't claim he had never fathered any children. He didn't have to worry about whether or not his bloodline would survive. But he had never fathered children with a Zetithian woman before, and if what he suspected was true, Kim wouldn't conceive with anyone but him. This wasn't so much a matter of his bloodline being lost, but of hers dying out.

Unfortunately, in this particular skirmish, Kim's life was in as much danger as his. He simply couldn't do it. Not now. Not when so much remained to be done.

Rashe moved in behind him. "Dude, you know what—"

"Yeah. I know." Onca blew out a sigh. "Believe me, I know. But not right now. We have work to do."

A glance at Roncas revealed an expression of mild disapproval—her silvery brow was only arched about half as high as he knew it could go. "I guess there's no denying Mother Nature, is there?"

"Mother who?" Onca echoed. "Never mind." He knew exactly what she meant. Pressing another kiss to Kim's forehead, he stood up. "Come on. We've all got jobs to do and not much time. We can't stay holed up in here forever. Sooner or later, they'll figure out how to shut down our power, and—"

Roncas's snicker cut him off. "You're forgetting something, Boss. We're not on the grid. We have our own power supply." She glanced at Rashe. "Our clients threw such a fit the one time the power went out, Jerden made sure it would never happen again."

"That's nice to know." Rashe shrugged. "A power failure wouldn't make any difference at my place, but I can see where your ladies might fuss if the risers didn't work."

"Whatever," Onca said with a dismissive wave. "We still need to get moving before they figure out how to disable our communication capabilities. Without them, we're screwed."

Val stuck his head through the doorway. "I talked to Anara. She'll be here tomorrow morning."

"Great. Now I just have to find some reporters." He frowned at Rashe. "What were you going to do?"

"Must've skipped me when you were handing out jobs," Rashe replied. "But I volunteer to be in charge of security."

"Just dying to use that tomahawk on somebody, aren't you?"

"First time for everything." He patted the hilt. "I'd dearly love to break it in on a Herpatronian's head. You know, we really should've dragged a Herp along with us last night. The interrogation would've been fun."

"Somehow I think the girls might've gotten further with that. Their threats would've been more...specific." Onca had only *twisted* the nuts on one of them. He doubted the girls would have been quite as forgiving.

"Probably would've had to lock the damned Herp up for his own protection." Rashe nodded toward the doorway to the forest. "We could put 'em up on one of the risers." Rashe's swift, downward glance proved that the Rutaran salami was clearly evident. "Sorry about the pants, dude. That was the only pair I had aside from my buckskins. Couldn't go there this time myself." Settling his belt on his hips, Rashe adjusted his loincloth with a grimace. "Don't know how I stood wearing them as long as I did."

Onca chuckled. "The loincloth shows off your ass better. The girls will love it."

"Hey, after all the creepy dudes those girls have had to put up with, a Norludian would probably look good."

"The Scorillian said she thinks Val is hot," Roncas put in. "Must be the wings—although it amazes me that any of them would even want to lay eyes on a man again. Maybe they're young enough to bounce back from this." With a slow wag of her head, she added, "I don't know how, though."

"Don't want to look at another man myself. Already got one."

Her voice sounded as though she was on the verge of sleep, but Kim was obviously still awake. She looked so tiny lying there on the red velvet daybed.

So beautiful... so completely adorable...

Onca had never fucked anyone on one of those beds, which had been placed there for ladies to relax and recover from the effects of Zetithian sex. He had seldom seen any of his clients lying on the plush velvet, covered with satin sheets while sipping wine and nibbling on chocolate—he'd always been busy with the next one. At the moment, however, he wanted nothing more than to rip off his restrictive pants and dive into her. Right here, right now.

I really need to get out of here.

"I'll, um, be in the office if anyone needs me."

"*I* need you." Her voice was so soft he could have pretended he hadn't heard her.

But he had. "I'll be back soon." He hesitated in the doorway. "I promise."

A faint glimmer of a smile touched her lips. "I know you will."

The trick would be staying away long enough to get anything done. Anara wouldn't arrive until morning, which gave him one more night with Kim. One night to make love with her on a grassy bower up in the trees where butterflies and twinkling lights hovered among the leaves. What would happen after that was anyone's guess. Depending on what Anara advised, he might give himself up or allow himself to be arrested and imprisoned—he might even be deported—but come what may, by morning Kim would be carrying his young, and she would know how much he loved her. That was one battle he refused to fight any longer.

I surrender.

Hell, he surrendered *now*.

In an instant, he was on his knees beside her. She was in his arms, and as his lips found hers every shred of his resistance crumbled. Everything about her cried out to him, drowning his senses—her scent, her flavor, the feel of her body against his, the beat of her heart, and the breath in her lungs. All of it came crashing down around him at once. He had fought against millions of years of Zetithian evolution and lost, and along the way, he'd lost his heart to a tiny woman with huge brown eyes and a smile that robbed him of breath.

Roncas squawked like a Resaneden goose about to become someone's dinner. Rashe mumbled something about security. The door to the main chamber slid shut behind them.

"I love you," he whispered against her lips. "Do you hear me, Kim? I love you. I can't explain it or fight it and I don't even want to try."

Her sigh flowed over his skin as her essence seeped in through his pores. The delicate aroma that was so uniquely hers filled his lungs and rushed through his bloodstream until he knew he could have identified her blindfolded from a hundred meters away. His own purr roared in his ears, blocking out any other sounds save for those made by his adorable Kim. Her sighs, her soft moans, her hums of pleasure. He relished every one of them. Vowing to draw more from her, he paused only a moment to rid himself of his clothing.

Onca had seldom had to undress a woman. His clients
had always come to him already disrobed. Nevertheless,
he made quick work of Kim's clothes and cast them
aside. Already her body seemed fuller, not quite as
painfully thin as it had been the first time he held her. It
didn't seem possible, but he'd fallen in love with her in
that same space of time—a span of days that seemed far
longer than the actual hours that had passed.

Softer than the velvet upon which she lay, her wet
warmth beckoned and she moaned as he sank into her.

"Mmm...love that." Nothing had ever felt so good or
so right as she wrapped her arms around him, drawing
him in, holding him close, and whispering words that
filled him with joy. "Love *you*."

He didn't leave me.

Kim held Onca's face in her hands, gazing up into
his glowing green eyes before pulling him down for
another kiss. An orgasm gripped her from within, dis-
rupting his rhythm.

He didn't seem to mind the distraction, kissing her
thoroughly before resuming his steady pace. "You do
love me, don't you?"

She frowned. "Always have, I think. Maybe even
before I met you."

Had she ever had a premonition or a vision of him?
If so, she couldn't recall it—at least not with any clarity.
Something had kept her going, even when she should've
given up hope. Perhaps it was him—or the idea of him.
At the moment, however, none of that mattered. The
ache in her heart had eased along with the ache in her

core. He was here, moving inside her, filling the emptiness in her soul with warmth and light—and he was Zetithian enough not to question her peculiar response to his query.

With a smile, he rocked into her again, moving his strong cock in sweeping circles, stimulating her sweet spots and drawing gasps of delight from her with every thrust. She hugged his cock with her inner muscles, seeking to give him as much pleasure as she could while intensifying her own.

"We're mates now, aren't we?" she asked.

"Oh, *yeah*…"

"Jack can't marry me off to one of her sons, can she?"

"No. And even if she could, I wouldn't let her. I tried being gracious and magnanimous, but there's nothing noble about me. Her boys can find their own women. You're mine."

Since this was in perfect accord with her own views on the subject, she saw no need to discuss it any further. "Should I bite you to seal the deal?"

"Sure. Bite me, smack me, kiss me—whatever you want—just don't ever leave me."

Kim knew she wouldn't leave him—at least not voluntarily. She wasn't so sure about Onca. "I won't—if you'll promise not to leave *me*."

"I promise."

"But what if they throw you in jail?"

"You'll have to come and visit me." He dropped another kiss on her lips. "Hourly."

Onca followed the kiss with a plunge of his cock that made Kim forget all about biting him. She felt no need to mark him as hers now. He had claimed her as his own, and she had his promise. A swipe of his tongue on her neck sent her dangerously close to another climax.

"If you keep doing that, they'll have to lock me up along with you," she warned.

"Not for long. After you have triplets, the guards will be begging the warden to release us."

"But I'm not pregnant."

His crooked smile promised she soon would be. "Wait for it..."

Arching his back, he sucked in a sharp breath as his head snapped back, sending his hair cascading over his shoulders. Was there ever a more glorious sight than her darling Onca at the height of ecstasy? She thought not. He was beautiful. No other word came close to describing him—he was beautiful in body as well as in soul.

As he reached his deepest penetration yet, her body imploded, drawing him in to the point that they truly became one. Still, she kept her eyes open wide, watching as his climax unfolded. She saw it all. The strong lines of his neck. The slope of his shoulders. The muscles of his chest and arms as they contracted. His explosive, purring exhale. The eventual dip of his head. The hair sweeping forward to frame his face. His glowing pupils dilated to their fullest as his gaze met hers.

Then the ecstasy shifted to her. Heated blood rushed through her vessels and time stood still as his essence overcame her senses, filling her with joy. Somewhere deep inside her, she became aware of a slight ping, followed by another and another. Her awareness expanded, surging to a peak before flowing down over herself and three new entities—the three fresh lives to renew the cycle.

"Did you feel that?" he whispered.

She replied with a nod. "We have children now." Pausing as additional knowledge slid into her mind from a source hitherto untapped. "Two boys and a girl."

"You say that like you know for sure."

Closing her eyes, she touched each of the tiny motes with a wisp of her psyche. "I do." Marveling at the wondrous nature of this new level of consciousness, she touched them again, watching them bounce away with a vibration that seemed to be...

Laughter? Perhaps. She couldn't distinguish their thoughts, but her own heart filled with the joy of simply being alive.

"This may sound crazy," she began, "but I can sense their emotions."

"Doesn't sound crazy at all. How do they feel?"

"Happy. Joyous. Thrilled."

Onca leaned down and kissed her—a kiss so achingly sweet and loving it brought tears to her eyes. "Me too."

Chapter 28

AFTER THE FIRST THREE REPORTERS HE CALLED ASKED if he could get them a date with Jerden, Onca began to question his decision to target only women. Nevertheless, by the time he had contacted every female reporter in Damenk and a few in the neighboring city of Kartous, he felt confident that public opinion would be in his favor. Most of the former slave girls had expressed their willingness to talk, and he had no doubt that the Herp's assault charges would look pretty stupid up against their testimony.

Deciding that male reporters might be more sympathetic when it came to being buggered by a Herp— unless they happened to enjoy that sort of thing—Onca went back to the listings and called a few of the men on the *Tribune* staff. Four of them shuddered and the fifth was openly envious.

Better scratch that one.

He was about to call a sixth when Kim came into the office. He didn't even have to look up to know it was her. The enticing aroma that preceded her told him all he needed to know.

"How's it going?" she asked.

"Not bad. I think we'll be okay."

"Glad to hear it." Leaning in close behind him, she slid her arms around his neck and nipped his earlobe.

One swift inhale sent his dick from flaccid to rigid in

the space of three heartbeats. "Mother of the gods, you smell incredible!"

"So do you." Purring, she licked his neck. "I'm getting a real kick out of being a mom."

"Can you still pick up on their emotions?"

"Seems that way. Then again, they don't have much to be unhappy about at the moment, so I doubt their attitudes would change any."

Onca couldn't remember a time when anything had been that simple, and he certainly couldn't recall being in the womb. As terrifying as his birth must have been, he considered the loss of that memory to be fortuitous— along with the memory of being handed over to Amelyana by his parents.

Or so he had always thought. Lately he'd begun to question whether being spared that trauma was worth the blow to his sense of identity. Although every child aboard the refugee ship had been orphaned, most of them at least knew who they were and where they came from. Onca had no idea. Looking back, it was a wonder he'd grown up as well-adjusted as he had—although some would argue that he hadn't. He knew Jack's opinion of him quite well. Fortunately, Kim didn't seem to share it.

Scooting his chair back from the desk, he pulled her into his lap, stroking his palms up and down her back. "What have you been up to?"

"Trying to figure out how to feed an army of kids out of such a tiny kitchen." A slow, wet kiss followed her reply—one that made his head spin and his dick ache. "Val hasn't complained, but he's bound to be getting tired of flying out for more groceries. Don't suppose we could call the Norludians again, could we?" Purring, she traced the curve of his ear with the tip of her tongue.

Onca didn't notice his own purr until he tried to speak. "I don't see why not. We could order some better equipment too. With a computer and a bank account, you can get damn near anything on this planet."

"If you trust the people who deliver it. Heard anything from Shemlak and Jatki?"

"Not a peep," he replied.

"The kids keep trickling in, so they must still be out there recruiting. Dunno where they'll all sleep tonight."

He grinned. "I know where *we're* going to sleep. Up in the trees on one of the risers."

She didn't pretend to miss his meaning. "I'll try not to make too much noise."

"Good plan." If he'd been in his typical state of undress, he could have slid his cock right into her tight pussy. Too bad she wasn't equally naked or at least wearing a dress. Onca had never considered the advantages of skirts before, but those damned jeans gave him no access to her at all. He sucked in another lungful of her incredible aroma. "What *is* it about you that makes me want you so much?"

Her impish smile made his heart turn somersaults. "Probably the same thing that makes me want *you*."

"No, wait. It's because you're pregnant. Pregnant women smell really good to Zetithian guys."

"So it's only my scent?"

He buried his face between her breasts. Even through her shirt, he could almost taste her. "That and everything else about you. How about closing the door and losing those jeans?"

—⁓—

Kim had thought that becoming pregnant would diminish her need for him. Not so. If anything, her craving for him had quadrupled.

At least I'm not dizzy anymore.

She wondered briefly about the origin of such a peculiar symptom and why conception had cured it almost immediately. Perhaps Zetithian women were impossible to catch unless they were so dizzy they couldn't stand up—normal-sized Zetithian women, that is. As little as Kim was, she had no doubt that Onca could easily outrun her. At the moment, however, running away was the very last thing on her mind. She tapped his nose with a fingertip. "Be right back."

Having closed the door securely, she gestured at the window that looked out onto the forest. "Can anyone see us in here?"

"Not if you push that button on the sill."

With a tap of the control, the window lost its transparency, becoming the same shade of green as the wall around it. By the time she turned around, Onca was already peeling off his pants. "Been dying to get out of these damn things ever since I put them on."

"As tight as they are, it's a wonder you can walk."

"No shit. I'm surprised my dick still works."

Her swift, downward glance revealed a perfectly functioning Zetithian penis—complete with the juice guaranteed to make the most disinterested woman imaginable moan with delight. "Looks fine to me."

His lips twitched into a smirk. "Better give it a thorough examination—just to be sure."

"Don't worry. I will." One lick sent her senses reeling. Taking him in her mouth had her squirming with anticipation. "Tastes okay. Not sure how well it'll hold up under pressure, though."

"Want to test its penetration ability?"

"Absolutely." Toeing off her shoes, she stripped off the rest of her clothing. "Go for it."

In an instant, she was in his arms, lifted easily off her feet. As she wrapped her legs around his waist, he set her down on his prick, the head unerringly finding her slit. "Nothing wrong with the targeting capability."

"Mmm...glad to hear it."

Rocking her side to side, he worked her tight sheath down over his shaft. "Far enough?"

"Almost." Lifting her hips, she sat down hard, taking his full length inside her. "Perfect."

He sighed. "Oh, *yeah*... Do that again."

She did as he asked, then began grinding against his groin until the scalloped ridge raked her sweet spot. "Seems stiff enough..." With short, precise moves, she brought herself quickly to climax.

"Neat trick," he said. "But I bet I can top it."

"No way," she murmured, savoring the pinnacle until his orgasmic juice triggered another rush of delight.

"There's something about having someone else do it *to* you, rather than doing it yourself."

Although she knew he was right, she opted for an adversarial stance. "Prove it."

A brief chuckle was his only response and her only warning as Onca sank to his knees, taking her down with him. A kiss stole her breath before he eased her backward until her head and shoulders touched the plush carpet. Holding her hips, he worked her sweet spot just as she had done, except this time, he was in control. The angle of his cock was perfect as his lazy, circular, seemingly random movements kept her guessing while driving her wild. She gazed up at him, enchanted by his cheeky grin and the auburn curls framing his face. Unable to reach him with her fingertips, she could only watch as muscles played beneath his skin and bask in the glow of his captivating green eyes. For her, he was the epitome of what a man should be. No others could even begin to compare.

The climb to her peak was so gradual every upward step registered clearly in her mind before rising to the next level. His purring added spice to the heady brew as he slowly ramped up the tension within her until her control finally snapped and sent her soaring.

"Okay," she gasped. "You win that round."

She ought to have known better. He was, after all, a professional.

But she had an advantage. She was Zetithian, and she was pregnant with his children. He couldn't resist her.

I've never been irresistible before.

Her only dilemma was what to do with this newfound power. Should she make him beg for it or beg him not to stop? She could ask him to do anything, and he would probably do it for her.

Let's not get cocky.

No, she wouldn't ask him for the moon and stars or a castle. All she wanted was him and his love. No limits, no reservations. If Jack objected to their union, she would simply have to get over it. Onca belonged to Kim, and she to him.

"Any special requests?"

Had he been reading her thoughts? If she could sense the emotions of their babies, why couldn't he feel hers?

She shook her head. "No. I only want you. All of you. All the time."

"Works for me." Onca held out his hands, and she placed hers in his grasp, allowing him to pull her into the warmth of his embrace. She flung her arms around his neck, holding him close while his rumbling purr filled her with delight. As his eyes met hers, a quirky little smile touched his lips. "My friends all said this would happen to me someday, and I didn't believe them. But by all the gods above—and I'm beginning to believe the gods really *do* exist—they were right. Tarq's wife, Lucy, told me how it would be once I found a mate—that your scent would drive me wild and being with me would make you insatiable. I scoffed at the idea—'a scent is a scent is a scent and it doesn't matter whose it is as long as it makes your dick hard,' I said. Jerden said I didn't understand because I'd never been in love. And damned if he wasn't right about that too." With a slow wag of his head, he added, "I'll *never* live that one down."

"I wouldn't worry about it," Kim whispered. Snagging his earlobe with a fang, she gave it a light bite. "By the time any of them get here, there'll be so much drama going on, they might not notice."

"Yeah, right," he said with a derisive snort. "Jack doesn't miss much, and neither does Cat. He'll know you're pregnant. In fact, he may already know."

"Yes, but will he tell *her* about it?"

"Maybe. Cat's an interesting character. Normally he's as honest as the day is long, but he can be devious

when it suits him." Onca grinned. "He may enjoy waiting until she's here and we can all see the look on her
face when she finds out." He turned his head. "Go ahead
and bite the other ear, babe. I love it when you do that."

"Mmm...my pleasure."

She nibbled his ear for only a moment before he captured her lips with his once again. She was hooked on
him, and he truly did make her insatiable.

"Ready to get fucked into oblivion?"

"Oh, *yeah*..."

"On the desk?"

"You bet." With his dick nestled so nicely inside her,
she hated to move. "Think you can stand up holding me
like this?"

He arched a scornful brow. "As little as you are? Of
course I can."

Seconds later, her bare bottom was perched on the
edge of the desk. "I'm impressed."

"Yeah, well, the fact that you don't weigh much more
than a puppy helps."

She patted her stomach. "Bet I'll weigh a lot more
than a puppy once these babies get bigger. I'm still having a hard time getting used to the triplet idea. How does
anyone take care of that many kids?"

Onca shrugged. "Guess we'll figure it out as we
go along."

Kim thought the topic required more discussion, but
once he began the fucking-her-into-oblivion thing, her
attention was diverted for quite a while.

This was something else she never would've expected.
Me? Insatiable?

She—who had positively disliked sex the few

times she'd tried it—was now as enamored with the
entire process as the typical Davordian. Onca wasn't
the only one who would have to eat his words. Kim
had been fairly vocal about her opinion of the sexual
act after that last failed attempt. Cassie had laughed
and said it was because she hadn't found the right
man. Kim doubted a man existed who could change
her mind.

But he *did* exist. He was right there in front of her
with pointed ears and fangs just like hers and a penis that
fit as though it was made for her. Perhaps it had been.
Perhaps he was too.

Her thoughts were diverted once again as his thrusts
became more vigorous—rocking, plunging, rotating,
and sweeping side to side. With each movement she lost
even more control of both mind and body.

Onca pulled her feet up to rest on his shoulders and
the angle altered once again, setting off new waves of
bliss. Funny, she didn't have to be with Jerden to know
that Onca was better. She knew it in her heart. He was
her mate, the only one who could give her—

His climactic cry sliced through her reverie as he
filled her with his essence.

—*joy*.

Seeing the joy in Kim's eyes extended Onca's climax
well beyond any pleasure he had ever known before.
At the Palace, he had done exactly the same thing with
up to eight women on any given day, never reaching
quite the same level of ecstasy. Was the difference due
to her pregnant state or was it simply because she was

Zetithian? His pleasure seemed to rely heavily on hers. He was satisfied, and yet he wasn't—her needs intensifying his.

How peculiar.

"Feel better now?" he asked.

Following a long, deep inhale, she nodded. "Oh, yeah—not that I was feeling terrible or anything."

"Lucy says Zetithian semen is like medicine for pregnant women—prevents morning sickness, aches, cramps—stuff like that."

"So if I feel like crap, sex with you will cure it?"

He grinned. "Convenient, isn't it? Your scent is impossible for me to resist, and you need me to get you through pregnancy without puking your guts out every morning." Onca had never considered sex to be therapeutic, but apparently, it was.

"And I'm sure you're more than willing to provide me with as much of your *snard* as I want."

"I can't imagine ever saying no to you." The truth of those words stunned him. Her lovely face, her intoxicating scent, the sound of her voice—all of those things and more—were as vital to him as the air he breathed. He pulled her up from the desk and into his arms, covering her face and neck with fervent kisses.

She threaded her fingers through the hair at his temples, somehow turning even that simple touch into a loving caress. "I can't wait to spend the night up in the trees with you. Whose idea was it to turn this place into a forest anyway?"

"Tarq's. He loves the outdoors, and he and Jerden remembered Zetith better than most of us." He shrugged. "This decor certainly sets ours apart from the other brothels in the district, but I have to take their word for it that this is what Zetith looked like."

Tipping her head to the side, she studied him with sympathetic eyes. "That bothers you, doesn't it?"

The sudden pang near his heart and the sting of tears spoke for him. Swallowing hard, he tried to turn away, but her light grasp prevented him.

She nodded slowly. "More than you're willing to admit." Her eyes took on a contemplative cast as she trailed her fingertips along the side of his face, tracing the line of his jaw. "I don't remember it, either. It was blown to bits before I was born. According to what Captain told me, if my family had been able to elude the bounty hunters for a few more months, they would probably still be alive. I wouldn't have grown up on the street, and you and I would never have met." She paused as a smile curved her lips. "At least, not like this."

He drew in a ragged, somewhat painful breath. "Then at least one good thing came out of all that tragedy." Her steady gaze soothed him like nothing else could. "I'm so sorry you lost your family, Kim. I know I can't replace them, and I don't even have a name to give you. But I—"

Tears pooled in her soft brown eyes as she pressed a finger to his lips. "How about if I give you mine?"

Chapter 29

OBVIOUSLY SHE'D BEEN RIGHT ABOUT HOW IMPORTANT his identity was to him because Kim's offer of her name brought more than tears to Onca's eyes. Deep, gut-wrenching sobs racked his body, and he clung to her like a lifeline. Stroking his hair, she spoke in soft whispers, promising her eternal love and everything that went along with it.

Every living Zetithian carried scars from their world's demise. Onca's were simply less obvious. Beneath his facade of casual indifference was a lost, wounded soul who needed love as much as anyone— perhaps even more.

Not that she'd had much experience with love herself. Her heart had been untouched when she met him, but now that she had found her mate, the attraction was impossible to deny. The bond between them was already so strong she couldn't imagine going on without him.

As his sobs subsided, she brushed away his tears. "Why can't we stay at the Palace until Jack and Leroy arrive? You said he was an arms dealer. With enough firepower, they could fight their way in here, pick us up, and take us straight to Terra Minor."

"Maybe," he conceded. "But they have their own livelihoods to consider. They're traders, and Rhylos is the hub of commerce in this sector."

"Doesn't being Zetithian count for anything? There

are so few of us left. Surely no one would risk killing more of us—would they?"

"Depends on who's calling the shots. Some people wouldn't give a damn."

"Guess that's why we need public opinion on our side."

"Yeah." He drew himself upright. "I'd better get back at it."

"Need any help?"

He winced. "I hate to say it, but we'd probably get more done if we didn't work together for now."

"You're right." With extreme reluctance, she released him and reached for her clothes. There would be plenty of time for that later.

I hope.

Truth be told, she didn't know what to expect from the days ahead. This lawyer friend of Val's seemed like the best person to help them, but since they truly didn't know who they were fighting, the outcome was anyone's guess.

"Want some lunch?" she asked.

"Sure. What've we got?"

"You'll have to ask Val. Given his fondness for nuts and berries, no telling what he's been bringing in."

Not bothering to put on his pants, Onca pulled up a chair, sat down at the desk he had so recently taken her to the stars on, and tapped into the comlink. "I'll call the Norludians. They'll know what to bring."

She bit her lip, unable to stifle a chuckle. "Maybe they should bring you some clothes."

"Not necessary," Onca replied, his gaze intent on the viewscreen. "I'm not cold."

"That's not what I meant. We have children out there.

Considering what my scent does to you, I think you'll need clothes."

The scowl he shot her should have set her on fire—and it did, although perhaps not in the manner intended. She was almost afraid to look at his dick.

"Oh, all right." He snatched up his pants, grumbling. "If I can get the damn things on, that is. Maybe I should get some of the stretchy kind Val wears."

"Stretchy might be more comfortable, but it wouldn't camouflage anything." Especially not something as hard to miss as his erection.

"True. Tight undies and a kilt might be better."

She arched a brow. "A kilt?"

"A plaid skirt worn by Scottish men on Earth. Very old school—but terribly practical, seeing as how they didn't wear anything underneath them." His cock folded neatly up against his belly as he zipped up the fly.

"How far away do I need to be for that to go back down?"

"I dunno." He glanced down at the huge bulge and shrugged. "On another planet, maybe?"

With an exasperated sigh, she headed for the door. "Not likely." She didn't even want to be in another room, let alone another planet. Being mates could be inconvenient at times.

"Kim?"

She paused in the doorway.

"Thank you. Shrovenach is a fine name. I'll try to be a credit to it."

"You already are." Smiling, she gazed at him through a shimmer of tears. "My father would've been very proud of what you've done."

"Sure he wouldn't think I'm too old for his daughter?"

"No. But he might have a problem with your tendency to harp on things that don't matter." With a wink, she added, "Work on it?"

"I'll do my best."

———

Onca wasn't sure crying like a baby was the most auspicious beginning for his new name. Then again, he didn't intend to make a habit of it.

He had never cried for the loss of his family name—or his family, for that matter. Having fond memories of people he'd never known didn't make any sense at all. Probably half the girls rescued from the Den were in the same boat. No family. No home. No names. At least their homeworlds still existed. Once he'd sorted out this mess, he would help each one of them to find their own way in whatever life they chose—on whatever planet they wished.

Dax and Jack would help. Dax specialized in taking people anywhere they wanted to go for no more than they could afford to pay, and Jack had a soft spot for strays. Now that she didn't have as many stray Zetithians to concern herself with, she might be willing to give him a hand with the orphans of other species.

In the meantime, he busied himself by calling up the Norludians for more food, ordering clothes and bedding for the children, and buying enough kitchen equipment to start a restaurant.

Rashe stood guard with his pistol in one hand and his tomahawk in the other while the jittery deliverymen installed the stove. "Bunch of chicken-shits if you ask me," he muttered as he marched them out the front entrance.

"Too bad Shemlak isn't here," Onca remarked. "We could use his help cooking for this gang."

"Shemlak?" Roncas echoed. "Darconians don't actually *cook* anything. All he does is wash the fruit and put it on a plate."

She had a point. "Guess I'm elected, then. It's been a while, but I still remember how to make enough pizza for an army."

Roncas shuddered. "Might want to stick with soup, Boss. I've tasted your pizza. Not sure their digestive systems can handle it."

"I can leave off the jalapeños," Onca insisted.

"The Scorillian wouldn't mind," Rashe pointed out. "They like spicy junk food."

"Junk food?" Onca gasped. "My pizza is *not* junk food. It's very nutritious. Tomato sauce, cheese, pepperoni, onions—"

"And about a kilo of Tumerlian pepper," Roncas said. "Took two days for the swelling in my lips to go down after the last time I tried it."

Onca threw up his hands. "On the ship we had to make do with whatever food we could get. Sometimes spicing it up was the only way to make it edible."

"Yes, but we don't have that problem now," Roncas said. "You can put all the pepper you want on yours. Just don't make the rest of us eat it."

"Oh, all right," Onca snapped. "You know, when I was a kid, we took turns doing the cooking. Might as well start now." He turned to the throng of children scattered about the grassy floor of the Palace. "Okay, gang! I need five volunteers for chef duty. Cassie, you take their names and we'll start a rotation. This is a cooperative venture, not a soup kitchen."

"Too bad we're not bringing in any money," Roncas muttered. "These kids will eat up your fortune in no time."

Onca had a feeling the current situation wouldn't last that long. "We'll cross that bridge when we get to it. Until then, we have to work together."

With any luck, the smell of baking pizza would over-power Kim's scent. Apparently the tryst in the office hadn't helped a bit because his dick still reacted with a vengeance anytime she passed by. He kept telling him-self he only needed to hold out until the kids went to sleep. Then he could be with her all night.

Damn. I sound like a parent already.

He was beginning to understand how Amelyana must have felt with so many children in her care. Granted, she hadn't done it alone—her Zetithian mate and another Terran couple had helped her—but the children had all seen her as their mother. She had dedicated her entire life to them, working tirelessly to keep them safe—even stealing when she had to—and doing her best to see that they were educated.

Onca spent the rest of the afternoon teaching the new cooks, thankful that he had something to occupy his mind—even something as simple as kneading pizza dough—otherwise the sense of unease would've been unbearable. Anara had given him no instructions, only telling Val that she would study the case while en route to Damenk. It was like waiting for a verdict he was powerless to influence.

At least, not *yet*.

—⁓—

Darkness fell over the Palace, leaving only the stars twinkling overhead as Kim gazed out over the sea of sleeping children, knowing that, like herself, they probably felt safer than they had in years—perhaps even for the first time.

Onca had given them that security. He was a hero to these young souls, whether he saw himself as such or not. True, he'd had help, but that didn't matter to them. *He* was the one who had gone into the Den alone. *He* was the one who had welcomed the slave girls and every other homeless child into the Palace, giving them more in one day than most of them had ever had in their entire lives. He was the one who had rescued *her*, capturing her heart and teaching her what it meant to love and be loved in return.

He'd kept one riser clear, and as she stepped onto the grassy platform, he activated the controls that took them up into the trees. Hovering high above the forest floor, they were alone, isolated on an island in the sky, surrounded by rustling leaves and tiny, winking lights.

"Oh, wow," she whispered. "The lights…are they alive?"

Onca shook his head. "The butterflies are real, but the lights aren't. They're supposed to be like fireflies. I've never seen the real ones. They're indigenous to Earth—something Amelyana told us about. We thought it would add a nice touch."

Kim agreed. The effect was magical, making the building an attraction in and of itself. "You know, people would probably pay good money to spend the night here," she said, recalling Shemlak's comment.

"I thought about that—which is another reason I haven't sold it yet."

"Do you think it could generate enough income to take care of all these kids?"

"I doubt it—at least, not the kind of money we made when there were three of us working here. We installed six platforms, hoping to recruit more guys from the ship— but no such luck. They were smarter than we were."

"How so?"

He rolled his eyes. "They found mates—and they weren't as greedy."

"Was it truly greed?"

"Maybe not," he admitted. "Growing up on a ship where the men outnumber the women kinda skews your perspective." He paused, frowning. "Did I ever tell you—? No, I don't suppose I did, although you might've guessed it. The girls on the ship never wanted me, and when Jerden came up with the idea, I jumped at the chance. I've never really been sure why. I wasn't the only virgin on that ship when it landed. We used to call Dax the Great Virgin—and he did just the opposite of what I did. Of course, his problem was that very few women ever smelled good to him, so he had no choice but to wait for the right girl. I fucked anyone willing to pay a thousand credits."

"I can't imagine anyone not wanting you as her mate."

He shrugged. "Maybe it was because they knew I didn't care whether they wanted me or not." His gaze shifted to become fixed on hers, his eyes shining in the darkness. "But I *did* care. My fault was in caring too much."

Kim understood him now. She had known the love

of a family—her mother had sacrificed her own life to save her daughter's—but Onca hadn't. He might have grown up knowing what his parents had done to save him, but the *idea* of being loved wasn't quite the same as the actual experience. Being one child among many, he'd never known the kind of unconditional love children need in order to thrive. Never having received it, he had shunned that love as something he didn't want and didn't need—but he craved it anyway.

"I'm not sure it's possible to care too much. How do you feel now?"

"Like I've finally found what I was looking for—*you*."

Holding out her arms, she smiled. "Then you *have* been waiting for me. You just didn't know it."

———~~~———

In an instant, Onca was in her embrace, covering her face with desperate kisses, holding her close as heat surged through him like a wildfire. Kim was his. He couldn't lose her now.

"We'll get through this," he promised. "Then we can be together forever."

He had no idea how long it would take. Being apart from her for a day or even an hour was unbearable, but he could endure anything as long as she would be waiting for him.

Lying on a grassy bower beneath the stars, he found solace in her smile, warmth in her embrace, and love in her kisses. She had changed him. In that one brief, shining moment when her eyes first met his, his fate had been sealed, his destiny determined. The past was forgotten. Their love for each other was all that mattered now.

Her touch excited as well as soothed him as she removed his clothing with tiny, deft fingers. She only looked like a fragile flower. There was fire and steel in her, and yet she had a softness about her that beckoned to him as he pushed her own clothing aside. As she welcomed him into the place where he was loved, her heat surrounded him, imbuing every stroke, every thrust, and every touch with pleasure.

When she reached her first climax, her slick inner muscles tightened around him, her scent engulfing him like a tidal wave. Purring, he let his cock dance slowly inside her, eliciting even more moans of passion and delight. He captured her lips with a kiss, tasting their sweetness before moving down the slope of her neck to her shoulder. Her delicate breasts begged for his caress, and he teased her nipples, noting that they already seemed larger, darker than before.

Her sharp inhale made him pause. "I'm not hurting you, am I?"

She dispelled that fear with a vigorous shake of her head. "No. Don't stop. That feels..." Her voice trailed off as she fisted her hands in his hair. "...incredible."

His cock slipped from her sheath as her scent drew him downward, seeking its source and the flavor that was inherently her own. As he flicked her clitoris with his tongue, she arched up from the grassy bed, giving him greater access to her intoxicating essence.

"And you *taste* incredible."

"Mmm...so do you." She gave his hair a tug. "Think you could turn around?"

Onca wasn't sure he could budge from the spot, but she was his mate. Refusing her was impossible. Growling, he rose up on his hands and knees and crawled over her. With the first touch of her lips on his cock, his head snapped back, sending his hair flying as his breath hissed in through his teeth.

Kim closed her mouth over his cockhead, sucking gently at first, then harder, raking the shaft with her fangs. Gliding her tongue along the coronal flange, she traced each serration, driving him to the edge of madness. A gentle bite to the head sent more of his coronal fluid gushing into her mouth, and she snarled as the orgasmic juice worked its magic, her hips curling up until her knees hit his shoulders. Mouth open wide, he went down on her pussy, devouring her like the delectable treat she was.

Unable to decide which was better—her mouth on him or his lips on her—he suckled her clit, doing his best to get her to explode before he lost his mind. She crossed her legs behind his neck, forcing his head down and his hips up. A puff of her breath on his scrotum stopped his protest before it began, her purr the only warning as she sucked a testicle into her mouth.

Onca stifled his ecstatic cry, not wishing to awaken any of those who lay sleeping far beneath them. Her hands were everywhere at once—stroking his cock, caressing his skin, dragging her nails over his bottom. Releasing her hold on his upper body, she let her legs slip past his ears as he rose upright on his knees. Wiggling his hips, he set his genitals swaying, brushing her face with his nuts, doing his best to entice her to—

"Bite me."

His balls twitched in anticipation as the night winds rustled the leaves surrounding the platform and wafted over his wet cock. With a snarl, she sank her fangs into the thick muscle just above his thigh, igniting yet another inferno of desire. His chin snapped upward, his hair tickling his buttocks and possibly her face.

Her face…

Reversing his position, he gazed into her fiery eyes as he lowered the tip of his cock to her lips. Her breath on his moist skin made him shiver, and the swipe of her tongue made him groan. Falling forward onto his hands, he fucked her mouth until he came, filling her with his cream. She swallowed—nearly taking his dick down her throat—then pushed him back and licked the remaining *snard* from his cockhead.

"Don't worry," he said. "There's plenty more where that came from."

"Good. Lie down on your back. I want to ride that rascal."

Onca sprawled beside her, waiting for her to mount him. Her lips curved into a smile as she straddled his hips, gazing down at him through pupils as round and glowing as hot embers.

"Mother of the gods," he whispered. "You're beautiful."

She shook her head. "No. You're the beautiful one—lying there with your hair all fanned out like that." She ran a hand through her own curls. "Should I let mine get that long?"

"If you like. Either way, you'll still be beautiful."

With a wink, she settled herself down on his cock. "Bet I look even better now."

"Not possible."

She began a steady, undulating movement of her hips. "How about now?"

"Nope. Still the same."

The tension began building within him again, faster and more powerfully than he had ever imagined. The swiftness of it stole his breath, making his head spin.

"Now?"

He gritted his teeth. "Not yet."

Time stood still as her body squeezed his with an orgasm that seemed to go on forever, her sighs filling him with elation and wonder. His own pinnacle was already in sight, and he gazed up at her, fighting to maintain his vision, his sanity.

When the moment of ecstasy came at last, his soul seemed to expand to encompass the entire universe—a universe of which she was the center.

"Now?"

He nodded. "Now."

Chapter 30

ANARA'S ADVICE WAS SIMPLE. "KEEP IT PUBLIC."

Onca hoped she meant talking to reporters rather than walking out of the Palace naked. That sort of exposure had ceased to be good for business several days ago. "How so?"

"Don't turn yourself in at the police station," she replied. "Tell them you'll meet them in front of the Palace later this afternoon. We'll be ready for them."

Anara Threlkind had arrived without fanfare, flanked by her two husbands, Lor and San. Tall, dark, and strikingly handsome, the men could have passed for identical twins, but were, in fact, clones of the same man, each possessing the same curly hair, green eyes, hawk-like noses, and cleft chins of the original. Anara appeared to be several years older than her spouses, though with her lush figure and thick brown hair, she was still quite beautiful.

"I think I can guarantee a big crowd," Roncas said. "I have an idea."

Noting the significant lift of the Zuteran's brow, Onca was almost afraid to ask. "What *kind* of idea?"

"I'd rather not say just yet," she replied. "I think the element of surprise will make it more effective."

Onca stared at her. "I don't know you at all, do I?"

"Better than you realize," Roncas said. "I'm a devious little bird."

"I knew *that*, but—"

"It doesn't matter how you get a crowd—or even the nature of it," Anara said. "All that matters is that there are enough to make a scene."

Roncas twittered. "I can promise you that."

"I'll need access to your information, Onca," Anara went on. "Immigration records, deeds, bank statements." She glanced at Kim. "And you, as well—full name, birth date, that sort of thing. Were you born on Rhylos?"

"Why does any of that matter?" Onca demanded as Kim nodded her reply.

Anara appeared to take no notice of his question. "Good. We should be able to find the records then—and I'll need you to sign a few things."

Onca was still in the dark, but Anara didn't seem inclined to enlighten him beyond commenting that she believed in being prepared for any eventuality.

"Yeah, right. Sounds like you're just making it easier for them to deport us."

Anara winked, favoring him with a slow, secretive smile. "Perhaps." Her attention returned to Kim. "You're pregnant, aren't you?"

"Mother of the gods!" Onca exclaimed. "How the hell could you possibly know that?"

"I didn't," Anara replied. "But you just confirmed it."

Onca gaped at her in dismay before rounding on Val. "And she's actually going to *help* us?"

Val didn't reply, merely regarding him with an arched brow and a flap of his wings.

"Don't just stand there ruffling your feathers at me," Onca growled. "I want—"

"Might be best to go with the flow, dude," Rashe

advised. "Something tells me she knows exactly what she's doing. And, um, congratulations."

"Thanks. Kim says there are two boys and a girl. Not sure how she knows that, but—oh, what the hell." Onca turned away, grumbling. "When you're ready to fill me in on the particulars, I'll be in my office." He stormed off, doing his best to ignore Roncas's twittering laughter.

He liked the idea that Anara believed in being prepared for anything; he only wished she was a little less cryptic. Originally a divorce lawyer excelling in getting the most for her clients, she had also been instrumental in establishing clone rights. She seemed savvy enough. She had already tricked him into admitting that Kim was expecting—a circumstance he'd thought it best to keep mum about until the legal crap was settled.

Kim didn't even follow him into the office. A glance at the window showed her still talking to Anara. Heaving a weary sigh, he sat down at the desk and began searching through his files. He found a copy of the deed to the Palace in a drawer, but the other documents Anara had requested were online—easily accessible with his identification chip. What was sad was that there were so few records to access. His life hadn't truly begun until Rutger Grekkor's death made it safe for the refugee ship to land. Before that, there was no proof of his existence anywhere. The officials on Terra Minor had assigned him a date of birth during the immigration process. His place of birth was simply listed as Zetith—the city and region unknown.

He still wasn't sure why Anara needed similar information from Kim—although he couldn't argue that it was best for her to know everything about him and everyone involved. Surprises of that sort in a courtroom could be costly.

Too bad this wasn't Zetith. Kim would already be considered his mate there. Here on Rhylos, she was only his girlfriend. Then again, maybe no one would care that he'd only known her three days before impregnating her.

Yeah, right.

He couldn't see that chain of events impressing anyone—except maybe Jack. If she hadn't intended to marry Kim off to one of her sons, she would have been tickled to death.

Funny how things turn out.

Anara might be able to put a "love at first sight" spin on his relationship with Kim, but he could also see the Herp's lawyer having a field day with it. He doubted the story would arouse much sympathy from a judge— especially if the bad guys had any influence within the judicial system. Given all that had happened thus far, he suspected they did.

The Herp's assault charge didn't worry him overmuch—how long a sentence could a person possibly get for beating up a Herp, anyway? On the other hand, inciting a riot might earn him some serious jail time. Deportation would be welcome, except that he would be kicked off the planet without a single credit to his name.

Unfortunately, none of those options would help them find Dalmet. Kim would never forgive him if he failed to exhaust every possibility to find her friend, nor would he forgive himself. Unsolved kidnappings caused sleepless nights for a lot of people. He was no different.

He scanned the deed and put it in a file along with the rest of his credentials and sent it to Anara's inbox.

Then he called the police.

———⁓⁓———

Kim eyed Roncas with skepticism. "Are you sure this will work? I mean, I know it'll draw a crowd, but I doubt it's the right kind."

"Anara said it didn't matter," the Zuteran replied. "And I'm taking her at her word. All we have to do is publicize it a bit." She paused, frowning. "Think you could get some pictures for me? For the ad, I mean."

If she was referring to the kind of pictures Kim guessed they were, Roncas had better *not* want them for herself. "Okay. But you'll have to give me a camera. Unlike everyone else on this planet, street people don't have that sort of thing on them at all times."

"No problem. Oh, and a headshot will do. I hate to admit it—and I've done my best to keep him from getting too cocky—but he *is* rather attractive."

"*Now* she tells me," Kim muttered. "Thanks for keeping him humble—although I'm not sure your efforts were necessary. The best I can tell, he has more reasons to be insecure than cocky."

"You weren't around when he was working. The way his clients used to look at him, trust me, he was in danger of becoming *lethally* cocky."

Kim could understand the looks he would've gotten, but cocky? Probably not. "Whatever. Just find me a camera and let's get on with it."

———⁓⁓———

Onca sat in his office trying to decide whether to risk getting anywhere near Kim again. His dick still ached from when she had popped in to take a few pictures—presumably to remember him by while he was locked up in the slammer. Or maybe she wanted them so their children would know what their father looked like. Either way, he was beginning to suspect a dismal future.

Roncas stuck her head in the door. "Hey, Boss, could you come here for a minute?"

Something in her tone made him fear the worst. Undoubtedly the police were already there, itching to clap him in irons and throw him in the dungeon or to the wolves or whatever it was they did to people who incited riots. "What's up?"

She motioned for him to accompany her. "Come on. You need to see this."

With a great deal of trepidation, he followed her to the main entrance. Pushing the door open, Roncas took his hand and led him outside.

A sea of females of every species imaginable erupted into a cheer as he crossed the threshold onto the landing at the head of the broad steps that led down to the street. Several of the ladies waved signs with his picture on them. Two women held a banner that read, *We love you, Onca!*

"Holy shit, Roncas! What the hell did you put in those ads?"

Roncas shrugged. "You said to drum up support. So I'm running a contest."

His eyes widened as he spotted Ganyn passing out tickets. "*Please* tell me the tickets are free."

Roncas nodded. "All they had to do was show up

and get a ticket for the chance to win a free fuck." She glanced at her watch. "Almost time for the drawing."

Onca groaned. "But I'm *retired*." Not to mention being mated to Kim. He wouldn't have been able to get it up for any of them—whether he wanted to or not. And he certainly didn't want to.

She nodded at the crowd. "Yes, but *they* don't know that."

Roncas waved her hands for silence, then held up a glass bowl filled with ticket stubs. "My young friend here will now draw the winning number."

An expectant hush fell over the crowd as Han came forward and stuck his hand into the bowl. Drawing out a ticket, he held it up. "Twenty-one eighty-seven!"

A squeal came from the center of the crowd. "I won!"

Before Onca had the chance to spot the winner, several police officers shouldered their way through the crowd. Coming to a halt at the foot of the steps, their leader pointed his weapon at Onca.

"So, the Zetithian man-whore hides behind children now?" he sneered. "That's even worse than hiding behind the skirts of women."

Onca knew the bastard was only taunting him into doing something rash—a ploy that might have worked if Val hadn't swooped down from the sky to land lightly at his side.

"And you, who stood by while innocent young women were raped and enslaved, have no claim to integrity," Val said. "We will not allow you to take him."

Onca had to admit, with his icy eyes and outstretched wings, Val was almost as intimidating as a pissed-off Darconian. The pistol in his hand was incidental.

Moments later, Jatki and Shemlak closed in behind the police along with about twenty more children and several other adults he didn't recognize—although judging from their rapt attention and recording devices, he assumed they were the reporters.

A smile touched Onca's lips as he locked eyes with Shemlak, who winked.

Anara came out to stand beside him, flanked, as always, by Lor and San. "You cannot take him without legal counsel. I shall accompany him."

"But what about my free fuck?" a familiar voice called out.

Following the sound, Onca spotted Kim in the crowd, grinning up at him.

"You'll have to wait until he gets out of jail," the policeman shouted back. "And you might be waiting a very long time."

A tall woman with short dark hair stood next to Kim. "Yeah, well, we'll see about that, bucko. You'd better take damn good care of him. He's one of the few Zetithians left in the galaxy—and you know what happens to people who harm members of an endangered species. The ZPA comes after them with a vengeance."

"ZPA?" the cop retorted. "Never heard of it."

"The Zetithian Protection Agency." Jack Tshevnoe patted the butt of her pistol. "That's me."

Onca rolled his eyes. "Take it easy, Jack. I'm not dead yet."

"And it's my job to see that you stay that way." Raising her voice, Jack addressed the crowd. "Ladies, I believe our friend Onca needs an escort to the police station. Shall we proceed?"

Chapter 31

ALONG THE WAY TO THE NEAREST POLICE STATION, more people joined in, giving the event all the trappings of a protest march. Onca led the procession with Jack and Anara. The police were obviously trying to at least appear to be the ones in charge, but they didn't fool anyone. Kim suspected Onca's arrest would turn out to be more of a formality than anything—or so she hoped.

Deeming it best to keep a low profile, she stayed back in the crowd, making the trek alongside Jatki and Shemlak. After hugging her friend until her joints popped, Kim asked about the night of the raid.

"Shemlak had to fight off the Herps that chased me," Jatki replied. "He figures that's when he lost his comlink. After that, we were running along together, and you won't believe where we wound up."

Considering the part of town they'd been in, Kim made a reasonable guess. "A brothel?"

"A *Darconian* brothel! The ladies spotted Shemlak and practically dragged him inside. You should've seen it. The place was *huge*—built of something called shepra stone and lit up with glowstones. It was like walking into a temple."

Kim chuckled. "What do they call that one? The Darconian Palace?"

"Yeah. Said they got the idea from the

Zetithians—only they say it looks more like a palace than Onca's place does. What's his brothel like?"

"More of a forest than a palace. It's pretty cool, actually."

Jatki nodded toward Onca. "How come you aren't up there with him?"

Kim cleared her throat, unsure of how much to say within the hearing of others. "I'm something of a distraction at the moment. It's best for me to keep downwind of him."

Shemlak barked out a laugh. "Bet I can guess why."

"Keep your suspicions to yourself for now," Kim advised. "If these ladies learn the truth, they might decide to desert him in his hour of need."

Shemlak swept his eyes over the crowd. "Not much chance of that. But if the police try to rough him up, they're liable to have a *real* riot on their hands." With an expression of chagrin, he added, "Wish women liked me that much."

Jatki stared at him, her wide mouth open in surprise. "Those Darconian ladies seemed pretty taken with you. They lied to the cops and everything."

Shemlak coughed as though he'd choked on more than his own spit. "Yeah, well, the less said about that, the better. Wouldn't want my wife to hear of it."

"Shemlak, you didn't!" Kim gasped.

"No," he replied. "But the temptation was strong."

Kim walked on for several minutes without further comment. She had other questions for Shemlak, none of which concerned his behavior in a brothel. "I have a confession to make," she finally said. "I suspected you of working with the enemy when we realized Draddut was still wearing that tracking device."

"Figured you'd think that," he said. "I wasn't working with them, but I did hope one of those creeps would try jumping Draddut. That way we would've known who we were dealing with. It was a calculated risk that backfired—a mistake I've been trying to make up for ever since."

Kim shrugged. "It might end up being a good move in the long run, but Onca was pretty upset at the time, and so was I. Ganyn swore you weren't that kind of man—and we believed her—but you've got to admit, it looked bad."

"He saved me," Jatki said as though that one act absolved Shemlak of any other misdeeds—and perhaps it did.

"I was more worried about you than anyone else," Kim said, noting that Jatki's skin had turned slightly yellow.

"Those Herps almost got me." She shuddered, cracking her knuckles in earnest. "I would've died if they'd locked me up in one of those places."

"No, you wouldn't," Kim said. "We'd have found you somehow. Just like we'll find Dalmet."

"Are you sure about that?" Jatki asked. "What if she's been sold offworld? For all we know, she might even be dead."

"That's what we're gonna find out." Kim laid a hand on her friend's shoulder. "We'll find her, Jatki. And we'll make sure no more girls are kidnapped off the street here ever again."

"I hope you're right. Scary business, though."

"Our entire lives have been scary. What we're doing now will change that."

If it doesn't destroy me completely.

Kim listened with half an ear as Jatki and Shemlak regaled her with the rest of their adventures. They'd both been a tremendous help, and she thanked them, but her mind had shifted to the man leading the march. A man she might never see again.

Losing Onca now would kill her. At least, she thought it might. Audrey's death hadn't killed Jerden, but Kim had heard enough of the story to know it had messed him up for quite a while. She wasn't sure she would even *want* to go on living without Onca. Maybe that was it. The loss of a mate wasn't lethal; it simply removed the will to live.

She reminded herself that Onca hadn't committed murder. He had done nothing but defend himself. No one had been killed during the so-called riot. Under ordinary circumstances, his punishment, if any, would be minor.

But the circumstances weren't ordinary.

Someone unknown but extremely powerful was doing their best to make an example of him—making sure that no one else tried to instigate the changes that would eliminate the Den and other brothels like it.

If only they knew who that someone was. Jatki had suggested that they follow the money to discover the identity of the ringleader. Thus far, they hadn't been able to do that. Anara might get the charges against Onca dropped, but that wouldn't solve the real problem. They needed someone on their side who was as powerful as the opposition.

Somehow, Kim didn't think it was Jack Tshevnoe.

Onca didn't have to look back to know where Kim was. He knew her precise location and could even sense her mood. She was uneasy but determined.

Plucky little woman.

He understood her reasons for not walking beside him, and though it was kind of her to consider his comfort, the only thing her actions did was keep his dick soft. Nothing else was affected in any way. She was his mate, and he felt lost without her. With backing like this, his chances of the police locking him up and throwing away the key were unlikely. Still, any kind of separation from Kim was abhorrent to him—no matter how brief.

"She's cute."

Jack's words may have startled him from his reverie, but he didn't pretend to misunderstand her. "Larry can eat his heart out."

"He'll get over it," Jack said.

"Where is he, by the way?"

"Ha! The less you know the better. Let's just say I didn't put all of my eggs in one basket."

"I don't suppose Lerotan or Dax have shown up."

Jack snorted a laugh. "Neither of their ships are a match for mine, but they'll be here soon enough."

Onca disagreed. "Yesterday would've been better."

"Hey, at least neither of them was making the run to Darconia, or they'd take weeks getting here. No worries, though—well, *almost* none. Kim told me her Levitian friend wasn't at the Den. Any idea where she might have been taken?"

"Not really—although Rashe said there are other brothels like that one."

"Any that cater to Levitians?"

"I doubt it," Onca replied. "Levitian culture has no history of prostitution or male dominance—they're a lot like Zetithians that way."

"Yeah, well, you and your buddies kinda broke with tradition there," Jack reminded him.

"Maybe. But if Levitians *did* have brothels, they'd be more like the Palace than the Den." Although, to the best of his knowledge, Onca had never done a Levitian woman. Not a single, solitary one. "What I mean is if anyone wanted a Levitian sex slave, it wouldn't be another Levitian."

Pursing her lips, Jack nodded. "The only Levitians I've ever known have been doctors or policemen—peculiar personalities, perhaps, but inherently honest. Can't imagine any of them putting girls in cages."

"Me, either. Hell, the majority of this city's officials are Levitian—and on the whole, Damenk is better run than most places. I can only think of a few offhand that—" Onca gasped as the pieces of the puzzle fell into place.

Mother of the gods…

"What?" Jack prompted.

"The police chief and the director of the brothel guild are both Terran."

"Well, what do you know?" Jack let out a low whistle. "Sounds interesting—maybe even a little fishy."

"You think? And now I'm headed off to jail with a bunch of—" He glanced over his shoulder, hoping the cops weren't listening. Obviously some of them had to be on the take, but the chief of police? *Can't say Rashe didn't warn me.* "See what you can dig up on those two. They just might be the ones behind this."

"No problem. I'll get Larry on the horn to Leroy and

have him do some checking. He knows some pretty shady characters who know a lot of other shady characters. I've met a few crooks myself. For example, the Nerik who sold you that speeder. I'm guessing his name was Veluka—right?"

Onca nodded reluctantly. "How is that significant?"

Jack chuckled. "Just proves my point. You Zetithian boys are so honest, you wouldn't know a scam if it hit you in the face—not streetwise at all. I'm guessing Levitian politicians are the same way. When it comes to corruption, they can't see the forest for the trees."

Whether he disagreed or not, Onca knew it was pointless to argue with Jack when she was on a roll—and from her indulgent smile, she apparently considered that honesty to be a large part of Zetithian charm.

Whatever.

He scanned the surrounding area and the street ahead. "Speaking of Zetithian boys, where's Cat? I didn't think you could be more than a few meters away from him without freaking out."

"Don't you worry about Cat. I know *exactly* where he is." Closing her eyes, she inhaled deeply. "I always do."

From that, Onca guessed that her husband was nearby, which undoubtedly meant that others of her crew were also within range. He had protection he couldn't even *see*—none of which would help him if he was attacked while in police custody. The station loomed ahead, making Onca feel as though he was being marched to the gallows. Lowering his voice, he said, "Got any ideas for helping me survive in there?"

"Matter of fact, I do," she murmured.

Trust Jack to be prepared.

When she came to a halt at the foot of the police station steps, Jack held out her hand. "Well, I guess this is it." With a firm handshake, she pressed two small stones into his palm. "Take care of yourself, bucko. We'll be rooting for you."

"Thanks for your help, Jack." He slid his hand into his pocket, grimacing as one of the officers grabbed his other arm.

"No rough stuff," Anara warned. "Or we'll press charges."

With a snarl, the officer released Onca and motioned for them to precede him into the station.

Onca knew exactly what to do with the stones. What he *didn't* know was whether or not they would show up on a scan.

If they did, he was screwed.

—∿∿—

Once Onca and Anara had disappeared inside the police station, Kim started talking to the reporters, telling them everything except the part about being Onca's pregnant mate. Rather than professing her love for him, she described in detail how he'd found her and taken her in. She told them of Roncas's involvement and Jatki's rescue, relating the facts without embellishment, leaving it to those who'd been imprisoned in the Den for the more graphic aspects of the tale. Each and every one of the former slaves painted Onca as a hero and the staff, clients, and owners of the Den as evil villains.

The reporters lapped up the stories as though nothing newsworthy had happened in years. They seemed sympathetic—the attack on Kim's family and her subsequent life on the street reduced some of them to tears—but their sincerity had yet to be confirmed, nor were they the ones responsible for enforcing the law.

And the police were definitely involved.

Kim hated the idea of turning Onca over to the cops when at least some of them held a grudge against him. She couldn't decide where he would be in the most danger—in jail or walking the streets. Still, the girls remained, and their stories were far more incriminating than any evidence Onca might give.

Unless they chose to kill him for revenge. Kim had lost everyone she'd ever loved because of money. Even if the police only questioned Onca and let him go, a price on his head would send all sorts of assassins gunning for him. He wouldn't be safe until they found the ringleader and put him out of business for good. She felt rather vengeful herself, but revenge wouldn't bring a dead man back. Death was final.

Unless it was staged.

If his death could be faked, everyone would stop looking for him. They would give up and—

She glanced up as Anara descended the steps from the station.

The lawyer's tight lips and narrowed eyes didn't bode well. "I did my damnedest, but they insisted on keeping him—for his own protection." She snorted in disgust. "I'll file an appeal, but God only knows how long it will take a judge to act on it."

"Guess we'd better get back to the Palace, then." Jack tapped a small stone pinned to her collar. "Okay, Cat. Let's roll."

"What about going to Onca's house instead?" Kim

suggested. "He's got a really smart computer who might be able to help."

"Good idea," Anara said. "We need all the computing power we can get. Rashe and Roncas can take care of the kids at the Palace. Val can do some checking from the computer there."

"We'll need Onca's speeder to access Captain," Kim said. "Otherwise, I have a feeling we might never get into the house."

"No worries," Jack said as four speeders approached. "Tisana is bringing it."

Two of the speeders were piloted by Zetithian men, while a Terran woman with dark hair and green eyes flew Onca's vehicle. Lor and San were in the fourth speeder, which presumably belonged to Anara.

"That gorgeous hunk is Cat," Jack said, indicating a man with black hair and a deep scar on his cheek. "The blond dude is Leo, and that's his wife, Tisana. Figured we might need an armed escort."

"I certainly wouldn't turn it down," Kim said. "I just wish we had some way to protect Onca." She shivered, remembering the horror of finding him beaten nearly senseless by that Herpatronian thug. If the cops didn't want to get their hands dirty, other prisoners could be bribed to rough him up or even kill him.

"No worries," Jack said with a wink. "Got a few tricks up my sleeve, but Onca's no dummy. If he keeps his head...well...he'll keep his head."

"Whatever *that* means," Kim muttered.

Cat chuckled. "I will explain later." He hesitated, cocking his head to one side as he peered at Kim. "Two boys and a girl?"

Jack let out a yelp as though Cat had pinched her. "Son of a fuckin' bitch! You mean to tell me—"

"Nothing," Kim snapped. "Nothing at all. At least, not yet."

Kim had seen loved ones used as pawns before, and even Jatki had been bait for a trap. Onca's life was at stake, and she didn't want their love or their children to be used as the means to manipulate him or anyone else.

"But Cat is *never* wrong," Jack insisted. "I just—"

She glared at Jack, praying she got the message before anyone else who might be listening figured it out. "Not. Yet."

Chapter 32

ONCA EYED THE SCANNER WITH CONSIDERABLE APPRE-hension. The stones Jack had given him might not be noticed in a physical search, but a scanner could still pick them up.

The officer stationed at the monitor motioned for him to pass through the device. Resisting the inclination to run through the archway, he sauntered to the other side.

"All clear."

Unable to believe his good fortune, he glanced at the officer for further confirmation and received, of all things, a sly wink.

Momentarily stunned, he took in the man's square, ridged jaw and had to swallow a gasp.

He's Levitian.

Jack's comment about Levitian honesty took on new meaning. Onca had already decided that their enemies probably weren't Levitian, but did that also mean they were potential allies? Had he ever mentioned to the press or the police that Dalmet was Levitian? He was pretty sure he had, and if so, this man would undoubtedly take his side in a fight. There might even be others like him.

"Thanks." He peered at the Levitian's badge. "Officer Lembic." The smile Onca gave him was genu-ine enough, but it wasn't returned.

Clearly Lembic saw no point in giving himself away. Then again, perhaps any Levitian officers were unaware of the corruption in their midst. If they had known, they might have already blown the whistle or been drummed out of the force. About the best Onca could hope for was that they would tend to be sympathetic to his cause.

After being issued prison clothing—happily, the pants were larger than those he had on—he was escorted to his cell. A casual hand in his pocket, a wipe of his lips, and the stones were easily hidden between his cheek and gum. They wouldn't help him escape or offer much in the way of protection, but at least he would always have light and a means of communication with the outside.

The Terran guard who locked him in his cell was unnecessarily rough about shoving him inside, and a few of the other prisoners jeered. While he did have some privacy—there was a partition in front of the toilet area—there were no walls or doors facing the main corridor, only force fields.

Guess I'll have to talk to Jack from the bathroom.

Any support from the other inmates seemed unlikely since a large percentage were Herps and Racks. He spotted several Davordians, Vessonians, and Terrans—along with a few other species he didn't even recognize—but no Levitians whatsoever.

Never realized they were quite so law-abiding.

His cell boasted only one bunk, a tiny table, and one chair, which meant he'd been spared a cellmate. The mattress was reasonably comfortable, and with nothing better to do, he stretched out on it to take a nap.

He was awakened a few hours later by the arrival of the evening meal and was about to take a bite of baked fish when a voice from out of nowhere said, "Don't eat that."

Glancing around, he saw no one.

"Oh, I see," he said. "Instead of poisoning me, you're going to scare me into starving myself to death?"

"Don't be ridiculous. Hold on."

Moments later, Officer Lembic appeared with a tray. "Don't take food from anyone but me, understand?"

"How do I know you're not the one with the poison?"

"You don't."

"My, how reassuring," Onca drawled. "And I should trust you because…?"

"You know why." Deactivating a slot in the force field, the tall Levitian pushed the tray onto the table. "Give me that one."

Considering Onca wasn't terribly fond of fish, he didn't have any qualms about trading it for a salami and cheese sandwich and a bag of Twilanan cookies.

"Pumpkin spice. My favorite. Thanks."

"Don't mention it. Word is you won't live long enough to go to trial. I'm making it my job to see that you do."

"Setting yourself up as my bodyguard?"

"If I have to." Leaning down from his superior height, Lembic spoke directly through the slot, keeping his voice low. "I read that article about how you're still looking for a Levitian girl named Dalmet. I have a cousin by that name."

Onca almost choked on a cookie. "The same girl?"

"No. But she could be." Lembic clenched his teeth, accentuating the bony ridges of his jaw. "Although I don't see how that other Dalmet ever wound up on the street in the first place. Seems strange for one of us to be orphaned and homeless. Someone would've taken her in. You're sure she's Levitian?"

"I've never actually seen her, but Kim said she was. She was the second of Kim's friends to disappear. We found the other two at the Den." He took a moment to consider his options before deciding it was worth the risk. "You might ask some of your buddies about that."

Lembic's gaze narrowed. "You think the police force is somehow involved with that abomination?"

"Think about it," Onca replied. "Who else would be in a position to make sure I don't go to trial?"

Lembic grinned, revealing his sharply pointed teeth. "Can you identify them?"

"Maybe, but Val would be the best one to ask—you know, the Avian clone? He's got an uncanny memory and incredible eyesight. He's probably gone back to the Palace."

Lembic nodded. "I'll speak with him. In the meantime, call me if you need me." In a seemingly insignificant gesture, he rubbed a fingertip behind his ear, drawing Onca's attention to a small, beaded earring.

Onca raised his brow in comprehension. Clearly he wasn't the only one carrying a Darconian comstone. "I'll do that."

―⁓―

"I managed to arrange for him to be in a cell by himself," Anara said. "Which only means they can't coerce his cellmate into killing him. Unfortunately, it also makes it easier for one of the guards to do it."

Kim wasn't sure whether to scream or throw up.

Although she'd felt increasingly queasy ever since Onca went into the police station, at the moment, her frustration level overrode it. "We've got to figure out a way to get him out of there."

"That's what we're doing," Anara assured her. "I'm trying to find a judge who'll rescind the order to keep him in protective custody." Her emphasis on those last two words was indicative of just how poorly *protected* she believed him to be.

Captain had let them into Onca's house without question, and though he had been given several tasks, he had yet to discover any useful information. Jack sent a message to Lerotan asking him to check with his contacts in the slave trade in an attempt to discover the identity of the ringleader. His ship was still almost a day away, but he promised to do some digging. Val was at the Palace, trying to hack into anything that might help them find Dalmet. Jack had told them about the two stones she had given Onca, but made the comment that he would have to use the comstone to contact *her*, rather than the other way around.

"No telling who else might be there with him."

Kim was within a hairsbreadth of snatching Jack's comstone and using it herself, just so she could hear his voice. She was back to that desperate, powerless feeling she'd had when her buddies first began disappearing. She needed to act, to *do* something, but there wasn't anything for her to do but wait.

Drifting into Onca's bedroom, she curled up on the bed. His scent still lingered on the sheets, offering her a little comfort. How long would it be before that aroma was reduced to a memory? Would she still remember his face when he was gone?

No. She couldn't allow herself to think that. *Never give up hope.*

Not yet, anyway. She wanted him there beside her. Not locked up in a prison cell—a cell he would leave only when he went to trial—or when he died.

She blinked back tears, staring blankly at the ceiling with its pattern of glowstones. Even if he was hurt, he would go into the regenerative sleep and heal himself the way Zetithians usually did.

A sleep that might mimic death—at least, to the uninitiated.

Or someone they could trust…

Kim scrambled from the bed and ran into the kitchen where most of the others sat at the table in front of a computer or a comlink. She spoke first to Anara. "If Onca were to get sick or die, what would they do with him?"

Anara frowned. "He would be taken to the infirmary for treatment. If pronounced dead, he would then be taken to the morgue for examination."

"Where's the infirmary? In the police station?"

"No. The nearest one is several blocks away. They would have to load him into an ambulance and take him there."

"Holy shit," Jack whispered. "We could hijack it."

"Breaking him out of jail would get him in even more trouble," Anara pointed out.

The comlink chimed, and Jack answered it.

Val's icy glare stared out of the viewscreen. "You'll never guess who just called me."

Jack snorted a laugh. "The chief of police?"

"Close. An officer by the name of Lembic—a

Levitian police officer. Apparently he's looking out for Onca's safety and wanted to know which of the officers was at the Den the night of the raid. He seemed... trustworthy. I gave him descriptions. He's pretty sure he knows who I saw."

"Great!" Jack exclaimed. "Think you could call him back? Kim has an idea."

When Lembic brought him his breakfast the next morning, Onca could scarcely believe his pointed ears. "You want me to *what*?"

"Keep your voice down," Lembic urged. "Just take one bite. My cousin's a doctor. He says a tiny amount won't kill you. It'll only make you sleep so deeply everyone will think you're dead."

"Yeah. I'll probably sleep forever," Onca said with a snort. "And Jack thinks this is a good idea?"

"She's the one who suggested it."

Jack had been involved in some pretty wild schemes in her time, but he doubted she would do anything to endanger a Zetithian. For her, the people of Zetith were practically sacred. But he only had Lembic's word that she was truly the one behind the plan. Retrieving the comstone from his pocket, he tapped it and whispered her name.

"Hey, bucko," came Jack's whispered reply. "Do what Lembic says. We're waiting to nab you as soon as they haul your sorry carcass out of there."

"Yes, but did you have to put the poison in oatmeal? I can't stand oatmeal."

"You'll never have to eat any of it again," Jack assured him.

"The way things are going, I may never eat *anything* again," Onca muttered. "Is Kim there with you?"

"Yeah, she's here," Jack replied. "Honest to God, we've got this figured out."

Onca had all sorts of suspicions, not the least of which was whether Lembic's cousin knew what the hell he was talking about. "Let me talk to her."

"Onca? It's me, Kim."

As if he'd needed for her to tell him that. Her voice was like a balm to his frazzled nerves. "Are you sure you can trust this guy not to kill me?"

"Absolutely. We talked to his family. He's related to a doctor on Terra Minor by the name of Vladen. Jack says she knows him. Her son Larry got a message through to Vladen during the night, and he says Lembic is a good man."

Onca glanced at Lembic. "Yeah. I thought so too, but that was before he asked me to voluntarily swallow poisoned oatmeal."

"Just one spoonful," Kim said. "We'll get you out of there. I promise."

"I love you, Kim. I want to see you again before I die. I want to see our children before I die."

"You will. I'll be right there with the antidote, and even if you don't get the antidote, Vladen says you'll recover on your own." She chuckled. "He says Zetithians are really hard to kill."

"Yeah. Took an asteroid to kill most of us." He took a deep breath. "All right. I'll do it. But keep talking to me."

"Vladen said it won't hurt. You'll just get sleepy and then pass out."

Somehow, Onca thought it might hurt a little, considering the fact that he was standing next to the table. "Maybe I'd better sit on my bunk."

"Good idea," Kim said. "No more bumps and bruises if you can help it."

Onca carried the bowl over to his bunk and sat down. "Here goes." Picking up the spoon, he scooped up a small amount and ate it. "Hmm...seems better than usual. What's the secret—" His vision dimmed and he fell back onto the mattress. The bowl of oatmeal clattered to the floor. "—ingredient?"

"Brown sugar," Lembic replied.

"Tasty."

Chapter 33

"WHAT IF SOMEONE DECIDES TO MAKE SURE HE'S dead?" Kim sat in Onca's speeder with Tisana, while Cat and Jack waited in their own vehicle.

"Lembic said he'd stay with him, along with a couple of others he trusts," Jack said over the comlink. "They won't let anyone else touch him."

"Wish we were doing this at night," Cat commented. "The cover of darkness would help considerably."

"I'm glad we're not," Jack declared. "Hell, we ought to just go and demand the return of his body. We could say it's against Zetithian beliefs to do an autopsy."

Cat cleared his throat. "There is no such belief."

"*We* know that, but *they* don't," Jack insisted. "I—"

"Shh. Here they come." Kim's heart clutched with horror as the police carried a body out on a stretcher, covered head to toe with a sheet. "They must think he's really dead."

"That's the idea, isn't it?" Tisana patted her medical bag. "Don't worry. I've got the antidote right here."

Regardless of Tisana's expertise, Kim was still scared stiff. She hadn't had much experience with Mordrial witches, but this wife of Leo's seemed to know what she was doing. So far, anyway.

Shemlak and Draddut were stationed a few blocks away with Leo, the route the ambulance would take having been verified with Lembic. Val circled in the air above them.

"Val says it's all clear," Jack reported. "Should be a piece of cake."

"Unless the ambulance driver gets creative," Tisana muttered. "Most of those guys are really good pilots."

"Maybe, but there's no need to go Code Three with a dead man," Jack said. "Even if they do, we'll catch them when they get to the infirmary."

The rear doors of the ambulance slid shut and Kim gasped as the oversized speeder took off like a shot, complete with wailing sirens and flashing lights.

"Guess I was wrong about that," Jack growled as she took off in pursuit. "We should've nabbed them before they left."

"We decided it was best not to do that in front of a building full of cops who would like to see us all dead," Tisana reminded her.

"Whatever." Seconds later, Jack's speeder slid in behind the ambulance just as it made a sharp turn to the right. "Dammit! They're taking a different route. I'll head them off."

Kim glanced behind her. "Holy shit! There are four police speeders after us!"

"Slow them down, Tisana!" Jack shouted.

Tisana looked back for only a second as a massive ball of flame erupted from her eyes. An explosion detonated behind them, flinging the police speeders aside like children's toys.

Kim gaped at her companion with newfound respect. "You can shoot *fireballs* from your eyes?"

"Sure can," Tisana said with a grim smile. "Haven't had to use that particular talent lately, but I haven't forgotten how."

Kim swallowed hard. "Glad you're on our side."

Tisana chuckled. "A common sentiment."

"Can you aim one in front of the ambulance? Just close enough to stop them or head them off?"

"No problem," Tisana said. "Two blocks to the east and they'll run right into our trap."

Tisana launched another volley and the subsequent explosions landed precisely on target. The ambulance veered to the left with Jack's speeder close behind.

"Perfect." Kim looked back over her shoulder. Two police speeders were still following them. "Behind us?"

Tisana took them out with pinpoint accuracy.

"You're really good at that," Kim said. "I'm impressed."

"That was nothing. Try doing it on horseback while galloping through a snowy forest with an army chasing you."

"I'd rather not," Kim said with a shudder.

Tisana shrugged. "That's how I learned."

As the witch banked the speeder around the next corner, Kim spotted Shemlak and Draddut ahead, standing in the street with pistols drawn. Leo was positioned on the right-hand sidewalk. The ambulance slowed briefly, then picked up even more speed as Leo got off several pulse blasts.

He must have taken out the pilot because the vehicle slowed again, enabling the two huge Darconians to catch it. Draddut punched out the rear door, extracted the policemen, and tossed them aside. Assuming one of them was Lembic, Kim hoped he didn't suffer any serious injuries. Leo and Shemlak dragged the unconscious pilot from the cockpit and Leo jumped in to take over the controls. The ambulance sped off in a new direction, with Jack and Tisana's speeders following in its wake.

"Is there any rush to give Onca that antidote?" Kim asked. "I mean, should we stop and give it to him now?"

"No time," Tisana said, shifting into another turn.

"But this speeder can be cloaked. We could put Onca inside it and you could give him the antidote."

Tisana glanced over her shoulder and shot another round of fireballs. "Just in case anyone is still following us."

"Might be best to abandon the ambulance," Kim suggested. "It's a pretty big target."

"True." Tisana tapped her comstone. "Leo. Pull over. We'll take Onca from here. Cat and Jack can pick you up."

"Will do," Leo replied. "But I think I'll head over to the Palace to put them off the trail."

"Okay, but please be careful."

"I'll ditch it when I'm getting close," Leo said. "Val can keep an eye out for trouble from the air."

The ambulance came to a halt in front of a Markelian deli with Jack's speeder alongside. Tisana pulled in behind it as Val landed on the sidewalk. With the Avian standing guard, Cat and Leo pulled the stretcher from the vehicle, and then gathered up Onca, mattress and all, and laid him in the cargo compartment of his own speeder.

"Cloak us, Captain!" Kim climbed in the back with Onca as Cat lowered the canopy. "Give me the antidote, Tisana, and get going!"

Tisana tossed her the medical bag. "It's a simple injection. Just press the nozzle to his neck and pull the trigger."

Onca truly did appear to be dead—his face pale, his limbs slack and lifeless—and Kim's hands shook as she followed Tisana's instructions. A quick hiss indicated the dose had been delivered.

She stared at him for a long, anxious moment. "Nothing's happening!"

The speeder lurched as Tisana slid her fingertip up the throttle, slipping past the ambulance and out into the flow of traffic. "Might take a while for him to wake up. You know how Zetithians conk out when they're sick."

"Yes, but I can't stand—"

"If you really want to bring him around, play with his dick. Trust me, it works every time."

"You've *got* to be kidding."

"Nope. Try it."

Kim felt like an absolute idiot reaching into Onca's pants. The fly on his prison garb was held together with sticky tape that made a ripping sound as she pulled it open. "But what if he's really dead?"

"Does he feel cold?"

"Well, no…"

"Then he's not dead." Tisana sounded slightly annoyed. Kim was about to retort when she remembered how tough it was to fly a cloaked speeder.

"Sorry."

"I know how you feel," Tisana said in a softer tone. "When we had our first adventures together, I pulled Leo's seemingly lifeless body out of the snow twice. Onca will be okay. I promise."

"It just seems like a weird thing to do to someone who's been poisoned and presumed dead."

"Yeah. I know." Tisana sighed. "Felt that way myself a time or two."

With no other alternative, Kim slipped her hand

inside Onca's pants and wrapped her fingers around his cock, giving it a firm squeeze. When that failed to elicit a response, she stroked it harder, then moved on to massage his balls.

Never having had her hand on Onca's dick when it was actually soft, she was about to give up until she noticed that his respirations had increased in depth and frequency.

Within moments, he was purring like a kitten.

—◊◊◊—

Onca didn't have to open his eyes to know who had hold of his dick. Kim's scent was like a rose in bloom, and as he breathed it in, his heart began to pound, pumping blood faster and faster until his head cleared enough for him to speak.

"Where are we?" he asked.

"In the back of your speeder, heading for your house," she replied. "Cat and Jack will meet us there. Roncas and Rashe are taking care of the kids at the Palace."

"Sounds good," he murmured. "Glad to be going home. Prison food sucks."

"I don't much care for the clothes they gave you, either."

"Better than Rashe's pants. Damn things nearly ruined my dick."

"Feels okay to me," she said. "In fact, it feels perfect." She gave his cock a light stroke before releasing him.

"Glad you think so, but I didn't mean I wanted you to stop." He hesitated, frowning. "Who's flying the speeder?"

"Tisana—and it's cloaked. We probably shouldn't distract her."

"Gotcha."

Kim nestled in beside him and he put his arms around her, holding her close to his chest.

"Nice to hear your heart beating," she said. "Don't know how much more excitement I can take." With a soft sigh, she threaded her fingers through his hair and kissed him. "Promise me you'll never die on me like that again."

"I can't promise I'll never die," he said. "But I *can* promise never to eat oatmeal again—poisoned or otherwise."

"Can't say I blame you for that."

Kissing the top of her head, he ran his hand down her back, reassuring himself that she truly was there with him. "Never realized how cozy the back of a speeder could be."

"That's because we're lying on a stolen stretcher mattress."

"Really?" He shifted his weight, noting that he was indeed lying on something relatively soft. "Sounds like an interesting story."

"Oh, it was quite an adventure. I'll tell you more later, but basically, we stole your body out of the back of an ambulance on the way to the morgue."

"Now, *there's* a cheery thought. Glad I wasn't really dead."

Her kiss was long and deep, making his toes tingle and his cock twitch.

"Me too."

~~~

When Tisana flew the speeder into his yard followed by Cat and Jack, Onca was surprised to find the property surrounded—not by police, but by a huge crowd of well-wishers. A cheer went up from the throng as he climbed out of the speeder.

"We're maintaining a constant vigil until we know you're safe," a Davordian woman announced. "It's our civic duty to protect you from any further harm."

"I appreciate that," Onca said. "You ladies are the best." He waved to the crowd, drawing another cheer. "I had no idea I was so popular," he whispered to Kim.

"Yeah, right," Kim said with a snort. "I'll bet half of these ladies are former clients from the Palace."

"Does that bother you?"

"Not a bit," she declared, giving him a hug. "As long as they help keep you alive."

Moments later, Leo arrived with more news. "We left the ambulance several blocks from the infirmary. The cops were combing the streets. After Val picked off a couple of them from the air, I figured I'd better get lost, so I took a cab. Val flew back to the Palace."

Anara was waiting inside the house along with San and Lor. "I've made a statement to the press regarding how poorly protected you obviously were while in police custody and our subsequent rescue of you. The comments on those articles in the *Tribune* are running about a thousand to one in your favor. Interestingly, the head of the Brothel Guild and the police chief are both keeping quiet. Whether we can prove anything remains to be seen, but I believe we've found our culprits. Now that everyone knows you're still alive, a judge has been chosen for your hearing."

Onca had received worse news in his life, but he suspected there was more to it. "Anyone you know?"

Anara pinched the bridge of her nose as though attempting to stave off a headache. "Buertha Salaxine. The toughest judge on the bench."

"Oh, great. Does she like Herps?"

Anara shook her head. "She doesn't like *anybody*."

"Then I guess there's no point in trying to charm her."

"No," Anara agreed. "But I do believe you'll get a fair hearing. She's incorruptible."

"Seems like a rotten choice if the bad guys had anything to say about it," Jack commented. "Doesn't sound like the type who'd support places like the Den."

"She isn't," Anara said. "At least, not that I've ever heard. Apparently she insisted on hearing the case—and pulled a lot of strings to do it."

"Think she's out to nail my ass to the wall or someone else's?" Onca asked.

"No way to know with her," Anara replied. "She's something of an enigma, but if I had to guess, I'd say she has nothing against your ass."

Kim giggled. "I can't imagine any woman who would."

If only it was that simple. "Let's hope she isn't the first."

Chapter 34

"I TOLD YOU TO KEEP YOUR HEAD DOWN AND YOUR mouth shut," Rashe said. "Didn't I?"

"Yes, but you couldn't stand the idea of girls in cages, either. So that's a moot point." Onca wasn't surprised when the police report implicated him and Rashe and everyone else involved in the raid at the Den, with the emphasis on prosecution to the fullest extent of the law. "Seems to me that being so nasty about it points suspicion at them."

The "them" were the two Onca and Jack had fingered as non-Levitians—namely, police chief Ramundo Calista and Brothel Guild director Schumann Temple, both of whom were Terran. They sat on the opposite side of the courtroom and appeared confident that their side would win. Onca longed to slap those smug grins from their faces. Granted, they were only there to provide information pertaining to the brothel licensing system and the poisoning of an inmate, but Anara intended to question them thoroughly.

She had also made sure that Lembic was there, along with several of the girls from the Den. Being too big to fit in the chairs provided, the Darconians were ranged around the room's perimeter. The Herpatronian Onca had allegedly assaulted fidgeted in his seat, doing his best to appear to be in severe pain—not that Herps ever looked as though they felt *good*.

"Not so bad for you," Rashe grumbled. "You're retired. Temple has threatened to revoke my brothel license."

"Yeah, and I'll just get thrown back in jail with people who want me dead," Onca snapped.

Anara had only been given a week to prepare her defense strategy, and granted, this was a preliminary hearing rather than a trial, but the charges against them were piling up. Val had hacked away at the computer files and found a few irregularities, but nothing definitive as yet. He was still working on them, risking contempt charges for missing the hearing. Onca hoped they could get this wrapped up soon, or between the legal fees and the cost of feeding over a hundred hungry mouths, he would be out of money in no time. Going back to work was not an option, whether he could get his brothel license renewed or not.

Kim sat far enough away that he couldn't pick up her scent. The past week had been nerve racking, but the nights with his mate had been heavenly. She told him repeatedly that he was in the right and that no honest judge could possibly see it any other way. Unfortunately, if Temple and Calista had the judge in their pocket, things could go very wrong very quickly. The plaintiff, he discounted. Somehow he couldn't imagine that anyone, short of another Herp, would be sympathetic toward such an ugly ape.

Onca had filed attempted rape charges against the Herp, but that was the subject of another hearing—and no one appeared to have arrested *him*.

Anara had insisted that the hearing be open to the public. Thus, the room was crawling with reporters, and most of the people in the gallery were female.

Somehow Onca didn't believe they were there to support the Herp.

Some official or other stood before the court and announced the case. "The Superior Court of Damenk City
will now hear the case of *Hunard v. Onca*, the Honorable
Judge Buertha Salaxine presiding."

Judge Salaxine swept into the courtroom in long
gray robes that matched her straight, bobbed hair. Her
bearing was imperious, with lips set in a grim line and
eyes like black ice. Certainly not a woman susceptible to
charm—from a Zetithian or anyone else. Onca had been
pleased to discover that the Rhylosian judicial system
was more like that found on Earth rather than someplace
like, say, Derivia, where they were still doing the battle
to the death thing. As a resident of Rhylos, Anara was
well-versed in the local court procedures. Still, with a
judge like this one…

I'm doomed.

He was momentarily heartened as her unyielding
gaze passed over the plaintiff and his compatriots as she
took her seat. Unfortunately, he now had to sit quietly
while those assholes ripped his character to shreds.
Anara had warned him against outbursts protesting his
innocence, but it was damn near impossible—especially
when Hunard made the comment that Onca had actually
requested his services prior to the assault.

Anara's grip on his hand got him past that, but the
blatant lies everyone else told only added more fuel to
the fire. About the best Onca could say was that, knowing the truth as he did, Temple and Calista couldn't have
demonstrated their guilt any better if they had confessed.
When Temple made the point that the girls in the Den

were well-paid volunteers who had been deprived of their livelihood because of the raid, Onca nearly exploded with rage.

He heard a low growl behind him—a growl that could only have come from his mate.

Kim. I've got to get through this for Kim and our children. Breathe, breathe, breathe…

Finally, it was over.

"Now it's our turn," Anara whispered. "We're gonna knock 'em dead."

Anara called Kim to the witness stand. She told her story with frequent interruptions by Hunard's lawyer, a sleazy Terran who kept licking his lips like he wanted to eat her alive. Following Rashe's testimony, they had a brief break for lunch, and the hearing resumed with the statements made by Cassie, Peska, and three of the other girls from the Den. By the time they finished and it was Onca's turn to speak, there wasn't a dry eye in the place. Several of the reporters were openly weeping.

When Anara asked him to give an account of his involvement, Onca did the best he could to explain the motives for his actions. "I couldn't rest until I found those girls and freed them. And there are others. One of Miss Shrovenach's friends—a Levitian named Dalmet—is still missing. We have to find her. I can't do that if I'm in prison."

Anara nodded her approval, then faced the judge. "Your Honor, the defense rests."

Onca sat in a daze during the brief recess, knowing he was in the right, but still not quite believing a reprieve was possible. Not with the chief of police testifying

against him. They had just called the courtroom to order
when Val flew in and handed Anara a large envelope.

Judge Salaxine returned to the bench. "In the case of
Hunard v. Onca, the court finds in favor of the defen-
dant." With a decisive rap of her gavel, she concluded,
"Case dismissed."

Hunard leaped to his feet. "But he bent my dick and
twisted my nuts!"

The judge arched a brow. "My dear fellow, when
faced with the threat of rape by another male, what
would *you* do? Quietly submit?"

And then she smiled.

Onca's jaw dropped as she tucked a lock of gray hair
behind her ear. A gesture he finally recognized—along
with *her*.

His last client.

With a shout of triumph, Kim launched herself into
Onca's arms, kissing him for all she was worth. "I knew
we'd win!"

Onca returned her kiss with equal ardor. "I'm glad
you were sure. I thought I was dead a dozen times over."

"Now comes the fun part." Anara waved a sheaf of
papers. "Hold on while I give these to the judge."

Kim shook her head as Anara handed over the documents to a beaming Judge Salaxine. "Didn't think that
woman could smile."

"Me, either," Onca murmured. "Well, not until the
end, anyway."

As Judge Salaxine sifted through the pages, her smile
disappeared. "Bailiff! Would you please detain Chief

Calista and Mr. Temple? I have just received some very interesting information."

"What is it?" Kim asked Anara.

"Val finally hacked into the system," Anara replied. "Seems that 'offworld owner' was actually a front for Calista and Temple. The profits from the Den were transferred from that account into their personal accounts on a monthly basis."

"Follow the money," Kim whispered.

Anara nodded. "There's also a mention of proceeds from three other brothels in the district. I believe we'll find Dalmet in one of them."

As the bailiffs escorted the two men from the courtroom, the judge made another request. "Will Miss Shrovenach and Mr. Onca please approach the bench?"

Kim frowned. "Are we in trouble again?"

"Go on," Anara urged. "She's not a woman to be kept waiting."

"I have here another interesting document," Judge Salaxine said. "One that I would very much like to have the honor of acting upon."

Kim shot a questioning glance at Onca, who merely shrugged in reply.

The judge held up one of the pages. "This marriage license has your names on it—all perfectly legal and just waiting for someone to make it official. I haven't performed a marriage ceremony in many years, but I believe I still remember how it goes. Shall I?"

The secretive smile Salaxine aimed at Onca spoke volumes, but Kim thought it best to question him about it later.

Onca grinned. "What about it, Kim? I'm game if you are."

Jack sauntered up. "I volunteer to be a witness." She slapped Onca on the back so hard he staggered. "Gotta get this rascal hitched before he gets into any more trouble."

Kim knew the ceremony didn't matter. They were already mated. Nothing short of death could separate them now. "I can't think of anything I'd like better. Yes, Onca. I will marry you."

The crowd cheered as Rashe held up a hand. "Can I be best man?"

Onca scratched his head. "Correct me if I'm wrong, but aren't Kim and I supposed to choose?"

"Well, yeah," Rashe admitted. "Figured if I didn't hurry up, Wings would get the gig."

Kim still didn't understand where the license had come from. "How did you—?"

Anara smiled. "Like I said, I believe in being prepared."

Judge Salaxine began the ceremony, one that Kim had never heard before. She gave the correct responses when prompted, and in a few short minutes, she was in Onca's arms for the best kiss of all.

The kiss that meant they would be together forever.

"Congratulations to you both," Salaxine said before sifting through more of the pages. "Ah, yes, and we have another one here…requesting that the surname Shrovenach be added to Onca's legal name. I can approve that one, as well."

"Okay. This is *really* freaking me out now," Kim murmured to her new husband. "How the hell would anyone know we talked about that?" She glanced at Anara. "Is she a witch?"

"No," Anara said—although her fiendish expression

seemed to contradict that assertion. "But I *am* observant. I caught him practicing his signature a few days ago."

Onca threw up his hands in protest. "I was just trying it out. You know, to see what it would be like to have two names."

Kim grinned. "How did it feel?"

"Fabulous."

~~~

Kim gave Onca a kiss that melted his bones, closely followed by a hug that stole what was left of his breath.

"So, what do we do now?" she asked.

Onca shrugged. "You got me by the short hairs—for real, now that I think of it. I dunno, live happily ever after?"

"I doubt we'll always be happy," Kim said. "Shit happens, you know."

Onca certainly couldn't argue with that. "Yeah, like rescuing damsels in distress and getting shot at by Racks." Then again, perhaps they had already faced the worst that life intended to throw at them. "I'm hoping for smooth sailing from here on out."

"I wish we knew where Dalmet was," Kim said. "This won't be over until we find her."

"I know where she is," Val said. "At least, I know where those other brothels are. I'll fly over and get her."

Onca snorted a laugh. "Yeah, right, Wings. Like she's gonna trust *you*. Those eyes of yours will probably freak her out."

"Maybe I should go with you," Kim suggested. "We need to get all those girls to the Palace as soon as possible."

"Good idea," Jatki said. "How about if I go with

Val?" She winked at Kim. "I'm sure you'd rather stay here with Onca."

"I know what *I'm* gonna do," Jack declared. "I'm going back to that Markelian deli—you know, the one next to where we ditched the ambulance? Never ate any Markelian food before, but I want to try it."

Onca never had, either. "Sounds good."

"Maybe we should invite the judge," Roncas said. "She's probably hungry after such a long day."

He glanced at Salaxine, who was still sorting through the pages Anara had given her. "Nah, she's busy. I'll, um, send her a thank you note when we get home."

Roncas blinked, her blue eyes blending nicely with her Val-enhanced purple skin. "You know...she seems kinda familiar."

Onca shrugged. "Seen one judge, you've seen them all." He arched a brow. "Spent much time in court-rooms, Roncas?"

"No," the Zuteran replied. "Maybe I've seen her at the market or something."

"Do judges *really* do their own shopping?" Kim asked. "Seems like she'd have a droid or someone to do it for her."

"Maybe," Onca said. "But there are some things you have to do for yourself."

"That's it!" Roncas exclaimed. "I've seen her at the—"

"Doesn't matter now, does it?" Taking Kim by the hand, Onca headed toward the exit. "I hear the Markelians make a great sandwich. Slow-roasted meat, aged cheese, fresh bread—that sort of thing—and they have this secret sauce that makes your hair grow really fast."

Kim ran a hand through her short curls. "Cool. My hair needs all the help it can get to catch up with yours."

"No worries." He pulled her into his arms for a kiss that left behind a lingering sweetness, a flavor he knew he would never grow tired of. "You've got the rest of your life for that." If he was lucky, he would be there for all of it—every single joyous moment.

She tapped his nose with a gentle fingertip. "Let's get started, shall we?"

Onca's vision altered slightly, revealing an older version of Kim surrounded by laughing children—her own along with dozens of others of every species imaginable. Clearly the gods had a happy life in store for her—and him.

"Lead on."

By the time they had all finished dinner, word came that the police, led by Officer Lembic, had raided the three brothels implicated in the records Val had discovered. True to his word, Val brought Dalmet and Jatki back, although he had to make two trips.

Kim embraced her friend, who seemed as shaken by the rapid turn of events as she had been by being kidnapped and enslaved.

"I could hardly believe it when the police came and let us out," the Levitian girl exclaimed as she returned Kim's hug. "I was beginning to think I'd never see you again."

"Same here," Kim said. "When you weren't in the Den, we were afraid you might've been sold."

"They threatened me with that," Dalmet said,

shuddering. "Said they'd sell me to a Scorillian if I didn't cooperate. Have you ever seen a Scorillian's dick? It looks like a long, pointed crystal—not like a Levitian's at all."

"At least it wasn't a Norludian," Jack said, turning slightly pale. "Damn things make me sick to look at them."

"You've been saying that forever," Tisana snapped. "But you've never told us why."

"That's because it makes me want to puke just thinking about it."

"Maybe it's time to get it off your chest," Onca suggested. "You know, venting your feelings and all that psychobabble bullshit."

"You might be right." Taking a quick swig of Markelian ale, Jack leaned back in her chair. "One of those weird little shits sucked his fingers onto my cheeks and tried to stick his tongue down my throat once." With a sharp exhale, she lurched forward as though about to lose her dinner. Snatching up a napkin, she pressed it to her lips.

Momentarily stricken with macabre fascination, Kim asked, "What did you do then?"

"Bit him." Jack shivered. "Believe me, Norludian blood tastes worse than anything you can imagine. Couldn't keep food down for a week."

Onca cleared his throat as though recalling something equally distasteful. "Sorry I asked." With a slight shudder, he turned to Dalmet. "Speaking of Levitians, Lembic wondered why you were living on the street. He seemed to think it strange that you wouldn't have been taken in by other Levitians when you were orphaned."

"I was a runaway, not an orphan." An expression of

chagrin tightened Dalmet's jaw, emphasizing the bony ridges. "A *stupid* runaway. I wanted freedom, and look where *that* got me."

"Well, you're free now," Kim said. "Are you hungry?"

Dalmet rubbed her flat belly. "Starving."

"You've come to the right place." Onca waved at a waitress. "You can order anything you like, but those *jharic* sandwiches are damn good."

Kim nodded. "As soon as I get my share of the Zetithian trust fund, Onca and I will make sure none of the street kids in this city go hungry again. We're gonna start a school too." She glanced at Rashe. "Think the brothel owners would donate to the cause?"

"I guess so," Rashe replied. "I can donate a free fuck once a week or so. Not sure about the Statzeelians—they're kinda tightfisted—but the others would probably chip in."

"Great," Kim said. "So we can put you down for— how much did you say you charged your clients?"

"Four hundred credits." He shrugged. "I know it isn't anywhere near what Onca used to charge, but, hey, I'm only human."

Jack let out an appreciative whistle. "Ooh, you're good, Kim. At this rate, you'll be hosting charity balls in no time. I could probably cough up a few credits myself."

"I shall speak to the restaurant owners," Shemlak said. "A great deal of food goes to waste on this world while children go hungry. We can do better."

"And we will," Onca said. "Amelyana only raised Zetithians. Kim and I will have children of all kinds, including our own." Enfolding Kim's hand in his, he gazed into her eyes, sending waves of warm contentment washing over her. "You've given my life purpose and filled it with love. I'll spend the rest of my days giving it back."

She smiled, her mind touching the lives deep inside her womb with the strength of her love for their father. "You already have."

"Sweetheart, that's only the beginning." Leaning closer, his lips met hers in the softest of kisses. "I promise to give you joy unlike any you have ever known—every day of my life."

Her vision altered, transforming his image to the man he would become, foretelling their long and happy future together. "I know you will."

Acknowledgments

When it comes to acknowledgements, I've never been terribly chatty. Lots of authors will tell you this, that, or the other about all the research they've done and where their ideas came from. I've never done that, and since *Rebel* is the tenth book in this series, I see no point in starting now.

Therefore, my sincere thanks go out to:

My loving husband, Budley

My handsome sons, Mike & Sam

My talented critique partners, Sandy James & Nan Reinhardt

My keen-eyed beta reader, Mellanie Szereto

My supportive agent, Melissa Jeglinski

My longtime editor, Deb Werksman

My amazing blog followers

My fellow IRWA members

My insane cats, Kate & Allie

My normal cat, Jade

My barn cat, Kitty Cat

My trusty horses, Kes & Jadzia

My peachy little dog, Peaches

But most of all, I'd like to thank my wonderful readers.

This *Rebel* is for you.

Escape to the world of the Cat Star Chronicles by Cheryl Brooks

READ ON FOR EXCERPTS FROM

Virgin

Stud

Wildcat

Available now from
Sourcebooks Casablanca

From *Virgin*

DAX HAD NO IDEA WHY DISCOVERING THE COLOR OF HER eyes should have affected him so strongly, but he'd never purred for a woman in his life. He'd finally gotten a good whiff of her; she smelled so damn good, he'd reacted before he had time to think.

The sound of a scuffle behind him diverted his attention and, turning around, he saw Lars headed their way with scratches all over him and a branch clinging to the seat of his pants. Blood covered at least half of his face, but he was still waving his pistol at Dax.

"You Zetithian scum!" he roared as he approached. "She's mine!"

"Not anymore, pal," Dax said. "So back off!"

"You've been fucking her, haven't you?" Lars yelled. "I tell you I won't let—"

Dax didn't often lose his temper, but he'd had just about enough of Lars. "I haven't fucked *anybody*," he shot back. "She's leaving because she doesn't like getting beat up. So why don't you just shut up and go home!"

Lars ignored him and continued to advance. Realizing that talking wasn't getting him anywhere, Dax grabbed Ava's hand, flipped the setting on her pistol to heavy stun, and squeezed the trigger.

"Well, I'll be damned," Waroun said as Lars fell in a heap. "You actually hit him."

"Amazing, isn't it?" Dax said with a sardonic laugh. "Let's get going before he wakes up again."

"Which won't be long," Ava warned. "The frying pan does a better job."

"Anyone that hardheaded must have a little Herpatronian in his bloodline," Waroun mused, still staring at Lars's inert form. "Or a touch of Darconian—though I'm not sure that's possible."

"Have you ever considered that hitting him in the head might be making things worse?" Dax said. "I mean, shit like that is bound to scramble his brains eventually."

"I've been hoping it would give him a lobotomy," Ava said. "But it hasn't worked so far." She tipped her head to one side, adding thoughtfully, "Maybe I wasn't hitting him in the right spot."

"Remind me not to let her anywhere near the galley," Waroun muttered. "We might all be lobotomized before we get her to Rutara."

"Hey, it was your idea to bring her along," Dax pointed out. "If anyone gets conked over the head, it should be you."

"Aw, come on, you guys!" Ava said. "I won't need to hit either one of you—unless you hit me first."

"I don't plan on it," Dax snapped. Actually, hitting her was the farthest thing from his mind at that point. Another moment spent gazing into her eyes and he would have kissed her! Striding off in the direction of his speeder and his other passengers, Dax made an interesting discovery. She'd not only made him purr; she'd made his dick hard.

And, not only that, it was also slick with the orgasm-inducing fluid for which Zetithians were famous. Dax

had been around lots of women, but very few of them
had ever given him an erection—not that they hadn't
tried—and none had made him want to purr. He hadn't
done it intentionally this time; it had simply happened.
It was all wrong, though—it was very clear that she
wasn't interested in him. But if that was the case, then
why had she smelled so good?

Anyway, it was supposed to be the other way around:
When males saw a woman they were attracted to, first
they purred and *then* they were aroused by her scent. At
least, that's what he'd always been told. The fact that a
woman's scent could be arousing whether he'd purred or
not surprised him. Then it occurred to him that drowning
in her eyes might have been the reason. After all, he'd
had to get pretty close to her to do that.

Proximity, pure and simple. As tall as he was, looking
right into a woman's face didn't happen very often. Most
females only came up to his chest, and some only to his
waist. Drells were somewhere around his knees—not
that he'd ever been able to figure out which of them was
female. One of his passengers was a Drell this time, so
he'd have to make a point of asking. The other two passengers were Kitnocks, and though they were nearly as
tall as he, Dax had long since decided that the only way
you could tell the sexes apart was by the color of the
body stockings they wore to cover their spindly limbs;
females wore blue, and males wore red. Always.

As they approached, Dax spotted three scantily clad
Davordian hookers waiting with his motley trio of passengers. Except for their luminous blue eyes, Davordians
looked essentially human, but Kitnocks and Drells were
humanoid only in the respect that they each had two

legs, two arms, and a head. If those girls had provided
the necessary services, they were either the toughest
hookers ever born or the most desperate.

One of the Kitnocks, Teke, inclined his tall, cylindrical head as he waved a hand in greeting. "These ladies
heard we were shipping out with a Zetithian and wanted
to know if you'd be interested—"

"I'm not," Dax said, not bothering to wait for the rest
of it.

"But they wanted to see if you had an aversion to blue
eyes," Teke said. "Apparently they've come to believe
that this is a trait among Zetithians."

"It's not," said Dax. "That's Trag's problem, not mine."

"No, his problem is that he doesn't like to fuck,"
Waroun said, aiming a sucker-tipped thumb toward
Dax. "I, on the other hand, would be happy to partake of
anything you ladies have to offer."

It might have been the light, but Dax could have
sworn the hookers lost what little color they had in their
fair-skinned faces.

"We have, um, other clients waiting," one of the
Davordians said, averting her eyes.

"That's right," the others chorused.

"Works every time," Dax said under his breath as the
hookers quickly withdrew.

Still recovering from her reaction to Dax, Ava barely
registered this exchange. No one, not Russ or Lars or
anyone else, had *ever* made her melt. She made herself a promise not to get that close to him again, but
she also knew that on a long space voyage this might

prove difficult—especially if it was a small ship. With no more passengers than he took on—not to mention their apparent lack of class and, at least in her case, funds—the odds were against him being the captain of a luxury space cruiser.

"We'll make introductions later," Waroun said. "Now, if you'll all climb into the speeder, we'll be on our way."

Following Waroun's gesture, Ava climbed into the backseat of the sleek speeder to sit next to the Drell. They were rude little rats as a rule, but she knew how to handle them. All you had to do was swear at a Drell, and they backed down instantly. Kitnocks were another problem altogether. These two were obviously male, and though she'd waited on plenty of them, she didn't care for them at all. Their huge mouths made them look like caricatures drawn by children, and they had some very odd habits. Cracking their knuckles was the most annoying of these and was something they did constantly, unless they were holding something in their hands.

She'd heard that the knuckle cracking was a secret language among Kitnocks—and the fact that they mostly seemed to do this while among others of their kind made the rumor seem likely—but Ava had never been able to confirm this. Not that she cared. She'd always tried to avoid them in the past, but the best she could hope for in this instance was that their destination was nearby, because she was pretty sure that Rutara would be the last stop.

The Drell shifted over as Ava sat down—not away from her, but toward her, barely leaving her a place to sit, let alone allowing room for her sack. Obviously, the swearing would have to begin immediately. "Move the fuck over."

The Drell screeched like a scalded cat and scrambled to the far side of the seat. "I merely wanted to—"

"I don't give a damn." She was watching Dax climb into the driver's seat, noting that he looked as fabulous from the back as he did from the front. She briefly considered what he might have thought if their positions were reversed—though, given his aversion to "fucking," she doubted that the sentiment would be mutual. She sat up straighter and gazed pointedly in another direction. She didn't need to be getting the hots for a Zetithian. She'd heard about them. They were like highly addictive drugs; one hit and you were hooked. And besides, she'd had enough trouble with bad boys; there was no need to get hung up on another one.

And Lars had been a very bad boy. What *had* she been thinking? At the time, he'd seemed daring and handsome and dangerous and sexy. Now he was just ridiculous and mean. She should have known better, but if she didn't get it back then, she certainly did now. She wasn't going to hook up with another one. Maybe she *should* go back to Russ. He was a good man. Not terribly exciting, perhaps, but excitement was rapidly beginning to lose its appeal.

The last she'd heard from her mother—perhaps six months previously—led her to believe that Russ was still single. Hopefully he'd waited at least another six months, but even if he hadn't, Rutara was still a better place to live than Luxaria. Glancing around at the dusty, weedy, unkempt excuse for a spaceport, she concluded that almost any place would be an improvement.

From *Stud*

TARQ SMELLED HER BEFORE HE EVER LAID EYES ON her—a glorious, delectable aroma that curled through his head and shot straight into his bloodstream. Closing his eyes, he inhaled deeply as the effect of her fragrance hit his cock like a pulse blast, obliterating his every thought with the instantaneous ecstasy of an erection so hard it made his head swim.

He glanced away from his menu, taking in the shape of her legs out of the corner of his eye—what he could see of them, that is. Her baggy trousers and apron concealed everything about her legs except the fact that she had two of them.

"Hi, my name is Lucy, and I'll be your server," she said. "Do you already know what you'd like, or do you need more time?"

Tarq smiled to himself as he shook his head. No, he didn't need more time. He knew exactly what he wanted. "You," he replied. "I'd like a full order of *you*."

"I-I beg your pardon?" she stammered.

He could hear the words catch in her throat and hoped he'd just done the same thing to her that she'd done to him. She was human—he could tell that much from her voice—but a human female who didn't mask her natural scent with heavy perfumes was rare. Tarq could never understand why they did that, but then, humans weren't the dedicated scent breeders that Zetithians were. It didn't matter what a woman looked like; if she didn't smell right, his cock was going nowhere.

This woman, however, wasn't hiding her scent and it assailed him full force. His mouth filled with saliva at the thought of tasting her—to the point that Tarq had to swallow before he could speak. With one more deep, satisfying breath, he looked up at her.

No, she wasn't beautiful, but the way she stared down at him, round-eyed and speechless, was enough to make him want to purr. She was young, but not too young to mate with a man of his age. Her dark hair was pulled back from her face, though a few soft tendrils had escaped near her temples, accentuating fair skin and round cheeks that needed no artificial enhancements to put a rosy blush on them—though his words might have been responsible.

The expression in her deep brown eyes intrigued him. It was as if she wasn't sure if she'd heard him correctly and was somewhere between laughter and astonishment. Tarq drank in her appearance just as he had done with her scent. Her nose was dusted with freckles, her dark eyelashes curled enticingly, and, as he watched, her generous mouth finally smiled.

Actually, it was more of a grin. Then, all at once, her face went blank and she recoiled slightly. Her eyes swept from his chest to the roots of his hair, with a darted glance at his features. He knew what she was seeing—blue eyes with catlike pupils, ears that curved to a pointed tip, eyebrows that slanted upward toward his temples, and blond hair that hung in spiral curls to his waist. She wasn't going to say it out loud, but the shock of recognition was clear; she knew *precisely* who he was and why he was there.

A nervous giggle escaped her. "Do you want to hear today's specials?"

Tarq shook his head and smiled, drawing her attention to his fangs as he slowly licked his lips. "What would you recommend?"

Swallowing hard, she blurted out, "The fish."

Nodding, Tarq exhaled with a loud purr. "Then I'll have the fish." Shifting his weight, he leaned back, shaking the hair back from his face. His dick was starting to hurt and his balls were tingling like crazy. It had been three days since he'd had a woman. One more whiff of her and he'd probably lose all control.

She tapped his order into her notepad. Without looking up, she went on, "Baked, broiled, or grilled?"

"How do *you* like it, Lucy?" Tarq put as much seductive emphasis into those words as he possibly could—a question he'd asked countless women, but in a far different situation.

Still not taking her eyes off the pad, she said, "Um... grilled."

"Then I'll have it grilled." Tarq let his own eyes roam over her round hips, ample breasts, and capable hands. She looked every bit as luscious as she smelled. A woman like that had to be mated already. Then he remembered the human custom of wearing rings on their left hand. He could see both of her hands clearly; there were no rings on either of them, but they were shaking.

"You get two sides with that." There was a tremor in her voice; Tarq knew he was making her nervous, which was the very last thing he wanted to do. He wanted her relaxed and receptive.

"Why don't you choose for me?" he suggested. "I don't recognize any of them."

"How about the Greek salad and eggplant with tomatoes and kalamata olives?"

"That sounds good."

"And to drink?"

Tarq couldn't say what he *really* wanted to drink; there were some things you didn't say to a woman you'd only met a few moments before—unless she was a client, of course. "Water."

"Anything else?"

Tarq had to bite his lip to keep from saying what was on the tip of his tongue, opting to reply with a shake of his head.

"I'll be right back with your drink."

Tarq smiled as he watched her go, her soft moccasins making no sound as she walked away. No wonder she had been able to sneak up on him like that. Tarq had excellent hearing—though his sense of smell was better—and there was nothing wrong with his eyesight, either. He'd lied when he said he didn't recognize the side dishes; the truth was he couldn't read the menu.

From *Wildcat*

SARA COULDN'T SAY SHE HADN'T BEEN WARNED. After all, Jerden *was* Zetithian, and though she'd expected his waist-length hair and stunning physique, when he came cantering up on her missing stallion—no bridle, no saddle, no *clothes*—with a black leopard bounding alongside, her breath caught in her throat. Ordinarily his good looks wouldn't have mattered to a woman like Sara, but the picture they presented was nothing short of spectacular. Even so, skuzzy Cylopean or Zetithian hunk, Jerden had her horse, and Sara wanted him back.

She'd heard the rumors that Jerden was dangerous, insane, and lived like a hermit in the wilderness. But although her good friend and neighbor Bonnie Dackelov had assured her those rumors were completely unfounded, he *did* look the part, especially with that huge cat shadowing his every move.

Closing her eyes, she gave herself a mental kick for going to his place alone. Bonnie was cute and kind, and Jerden already knew her. She could've easily convinced him to part with Danuban, simply by being her pretty little self. Sara was out of her league.

Still, she did have the law on her side and documentation to prove she was the stallion's owner, giving her a bona fide excuse to finally meet her newest and nearest neighbor without being introduced as a potential love

interest. She was there to get a horse that, as part of the
carefully overseen equine importation program on the
recently colonized planet of Terra Minor, was a very
valuable animal.

Black as night, standing sixteen hands high with a
long, flowing mane and tail and a high, arched neck,
Danuban had a bloodline that could be traced back over
a thousand years, and the Andalusian breed itself dated
back to Earth's fourteenth-century Spain. Moving with
an elegance few other breeds could match, he looked
like something straight out of a romantic fairy tale.

Unfortunately, horses were the only things about
those old tales that interested Sara. She had no use for
romance and had stopped trying to be charming long
ago. It never worked for her. Even as a teen, any time
she made the attempt, the boy in question stared at her
almost as though another guy had displayed interest—
and the only time a male classmate *had* shown interest
had backfired on her in a way she still didn't care to
think about, nor had she ever shared that experience
with anyone.

She'd heard all about this Jerden—how he used
to sell himself in a brothel on Rhylos for a thousand
credits per session—and had avoided Bonnie's attempts
to introduce her to him. She had no desire to meet yet
another man who wouldn't give a damn if he ever saw
her again.

A thousand credits. A man would have to be awfully
good at what he did to charge that much for an hour's…
work. Sara didn't even want think about how much she
would have to pay him to look at her twice. She knew
there was nothing feminine about her—with the possible

exception of an affectionate heart. Unfortunately, only animals seemed to appreciate that quality.

Though Andalusians were characteristically docile and gentle, the long voyage from Earth had left Danuban wild and unmanageable, and he'd broken away from his handlers in Nimbaza before his tracking implant could be placed. Impossible to track, where he'd run off to was a mystery until Bonnie, whose farm lay to the north of Sara's land, reported that Jerden had acquired another stray.

Which was apparently something else he was good at. She'd heard about the leopard that followed him everywhere, as well as the pack of dogs and domestic cats he'd managed to accumulate in the short time he'd been living on Terra Minor. According to Bonnie, the murder of a woman on Rhylos had affected him so strongly that he'd become a recluse. But though he might have been avoiding people, animals seemed to be welcome, which might explain why Danuban had wound up on his land.

At least he hadn't ended up on Nathan Wolmack's ranch. Nate had a decent herd of horses and was one of only two men who'd ever sought her company, but, like the first one, he gave Sara the creeps. Thankfully, his land was even farther north than Bonnie's, or Sara would have had more visits from him, though she did have to pass by his place on the way to Nimbaza. Rumor had it that he was trying to buy the spread to the east of hers, and Sara prayed that the deal would fall through. The last thing she needed was Nate showing up whenever the spirit moved him.

She'd had no such problems with Jerden, though there were plenty of women in the district who would've loved to have a problem like that, and for that matter, quite a few who wouldn't mind if Nate came sniffing around. Sara would've preferred to avoid dealing with either man, but in this instance, she had no choice.

Having parked her dusty speeder in front of Jerden's rustic lakeshore home, she stood waiting by the porch, taking in the scenery. A picturesque lake stretched out behind the house, mirroring the snowcapped mountains that loomed above it. Open grassland lay to the north, ending where Sara's fences began. Surrounded by a grove of tall conifers, the ranch-style house was built of logs, with two steps up to a wide veranda where at least six dogs and as many cats lay sleeping, both on and under the chairs that were scattered about. All appeared to be healthy and well-fed, in addition to being surprisingly well-groomed. Two of the dogs got up to greet her with panting smiles and wagging tails, but the rest didn't bother. The cats didn't even wake up.

Sara had been confident that her experience with horses would make a difference in Danuban's unruly behavior, but she couldn't help envying the way Jerden rode without benefit of bridle or whip. The stallion seemed to do his bidding without question, and he sat on the Andalusian's broad back as if he'd been born there. With horse whisperers scattered throughout human history, it should have come as no surprise that members of some alien species—such as the Mordrials, some of whom could communicate with animals through telepathic means—might possess the same abilities. Nevertheless, a tingle tightened the back of Sara's neck as she watched him ride.

But Jerden Morokovitz was a Zetithian, not a

Mordrial. The only things his kind were noted for were the occasional prescient vision, their attractive feline characteristics, and, if the reports were correct, sexual abilities that were second to none.

Not that Sara would have been a good judge of anyone's sexual prowess. Bonnie, on the other hand, was married to Lynx, who was not only Zetithian, but a former harem slave. She could have enlightened Sara, but the fact that Zetith and nearly all of its people had been destroyed at the instigation of one insanely jealous and very powerful man was proof enough. Zetithian males were irresistible, particularly to human women, which was what Sara feared far more than the leopard by Jerden's side. She had no desire to develop an interest in another man only to be ridiculed or ignored—or even abused.

Determined to keep this meeting friendly, Sara waved at Jerden as he approached. When he dismounted with a catlike grace that many a rider would envy, she saw that her eyes hadn't been deceiving her. He wasn't wearing *anything*. Not even a ring or a watch. She reminded herself that her visit was unannounced and that this was *his* land. She couldn't fault him for his nudity, but his total lack of modesty surprised her. He made no attempt to cover himself, though Sara was at a loss to explain how he would have accomplished this. She doubted he could have done it successfully even if he'd used both hands.

Outcast

by Cheryl Brooks

———————

Sold into slavery in a harem, Lynx is a favorite because his feline gene gives him remarkable sexual powers. But after ten years, Lynx is exhausted and is thrown out of the harem without a penny. Then he meets Bonnie, who's determined not to let such a beautiful and sensual young man go to waste…

———————

"Leaves the reader eager for the next story featuring these captivating aliens." —*Romantic Times*

"One of the sweetest love stories…one of the hottest heroes ever conceived and…one of the most exciting and adventurous quests that I have ever had the pleasure of reading." —*Single Titles*

"One of the most sensually imaginative books that I've ever read… A magical story of hope, love and devotion" —*Yankee Romance Reviews*

For more Cheryl Brooks, visit:

www.sourcebooks.com

Fugitive

by Cheryl Brooks

—⫸w⫷—

A mysterious stranger in danger...

Zetithian warrior Manx, a member of a race hunted to near extinction because of their sexual powers, has done all he can to avoid extermination. But when an uncommon woman enters his jungle lair, the animal inside of him demands he risk it all to have her.

The last thing Drusilla expected to find on vacation was a gorgeous man hiding in the jungle. But what is he running from? And why does she feel so mesmerized that she'll stop at nothing to be near him? Hypnotically attracted, their intense pleasure in each other could destroy them both.

Praise for The Cat Star Chronicles:

"Wow. The romantic chemistry is as close to perfect as you'll find." —*BookFetish.org*

"Fabulous off world adventures... Hold on ladies, hot Zetithians are on their way." —*Night Owl Romance*

"Insanely creative... I enjoy this author's voice immensely." —*The Ginger Kids Den of Iniquity*

"I think purring will be on my request list from now on." — *Romance Reader at Heart*

For more Cheryl Brooks, visit:

www.sourcebooks.com

Hero

by Cheryl Brooks

—◦◦◦—

He is the sexiest, most irksome man she's ever encountered...

Micayla is the last Zetithian female left in the universe. She doesn't know what's normal for her species, but she knows when she sees Trag that all she wants to do is bite him...

He has searched all over the galaxy for a woman like her...

Trag has sworn he'll never marry unless he can find a Zetithian female. But now that he's finally found Micayla, she may be more of a challenge than even he's able to take on...

—◦◦◦—

Praise for the Cat Star Chronicles:

"Sexy and fascinating... leaves the reader eager for the next story featuring these captivating aliens."—*RT Book Reviews*

"The kind of delightfully hot read we've come to expect from Ms. Brooks."—*Star-Crossed Romance*

For more Cat Star Chronicles, visit:

www.sourcebooks.com

About the Author

A native of Louisville, Kentucky, Cheryl Brooks is a former critical care nurse who resides in rural Indiana with her husband, two sons, two horses, four cats, and one dog. *Rebel* is the tenth book in her Cat Star Chronicles series, which includes *Slave*, *Warrior*, *Rogue*, *Outcast*, *Fugitive*, *Hero*, *Virgin*, *Stud*, and *Wildcat*. She has self-published one ebook, *Sex, Love, and a Purple Bikini*, and one erotic short story, *Midnight in Reno*. Her self-published erotic contemporary romance series, Unlikely Lovers, includes *Unbridled*, *Uninhibited*, *Undeniable*, and *Unrivaled*. She has also published *If You Could Read My Mind* writing as Samantha R. Michaels. As a member of The Sextet, she has written several erotic novellas published by Siren/Bookstrand. Her other interests include cooking, gardening, singing, and guitar playing. Cheryl is a member of RWA and IRWA. You can visit her online at www.cherylbrooksonline.com or email her at cheryl.brooks52@yahoo.com.